THE MARRIAGE METHOD

Mimi Matthews

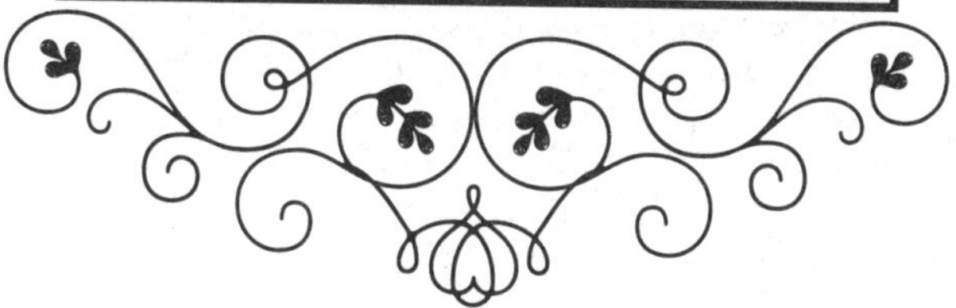

BERKLEY ROMANCE | NEW YORK

BERKLEY ROMANCE
Published by Berkley
An imprint of Penguin Random House LLC
1745 Broadway, New York, NY 10019
penguinrandomhouse.com

Book design by Kristin del Rosario
Interior art: Victorian silhouette © dariodraws/Shutterstock

Library of Congress Cataloging-in-Publication Data

Names: Matthews, Mimi author
Title: The marriage method / Mimi Matthews.
Description: First edition. | New York : Berkley Romance, 2025. |
Series: The Crinoline Academy
Identifiers: LCCN 2025007195 (print) | LCCN 2025007196 (ebook) |
ISBN 9780593639313 trade paperback | ISBN 9780593639320 ebook
Subjects: LCGFT: Fiction | Romance fiction | Novels
Classification: LCC PS3613.A8493 M37 2025 (print) |
LCC PS3613.A8493 (ebook) | DDC 813/.6—dc23/eng/20250502
LC record available at https://lccn.loc.gov/2025007195
LC ebook record available at https://lccn.loc.gov/2025007196

First Edition: November 2025

Printed in the United States of America
1st Printing

The authorized representative in the EU for product safety and compliance is Penguin Random House Ireland, Morrison Chambers, 32 Nassau Street, Dublin D02 YH68, Ireland, https://eu-contact.penguin.ie.

Praise for Mimi Matthews

"Shiveringly gothic. . . . Watching Julia blossom away from prying eyes is almost as satisfying as seeing Jasper Blunt pine for her from nearly the first page. . . . For best effect, save this one for a windy night when trees scrape against the windowpanes."

—*The New York Times Book Review*

"No one writes Victoriana like Mimi Matthews! In *Rules for Ruin*, she introduces us to an outwardly respectable academy for young ladies [that] trains its pupils in a secret agenda: disrupt and discredit the powerful men of London who seek to keep women in their place. The academy's best pupil, Effie Flite, embarks on a bold plan to discredit a ruthless politician, but locks horns with underworld kingpin Gabriel Royce, who needs her target safe in Parliament and not discredited in the newspapers. Sparks fly between Effie and Gabriel in a thoroughly enchanting romance that promises the start of a new series—I can't wait for the next installment from the Crinoline Academy!" —*New York Times* bestselling author Kate Quinn

"Mimi Matthews never disappoints, with richly drawn characters and couples whose individual shortcomings become strengths when paired together. In this 'Beauty and the Beast' retelling, we get to root for two underdogs who get to rewrite their own stories."

—#1 *New York Times* bestselling author Jodi Picoult

"Mimi is truly a national treasure. All of her books are filled with such delicious chemistry and heart, and her writing is superb. This one is another winner. Highly recommend."

—#1 *New York Times* bestselling author Isabel Ibañez

"Mimi Matthews has become one of my favorite authors. She never disappoints." —*New York Times* bestselling author Mary Balogh

"What I love about Mimi Matthews is that in the crowded field of historical romance, she always finds new and interesting slants for her plots and characters. That, along with her wonderful writing and meticulous research, makes every book she puts out a rare treat to enjoy and savor. Highly recommended!"

—*New York Times* bestselling author Kate Pearce

"Thrilling, poignant, and romantic, *Rules for Ruin* is a delight! Mimi Matthews's evocative prose carries readers on an unforgettable adventure through London's bustling streets and elegant drawing rooms. Euphemia and Gabriel's romance simmers with electric chemistry, witty banter, and powerful emotion. Readers will love *Rules for Ruin*!" —*New York Times* bestselling author Chanel Cleeton

"*Rules for Ruin* is the ultimate cat-and-mouse romance with witty banter, sizzling attraction, and twists of excitement—a perfect first installment to kick off Mimi Matthews's new Crinoline Academy series." —*New York Times* bestselling author Madeline Martin

"A delicious crumpet of a novel: sparkling characters, lush romantic chemistry, and a woman on a mission made me fly through the pages!" —*USA Today* bestselling author Evie Dunmore

"*Rules for Ruin* is a thrilling page-turner that has everything fans of Victorian romance could wish for: a smart, strong, yet vulnerable heroine you'll adore; a tough-as-nails, self-made hero who proves to be her perfect match; swoonworthy, sizzling romance; nonstop action; secrets to uncover; and a baddie to bring down—all wrapped up in Mimi Matthews's rich, evocative writing and a gripping, impeccably researched plot. One of my favorite Mimi Matthews novels ever. I *loved* it and couldn't put it down!"

—*USA Today* bestselling author Syrie James

"Mimi Matthews is in a class of her own. I adored Effie and Gabriel's romance, and I continue to be so impressed by the way Victorian London effortlessly comes alive through Matthews's meticulous research. I am very much looking forward to the next book in the Crinoline Academy series!"

—Hester Fox, author of *A Magic Deep and Drowning*

"A mysterious debutante, a lord of the underworld, and the most romantic proposal ever—*Rules for Ruin* is the first book in what promises to be a fabulous new series by one of my favorite historical authors. Mimi Matthews consistently delivers achingly tender love stories set against a rich Victorian backdrop."

—Harper St. George, author of *Eliza and the Duke*

"Lush, seductive, original—*The Siren of Sussex* drew me in from the first page and wove its magic. A fresh, vibrant, brilliant Victorian romance, making it an unforgettable read."

—*New York Times* bestselling author Jane Porter

"I've long been a devoted fan of Mimi Matthews, and with *The Lily of Ludgate Hill*, the delightful continuation of her Belles of London series, my admiration of her work has only increased. Her command of historical detail is faultless. . . . I loved Anne and Hart, was instantly and completely consumed by their tangled past and seemingly impossible future."

—International bestselling author Jennifer Robson

"This story unfolds like a rose blooming, growing more and more beautiful as each delicate layer is revealed. A tender, luminous romance. I loved it more and more with every chapter!"

—*USA Today* bestselling author Caroline Linden

"The best book I've read in a long time: gorgeously written, thoughtfully considered, swoonily romantic, and unafraid to examine issues of class, race, and gender." —National bestselling author Olivia Dade

"A moving love story and a vivid re-creation of Victorian life, *The Siren of Sussex* by Mimi Matthews is a treat of a book for the historical romance lover." —Award-winning author Anna Campbell

TITLES BY MIMI MATTHEWS

BELLES OF LONDON NOVELS

The Siren of Sussex

The Belle of Belgrave Square

The Lily of Ludgate Hill

The Muse of Maiden Lane

THE CRINOLINE ACADEMY NOVELS

Rules for Ruin

The Marriage Method

For Lura

The female world is sinking fast to strangely wicked ways,
When ladies steel their petticoats, and daily bone their stays;
And menace thus with danger the threatened public weal,
Bound firm and fast unitedly in bands to bone and steel.

—James Hain Friswell, *The Glories of Crinoline*, 1866

A NOTE TO THE READER

This book is a swoony Victorian romance, with lots of sweetness and tender moments. It also contains a secondary mystery, with references to off-page acts of violence, abduction, and an incidence of mutilation. There are several on-page fight scenes, some ignorant remarks about a main character's disability (made by the villain), and discussions about parental abandonment (in the past), death of a parent (in the past), and a traumatic injury suffered by a main character (in the past). If you are sensitive to any of these topics, please proceed with care.

The Marriage Method

1

August 1864

Penelope Trewlove followed the harried young clerk down the hall of the Fleet Street offices of the *London Courant*. Similarly harassed-looking newspapermen bustled in and out of the small offices they passed, shuffling papers and addressing one another in urgent tones. At the sight of her, some of them faltered, their attention caught between the fluttering black veil that shrouded her face and the limp that marred her gait.

Nell's gloved fingers tightened reflexively on the raven's head handle of her ebony cane. It was her first visit to London, and not a willing one by any means. She had been putting off the paper's editor, Mr. Quincey, for weeks, each of her exceedingly formal replies to his letters penned with an effort to discourage his relentless curiosity. But she could put him off no longer. His last letter had made that abundantly plain. Either Nell travel to London to answer his questions about Miss Corvus's Benevolent Academy for the Betterment of Young Ladies, or Mr. Quincey would come to the isolated stone manor house at the edge of the Epping Forest and put his questions to Miss Corvus herself.

As if Miss Corvus would ever risk allowing a journalist inside the charity school's iron gates! She had, instead, sent Nell to deal with the situation. To come here today, in her role as deputy headmistress, and put an end to Mr. Quincey's problematic inquiries once and for all.

A painted door at the end of the hall bore the vexing man's name in stenciled letters. The clerk opened it without knocking. He ushered Nell into a moderately sized office, distinguished by a wall of overstuffed bookcases, a small, threadbare sofa with a fringed skirt, and a massive desk, covered with chaotic piles of papers and three open bottles of ink. The great leather chair behind the desk was conspicuously empty.

"Mr. Quincey is engaged at present," the clerk said. He gestured to one of the two slat-back wooden chairs that were arrayed in front of the desk. "If you would care to wait?"

"Not at all." Nell gratefully availed herself of a seat, propping her cane beside her. After two hackney cab rides and a railway journey of nearly twenty miles, her left hip and thigh were aching like the dickens. She did her level best not to betray the fact. Her spine remained ramrod straight, her veil still firmly in place as she arranged the full skirts of her black bombazine carriage gown over the imposing frame of her wire crinoline.

Miss Corvus wasn't a woman given to fashionable indulgences, but she had made an exception for the controversial cage-like undergarment. All of her teachers donned them like armor, as did many of the older orphans. It was no mystery as to why.

The sheer circumference of a crinoline kept its wearer separate and apart, protected from all but the most determined encroachments. Not only that. She took up space for herself—demanded space—on the pavement, in a crowded conveyance, and in every sphere through which she traveled. The greater world must step aside and let her pass. They dare not stop her.

The clerk bowed and withdrew, shutting the door after him.

Nell took the opportunity to cast an eye over the room. *Know your surroundings. Know your opponent. Know yourself.* They were the three most important rules she had learned at the Academy. Rules meant to keep young ladies safe. To ensure they were prepared for anything, never overmatched or left unable to defend themselves.

It was the first rule that occupied her now. Unlike men, women didn't have the luxury of entering a situation blindly. A female must know the four corners of where she stood—the entrances, the exits, the problematic terrain. She must, at all times, think both defensively and offensively.

Fortunately, Mr. Quincey wasn't a complete unknown. Nell's recently married Academy sister, Effie Royce, had a passing acquaintance with him *and* his premises. Among other things, she had warned Nell to anticipate cats.

There appeared to be none in residence today. The room was seemingly empty. Although . . . Was that a faint rustle of movement beneath the sofa?

The door jerked open before Nell could investigate the matter. A deep male voice sounded behind her. "Miss Trewlove?"

Nell's head turned sharply. Never mind that she'd been expecting him, the sight of the tall, raven-haired newspaper editor still served to send a jolt through her. She stared up at him from behind her veil. "Mr. Quincey?"

He was in his shirtsleeves, his cravat askew and his black waistcoat rumpled. It did nothing to lessen his air of command. Self-assurance radiated from every inch of him. "Apologies for the delay. One of my reporters has gone missing and my staff is up in arms." He entered, closing the door behind him. "I trust you don't mind my not leaving it open? I've no wish to let the cat out."

"The cat?" She flicked another glance to the sofa as she moved to rise. "I didn't see any—"

"Pray don't get up. We're not much for formalities here. We've precious little time for them." Rather than bow, he reached to shake her hand. "I am, however, very pleased to meet you."

Nell's mouth went dry as his fingers engulfed hers. His hand was easily twice the size of her own, surely better suited to holding a steel broadsword than a steel-nibbed pen. His shoulders were quite broad, too, lending an unmistakable power to the leanness of his long-limbed frame.

Alarm bells jangled in her head, inspired as much by his physical presence as by the peculiar intensity that gleamed at the back of his dark brown eyes.

This was the gentleman who had penned the explosive series of articles that had lately brought down a powerful politician. A dogged and indefatigable reporter, possessed of an unassailable firmness of character, unafraid of retaliation or threats.

For the first time, Nell considered the possibility that she might be out of her depth.

"As to the cat," Mr. Quincey continued, releasing her hand, "she's barely civilized. She'll be hiding here somewhere." He crossed to his desk, taking a seat behind it in the large leather chair. "Did Higgins offer you tea? I can have some brought in for you."

"I thank you, no," Nell said. She made an effort to regain her composure. In truth, she was astonished she'd lost it—even if it *was* only for the space of a heartbeat.

She wasn't accustomed to dealing with men, that was the trouble. She'd spent the majority of her life at the Academy, first as an orphan, then as a teacher. Nearly the whole of her three-and-twenty years, surrounded by girls and women. The only gentlemen to ever set foot through the gates were the antiquated members of the parish council, and then but rarely. Miss Corvus saw to that.

Nell couldn't recall when she'd last been obliged to deal with any gentleman under the age of fifty. Unless one counted the stripling lads from the village who sometimes attempted communication with the orphan girls. And Mr. Quincey was no stripling. He must be thirty, at least.

He regarded her from across his desk's cluttered surface. He wasn't a handsome man. Not in the classical manner. His face was too angular and severe—his brows too stern, his clean-shaven jaw too hard, and his bold aquiline nose a fraction too large. But his features hung together in such a striking way that one could easily forget their asymmetry.

"Your journey wasn't too taxing?" he asked.

"Not terribly," she said.

"Yet still a lengthy business. I'd have preferred coming to you. It would have saved you the trouble."

"I have multiple reasons for coming to London," Nell said. "My trip won't be wasted."

She was to visit Effie when she and her new husband returned to town in two days' time. Until they did, Nell had other Academy business to attend to. *Important* business. It was that which should rightly be occupying her thoughts, not the solemn countenance and unusually broad shoulders of a prying newspaperman she would likely never see again after this morning.

"I'm pleased to hear it," he said. "I won't keep you overlong. There are just a few matters about the charity school that I'd hoped you might clarify." Small talk dispensed with, he picked up his pen, giving every indication that he intended to take notes of their conversation.

Nell would have expected nothing less. "By all means," she said. "Miss Corvus's Academy has nothing to hide."

It was a falsehood, to be sure. And one Nell didn't blush to utter. The Academy was her vocation, her life, her home. She wouldn't quail at defending it, even if it meant occasionally speaking something less than the truth to those who threatened its well-being.

Gloved hands folded neatly in her lap, she waited for Mr. Quincey's questions. But he didn't give voice to them. Not immediately. He only looked at her with a pensive frown, as though something about her person prevented him from pursuing his logical course.

"Forgive me," he said at length. "Mrs. Royce failed to mention that you were lately bereaved. Had I known of your loss, I would never have pressed you to—"

"I am not bereaved," Nell said.

"No?" He swept a glance from her black-veiled hat to her lusterless black mourning dress with its tight-fitting bodice and wide, untrimmed skirts. "You can doubtless understand my confusion."

Nell would have thought it plain enough. "I traveled alone from the Academy. I preferred to do so unmolested." She paused, adding, "Widows are generally accorded a degree of respect not offered to unaccompanied young ladies."

Mr. Quincey didn't bat an eye at her explanation. She suspected he was a man who wasn't easily surprised. "In other words, it's a disguise."

Nell's expression tightened. Leave it to a man to reduce a woman's desire to protect herself to a childish pantomime. "It's a practical necessity," she said.

"I see. And do all teachers at Miss Corvus's Benevolent Academy for the Betterment of Young Ladies employ such arts? Or is it only you who . . ." His words died away as she pushed back her veil.

Ah. Perhaps he was capable of being surprised after all.

Nell met his gaze, a hint of a challenge in her own. She wasn't vain. Neither was she guilty of false modesty. She knew herself, both her weaknesses *and* her strengths. "Feminine ingenuity isn't limited to the staff room at the Academy," she informed him. "Though, I assure you, it's in no short supply there."

Mr. Quincey collected himself in a blink—so quickly Nell wondered if she'd imagined the look of masculine alertness that had flared in his eyes on first seeing her face. Clearing his throat, he very slowly and very methodically returned his pen to the brass holder on his desk. "Something else Mrs. Royce failed to mention."

"What might that be?"

"How young you are."

Nell stiffened at his tone of disappointment. She wasn't used to anyone implying that she was lacking in wisdom or experience. Quite the reverse. In times of crisis, people generally looked to her for guidance. During Miss Corvus's recent illness, Nell had been all but running the school. "Is my age of importance to your inquiries?"

"Only as it pertains to your tenure," he said. "You can't have been in your position long."

"I have been employed as a teacher for five years, sir."

He sat back in his chair, frowning at her again with an attitude of impatience. One would think she had wasted his precious time. "Mrs. Royce led me to believe you had been present at the Academy's founding, nearly twenty years ago. It's why I consented to meet with you instead of pursuing an interview with Miss Corvus herself. I had anticipated your providing certain information about the institution's origins."

Nell at once grasped the cause of his irritation. He'd wrongly presumed she would be a much older woman. One who had spent the whole of the past eighteen years teaching at the charity school. "Mrs. Royce did not mislead you."

"Not only Mrs. Royce," he replied. "You, as well, Miss Trewlove. Your letters gave me to understand that you had decades of experience at Miss Corvus's Academy."

"I do," she said. "Or nearly that long. I was one of its earliest students."

Understanding registered on his face. He stared at her with renewed attention. "You were an orphan?"

Nell's chin ticked up a notch. "That's correct."

There was no shame in it. Not as far as she was concerned. It was just as she often told her girls. One wasn't accountable for the circumstances of one's birth, only for the choices they made and the actions they took. It was that which defined a person, not pedigree.

"As are all the students at the Academy?" Mr. Quincey asked.

"To a one," she said. "They come to us from all over the county. I flatter myself that we do our best for them."

"Your best being . . . ?"

She lifted one shoulder in an artfully casual shrug. "We feed them, house them, and provide them with an education that will best help them meet their potential."

Mr. Quincey narrowed in on the word with single-minded precision. "Their potential for what, exactly?"

Nell's mouth curved in a slow smile. She comprehended the unspoken crux of his question. He believed the Academy was a home for dangerous revolutionaries. Budding feminists and crusaders for equality, willing to go to any ends to achieve their goals, even if that meant destroying the occasional man who got in their way.

He wasn't wrong.

• • • • •

Miles was *not* amused.

He might have known Miss Trewlove would turn out to be some manner of goddess. It was, after all, Gabriel Royce's wife who had pointed Miles in her direction. And the newly minted Mrs. Royce was nothing if not trouble personified.

Miles was in no mood for it. Not this morning. Lawrence Cowgill had been gone for three days straight, leaving nothing behind in his desk but a notebook marked with a series of meaningless dates. In his absence, Miles had been forced to assign the paper's famous gossip column to another of his reporters. A poor salve on a potentially fatal wound, but it was either that or go to press without it. The latter hadn't been an option. Like it or not, the majority of the *Courant*'s dwindling circulation was owing to that cursed column.

They couldn't afford to lose any more subscribers. They'd already lost too many as it was. In the aftermath of Miles's series of articles exposing the treachery of a once-revered politician, Viscount Compton, many in society had closed ranks against the paper, no doubt frightened that they'd be targeted next—exposed and ruined by one of the *Courant*'s notoriously ruthless exposés.

It was only the gossip column that kept the fashionable public coming back. Without Cowgill to write it, the paper stood to lose a fortune. No one else was in possession of the secret sources that enabled him to deliver such unusually incisive tittle-tattle.

And now this.

Another disappointment, albeit one disguised in a rather beguiling package.

Miles ran a hand over the side of his face, wishing like the devil he'd followed his instincts and gone to Miss Corvus's Academy himself. Instead, he'd wasted months, engaged in correspondence with a woman he had foolishly assumed was an antiquated spinster.

But she wasn't.

Antiquated, that is.

With her flaxen blond hair, heart-shaped face, and graceful figure, Miss Trewlove had more in common with an angel than she did with his, admittedly narrow, preconception of a schoolteacher.

A sultry angel, at that.

Her hooded, long-lashed gray eyes had a deceptively sleepy quality to them. Like a tigress drowsing in the sun, as languorous as it was lethal. The effect was intensified by the elegant curve of her high cheekbones, and the voluptuous fullness of her lush Cupid's-bow lips.

A small jet brooch in the shape of a butterfly sparkled at her throat, the only spot of brilliancy in her dull black mourning ensemble. "It's a personal calculation," she replied to him. "Every girl has a different set of strengths. A head for mathematics, for example. Or an aptitude for writing, or a skill for sport."

"Sport," Miles repeated. "Such as hunting down corrupt lords like Viscount Compton?"

Miss Trewlove lifted her winged brows. They were thick and arched, a shade darker than her hair. "You presume the Academy is connected to his downfall?"

"I more than presume it. Miss Corvus's name came up often during my investigations. Or rather, the name she went by at the time she was connected to Lord Compton, some two decades ago."

Miss Trewlove noticeably did not refute that connection. "A man has done wrong and has finally been punished for it. What benefit can there be in violating his victim's privacy—whomever that victim might be?"

"I don't mean to publish her story," Miles said. He'd promised Gabriel he wouldn't. He hadn't, however, promised to forgo further inquiry. The mystery of Miss Corvus and her charity school was the single loose thread in his investigation into Lord Compton's crimes. And Miles couldn't abide a loose thread.

"Then what does it matter?" Miss Trewlove asked.

"Call it professional curiosity," he said.

Disapproval darkened her gaze. "At a lady's expense? That isn't very gentlemanly."

Across the office, the fringe on the bottom of the sofa twitched. Shadow poked her gray striped head out to listen to their conversation.

Miles cast an absent glance in the little tabby's direction. He had found her only last week here in Fleet Street. Small and thin, with a battered ear and weeping eye, she had summoned up the bravery to eat from one of the dishes he regularly put out for the other street cats. He'd really had no choice but to rescue her.

She'd been living in his office ever since, spending most of her time hiding while she healed from her wounds. Miles intended to remove her to his house in St. James's Square as soon as she was stronger. He had four strays already in residence. Cats were his weakness.

His *only* weakness.

"Not just any lady," he said. "The lady who Compton jilted and defrauded. His crimes against her are what ultimately led to his undoing."

"Elizabeth Wingard," Miss Trewlove mused. She adjusted her voluminous skirts. "Yes, I read your articles. She was treated abominably, as far as I can tell."

"She was," Miles acknowledged. "Rumor has it that she died abroad. Instead, as I discovered, she returned to England, armed with a new identity, and a new purpose."

"This is all quite fascinating—"

"She founded a charity school for girls. One of those girls—now Mrs. Royce—played a role in bringing about Compton's political demise. Do you dispute that there was a relationship between her actions and the mission of Miss Corvus's Academy?"

"I'm sorry, are you implying that Miss Corvus founded a school solely to raise up a generation of girls to settle a score with her former fiancé?" Miss Trewlove smiled, revealing a startling glimpse of a crooked front tooth. The unexpected flaw lent a roguish quality to her expression. "I am not a worldly woman, Mr. Quincey, but that does seem excessive."

"Not only Compton," Miles said. "All men who have wronged women."

"*All* men? How very ambitious of her."

"You don't deny it?"

"On the contrary. It sounds an admirable goal. I heartily endorse it." Her face reverted to solemn lines. "Truly, sir, in all seriousness, if that is what you believe, your imagination has run away with you."

Miles repressed a flare of aggravation. He had long learned not to judge people too quickly, and Miss Trewlove provided ample evidence as to why. She sat across from him, ladylike and subdued in her faux widow's weeds, and yet she was sparring with him as effectively as one of the bruisers he often faced in the ring at the boxing saloon.

"I have no imagination," he said. "I concern myself with facts and only facts. It's what makes me so good at my job."

"Facts, then," she said. "It's just as I told you in my letters—"

"Your very brief letters." None of them had been more than a few sentences in length.

She ignored the criticism. "Our charity school is wholly reputable, and the character of both our students *and* our teachers is beyond reproach. Any member of the local parish council can verify that fact, and that body is uniformly male and hardly what one would label progressive."

That much Miles *did* know. He had an appointment with one of its members later this morning. A Reverend Pettiman. Miles had arranged the meeting the prior month in a last-ditch effort to get information about the Academy after Miss Trewlove had repeatedly rebuffed his requests for an interview.

"As to the role of our girls once they enter society," she went on, "I can give you the current locations of as many as ten of them who have, after leaving our care, found genteel employment. They are governesses. Schoolteachers. And one is private secretary to a gentlewoman of some stature. None of them can be classed as avenging furies."

"What about the rest of your graduates?"

"You already know Mrs. Royce." Miss Trewlove's impossibly provocative mouth tipped slowly at one corner. The expression was uncannily feline. "And now you know me."

Miles held her gaze, ignoring the pulse of heat that threatened to dull his senses. He could see what was happening here. Miss Corvus and Mrs. Royce had clearly believed that Miss Trewlove's astonishing beauty would be sufficient to distract him from his questions. And it *was* distracting. But he'd faced worse obstacles in getting a story, and overcome them, too.

"Not yet, ma'am," he said. "But I intend to." Again, he picked up his pen.

Miss Trewlove may not be the proprietor of the charity school, but she had been one of its orphans and was now one of its teachers. If there were secrets to be had, she must be in possession of a few of them. All that remained was to wrest them from her.

"At what age did you come to the orphanage?" he asked briskly. "And under what circumstances?"

"I doubt my humble history can be of interest to your investigations."

"Quite the opposite. You interest me exceedingly. If Miss Corvus has deployed you to the front lines—"

"A troubling metaphor."

"But an apt one, I discern. You're the heavy artillery."

She didn't smile this time, but a dimple formed to the right of her mouth. *"Me?"*

"You," he said.

As they spoke, Shadow emerged from her hiding place, step by cautious step. Encouraged by Miss Trewlove's stillness, she slowly crossed the carpet to inspect the edge of her skirts.

"If it's a case study you're after," Miss Trewlove said, "I must surely be the least interesting subject of all our graduates. Unlike the other girls, I chose to remain."

"You had no desire to strike out on your own as a governess or secretary?"

"None at all."

"Teaching is your prevailing passion?"

"It is, though I wouldn't describe it in such lofty terms. I—" She broke off, her attention caught by the sight of the little tabby bestowing a delicate sniff to her hem. Her face lit with genuine pleasure. "Why, hello, little one," she said. "I was beginning to doubt your existence." She glanced at Miles. "Does she have a name?"

Miles required a full three seconds to recollect it. The look Miss Trewlove had given the cat had knocked him off his axis. It was so frank. So authentic. The whole of her countenance was transformed by it. A strange sort of alchemy, but in that moment, she changed from an untouchable goddess into an infinitely more desirable human girl.

He swallowed hard. "I've, uh, been calling her Shadow."

"How appropriate." Miss Trewlove stretched her gloved hand down as if to administer a pet.

Shadow's eyes widened to the size of twin saucers. The sofa being too far away, she darted for cover under the only shelter available—the billowing expanse of Miss Trewlove's skirts.

A rosy blush seeped into Miss Trewlove's cheeks as the cat disappeared beneath her hem. "Goodness," she said. "This is rather alarming."

"She means no offense," Miles said. "She's attempting to hide, that's all. She's still quite wild. You'll have to shake your—"

Before he could finish advising her, Miss Trewlove reached under her skirts to remove the cat herself. She jerked back her fingers with a cry of pain.

Miles was up from behind his desk in a flash. He strode around it. "If you would permit me—"

"Heavens!" Miss Trewlove leapt from her chair before he could reach her. She staggered backward. Shadow's small form was visible beneath the swell of her skirts, thrashing wildly. "I think she's caught!"

He closed the distance between them. "Caught in what?"

Miss Trewlove's face flamed. "In my *crinoline*." She took another stumbling step back, losing her balance.

Miles extended a hand to steady her, but he was a split second too late. Miss Trewlove's left leg inexplicably gave way. He caught her an instant before she dropped to the floor, breaking her fall with his body as the two of them landed with a thud on the office carpet.

She struggled up on her elbows. Her veiled hat had been knocked askew and a stray lock of blond hair had come loose from its pins to curl around her face. "She's still tangled up in it!" she gasped. "And her claws are quite sharp!"

Miles grasped a handful of Miss Trewlove's skirts, hesitating only long enough to ask permission to inflict what would, in other circumstances, be a reputation-ruining indignity. "May I—"

"Yes, yes," she said breathlessly. "Anything. Only remove her!"

Miles hoisted up the layers of black silk and starched petticoats, revealing the enormous cage crinoline Miss Trewlove wore underneath (and a pair of shapely, stocking-clad legs he pretended not to notice). Shadow had woven herself through the wire and fabric tapes of the undergarment's frame. The little cat looked at him, panicked, her chest vibrating on a low, continuous growl.

"Easy," Miles said to her. "I won't hurt you." He covered the cat's body with his hand. She responded by sinking her teeth into his finger. He sucked in a breath. *"Bloody hell."*

"Did she—"

"She's fine."

"I didn't mean the cat," Miss Trewlove said in a strained voice. "I meant *you*."

"I'll live." He slowly untangled Shadow's legs from the wires, ignoring her continued hissing and spitting. Extracting her from the crinoline, he set her down on the carpet. The little cat tore free of his grasp the instant she was able. Streaking across the office, she plunged under the sofa.

Miles exhaled. "There," he said, sitting back on his haunches. "No damage done."

No sooner had he uttered the fateful words than the door was thrust open and Higgins burst in carrying a small box in his hand.

"Mr. Quincey? This was just delivered at the front desk. Bob said as how you'd want to be notified directly . . ." The newspaper clerk's words trailed away as he beheld the scene before him—Miss Trewlove on the floor with her skirts above her knees and Miles looming over her like some vile seducer.

Higgins wasn't alone. An older, distinguished-looking gentleman stood a short distance behind him in the hall. The esteemed member of the parish council, presumably, come early for his appointment.

Seeing him, the color drained from Miss Trewlove's face. She scrambled to a sitting position, hastily pulling her skirts into some semblance of order. "Reverend Pettiman!"

Pettiman's florid countenance went crimson with outrage.

Miles didn't flinch. Neither did he hesitate. "I'll be with you in a moment, Higgins," he said in the same curt, businesslike tones he employed when dealing with any other workplace catastrophe. "See to my next appointment before he has an apoplexy, would you? And if you wouldn't mind closing the door?"

"Yes, sir. Apologies, sir. Completely my fault." Higgins backed out of the office, shutting the door after him with a power that rattled the doorframe.

To Miles, the sound was as significant as the crash of the gallows' trapdoor. His fate was plain. He accepted it with a grim sense of resignation.

Miss Trewlove's eyes found his. "Mr. Quincey—"

"Given our current predicament," he said, "I believe you had better accustom yourself to calling me Miles."

2

Nell permitted Miles to assist her to her feet. The pale-faced horror she'd felt on seeing Reverend Pettiman in the hall rapidly gave way to an ungovernable rush of anger. "Of all the despicable tricks! What is a member of the parish council doing *here*?"

"I have an interview with him," Miles said, sounding as infinitely calm and rational as he had when the clerk had burst in on them.

"*What?* But . . . why? I said I'd answer your questions. There was no cause to—" Nell stopped herself, hearing the shrill note of hysteria creeping into her words. She brought her voice down to a normal register. Whatever else happened, she was *not* going to panic. "This was uncalled for, sir."

Miles's hand remained at her elbow. "Unfortunate, certainly, insofar as timing, but I wouldn't say it was uncalled for. When you wouldn't agree to meet me, the logical next step was to seek out another person affiliated with the charity school."

"Logical, you say? And I suppose it was logical to ask your clerk to close the door after we were discovered together?"

"It seemed the reasonable course until I'd assisted you up," Miles said. "It was either that or have the whole of my office witness you flat on your back."

A blush threatened. "But the reverend did witness it. If you only knew— Oh!" She gave a startled cry as his hand left her elbow, feeling her leg give way beneath her for the second time today.

Miles's arm was instantly around her waist, strong as a band of iron. A fierce concern darkened his brow. "Did you injure yourself?"

She glared at him, heat stealing into her cheeks despite her best efforts to contain it. He was holding her far too close. Her bosom was pressed indecorously to his side, and her skirts—already rumpled beyond bearing—were crushed against his legs. "Yes," she said tightly, drawing as far back from him as she was able. "Some time ago. If you would be so good as to help me find my cane?"

He stared down at her, frowning. "Your cane," he repeated.

"It was leaning against the chair beside me. It must have fallen when I jumped up." She looked around the office, exerting every resource she possessed to quell the rising tide of panic that clawed at her throat.

That had been Reverend Pettiman out there. *The* Reverend Pettiman. The same insufferable man who had the gall to dictate official Academy policy to Miss Corvus. And now he had seen Nell with a man under her skirts.

How on earth was she to explain it?

Miles helped her back to her chair. His hand remained at her waist until she was seated, even as he scanned the room for her missing cane. "It's there," he said. "Beneath the desk."

"If you wouldn't mind—"

"Of course." He promptly retrieved her cane. His eyes lingered a moment on the raven's head handle. "Here you are."

"Thank you." She took it, feeling at once more herself.

She hadn't always used a cane. Indeed, when at the Academy, she generally refrained from relying on one. But it was different today. The train to London had rattled dreadfully, the streets were uneven and unfamiliar, and the chances of stumbling while climbing in and out of a hackney cab had been exponentially greater than the risk of losing her footing on the Academy's staircase. The last thing she'd wanted was to end up in a heap on the ground.

And yet, despite all precaution, that's exactly where she'd found herself.

Closing her fingers around the handle of her cane, she took a deep, steadying breath. Nothing could be gained by losing her composure. This was a catastrophe, to be sure. And one of epic proportions. But it wasn't beyond mending. All she had to do was think rationally, and—more importantly—behave rationally.

"I don't suppose you have any sherry?" she inquired.

Miles didn't blink at the request. He went behind his desk. Opening a drawer, he extracted a small silver flask. "Will brandy suffice?"

"It will do nicely, thank you." She held out her hand to him. "If you please?"

He passed her the flask, watching her with that same inscrutable expression as she uncapped it and took a swig straight from the spout. It scorched down her throat like wildfire, setting her midsection alight.

She grimaced mightily. "Ugh."

"Better?"

"Quite." She screwed the top back onto the flask and returned it to him. "Now, if you wouldn't mind fetching Reverend Pettiman?"

Again, Miles obeyed. If Nell didn't know better, she'd suspect he was humoring her.

He crossed to the door and opened it. "Higgins!"

The same clerk who had escorted Nell to Miles's office, and who had burst in on them mere moments ago, trotted forward. He was a stocky young man, with neatly pomaded hair and a highly polished pocket watch. "Yes, sir?"

"Where did you put my next appointment?" Miles asked.

"The gentleman in the beaver hat? He left, sir."

"Left?" Miles echoed flatly.

"I did explain things to him," Mr. Higgins replied. "Said as how the lady must have come over in a faint, and that we keep the door closed on account of the feral cat, and how you're a gentleman of the utmost integrity. But the man wasn't interested in facts, sir. He asked if I took him for a fool, then he hurried off, muttering something about needing to write a letter before the next post went out."

Nell's stomach sank. Good gracious. The reverend wasted no time, did he? And to think, she might have been being ravished in this room!

With an effort, she stood from her chair. Her leg was still throbbing, but she could manage with her cane. Just.

Miles flashed her a piercing glance. "A moment, Higgins."

"Yes, sir." The newspaper clerk dutifully remained in the doorway, pointedly avoiding Nell's gaze as he awaited his orders.

Miles returned to Nell. His deep voice lowered, pitched for her ears alone. "You're going?"

"I must," she replied under her breath. "If Reverend Pettiman is thinking to report me for wanton conduct—"

Miles made a scoffing sound. "Hardly that. It was an innocent encounter. Wholly explainable, though admittedly embarrassing to all parties involved. The reverend must have realized that on some level."

She gave him an incredulous look. "How do you come to *that* conclusion?"

"If he thought your virtue was in danger, he'd have stormed in to rescue you. He'd never have left while we were still . . . doing whatever it was he imagined we were doing."

Nell was beyond blushing. "Yes," she said emphatically, "he would."

"I disagree," Miles said. "It makes no sense."

"Not if you understand his motivating force. These suffocating rules of behavior that men like Pettiman espouse aren't about protecting women. They're about punishing them. He's more concerned with me being held to account for some imagined moral crime than he is in saving me from being ravished."

"I can hardly call what happened—"

"You might have been doing *anything*, and rather than burst in and demand you unhand me, he rushed off to telegraph my crimes to . . . whom? The other members of the council? The gentlewomen who contribute funds to the school? Miss Corvus herself?"

It was the latter possibility that alarmed Nell the most.

She turned toward the door. "I must go."

"If you insist," Miles said. "I'll see you back to Mr. and Mrs. Royce's house myself."

"I'm not staying with Mr. and Mrs. Royce."

His brows knit. "I thought—"

"I had planned to, but they were called to Paris unexpectedly. Mrs. Royce's former employer, Madame Dalhousie, is ailing and she asked for Mrs. Royce particularly. They won't be back until Friday."

Miles didn't appear to care about the Royces' whereabouts, or about the precarious health of Madame Dalhousie. "Then where—"

"At a ladies' hotel in Commercial Street."

His dark gaze sharpened to attention. She may as well have informed him that she'd taken lodgings on the moon. "The East End? Are you out of your senses?"

"Not at all. I have business there." *Had* business, Nell silently amended. Given what had just occurred, she could no longer reasonably hope to complete her assignment.

"I am not escorting you to one of the worst slums in London," Miles said.

"Forgive me, but I don't recall asking you to." Yanking her veil back down over her face, Nell crossed to the office door.

Mr. Higgins moved aside, allowing her to pass through it.

She didn't look back.

• • • • •

Miles stared after Miss Trewlove for a moment, before rallying himself. "Higgins—"

"Shall I send one of the lads ahead to fetch your carriage, sir?" Higgins asked.

"Sharpish," Miles said. "And bring me my hat and coat."

"Yes, sir. Right away, sir." Higgins dashed off at a trot.

Miles exited his office, shutting the door after him.

Bob Flack, Higgins's junior, hovered nearby. He was gawking at Miles, jaw slackened, as though he'd just made the jarring discovery that his esteemed editor in chief was not the highly principled man he'd believed him to be.

Miles's conscience twinged. But there was no time to correct Flack's misapprehensions. Ignoring the man's air of disappointment, Miles looked him straight in the eye. "See that this door remains closed, and the cat left undisturbed," he commanded. "I'll be back within the hour." With that, he stalked down the hall after the swiftly disappearing figure of Miss Trewlove.

More was at stake than her reputation. Miles had his own to think about.

He had come to the *Courant* over a decade ago as a junior reporter. He'd worked his way through the ranks, toiling night and day without complaint—diligent, relentless, reliable—first advancing to a position as an investigative journalist, then a foreign correspondent, then an assistant editor, then a city editor, all the way up to the position he occupied today as editor in chief.

His staff looked up to him. They believed in him. He was seen by them, just as Higgins had described him, as a gentleman of the utmost integrity.

As of now, only Higgins and Flack were aware of Miles's apparent misconduct. Miles didn't like to think how the rest of the paper would react on hearing that he'd been discovered in a compromising position with a source for one of his stories. And in his office, no less, during the height of the business day.

It didn't matter that Miles could explain it all. Middle-class morality demanded more than excuses and apologies. It was an exacting arbiter, defined by suffocating conventionality and a hidebound adherence to proper behavior. A workingman—a self-made man—had little else but his good name to recommend him. To lose that was to lose everything.

Higgins caught up with Miles in seconds. "Your hat, coat, and gloves, sir," he said, passing the items to him.

Miles took them. He shrugged on his coat as he walked. His gloves came next, obscuring the evidence of where Shadow had bitten him. He made a mental note to apply a poultice to the wound at the first opportunity—whenever that might be.

Higgins hurried along at his side, matching every one of Miles's long strides with two of his own. "And here's that package that was delivered for you." He extended a small box, wrapped in brown paper and twine.

Miles accepted it with a distracted frown. "Who did you say—"

"A street boy, sir. Claimed a beggar woman paid him a penny to give it to you. He didn't know who she was—or who might have put her up to it."

"Of course not," Miles said irritably. He tucked the box in the inner pocket of his coat. Up ahead, Miss Trewlove vanished through the door at the end of the hall, moving extraordinarily briskly for a lady obliged to rely on a cane.

A cane.

Miles hadn't even noticed it when he'd first entered the office and seen her seated there. And he prided himself on noticing everything.

It wasn't the first mistake he'd made with her. It had been misstep upon misstep since the instant she'd lifted her veil, all of it culminating in that ultimate moment when they'd been caught, compromised.

And he didn't even know her given name.

Yet.

He overtook her on the stairs as she descended to the ground floor. "Miss Trewlove—"

"Do you have any idea where he's staying?" she asked abruptly.

"Pettiman? No. I presumed he lived near enough not to require a hotel. As I recall, I wrote to him at his premises in—"

"In Waltham Abbey, yes. But he'll have taken a room for the night somewhere. He values his comforts too much to travel to town and back in the same day." She opened the door to the street before Miles could do it for her.

He caught it with his hand, holding it for her anyway. It was impossible to tell whether she appreciated his effort at chivalry. That dratted veil was covering her face again. She walked under his arm without breaking stride.

She didn't stop until she reached the pavement facing the busy street. Private coaches rolled past, interspersed with teeming carts and an overcrowded omnibus. "I must hail a hackney."

"I've ordered my carriage," Miles said, coming to a halt beside her. "You'll find it more comfortable than a cab."

Her head jerked in his direction. "I told you—"

"I heard you," he said. "And I trust you heard me."

She drew herself up to her full height. It wasn't much. Even with her hat on, she scarcely reached his shoulder. "It's no business of yours, sir. I'm the one who will be obliged to face the consequences of this disaster, not you."

"I wouldn't be so sure of that," he said grimly.

She didn't seem to comprehend his meaning. Either that or she was being willfully blind to it. "It's always the women who must pay the price," she continued. "But I won't refine on it. Whatever happens next—"

"Concerns us both now."

"Really, sir," she protested.

"Really, Miss Trewlove," he volleyed back, rapidly losing what was left of his patience. "I don't know what sort of gentlemen you've been used to dealing with, but I don't shirk my responsibilities to a lady. *Any* lady."

His carriage rolled up in front of them before she could supply a suitably sharp retort. Miles had no doubt that she wanted to. He could feel her efforts at self-restraint vibrating through her crinoline-clad frame.

He opened the carriage door. Stepping back from it, he offered his hand to assist her in. "If you would allow me, ma'am?"

Miss Trewlove hesitated a fraction of a second before grudgingly setting her hand in his. "It's Penelope," she informed him tightly. "Or Nell, rather, since it seems we must be intimates."

Nell.

Miles's jaded heart performed a troubling double thump.

He was already weighed down with too many burdens. Societal backlash from his articles, dwindling newspaper sales, a missing reporter, and an as-yet uncongenial street cat residing in his office, to name a few. He had neither the means nor the desire to take on another troublesome concern. And yet . . .

As he handed Nell into the carriage, he felt all at once the profound responsibility he had for her. He hadn't asked for it. Hadn't wanted it. But after today, it was his.

She was his.

The prospect, he found, wasn't as repellent as he had earlier imagined it.

3

Nell sat back in the leather-upholstered seat of Miles's carriage as his matched pair of jet-black horses sprang into motion. She wasn't an idiot. She knew what he meant when he referenced his responsibilities.

Were she not already consumed with worry at the inevitable repercussions of this morning's cat-induced debacle, she might have had some capacity left to be shocked by his sentiments.

Leave it to her to have been compromised by who had to be the last truly honorable gentleman in greater London. Surely, no other man would feel obliged to own up to his so-called responsibilities in such a way. Not if the lady he'd compromised was no lady at all.

Nell had no illusions on that score. She was an orphan girl, with no money or connections. A humble teacher at an obscure charity school, and a lame one at that. Most gentlemen would have fobbed her off with a wooden apology, and—if they were generous—an offer of some meager financial compensation. They certainly wouldn't have been contemplating anything more.

But Miles Quincey wasn't most gentlemen. He was the childhood best friend of Effie's new husband, Mr. Royce. Perhaps that's why he was behaving with such unusual consideration?

He sat across from her in the carriage, his tall black hat resting on his knee. He was, in every outward respect, no different from the man who had shaken her hand in greeting less than an hour ago, rumpled and impatient, as though he had a million obligations pulling on him at once and not enough time in the world to see them straight.

Yet, he wasn't the same at all.

She'd since felt the strength of his arms. The long length of his leanly muscled body pressed to hers. And she'd submitted, quite willingly, as he'd lifted her skirts, giving him full view of not only her ankles (which would have been scandalous enough) but her calves and—heaven help her—her *knees*.

Facing him now, any other young lady would be forgiven for swooning. But Nell had neither the time nor the temperament for lapsing into a fit of the vapors.

She pushed back her veil. Her hat was still partially askew on her head, her hair coming loose from its pins. "Have you any way of locating Reverend Pettiman?" she asked. "One of your newspaper sources or something of the like?"

Miles looked at her steadily. There was an expression in his eyes that was difficult to read. "I can try."

"I would be grateful," she said. "If you can but find him and explain things, we may yet avert the worst of this disaster."

"You prefer I speak with him?"

"It must be you. He'd never listen to my excuses. And if he did, he wouldn't believe them. As a man you'll be given the benefit of the doubt."

"A cynical viewpoint."

"An accurate one. It doesn't behoove me to fool myself. Pettiman must be made to see reason. Otherwise . . ."

The possible consequences pressed in on her from every side.

A truly liberated female would laugh in the face of them. But Nell knew better. Though the Academy's mission was firmly progressive, it must still present a public appearance of conformity. It was that outward veneer that was susceptible to crack if Pettiman's accusations about Nell were made public. No charity school could ever hope to remain reputable if its deputy headmistress had her character impugned by such a prominent local figure of morality.

Miles seemed to grasp her unspoken concerns. "You've done nothing wrong."

She reached up to remove her hatpin. "That doesn't signify. It's not the wrongdoing society concerns itself with, but the impression of wrongdoing. And you and I have provided ample evidence of that."

He ran a hand through his disheveled black hair. There was a slight wave in his locks that was not unbecoming. "It was a perfectly justifiable interaction, however it looked. Far more comical than immoral, if you think of it."

Nell lifted her hat from her head. "Yes, I'm sure Reverend Pettiman will be heartily amused. Perhaps we should introduce him to your cat?"

Miles's brows lowered. "Shadow is as innocent in this as you are."

Nell flashed him a speaking glance as she smoothed her hair back into its chignon. He was defending his cat. And from her of all people. She hated that she found it endearing. "I know *that*," she replied. "I'm not blaming her."

Miles didn't seem to fault the little beast either. Never mind that she'd bitten him. And severely enough to draw blood if the damp streaks of crimson that stained the front of his waistcoat were to judge. "No one is to blame," he said. "Unless—"

She paused in the act of resettling her hat back on her head. "Unless what?"

"Nothing." He glanced away from her to the carriage window. Outside, the city rolled by at a steady clip as the horses weaved through the crowded streets.

"Oh no," Nell said. "Please don't refrain. If you have a criticism to bestow upon me—"

He turned back to her. "Not on you. On that wire cage contraption of yours. It's the true culprit in this."

Heat threatened to flood Nell's cheeks once again. This time she failed to suppress it.

It was bad enough that he'd lifted her skirts. That he'd seen her stocking-clad limbs, with the darning on her right knee. Now he was criticizing her undergarments? The unmitigated nerve!

"Don't you dare speak another word," she said in the same perilous tones she sometimes employed with the more insolent of her students.

Miles was undeterred. "No one requires skirts of such astounding circumference. They're impractical, as well as being dangerous."

Nell's eyes narrowed. The man clearly had a death wish. "Let me guess, in addition to being a brilliant editor, a fearless reporter, and a champion of truth and justice and cats, you're also a member of the anti-crinoline league?"

He snorted. "Don't be absurd. I've rarely given the things a second thought."

She stabbed her hatpin back into place, securing her hat in its correct position. "Until this moment, it seems."

"Yes, well . . . the device is hard to ignore on direct acquaintance."

Her blood simmered with mingled embarrassment and indignation. "You have no acquaintance with my undergarments, sir, direct or otherwise. I'll thank you to keep your opinions about them to yourself."

A shadow of a smile edged his lips. It vanished as swiftly as it appeared. "I beg your pardon. I have been unforgivably rude."

"Yes. You have." She paused, adding dourly, "A gentleman wouldn't have looked at it at all."

"If that's so," Miles said, "a gentleman would have been precisely zero use in removing that cat."

Nell privately conceded the point. She only hoped that Reverend

Pettiman would prove to be as rational-minded about the matter when Miles found him.

If Miles found him.

Whether he did or he didn't, Nell's own course was plain. She had no choice but to return to the Academy on the next train.

Miss Corvus would require fair warning, and Nell would be remiss if she didn't give it to her as expeditiously as possible. It would have to be in person. There wasn't time to stitch one of the coded sewing samplers Nell and her Academy sisters used for confidential communications. And Nell could scarcely commit this morning's events to a telegram that any nosy clerk at the telegraph office might read.

She turned to stare out the carriage window, her stomach twisting into an inextricable knot. Good lord, but this was a mess.

No, not a mess, she amended bitterly. A *failure*. And on her first mission, too. For that's what this was, and no mistake.

She hadn't come all this way simply to answer Miles Quincey's questions. Important as it was to the Academy that she put his inquiries to rest, there was another matter that was more important still. It had arisen in the days directly preceding Nell's imminent departure for London. A pressing enough issue that Miss Corvus had summoned Nell to her private chambers and given her the assignment herself.

"I wouldn't normally send you on such an errand," Miss Corvus had said. *"But as you'll already be in town, you'll be well placed to investigate the matter."*

Nell had shaken her head. Much as she'd have liked to take charge of the situation, she knew she wasn't best suited for it. She wasn't Effie. She hadn't spent years abroad, mastering the art of gliding, sharklike, through the treacherous waters of fashionable society. From childhood, Nell's feet had been planted firmly on the shore.

"I wouldn't know where to begin," she'd said.

As ever, Miss Corvus had anticipated her. *"There's a seamstress in Whitechapel with whom I once had an acquaintance. She can't read. It makes writing to her an impossibility. You must visit her in person. Speak with her. Persuade her to introduce you to the madams at the brothels thereabouts. She does a steady trade for them, and will know where to direct you."*

"But I have no experience outside of the school," Nell had objected. *"I can deal with Mr. Quincey well enough. That calls for strategy and diplomacy. But for something of this nature, surely you would do better to send Miss Sparrow."*

Along with Effie and Nell, ginger-haired Gemma Sparrow was one of the earliest of the Academy's graduates. Now a teacher at the charity school, she instructed the girls in self-defense with her trademark brand of ruthless gusto.

"Miss Sparrow is a blunt instrument," Miss Corvus had replied. *"It's your soft touch that's required here. You have a gift for inspiring women and girls to trust you. It's time you put it to use."*

The compliment had been double-edged. Nell had once been destined to use her beauty as a weapon in the Academy's service. But after the girlhood accident that had injured her leg and damaged her smile, she had instead poured all of her energies into being a faithful friend, a devoted teacher, and an enthusiastic mentor. Admirable qualities, to be sure, but they weren't the roles Miss Corvus had originally envisioned for her.

Indeed, it seemed to Nell that she'd begun this mission with her credit already in the red. Success would have balanced the books for her. While failure would only prove to Miss Corvus, once and for all, that Nell had no value outside the walls of the school.

Nell refused to accept that.

She turned back to Miles. "How long do you expect it will take you to find Reverend Pettiman?"

"With luck? Not long. When I return to my offices, I'll send a man to inquire at a few of the nearby hotels. If Pettiman's taken rooms in one of them, it shouldn't be difficult to track him down."

"You might have done so immediately if you hadn't insisted on accompanying me," she remarked, a touch ungratefully.

"I didn't realize you wanted him found until we were already approaching the street," Miles said.

Neither had Nell. In the aftermath of being compromised, her first concern had been to get to the hotel. She'd sent her bags ahead from the station. She couldn't depart London without retrieving them.

"Given the fall you took," Miles continued pragmatically, "and the fact that you were overset, it seemed more important that I escort you to your lodgings."

Overset!

Nell bristled at the description. She didn't get overset.

Then again, it wasn't every day that one's reputation was effectively ruined.

"You needn't have," she grumbled.

"On that," he said, "we'll have to disagree."

Nell subsided into silence. There was no point in quarreling with him. She didn't require his agreement any more than she required his chaperonage. She had greater concerns weighing on her mind.

As the carriage turned down Commercial Street, her thoughts began to coalesce into something like rational order. She reminded herself that when Effie had encountered an obstacle to her first mission it was Nell she had turned to for advice. It didn't matter one whit that Nell had never been outside the school. She was still intelligent, resourceful, generally unflappable. Why else would Miss Corvus have appointed her as deputy headmistress?

There was no reason Nell couldn't handle this situation as capably as she handled every other crisis that had come her way. All she had to do was approach things sensibly, and she may yet avoid returning to the Academy empty-handed.

The carriage came to a halt outside a crooked black building squeezed between a greengrocer's establishment and a forlorn-looking chandler's shop. A paint-chipped placard proclaimed its name: MRS. MARIGOLD'S HOTEL FOR WOMEN.

Miles gave the place a doubtful look. "Are you certain I can't convince you to remove to a more reputable establishment? It would be safer."

"I'll be safe enough, thank you," she said. "I'm only remaining long enough to collect my luggage."

"You mean to return to the charity school?" he asked.

"I believe I must," she replied. "I shall catch the next train from Shoreditch."

Miles didn't argue with her, though it looked as though he very much wanted to. He opened the door and climbed out. "I'll walk you in," he said as he handed her down from the carriage.

Nell stepped onto the pavement. She gave her skirts a shake. "You may escort me to the lobby. I expect it's the only place gentlemen are allowed."

"Fair enough." He offered her his arm and she reluctantly took it, allowing him to walk her inside.

She was painfully conscious of her limp. It was far more noticeable than it had been when she'd arrived at the *Courant* this morning. The fact didn't escape Miles's attention. He cast her more than one troubled glance as he escorted her through the front doors of the hotel.

As it transpired, there was no lobby, only a small—and presently empty—foyer. It stood adjacent to a cramped visitors lounge, furnished with worn couches and chairs, and two strategically placed potted palms.

Miles drew Nell to the lounge's entrance. The air was stale, with a lingering aroma of dampness and rot. "There will be several trains leaving from Shoreditch this afternoon," he said. "You would do better to take a later one."

She stilled. "Oh, would I?"

"You already have a room reserved. Allow me to summon a doctor for you. There's time enough, if you'll take it."

Nell recoiled at the suggestion. She'd had her fill of medical men as a girl. Officious imbeciles all, with their leeches and lancets, and their endless poking and prodding. They inevitably made things worse. "I don't require a doctor," she said. "Whatever you might think."

"I think you worsened your injury when you fell," he said. "It would set my mind at ease if you would have it looked at."

It.

Her leg, he meant. For surely it was obvious to him that it was the source of her discomfort.

She ignored her embarrassment. "My injury is none of your affair," she informed him. "In any event, it will right itself with a little rest."

"Rest awhile, then," he said. "Give me a chance to find Pettiman. I'll return this afternoon with any news. Our heads will be clearer. It will give us an opportunity to talk."

Nell drew back from him, understanding what the subject of this talk was likely to be. She shook her head. "There's really no need."

Miles closed the small distance between them. "There's *every* need," he said with sudden intensity. "You and I still have an issue to settle between us."

Her heart gave an uncharacteristic quiver. It wasn't only apprehension. It was—

She didn't know what.

She dismissed the feeling. This wasn't the time to interrogate girlish palpitations. Miles wasn't being romantic. Whatever method he suggested to settle the issue of having compromised her—and there could only be one method, she knew—it would be compelled by duty, not attraction.

"Mr. Quincey—" she said. "Miles—" Again she stopped herself, seeing a flicker of some unidentifiable emotion at the back of his gaze. She continued with an effort. "I'm not insensible to the issue you're referencing, nor to its obvious solution. But believe me when I say that, where I'm concerned, such a remedy would be impossible."

He studied her face, brows notched in a frown. "You're not a widow after all?"

She bent her head. "No, indeed, but—"

"And you're not wed already? Or engaged to be wed?"

"No, but—"

"Then I don't see how there's any impossibility to what I must propose."

Propose.

The word was enough to make Nell's insides tremble. She had no experience with men, let alone proposals. Not unless she counted the ones in the novels she sometimes read in the evenings in the privacy of her small bedroom in the staff wing of the charity school. Even that much was an indulgence, and one she could scarcely afford given the weight of her responsibilities.

She forced herself to meet his eyes. "My life is at the Academy," she said. "I wouldn't alter it, not for any inducement. I'm happy as I am."

"So am I," he replied with harsh candor. "But my happiness doesn't matter any longer. This involves more than our own inclinations. We have our reputations to think of—*and* the reputation of the *Courant*. It's already been negatively affected by my articles exposing Lord Compton's crimes. A scandal like this one could damage it even further."

Had he said anything even remotely sentimental, Nell might have found it harder to withstand him. But this . . . this was bitter truth, however painful to swallow. He didn't want to join his future with hers. He didn't want her full stop.

And she didn't want him.

"Quite so," she said with forced briskness. "Which is exactly why you must run Reverend Pettiman to ground and convince him he didn't see what he believes he did. As for all the rest—"

"Nell—" Miles interrupted gruffly.

Her heart spasmed on an ache of regret. She couldn't recall when a gentleman had ever before used her given name. It was an extraordinary intimacy, and one she doubted she would experience again.

"I release you from any further obligation," she cut in before he could finish whatever it was he had been about to say. "Now please, sir, go and find Pettiman. And do see to the wound your cat inflicted before it festers."

Miles dropped a glance at his gloved hand. "It's nothing. She didn't even draw blood."

"No?" Nell directed a pointed look at the crimson streaks on the front of his waistcoat. "Then where did that come from?"

• • • • •

Miles followed her gaze. A jolt of alarm shot through him. *What in blazes?*

He immediately reached inside his coat and withdrew the small, brown-papered box. Blood was slowly leaking through its wrappings.

Miles met Nell's eyes. As if in silent agreement, they swiftly repaired behind the nearest potted palm. There, they sank down in unison on one of the lounge's badly sprung sofas, so close to each other that Nell's wide skirts bunched against his leg.

"Did someone send you a gift from the butcher?" she inquired quietly.

"I suspect not," Miles said.

The *Courant* wasn't above inspiring the basest of responses to some of its articles. During his time as editor in chief, he'd seen his share of dog excrement and rotting fish. Had he not been so preoccupied by this business with Nell, he'd have refrained from taking the package from Higgins in the first place. But, small as it was, it hadn't occurred to Miles that it could be anything harmful.

He withdrew his handkerchief from his pocket. Shaking it open, he spread it over his knee. Setting the box upon it, he methodically untied the twine bindings and stripped away the bloodstained paper. He paused before opening the box itself to look at Nell. "It might be anything," he warned her. "If you'd prefer—"

"I'm a teacher," she replied. Her countenance was surprisingly businesslike. "I've seen all sorts of vile anonymous gifts. Nothing could possibly shock me."

Miles gave a stiff nod. He opened the box. The item within was wrapped in a handkerchief of its own. The blood-soaked square of linen bore an elegant monogram that the anonymous sender had prominently displayed.

L. C.

"Lawrence Cowgill," Miles murmured.

"Who is Lawrence Cowgill?" Nell asked.

"My missing gossip columnist." Miles unwrapped the bloody handkerchief.

Nell sucked in a horrified breath. "*Good lord.* Is that—?"

"His tongue," Miles said with a sinking sense of realization. It appeared to have been cut out, possibly with a razor. And not too long ago, judging by the still-seeping blood.

He swiftly closed the box, hiding the contents from her view. He stood. "Forgive me, I must return to my office at once."

Nell rose. Her face was pale, but resolute. "Naturally, you must. But shouldn't you first notify the police?"

"Quite," Miles said. "I'll be back as soon as I'm able." He bowed to her, and turning on his heel, strode out of the hotel.

4

Miles stood beside Higgins outside the door of Lawrence Cowgill's ground-floor flat in Carey Street. It was difficult to believe that, only a short time ago, he'd been on the verge of proposing marriage to a lady he'd compromised. And now here he was about to commit what was inarguably a crime.

Then again, Miles had always been good at compartmentalizing.

His life was organized into rigid boxes—work, friendships, women, cats. Everything orderly and methodical. Thus far, only the cats had managed to escape the confines of their category. Nothing else threatened to do so. Certainly not a lady who was still virtually a stranger to him.

A stranger whose stocking-clad limbs he'd been privileged to admire. One he'd held close against him, feeling the narrow, corseted curve of her waist in his hand and the soft fullness of her rounded bosom pressing to his chest.

Penelope Trewlove.

The recollections of her nagged at Miles, threatening to divert his attention.

He mentally consigned her to one of his many boxes. Not the cobweb-strewn one labeled *Women*. That derelict space had been empty for ages, and even before that, it had never been occupied for long, and never by anyone who truly mattered to him.

In any case, it wouldn't do for her. She required a box of her own, one marked *Nell.* He would return to it and the inevitability of their engagement at a later time. For now, it was work that must take priority, just as it always did.

"I really do think we should have notified the police," Higgins said for what had to be the hundredth time.

Miles gave his clerk a distracted glance. Higgins was young, but he was trustworthy. More importantly, he knew how to follow orders. Miles had returned to his office only long enough to fetch him—and to dispatch a reporter to track down Pettiman—before proceeding to Cowgill's lodgings without further delay. They hadn't taken Miles's carriage. They'd used a series of hansom cabs to convey them as far as Portugal Street. The remainder of the way had been traversed on foot, much to Higgins's consternation.

"We will," Miles assured him. "But first—" He rattled the doorknob.

"There's no one here, sir," Higgins objected. "I came myself only yesterday, on your orders, and Bob the day before that. The flat was empty."

Miles stepped back from the door to examine the strength of its hinges. "You didn't go inside."

"Of course not. There was no one to admit us. As for Mr. Cowgill, why . . . he might even now be in the gravest of danger. Scotland Yard would—"

"Cowgill is dead," Miles said. "And once the police are involved, we'll lose any opportunity to find out why."

Higgins's face went ashen. "Forgive me, sir, but isn't that a question best answered by them?"

Only half listening, Miles glanced down the street, first to the left and then to the right, keeping a lookout for anyone who might raise the alarm.

It had been a long while since he'd stooped to breaking into someone's house. Decades, in fact. Then, he'd gone in quietly, usually through a window, in company with Gabriel and the other street children who haunted the alleyways of the St. Giles slum. Miles had grown up among them. Had circumstances been different, he might have ended up as Gabriel had—a dangerous underworld demigod, possessed of questionable wealth and a flexible sense of morality.

But there was a fundamental difference between Miles and his childhood best friend. Unlike Gabriel, Miles had had a mother.

A *formidable* mother.

Catching him shimmying down a drainpipe one evening, she'd dragged him home by his ear. *"We may be poor, Miles Quincey,"* she'd scolded him, *"but we aren't thieves. We don't go into strangers' houses. And we don't steal from anyone."*

"It was only a lark, Mum," Miles had answered back. *"Gabriel—"*

"And do you do everything Gabriel Royce tells you? Have you no mind of your own? No reason?" She'd shoved him into the single room they'd shared at the end of a fetid alleyway. It was where she'd raised him on her own since his birth, teaching him to read and write at her knee. *"As soon as I can scrape up the remaining funds, you'll be gone from here for your apprenticeship. It won't be a moment too soon."*

Miles well remembered both her words and the sharp sting of her smacks.

Rose Quincey had sacrificed everything to get him out of the Rookery and to ensure that he became a respectable, educated gentleman. She would turn over in her grave to see him now.

Miles sent up a silent apology to her as he forcefully applied his shoulder to the door. It gave on the first attempt, bursting open at its hinges.

"Mr. Quincey!" Higgins gasped. He shot a horrified look at the street behind them as though expecting a policeman to materialize out of thin air and haul them straight to Newgate.

"Don't just stand there," Miles said, entering the flat. "We haven't much time." He waited only long enough for Higgins to scurry in after him before propping the door shut.

The apartment was dark and dismal, but even in the dim light seeping through the cracks of the curtains one could see the state of the place. Drawers had been pulled out of a large bureau and turned out on the floor. The bookcase had been cleared, cushions slashed, and pictures removed from the walls. Clothing and books lay in heaps all over the green-and-blue floral carpet.

Higgins collected himself. As an office clerk, he wasn't accustomed to braving danger in the field. He was nevertheless possessed of good sense. "I'll light a lamp."

Miles scanned the cluttered room. It was composed in a largish square, with a bedstead, a sitting area, and an approximation of a kitchen, complete with a cast-iron range. A small part of him had expected to find Cowgill's body here, but there was no sign of it. Nor was there any evidence of blood. Not that Miles could yet discern.

Higgins managed to locate a tinderbox and used it to light the glass oil lamp that stood on a table beside Cowgill's sofa. "What are we looking for?"

"Something that might tell us what he was working on," Miles said.

"You believe his death is connected to it?"

"When someone cuts out the tongue of my gossip columnist, I can only presume." Miles stooped to pick up one of the books from the floor. He was flipping through the pages when a faint movement caught his eye from across the room. It was a breeze softly stirring the curtains.

Walking to the window, Miles pulled back the drapes. He wasn't entirely surprised to discover the glass cracked open and the latch on the casement broken.

Higgins wrinkled his nose at a heap of clothing on the floor. "I wouldn't have guessed Mr. Cowgill would be this untidy."

"He wasn't." Miles let the curtain fall closed. "Someone's been here before us."

Higgins blinked in dismay. "They broke in?"

"And turned the place over."

By the looks of it, they'd shaken out every book, rifled every drawer, and examined the innards of the pillows and the mattress. They had also checked the backs of the pictures and mirrors, likely looking for a notebook or a sheaf of papers containing whatever damning evidence Cowgill possessed against them.

There were few places left to search.

Miles's gaze once again drifted over the room, recalling everything he'd ever learned during a childhood spent fraternizing with the criminal elements of the Rookery. "Focus on the floor and the baseboards," he said. "Look for loose joints or cut sections of wood."

Higgins got straight to it, though not without grumbling. "Seems no point to me. They'll have already found what Mr. Cowgill had hidden here."

"They haven't," Miles said. He rolled back the carpet as far as he was able. "Doubtless they believe I have it."

Higgins paused in the act of feeling along the baseboards behind the sofa. "I don't quite—"

"They sent his tongue to me as a warning. They obviously think I know something. If they didn't, they'd never have risked exposing their crime. Cowgill's disappearance could have remained a mystery."

"With all respect, sir, it still is one."

"Only until we piece it together."

Higgins furrowed his brow. "Is that why we had to come here in such a roundabout way? Taking those hansom cabs and cutting through those alleyways on foot? You suspected we might be followed?"

Miles continued searching under the carpet for any sign of a loose floorboard. "I wouldn't rule it out."

Higgins's lips thinned. "We're not police inspectors, Mr. Quincey."

"No," Miles said. "We're investigative journalists. And some stories are more dangerous to report than others, as Cowgill clearly discovered."

"But Mr. Cowgill wasn't a reporter. He wrote harmless tittle-tattle about nameless lords losing their fortunes and unidentified ladies having love affairs. That isn't serious journalism."

"Yet Cowgill took it seriously. He was a veritable vault when it came to his methods. He wouldn't divulge them to anyone, not even me."

"There's some who say he cultivated relationships with the valets and ladies' maids of the gentry," Higgins said.

It wasn't the first time Miles had heard the rumor. "He may have done," he acknowledged. "The point is, he protected his sources. I don't expect he'd have been any less protective when it came to his notes."

"The notebook we found in his desk at the *Courant* didn't contain anything of value," Higgins pointed out. "Only three dates, as I showed you—two already past, and one next month."

Miles remembered. They had been written in an ink-splattered line: ***19th March, 28th March, 3rd September***. He hadn't paid them much attention at the time. He'd been too irritated not to find a draft of an actual gossip column tucked away in Cowgill's desk—something they might run in the cursed man's absence. A few scrawled dates had been useless, as well as meaningless.

"They must have meant something to him," Miles said. "Either they were sufficient alone to jog his memory, or they're a companion to another written record." He cast a glance at Higgins. "How well did you know him?"

"Not well," Higgins admitted.

Miles could say the same. As editor in chief, he didn't have direct supervision over the columnists. His attention was focused on larger issues—circulation, advertising, and the serious investigative articles he edited (or sometimes wrote) himself.

The truth was, he'd rarely read Cowgill's column. He'd only been notified by his managing editor, Mr. Griffiths, when there had been none available for Monday's issue. And then, not because Miles might know something about Cowgill or his whereabouts, but because the absence of the gossip column would affect the paper's bottom line.

"I *have* heard that he had a taste for fine things," Higgins went on. "He once boasted to me that his evening coats were made by the finest tailor in Bond Street."

That, Miles could believe. Indeed, it had been the impetus for the few meetings he'd had with Cowgill—harsh reprimands in Miles's office relating to Cowgill's repeated conflicts of interest.

The man had been notorious for taking advantage of the perks of his position. He'd relished moving in fashionable circles, and had wallowed in the favorable treatment he received there from society figures seeking to influence him. Miles had had to warn him more than once about accepting invitations from the people on whom he was meant to be reporting.

"I only accept the ones for lunches, dinners, and the odd house party," Cowgill had said in his own defense. *"If I didn't, I'd starve. You know I'm incapable of cooking a morsel."*

"Get yourself a housekeeper," Miles had replied, unmoved.

Recalling the terse conversation, Miles's attention flew to the iron range in the corner. Cowgill didn't cook. And given the fine layer of dust that had settled over the cooking surface, Miles doubted whether the man had heeded his advice to find a housekeeper.

Abandoning his search of the floorboards, Miles went to the range and sank down in front of it. He opened the hinged door. The inside of the cold oven was empty except for a heap of ashes at the bottom that appeared as though they hadn't been cleared away in some time.

Miles's pulse accelerated. Reaching into the ashes, he felt the unmistakable form of a book. "Eureka."

Higgins's head lifted. "Sir?"

Miles carefully dusted off the ashes before removing the small, leather-bound book from the stove and opening it. The pages were filled with Cowgill's characteristic scrawl. Satisfaction coursed through him. "I've found it," he said.

Higgins came to join him. "His notebook?"

"It appears to be." Miles thumbed through the pages. "The dates go back some time."

"The earlier notes must be in reference to his previous columns," Higgins mused, peering over Miles's shoulder. "Is there nothing more recent?"

Miles turned toward the end. "This is dated last week," he said. "The last entry before he disappeared."

The ink-splotched notes beneath the date were sparse and not readily understandable. Only random names, broken phrases, and a few seemingly unrelated scraps of information.

Fawn-Purvis, Innes
From Hertfordshire to Brothe
Depot
Sleep/Tea
5000 pounds.

Higgins beetled his brows. "What does it mean?" he asked. "Hertfordshire to brother?"

Miles examined Cowgill's notes with an editor's eye. He didn't understand what they meant yet, not in totality, but he did know one thing. "That word isn't brother," he replied. "It's brothel."

• • • • •

The bell over the door rang as Nell entered the dilapidated little rag-and-bottle shop. Located at the end of one of the narrow, intersecting alleyways that branched off of Commercial Street, it stood at the entrance to the slum—a fact announced by the refuse that littered the ground and the putrid air that rolled in from the docks.

An old woman poked her head out from behind a pile of discolored garments she was sorting. "Who's that?" she demanded, looking from Nell's face to her cane and back again. "Have something to sell?"

"I've come to visit the seamstress, Miss Jean," Nell said. "I understand she resides at this address."

Immediately losing interest in Nell as a potential customer, the old woman jerked her chin toward a curtained doorway behind her. "Second room on the right."

Nell inclined her head to the woman before passing through the curtain into a dimly lit passageway. She had remained in her room at the ladies' hotel only long enough to calm the pain in her aching leg before setting forth on her commission for the Academy. There was little enough time for it. According to her railway guide, the next train was departing at two o'clock. Nell intended to be on it.

If Miles was back before then, she might consent to speak with him. But she wasn't waiting around for hours merely to rebuff some misguided masculine attempt at redeeming her honor. She'd already made up her mind.

In any event, she doubted whether Miles *would* return. The man had been sent a severed tongue, for heaven's sake. She must be the last thing on his mind at the moment. Indeed, he'd scarcely managed a bow before abruptly taking his leave from her.

Not that Nell blamed him. One of his reporters had been killed. That obviously took precedence over her own ruination.

As for the state of her honor, Nell sincerely hoped that her present errand might go some small way toward repairing it. At least, that is, in Miss Corvus's eyes.

Reaching the second door on the right, Nell rapped on it firmly.

"Come in!" a woman called.

Nell opened the door, entering a room that was even tinier than her own small chamber at the Academy. It contained a narrow, neatly made bed, a dainty table with a chipped vase of violets upon it, and two faded chairs on either side of a window. A handsome woman in a printed floral dress sat in one of them busily stitching the hem of a linen dress. Her skin was as dark as rich mahogany, her black curly hair twisted back under a muslin cap.

"Miss Jean?" Nell inquired.

"Aye, that's me," the woman replied, a cockney accent edging her words. She appeared to be in her middle thirties. Poised and self-confident, her back not yet bent by a life of hardship. "I've got no time for any more mending if that's why you've come. Not 'til next week. I've dresses to make, as you see."

Nell shut the door behind her. "I haven't come to hire you. I've come to speak with you."

"You what?" Miss Jean looked up from her sewing to examine her unexpected guest. "And who might you be, milady?"

Nell came forward. She offered her hand in greeting. "Penelope Trewlove," she said. "Deputy headmistress of Miss Corvus's Benevolent Academy for the Betterment of Young Ladies."

Miss Jean's hand froze halfway to Nell's. "Miss Corvus?" She snorted. "That's a name I ain't heard in a long time."

"She sends her regards," Nell said, hand still extended.

Miss Jean shook it at last. "I bet she does." She gestured to the empty chair. Scraps of fabric and trimmings littered the seat. "Move those aside, and sit yourself down."

Nell cleared away a place before taking a seat. "I hope I've not come at a bad time."

Miss Jean chuckled as she resumed her work. "It's all bad times here, Miss Trewlove. Or hadn't you noticed?"

"But excellent craftsmanship, I see." Nell reached to examine a section of the linen dress. "Your stitching is flawless," she observed with genuine admiration.

Miss Jean's mouth quirked with dry humor. "Miss Corvus tell you to say that?"

"No, indeed. I can recognize good work when I see it. I have the honor of teaching a sewing class at the Academy. Needlework is one of my favorite subjects."

"A favorite subject, you call it? Teaching orphans to mend rich folks' clothes?"

"We don't focus a great deal on mending," Nell said. "We spend more time on samplers."

"Samplers? Huh!" Miss Jean scoffed. "Won't earn them no money, sewing samplers." Her needle flew as she spoke, stabbing in and out of the linen with unrelenting precision. "More of Miss Corvus's crackbrained ideas, in't it? Instructing girls on samplers, lock-picking, fencing, and fisticuffs, as though any of those are the means to making a living."

Nell's mouth tipped with amusement at Miss Jean's unflattering characterization. "I see you've some familiarity with our special curriculum. Was it Miss Corvus who shared it with you?"

"Oh, aye. She confided all about the classes she offered to her best and brightest. That's rich people for you, I said. They've the coin to indulge any odd notion, and all the rest of you fine folk go along with their fancies instead of telling them they've lost their bloody minds. But I told her, and all." Miss Jean glanced up again, an ironic set to her smile. "So, why'd she send you to me after all this time? She already knows I ain't coming to work for her."

Nell failed to contain a flash of surprise. "She offered you a position at the Academy?"

"Aye, she did, the madwoman. She said as how I could be a teacher."

"You certainly could be," Nell said.

Again, Miss Jean scoffed. "Teaching what, I ask you?"

"Needlework, for one. As to anything else—I daresay you have your talents. Miss Corvus is adept at choosing teachers who can convey some useful skill to our girls."

"I don't read or write, Miss Trewlove. Can't be taught. The letters are all backward and upside down to me. Happen you know that, else you'd have sent a note instead of coming here yourself. And without a chaperone, too." Miss Jean looked Nell over with a critical eye. "You think that mourning costume will protect you from the worst of this place?"

"No," Nell said. "I don't imagine it will." She smiled again. "Fortunately, I can protect myself."

Miss Jean laughed. "Miss Corvus said much the same when she come here all those years ago." At last, she put aside her mending. "So, what is it she wants?"

Nell studied her for a moment. She knew various ways of dealing with people—flattery, manipulation, outright intimidation. But none of them would serve here. If Miss Corvus had offered Miss Jean a position as a teacher, then she was an equal in the fight. It would have to be the truth.

"We were expecting a new pupil at the charity school two days ago," Nell said. "Her name is Flora Brent."

The health records the workhouse had forwarded to the Academy had given a brief description of the girl. It wasn't much, but it would have to do.

"She's but fourteen," Nell said. "Dark-haired and exceedingly pretty for her age. She never arrived."

Miss Jean was quiet a moment. "Happen she changed her mind."

"She could have done," Nell allowed. "But we don't think so."

"No? Not everyone wants to be saved by an eccentric gentlewoman, Miss Trewlove."

Nell wondered if that was the very issue that had prevented Miss Jean from joining their ranks. Did she believe Miss Corvus was some patronizing would-be rescuer? That her aims were any less valid simply because she'd been born into a life of wealth and privilege?

"We don't save people," Nell said. "We give orphan girls the education they need to effect a better future for themselves—and for all women."

"Don't mean a girl of fourteen had any desire to be part of it. Not if she could run off and make her own way."

"You're wrong. Miss Brent wanted to come to the Academy. She has a unique potential, one well suited to our aims. I corresponded with the matron at the workhouse about her myself. It was I who arranged for her to come to us."

"You feel responsible?"

"I *am* responsible. The matron put her in a third-class railway carriage in Surrey on Monday morning at my request. Miss Brent was to change trains at Shoreditch. We can trace her as far as that, but no further. Something appears to have happened to her here. Miss Corvus suspects it's the same thing that happens to many a pretty lass who ventures into London unaccompanied."

Miss Jean's countenance grew serious. She comprehended Nell's meaning.

Disturbing reports abounded of sinister madams preying on pretty village girls who traveled into town to find domestic work. They coaxed them from the rail stations with tea and cake, and promises of respectable employment. The next thing the poor girl knew she was ensconced in a brothel somewhere, her life—and her innocence—effectively at an end.

"You thinking she fell victim to some procurer?" Miss Jean asked. "Here, in the East End?"

"It's a distinct possibility," Nell said.

"Aye," Miss Jean replied darkly. "It is." A troubled frown clouded her brow. "Madams is hard people. And some of the hardest are hereabouts."

"You sew for them?"

"I sew for all sorts."

"And have you heard anything of a new girl being brought in? A girl who may have come unwillingly?"

Miss Jean's expression shuttered. "I've heard nothing."

Nell wasn't without sympathy. But it wasn't Miss Jean she was responsible for. It was Flora Brent. Whatever else happened, the girl must be found.

"I don't ask you to put yourself in peril," Nell said. "I only ask that you point me to some of these brothels where the madams are known to employ such tactics."

"And you aim to go there? With that face?" She gave Nell an incredulous look. "They'd snap you up faster than one of them foolish country lasses."

"Oh no," Nell said. "I won't be going myself. I must return to the school this afternoon. I'd be grateful if I had names and addresses to convey to Miss Corvus. She'll send someone to make further inquiries without delay."

"Names, that's all?" Miss Jean repeated.

"That's all," Nell assured her.

At length, Miss Jean gave a reluctant nod. "All right, then. If you're set on it, you may as well start with Mrs. Pritchard."

5

It was three o'clock when Nell's train reached Waltham Station. She hired a hackney to take her the remainder of the way. Not half an hour later, the driver set her and her bags down outside the pair of black wrought iron gates that guarded the grounds of the bleak stone manor house beyond.

A profound sense of relief settled over her.

Perhaps she was a coward. A frightened fledgling returning to its nest prematurely. In that moment, she didn't care. Whatever crisis had brought her back, all she wanted now was the safety and familiarity of the only place she'd ever called home, and the only people she'd ever known as family.

She had little enough memories of the years before. Of the small, hidden house in the country where she'd been lodged in the care of two elderly servants. The shameful secret of a fine, expensively perfumed lady who sometimes came to visit her—all silken gowns, pale powdered skin, and the singular fragrance of jasmine, tuberose, and honey. Her mother, Nell supposed.

But that had ended long ago. The elegant lady had eventually stopped coming, and one day, a short while afterward, those same aged servants had brought Nell's nearly five-year-old self to these very gates. She'd been clutching a toy loom in her hands, the only remnant of the life she was leaving behind. There had been fear—which she well recalled—and copious tears, too. But now . . .

There was only the Academy.

Alas, Nell had no key to let herself in. On any other occasion, she might have easily picked the lock. She and her Academy sisters were well-versed in such skills, just as Miss Jean had intimated. But Nell didn't feel equal to clever feats at present. She was too weary. Too dashed anxious. Instead, she waited like the veriest visitor, until one of the junior teachers emerged from the house to admit her.

But it wasn't a junior teacher.

It was Gemma Sparrow. Ginger curls springing from their pins, she marched down the long, pebbled path to the gates, the skirts of her gray woolen dress swaying wildly.

Nell watched her come with a reflexive smile. No one wore a wire crinoline like Gemma did. She didn't glide about in it as sophisticatedly as Effie, or arrange it about her with as much practiced grace as Nell. No. Gemma's garments were as alive and unpredictable as she was.

Gemma was, like Nell and Effie, one of Miss Corvus's special girls. A member of the earliest class of orphans, handpicked from among the Academy's inmates to attend lessons focused on stealth, strategy, and self-defense. It was knowledge not shared with all of the girls. At least, it hadn't been when Nell was a child. It was only recently, under Nell's rule as deputy headmistress, that defense classes had been opened to everyone.

"Back so soon?" Gemma asked, unlocking the gate with its enormous black iron key.

"As you see," Nell said.

"In less than a day?" Gemma's freckled face spread into a droll smile. "That must be a new record for one of our graduates." She opened the gate with a scraping groan of metal. "Let me guess. There's been a development?"

"Regrettably so." Nell collected her carpetbag, leaving her portmanteau behind as she entered the grounds. She only had one hand to spare when using her cane. "Is Miss Corvus at liberty?"

"She's in her study." Gemma gamely fetched Nell's portmanteau. Locking the gates behind them, she accompanied Nell up the path to the house. "*And* she's in a foul mood."

Nell gave Gemma an alert look. "Why? What's happened?"

"A letter came express not twenty minutes ago from that odious Reverend Pettiman of all people. It must have contained bad news. Corvus nearly bit my head off when I inquired about it."

Nell's face fell. "An express? From Pettiman?"

She hadn't even considered the possibility. Pettiman had specifically mentioned wishing to catch the next post. Nell had thought any letter he might send wouldn't arrive until the morning.

"I recognized his writing on the envelope," Gemma said. "Those pompous flourishes he puts on the A's and B's in the Academy's name, and the way he nearly closes the C in Corvus."

Among her other skills, Gemma was a gifted forger. She knew more about handwriting than anyone else of Nell's acquaintance.

"He's never sent an express before," Gemma reflected. "Who would have imagined he'd stump for anything other than the penny post? I suppose someone must have died." She cut Nell a shrewd glance. "Or worse."

Nell didn't ask what could be worse than dying. She already knew the answer.

"Might this express have any connection to your all-too-precipitate return?" Gemma asked as they climbed the front steps to the house.

"It might," Nell said. She waited for Gemma to admit them into the entry hall. It was empty at this time of day, only the faded carpets, moth-eaten tapestries, and large, gilt-framed oil paintings giving color to the aged stone walls and floor.

The two paintings had been hanging in their present location since Nell had first come to the Academy. One was a reproduction of Gentileschi's *Judith Slaying Holofernes*. The other was a portrait of a dark-haired lady in a plain black dress, standing strong and resolute in the silhouette of an open door, her back to the viewer.

"A woman looking through a doorway, not behind her," as Effie had once described it. *"Her true face hidden from the world."*

It might have been a portrait of Miss Corvus herself. Nell took comfort in its familiarity, just as she did the sounds and smells of the school—the buzz of girlish voices filtering from the floors above and the fragrances of parchment, ink, and the sawdust used to fill the canvas sparring bags in the athletic room.

"You'll be wanting to see her at once, I gather," Gemma said. They approached the broad, blackened oak staircase at the edge of the hall. "Shall I take your bags to your room for you?"

"That would be kind of you." Nell passed Gemma her carpetbag. "Thank you for standing in for me, even if it was only for one day."

Gemma made a dismissive sound as she mounted the steps. "No trouble at all. The girls in your morning classes are exceptionally well-behaved."

Nell should hope so. She'd specifically told them that they were to be on their best behavior for Miss Sparrow and the other teachers who had agreed to take over Nell's classes in her absence.

Gemma trotted up the stairs with Nell's bags and was soon out of sight. Nell ascended behind her at a more sedate pace, using her cane to steady herself when her leg began to feel weak. She'd asked a lot of it today, pushing her muscles to the limit. It wasn't surprising that it had given her so much trouble.

By the time she reached the fourth floor, her hip was twinging with every step. Miss Corvus's study was located at the end of the corridor—a remote tower room overflowing with books, private papers, and a convoluted filing system to which only Nell and Miss

Corvus held the key. Nell entered to find Miss Corvus seated at her large, carved walnut desk furiously writing a letter.

Clad in unrelieved black, she was as coldly elegant in form and manner as she'd been since Nell's childhood. A slender woman, with porcelain pale skin and silver-threaded ebony hair, she had recently marked her fiftieth birthday. The years sat lightly on her. Only the fine lines by her eyes and the grooves at her mouth betrayed the hardships she'd suffered as a young woman—alone and unprotected, the unwitting victim of unscrupulous men.

But that was a long time ago. The Artemisia Corvus that Nell had come to know was neither innocent, nor naïve. She was determined. Pragmatic. Arguably ruthless. Ever looking forward, and never back.

Nell paused at the threshold, waiting.

At last, Miss Corvus glanced up. Her lips compressed in a hard line. "Miss Trewlove."

"Ma'am," Nell replied.

Miss Corvus didn't rise. She gestured to the upholstered chair opposite her desk. It was the very place a teacher or student might sit if they'd been summoned in order to be called to account for something.

Stiffening her spine, Nell crossed the study and sat down. She saw no need to beat about the bush. "Miss Sparrow informs me that you've had an express from Reverend Pettiman."

Miss Corvus wordlessly picked up a letter from her desk. She offered it to Nell.

Nell took it. Her blood went cold as she read the reverend's unvarnished report of what he'd seen in the editor's office of the *London Courant*. The words *immoral*, *shameless*, and *disgrace* jumped out at her from the page.

"Well?" Miss Corvus prompted. "I presume you deny his account?"

Nell returned the letter to Miss Corvus's desk, relieved at the steadiness of her hand. Miss Corvus prized self-control. She had taught them, as Nell now taught her own students, that a lady's greatest strength lay in keeping her composure. "I can't deny what he saw," she said, "only his interpretation of it."

"Then you *were* on the floor of the newspaper office, with your skirts lifted, and a gentleman between—"

"Yes," Nell cut in. Mortification burned in her veins. "But not for the salacious reasons Pettiman imagines."

Miss Corvus sat back. Her face was tight. "Pray enlighten me."

Nell didn't prevaricate. She described the events that had led up to her being discovered by Reverend Pettiman as swiftly and succinctly as possible.

Miss Corvus listened, revealing not so much as a glimmer of amusement. Rather the reverse. Her expression seemed to grow harder and more forbidding by the second.

Nell continued with an effort. "So you see," she concluded, "it was all an unfortunate accident, caused by a frightened cat caught in the tapes of my crinoline. Mr. Quincey took no liberties in removing her. He was perfectly gentlemanly."

Miss Corvus met Nell's explanation with ominous silence.

Apprehension coiled in Nell's stomach. By some miracle she kept it from creeping into her voice. "Do you doubt me?"

"You've never given me any reason to," Miss Corvus said. "Yet it doesn't change the facts."

Nell's already sagging spirits sank still further. "I know. I *know*. It's why I came back immediately. I thought to warn you before—" She stopped herself. "But I didn't consider he'd send an express to you."

"Not only to me. If he's sent one here, you can be assured he'll have sent something similar to one or more of our patrons."

Nell had contemplated that very possibility during those frantic moments after she'd been caught in Miles's office. It made it no easier to hear.

"We rely on their generosity," Miss Corvus said. "Many are women like us—forward-thinking, subversive—but not all. It's the latter that concern me. Specifically, Lady Summers, Mrs. Crookshanks, and Mrs. Weaving."

Lady Summers, Mrs. Crookshanks, and Mrs. Weaving were their three largest benefactors. Respectable Christian women all, none of whom knew the true purpose of the Academy.

"How long do you think their annual donations will continue if they are persuaded my deputy headmistress is a light-heeled wench who's no better than she ought to be?" Miss Corvus asked.

Nell flinched at the coarse description. "I will explain the circumstances to them myself."

"It won't matter."

"I'll tell them—"

"It won't matter," Miss Corvus bit out. She stood abruptly. Arms folded, she paced across the study, her black crepe skirts swishing with bottled fury. "We are held to a higher standard here. Higher still because our outward show of modesty protects the true purpose of our work. What you have done, however inadvertently, puts us all at risk."

Nell clasped her hands tight in her lap. During all her years at the Academy, she had never received a dressing-down. The worst of Miss Corvus's ire had always been reserved for Effie and Gemma. Nell, by contrast, had rarely merited a single word of rebuke.

She had spent her life doing her duty as best she knew how. Always looking out for her sisters, her students. Always putting the Academy first. It's why she'd gone to London in the first place. And all for this to happen. It wasn't right. It wasn't fair.

"Would that I was rich enough to subsidize all this myself," Miss Corvus went on. "But we rely on these charitable ladies and their ilk.

When they come to me, along with Pettiman, demanding that I dismiss you—"

"*No!*" Nell objected, shocked.

Miss Corvus glanced over her shoulder to meet Nell's stricken gaze. Her mouth curved in a bitter smile. "Had that possibility not occurred to you yet, my dear?"

Nell could supply no answer. Her chest tightened so that for a moment she could scarcely breathe.

"No, I don't suppose it did," Miss Corvus mused. "All you could think of was returning home."

Tears stung at the back of Nell's eyes. "What else could I have done?"

"Nothing," Miss Corvus said. "Indeed, returning to the Academy is exactly what I expected you would do should trouble cross your path during your visit to town."

Nell stilled, hearing the unmistakable note of censure in Miss Corvus's arctic tones. "I don't know what you're implying—"

"I imply nothing. My meaning is plain. You had no wish to leave the school. You never have had since your accident. It surprises me not at all that you would return at the first opportunity."

"You make it sound as though I'm making excuses. Surely, you must see that the events of this morning—"

"Oh, they're a scandal. There's no doubt of that." Miss Corvus walked to the tower window. She stopped in front of it. There was an endless pause. And then: "What is Mr. Quincey like?"

Nell's heart beat an uneven rhythm. "A good man, I suspect," she said. "But unknowable."

"What is there to know? So long as he's honorable. And his exposés on Compton's crimes would lead one to believe he is. No one else would have risked so much to reveal the truth." Miss Corvus looked out the window, her posture as resolute as the woman in the portrait that hung in the hall. "You will, of course, have to marry the man."

Nell stared at Miss Corvus's rigid back. She was certain she'd misheard her.

"I will inform Pettiman and any others who inquire that you are already engaged," Miss Corvus said. "An excess of enthusiasm can be forgiven if a couple is soon to be wed. It will not expunge the crime, but it will go some small way toward ameliorating the damage." She turned. A muscle twitched at her eye, the only sign of the effort it took for her to maintain her control. "Perhaps, when enough time has passed, you may come back and resume your duties. Married teachers are not out of the common way. You might even live here again if Mr. Quincey will permit—"

"Stop," Nell cried, springing up from her chair. An image of Miles leapt into her mind—tall and commanding, with his broad shoulders and penetrating brown eyes. A hot flush swept over her skin. "You can't be serious."

"Do I look like I'm in jest?"

"But I don't understand why—"

"You do understand. You of all my girls know what it means to put the Academy first."

"I *have* put it first." Nell went to her, all thought of keeping her composure gone. She reached into her reticule, withdrawing the scrap of paper containing the names Miss Jean had given her. She offered it to Miss Corvus. "I did as you bid me. I went to Whitechapel. I saw Miss Jean."

Miss Corvus took the paper. She scanned the names, frowning. "And these are?"

"The brothels where Flora Brent is most likely to have been taken. I hadn't time to go to them myself. But I can return if you wish it. I can fix this. Make amends somehow for having allowed things to go so very—"

"No," Miss Corvus said. The expression in her eyes softened almost imperceptibly. "I was wrong to send you. I should have kept you close. All this might have been averted." She slipped the paper into the pocket of her skirt. "I shall send someone else. It need not concern you any longer."

A lump formed in Nell's throat. She knew what this was. She was being cut out. Dismissed. She couldn't allow it. "Send me," she said. "Let me return to London. Let me prove myself."

"You will be returning, but not to pursue Miss Brent. You shall have to meet with Mr. Quincey to formalize your arrangement. I presume he'll be agreeable?"

"*I'm* not agreeable," Nell said.

Miss Corvus took a step toward her. "You'd prefer exile? At least with marriage you would have a path back to us. A chance to return to your role at some later time, your reputation restored." She passed a hand over her brow as though staving off a headache. "No. There is no other remedy I can find. None that would serve the school."

Nell shook her head in reflexive disbelief. She refused to accept that her only choices were marriage or exile. Surely, there must be another way. A better way. She had only to think of it.

But she couldn't think at the moment.

Her emotions were in turmoil, her mind in a complete muddle.

"Take dinner in your room this evening," Miss Corvus said. "Recover your strength. We will plan your exit in the morning. There is no escaping it."

Nell was beginning to comprehend that. All that remained was to decide what form her exit would take. The frightening prospect of it—of her, existing somewhere, anywhere, outside of the school—gripped at her trembling vitals like a steel vise. "What about my students?" she asked.

"I'll tell them myself after you've gone," Miss Corvus answered. "They will be grieved to lose you, to be sure, but many will see it as a romantic adventure. As for the special girls . . . we might present it as a cautionary tale. Either way, I see no need for prolonged farewells. It would only upset them unduly."

Nell agreed in principle, though her heart was breaking. Like Miss Corvus, Nell desired what was best for the school. She wanted to be part of the new generation of women advancing forward, not the cause of their being hamstrung and held back. If that meant she must withdraw from the field . . .

Miss Corvus clasped Nell's arm briefly as she passed her on the way back to her desk. She didn't speak, but the fleeting touch of her hand spoke volumes.

The last of Nell's self-control crumbled. Hot tears spilled onto her cheeks. She swiped them away. "Yes, of course," she said. "I-I have much to think about."

She departed Miss Corvus's office without looking back, blindly descending the stairs to the staff floor. Somehow, she found her way to her room, to the small, safe world she'd built for herself within the Academy's impenetrable walls—the soft bed, the pink-painted wardrobe, and the little chair with the needlepoint pillow she'd stitched with such love and attention. It bore the unofficial symbol of the school—a raven with a white-tipped wing.

"An intelligent and prophetic bird," Miss Corvus had once explained to Nell and Effie. *"Ravens don't abandon their young. They remain with them into early adulthood, flying beside them."*

But no more, it seemed.

Henceforth, Nell must fly alone.

• • • • •

By the time Miles found his way back to Mrs. Marigold's Hotel for Women in Whitechapel, it was a quarter past four. His suit was stained, his hair rumpled, and his spirits decidedly worse for wear.

The news of Lawrence Cowgill's murder had spread through the offices of the *London Courant* like wildfire. A wave of intense demoralization had followed in its wake. It was made worse by the growing whispers that the paper's editor in chief—a man whose reputation the staff had formerly believed to be beyond reproach—had only that morning been caught beneath the skirts of a mysterious woman in black.

As if all that weren't bleak enough, the reporter Miles had dispatched to track down Reverend Pettiman had been unable to find the man. There had been no trace of him at any of the nearby hotels or guesthouses. Which could only mean one thing: Pettiman had already returned home, possibly by the next train, his scandalous tale ripe for the telling.

There would be no mitigating the damage now.

It was crisis upon crisis, with no end in sight. Miles was dealing with it the only way he knew how—one catastrophe at a time.

Lawrence Cowgill's tongue was now in the custody of Scotland Yard. It had been accompanied not by Cowgill's notebook (which was presently locked in Miles's desk at the *Courant*), but by the tissue of lies Miles had concocted to explain why he'd broken into Cowgill's flat.

"Leave it with us," the police inspector had told Miles and Higgins. *"We'll find who's responsible."*

Miles took leave to doubt it. The London police were overworked and overwhelmed. Even if they did by some miracle solve Cowgill's murder, they would have neither the time nor the resources to pursue the story that had led to it.

No. That was Miles's job. He had no intention of shirking his duty. Not to Cowgill, the *Courant*, or anyone else to whom he owed the burden of loyalty.

He approached the reception desk in the hotel's small foyer. A vinegar-faced older woman in a dark dress stood behind it, sorting letters into the rack of pigeonholes that hung on the wall, each of them numbered to their corresponding room.

"Can I help you, sir?" she asked without breaking her task.

"Miss Trewlove is expecting me," Miles said.

"Miss Trewlove is no longer in residence," the woman replied.

Miles froze. "She's checked out of the hotel?"

"She departed this afternoon. I summoned a hackney to take her to the railway station myself." The woman turned, eyes squinted in inquiry. "You're not Mr. Quincey, are you?"

"I am."

"She's left a note for you. I put it here somewhere or other." The woman searched through the stacks of papers on the desk. "Ah. Here it is." She passed him a folded note card stamped with the hotel's name in blue ink. "Miss Trewlove said I was to give this to you if you should come calling."

If?

Miles suppressed a harsh surge of annoyance. As though he couldn't be relied on to keep his word! Temper simmering, he unfolded the note, scanning Nell's familiar elegant script.

Dear Sir,

I have returned to the Academy. You may write to me there in regard to anything relating to Reverend Pettiman. As to the other matter you referenced, you will agree it is impossible.

Yours,
P. Trewlove

Reading her words, Miles's brow contracted in a furious scowl. He most assuredly did *not* agree. Whatever Nell's qualms, it didn't change the fact that he'd compromised her this morning—and himself in the bargain. It was incumbent on him to make things right. His reputation depended on it, even if hers didn't.

Tucking the card into his waistcoat pocket, he strode out of the hotel.

6

Nell folded a shawl and placed it into the open portmanteau on her bed along with the rest of her meager belongings.

Yesterday morning, on setting out for London, her future had been settled. She would continue teaching, remaining in her role as deputy headmistress, until Miss Corvus decided to retire. When that day finally came, it would be Nell who took over the charity school.

But no longer.

Fate had seen fit to give her a new future. Nell had no choice but to face it.

After a restless night, she'd woken this morning clearheaded and resolute. Rather than join the students and staff in the dining room for breakfast, she'd washed and dressed, and immediately begun the painstaking process of packing her things.

Her options were admittedly limited, but she wasn't without them entirely. Effie would be back from Paris tomorrow. Nell would go to her then, as she'd originally planned to do. But tonight . . .

Tonight, she would return to Mrs. Marigold's Hotel in Whitechapel.

Miss Corvus had tasked Nell with finding Flora Brent. Not Gemma, not Effie, but Nell—a person with a knack for dealing with women and girls, just as Miss Corvus had claimed. *That* was Nell's talent. She may have to leave the Academy for a time, possibly forever, but she wasn't abandoning her vocation. Whatever else happened, she was determined to finish her first mission. Even if it should prove to be her last.

"There's a gentleman to see you, Miss Trewlove."

Nell cast a distracted glance up from her packing, too lost in her own thoughts to hear what the junior teacher standing at the door of her room had said. "What's that, Miss Hanem?" she asked absently as she placed a stack of folded petticoats into her case.

Miss Hanem fidgeted in the doorway, the iron gate key clutched in her hands. A former orphan of sixteen, she had only recently been promoted to her position. "A gentleman," she repeated. "A great, tall, stern man with black hair. He's asking for you."

Nell slowly straightened, the girl's words sinking in to pulse-quickening effect.

Miles is *here*?

For it must be him. Nell didn't know any other gentleman who would fit the description Miss Hanem had supplied.

"Indeed?" she replied with creditable calm. "And you've admitted him, have you?"

"Oh no, Miss Trewlove," Miss Hanem said.

Nell nodded her approval. "Well done."

"Shall I tell him you're coming?"

"No need. I'll deal with him myself." Nell crossed to the doorway. She was dressed sensibly in a blue cloth skirt and a white Garibaldi blouse, her thick blond hair twisted into a plaited roll. Not a glamorous ensemble, but neat, clean, and pressed. It would have to do.

She gave Miss Hanem a reassuring smile as she passed, pausing only long enough to retrieve the key from her. "You may return to the dining room, my dear."

"Yes, Miss Trewlove." Miss Hanem obediently hurried off.

Nell smoothed her skirts as she descended the steps. She didn't use her cane. A night spent in her own bed had calmed the muscles in her leg enough that she could make do without it. It didn't mean that her limp was any less pronounced. Her gait hitched with every step.

Exiting the manor house to make her way down the pebbled drive, she felt a distinct flare of self-consciousness. Miles was watching her.

He stood on the other side of the gates, looking tall, dark, and imposing in a black three-piece suit and a hat. He must have traveled up on the first train from London to have arrived so early. A one-horse cab was parked not far behind him, the driver hunched on the box.

"Mr. Quincey," Nell said. "This is a surprise."

"Is it?" Miles returned with no trace of humor. "Then you must not have been listening to anything I said to you when last we met."

She stopped at the gates. "If you've brought news of Reverend Pettiman—"

"I couldn't find him," he cut in brusquely. "He must have left town immediately. It scarcely matters anymore."

"No, as a matter of fact, it doesn't. So, if you've come to pick a quarrel with me—"

"I shouldn't have had to come at all. If you'd done as I asked you and waited—"

"I never agreed to wait for you."

"No. But you might have—" He broke off, his heavy black brows notching in a scowl. "Must this conversation take place with a gate between us?"

Nell cast a wary glance back toward the manor house. She half expected to find Miss Corvus peering out her tower window. There was little that took place at the Academy that its redoubtable headmistress didn't know about.

"I can't permit you to enter the school," Nell said.

"Can't or won't?" Miles asked.

"Both."

"Very well. Then come out and join me."

Nell chewed her lower lip. Her leg was feeling stronger, but she doubted it was equal to bearing her weight on the stones for a prolonged period of conversation. Not to mention the fact that the jarvey would be right there, listening from his perch to everything she and Miles said.

Coming to a sudden decision, she produced the iron key and unlocked the gates. She opened them just wide enough to admit him. "We can talk in the garden," she said curtly. "There's a bench there, far enough removed from the house."

Commanding the jarvey to wait for him, Miles entered the grounds. He stood in grim silence as Nell locked the gates behind him. "You're without your cane," he observed as he accompanied her back up the drive.

She led him to the right, across the damp grass, to the small patch of wilderness that stood in the shadow of the tower. "I don't always use it."

"Why not if you need it?" he asked.

"I prefer not to rely on it too heavily when I'm at home." She gestured to the curved stone bench beneath the old oak tree.

Miles remained standing. He looked up at the weathered edifice of the school. "Home," he said doubtfully.

Nell sat down. Just because he wouldn't avail himself of a seat didn't mean she must be uncomfortable. She arranged her skirts about her, vaguely registering that her hands were trembling.

Miss Corvus was to blame—and Miles, too. All that talk about Nell marrying him. It added a palpable tension to their encounter. She could scarce be near him without unsettling thoughts creeping into her head about what it might be like to be his wife. To take his name. Live in his house. And . . . all the rest of it.

Nell pushed the troublesome images out of her mind. "It has been," she said. "For as long as I can remember."

"It's quieter than I'd expected."

"You anticipated chaos?"

"I anticipated children."

"The girls are at breakfast. After that, they'll disperse to their classes. Reading, writing, arithmetic. And so forth."

"And so forth," Miles repeated. "Naturally."

Nell tensed as his too-perceptive gaze drifted over the house and the grounds. He may have come here to see her, but he couldn't help himself, could he? He wanted to crack open the secrets of the Academy. To tie up the final threads of his exposé on Lord Compton, sating his journalistic curiosity about Elizabeth Wingard and all the rest of it.

And now Nell had let him into the gates.

"We are not anarchists, sir," she said.

"I didn't expect you were. That would imply a lack of purpose."

She folded her hands to mask their shaking. "Purpose we have in abundance. And warmth, and community, and the bonds of sisterhood. The Academy provides all those things for the orphan girls who come here. For the teachers, too."

Miles glanced back at her with solemn attention. "You're loath to leave it?"

The tension in her coiled tighter. "Who says I must?"

"Given what transpired yesterday, you must have considered it."

Nell had been considering little else since her interview with Miss Corvus yesterday afternoon. It served no purpose to discuss it with him. He had no part in her future. Not even if Miss Corvus commanded it. Not even if marrying him meant that Nell might one day return to her role as deputy headmistress of the Academy.

She moistened her lips. "Speaking of yesterday, did you go to the police? About Mr. Cowgill?"

He gave a stiff nod.

"What did they say?"

"That they'll investigate the matter."

"You don't sound convinced."

"London is rife with crime. My reporter's murder is but one of many." Removing his hat, he ran a hand over the back of his neck. "It doesn't signify. I'll be investigating Cowgill's death myself."

Nell's brows swept upward. "Isn't that dangerous?"

"Probably." He met her gaze. "I didn't come here to discuss the fate of my late gossip columnist."

Her stomach quivered at the gravity in his expression. "Yes, I gathered that."

"The matter we discussed yesterday—or rather, began to discuss—" He stopped himself before continuing, his voice taking on a gruff edge. "I'm aware you released me from my obligation to you, but the fact remains . . . You have an obligation to me."

She stared up at him, temporarily speechless. Of all the extraordinary reversals. Was he implying that *she* had ruined *him*?

"I *beg* your pardon?" she managed.

Miles soldiered on as though he'd prepared a speech and was committed to reciting the whole of it. "I don't exist within these gates," he said, "in this alternate world you've created for yourselves. I live in the real world. And in that world, actions have consequences that can't be ignored."

"I assure you—"

"I'm speaking about my reputation. My *professional* reputation. What happened yesterday took place at the *Courant*. It may not affect your life in here, but it's already affecting mine out there, and decidedly for the worse."

"You're wrong," she informed him.

His face hardened. "Shall I provide examples?"

"Wrong about me," she amended. "It *has* affected my life here." She gave a short, hollow laugh. The sound stuck in her chest. "Indeed, it's ended my life here."

Miles stilled.

"The fact is," she said, "I'm leaving the Academy. I'll be gone within the hour."

An inexplicable look crossed his face. But he didn't speak. He didn't question her. He only waited, his gaze fixing on her face with uncommon attention.

It struck Nell that this was exactly how he must deal with one of his skittish feral cats—all immobility, patience, and quiet. Biding his time in silence until they willingly came to him.

In that moment, she understood why they might.

He stood there, so stoic and capable, an intrepid defender poised between her and an uncertain future. The urge rose up in Nell to confide in him. To lean on him a little.

She sensed that he wouldn't think less of her for it. Wouldn't see it as a sign that she was weak or lacking in some way.

And she wondered . . .

What if she *did* join her fate to his? Could it really be worse than forging ahead on her own? Or was it the only rational answer? The single, solitary course that would ultimately lead her back to the Academy, the one place in the world where she truly belonged?

She clasped her hands tight in her lap. The certainty she'd always possessed as a teacher had left her. In its place was only fear and indecision, and the desolate, dreadful feeling that she was completely and utterly on her own.

"It seems I was mistaken," she said. "The situation is rather more serious than I'd allowed. Which is to say that you were right. Our happiness doesn't matter. We must salvage our reputations, however we can. Both of our reputations."

Miles regarded her steadily. His expression was as unreadable as it had often been in town. Then, Nell had born it because she'd had to. He'd been a stranger and an adversary. But not now.

"Don't do that," she said.

"What?"

"Don't be so . . . so dashed inscrutable. This isn't easy for me. And it's more difficult still when I feel I'm alone in my distress—"

"I don't mean to distress you."

"Whether you mean to or not—"

"Nell," he said gently.

Her throat clogged on an unexpected swell of emotion. She fought tears, reflecting that perhaps an unfathomable Miles was preferable if the barest kindness from him could provoke such an ill-timed reaction.

"Pettiman sent an express to Miss Corvus," she told him. "She says that the Academy's benefactors may soon call for my dismissal. If I remain, it will harm the school. Which I've no wish to do. I packed my things this morning. As I see it, I have but two choices. I can either go to Mrs. Royce in hopes that she'll take me in or . . . or I can go to you."

Miles drew closer to her, blocking out the tower window and the stone manor house, too, shielding her from everything and everyone but him. "To me," he said. "Obviously."

• • • • •

Miles waited for Nell to answer, his heart thudding with unusual heaviness in his chest. She'd accused him of being inscrutable. And he was. He *knew* he was. It was a skill he'd learned in hard school. Never showing his rivals what he was thinking. Never betraying weakness, or an excess of strength. Being, in short, something next door to invisible.

"It's the work that matters," his mother had taught him. *"That's where you must shine. It's the only way for people of our class to excel—by being better than all the rest. You just keep your head down and forget about anything else."*

Miles had taken her words very much to heart. He'd seen the truth of them during his apprenticeship, and later when he'd signed on at the *Courant* as a junior reporter. Work was how he distinguished himself, not through physical intimidation of his enemies, eloquence with young ladies, or an overzealous investment in social causes. He'd learned to be cold, methodical, abstract.

None of which served him now.

Nell sat before him, eyes luminous with unshed tears and her plaited flaxen hair glinting with threads of gold in the sunlight that shimmered through the branches of the tree. Standing over her in that moment, Miles was entirely at the mercy of emotion—both hers, and his own. A baffling state, and one to which he was completely unaccustomed.

As ever, when confronted with anything he couldn't rationalize, he reacted by over-rationalizing it.

He sank down on the stone bench beside her, close enough that he caught the elusive fragrance of her perfume. Some delicate floral something (gardenia, possibly?), applied so lightly as to be little more than a secret. It tickled at the back of his consciousness, faint but persistent, reminding him that this wasn't a typical business contract he was negotiating.

"You can't deny the logic of it," he said. "The Royces are still abroad. But I'm here. I have a house. A carriage. Adequate means. And there's the scandal itself to be addressed. Going to live with Mrs. Royce won't quell it. While if you married me—"

"Yes," she said softly.

"—we might begin to stanch some of the talk. We can start with my staff at the paper, and then . . ." Miles trailed off, belatedly registering her reply. He stared at her, his pulse thrumming in his ears. "I'm sorry, did you say *yes?*"

She gave him a stricken look. "Oh God. Were you not proposing?"

"I was," he assured her. "I just . . ." He bent his head on a huff of incredulity. "I hadn't anticipated you would accept me."

Not so quickly. Not without a great deal more in the way of rhetorical persuasion.

"Neither had I," she admitted. "But circumstances being what they are—"

"Quite," he agreed.

"It's the logical course, as you say."

"Eminently logical."

Her mouth trembled. "I only wish . . ."

Miles impulsively took her hand. Feeling her fingers curving tentatively around his in return, he was overcome by a feeling he couldn't begin to interpret. It was some bewildering mix of protectiveness and possessiveness. A fierce and powerful elixir that tightened his muscles and deepened his voice.

"Social pressure may have precipitated this match," he said, "but it needn't define it. Our marriage can be anything we want it to be. You need only dictate the terms and I will respect them."

Her brows knit. "Do you mean that?"

"Try me," he said.

She looked at him for a long while. "There is one thing."

"Name it."

"Miss Corvus has indicated that, in time, I may resume my teaching duties. When that day comes, you wouldn't object, would you?"

Miles sensed an unspoken question within her question. A hidden catch he couldn't yet discern. He studied her face. She was still so much a mystery to him. It didn't put him off. Rather the opposite, much to his consternation. "No," he said. "I wouldn't object."

Relief glimmered in her eyes.

"Anything else?" he asked.

She shook her head. "I don't know. I can't think now. Not clearly."

"There's no expiration on my offer," he said.

He meant it. Despite his imposing size and his frequent bouts of bad-tempered impatience, he wasn't a brute. Once they wed, Nell could remain safe in her box and Miles in his. He spent most of his time at the office. She need hardly see him if she didn't want to.

It was the normal way of fashionable marriages. Each party existing in their individual spheres. Only meeting at night, and sometimes not even then.

Why should his marriage to Nell be any different? Indeed, once they got over the initial upheaval of the arrangement, they could both go on with their separate lives, as countless other couples did.

Except that Nell wasn't a typical society bride. She was a member of the same secretive organization as Mrs. Royce. And not only a member. Until now, Nell had been deputy headmistress of Miss Corvus's Academy.

Miles had an idea of what that might mean. His research into the place hadn't been completely unproductive. He'd learned enough to understand that the Academy wasn't just a charity school, raising orphan girls to exceed their expectations. It was, he suspected, a training ground for formidable females intent on upending the patriarchy one uncooperative man at a time.

They had begun with Viscount Compton. Who knew where they might end?

And now Miles was proposing to marry one of them.

Nell seemed to read his thoughts, and to echo them in her own uncertainty. Her gaze fell to their clasped hands—his encased in a large black glove and hers small and bare and vulnerable. A frown worked its way across her brow. "I don't know anything about you outside of your work."

"Nor I you," he said.

A thoughtful line etched her forehead. Several seconds passed. "It was here I fell," she said.

"Fell? When?"

"When I was a girl. I was there, on the roof of the tower, helping a friend down, when I lost my grip."

Miles followed her gaze to the roof's edge. Understanding came, and with it a swift sense of dismay. Was this the cause of her limp? A four-floor drop to the ground? His hand tightened instinctively on hers. "Good God, Nell. What in blazes were you doing on the roof? You might have been killed."

"But I wasn't. I only concussed myself." Again, she paused, her gray eyes troubled by memory. "I woke a long while later, with an injured leg, some of my teeth knocked loose, and several other cuts and bruises. I'd saved my friend, but destroyed by own future in the bargain."

"How do you mean?"

"At your office yesterday morning, you asked me if I'd ever wanted to leave the school and go out into the world. The truth is, I did before I fell—quite desperately. I had so many dreams. But not afterward. Since that day, the school has become the whole of my life. I don't know who I am without it."

Compassion stirred in Miles's breast. "You're the same, surely."

"Am I?" she wondered. "All of my learning has been theory rather than practice. My visit to the *Courant* was the first time I've left these grounds since the day I arrived as a child. And we saw how swimmingly that went."

"You're afraid," he concluded.

She didn't deny it.

Miles hesitated. Duty had brought him to this moment, not infatuation or affection. But he couldn't deny that he felt something for her, even if it was only that same nagging ache of responsibility he'd experienced when he'd handed her into his carriage in Fleet Street. It prompted him to share something he'd never shared with anyone before.

"I was thirteen when I left the Rookery," he said. "My mother purchased an apprenticeship for me with a printer in the West Country. I had no wish to go. To live among strangers—my betters, supposedly. It meant leaving the one person I loved. Altering everything I was, my whole identity. I was frightened, too. Change *is* frightening. But that change . . . It was the making of me."

Her mouth curved with bitter irony. "And this one will be the making of me, is that it?"

"It will be whatever we make it," he said.

We.

The single word didn't appear lost on her. She wasn't alone in this. For better or worse, they were in it together.

Her bosom rose and fell on an unsteady breath. She lifted her chin. "Well," she said. "What now?"

"That depends. Do you require a grand wedding? A gown, guests, and so on?"

"No."

"Good." Releasing her hand, Miles reached into the inner pocket of his coat and withdrew a piece of paper. He presented it to her without comment.

"What's this?" She took it, scanning the printed text and signature. Her face drained of color. "A special license?" Her eyes flew to his. "How on earth did you manage it?"

"I went to Doctors' Commons yesterday afternoon," he said.

"But this means—"

"That we can marry anywhere, at a time of our choosing, without the necessity of calling the banns."

Her throat worked on a swallow. "Anywhere and anytime being . . . ?"

"On the return journey to London," he said decisively. "If we leave now, we can stop off along the way. There's a vicar I know of in Enfield who will oblige us. We can be married by the time we arrive at my house in St. James's Square."

Nell slowly refolded the special license. Her slim shoulders squared like a brave but unwilling recruit about to march into battle. "Very well," she said. "I'll collect my things."

7

Nell couldn't recall if she'd ever imagined her wedding day as a girl. Marriage had, for so long, seemed an impossibility; so unlikely *and* unwanted as to make fantasizing about it an exercise in futility. When the moment finally came, when she stood with Miles Quincey—a gentleman she'd known less than forty-eight hours—in the small North London church, hearing the aged vicar pronounce them man and wife, it seemed very much a dream.

And not for any romantical reasons.

The illusion of closeness they'd shared when Miles had taken her hand in the garden had ended as quickly as it had begun. Indeed, to say that their wedding was a businesslike affair would be to vastly understate the matter. Miles had been from the start as logical and unsentimental as Nell had observed him being in most every other respect. When addressed by the vicar, he'd brusquely admitted to not having a ring, equally brusquely answered "I will" at the appropriate place, and then dashed off his name in the register with all the impatience of a man who was late to catch an omnibus.

Nell was relieved that the words from the *Book of Common Prayer* hadn't instructed Miles to kiss his new bride. She'd undoubtedly have been subjected to the same variety of unwilling peck on the cheek that a reluctant guardian might bestow on a burdensome ward.

She didn't let it affect her. She had larger concerns than the questionable sentimentality of her new husband. Even as she signed her maiden name for the final time—*Penelope Trewlove*—her thoughts were on Academy business.

For that was one thing that marriage could *never* change. Whatever her new name, she was still an Academy girl. Miss Corvus's belief in her may have begun to waver, but Nell was determined that her own purpose never would. She would be passing through the East End within the hour. It was the ideal opportunity to pursue her mission.

She waited only as long as it took to board the next train to broach the subject.

"I have some business I must attend to in Whitechapel," she said as she entered their first-class compartment. "I'd rather it were done in daylight. If you wouldn't mind us parting at Shoreditch?"

Miles followed behind her. He had been unusually quiet since they'd left the church, saying hardly anything at all on the cab ride to the depot and during their short respite at the railway's refreshment room. Doubtless he was thinking of Mr. Cowgill, or some other pressing matter related to the *Courant*. He'd stopped in at the telegraph office before they'd departed the station in order to send a wire to one of his staff. She could only guess at what it might say.

"What business?" he asked.

Nell sat down in one of the cloth-upholstered seats, smoothing the skirts of her plain, dark brown traveling dress. She'd never ridden in a first-class railway carriage before. It was bordering on luxurious, with its wood-paneled walls, shuttered window, and gleaming brass parcel racks. Up to now, she'd always been content with second class. It was Miles who had booked the more expensive fare. She hadn't questioned him as to why.

"For the Academy," she answered.

Miles muttered something as he took a seat across from her. It sounded very much like "And here it begins."

Nell paused in the act of tucking a loose strand of hair back into the confines of her fanchon bonnet. "Do you object?"

"I wouldn't know what I was objecting to."

"Does it matter?"

"It matters." Frowning, he removed his hat, placing it on the seat beside him. "I'm sorry I didn't have a ring for you."

Nell blinked. "Oh," she faltered. "Well, that wasn't . . . That is, I didn't expect . . ."

"I hadn't time to go to the jewelers before this morning," he said. "Trust that I will at the first opportunity."

The conductor's whistle sounded. It was followed by a lurching jolt and a great grinding of metal as the train heaved into motion.

Nell hardly noticed. She was staring at the man she'd just married, oddly flustered. A quiet, closed-off Miles she could handle, but not one promising to purchase her something from a jeweler's shop. Not even if that something was a wedding ring.

Thus far, she'd survived the day by setting emotion aside. She hadn't concentrated on the restrained goodbyes she'd said to Miss Corvus and the other teachers, or the desolate feeling she'd had as she'd walked out the gates of the Academy for what might be the final time. To look backward was to risk losing her hard-won composure.

To look forward was equally perilous. To think of where she was going to live now, and with whom.

"Er, how did you know the vicar?" she asked for lack of any better response.

Miles ran a hand over his rumpled black hair. "A story I wrote last year on a series of thefts in Enfield. His church was robbed."

"How dreadful."

"The goods were found during the course of my story. I had some small part in their recovery—a lead of mine into a gang operating in North London. The vicar was grateful. He invited me to attend services when next I was in the vicinity."

"I'll wager he didn't mean a marriage service," Nell said with a fleeting wry smile.

Miles's mouth hitched briefly in return. "Probably not."

"In any case—"

"Yes."

"We *are* married now."

"That we are," Miles said gravely.

"And you did promise that I might dictate my own terms," she reminded him.

His brows sank in another frown, but he didn't dispute the fact. "What business does the Academy have in Whitechapel?" he asked.

"Why?" Nell asked in return. "Have you changed your mind about publishing a story about the school? Or is this simply more information you require to sate your boundless curiosity?"

His frown transformed into a swift scowl. "You do realize that I have a reporter's murder to solve, a newspaper to run, and a staff to convince that I'm not a conscienceless ravisher? Whatever curiosity I had about the charity school yesterday has been amply exhausted in those regards."

"Not all, obviously," she said.

"I'm concerned about *you*," he retorted. "We *are* married, as you said."

"Yes, but—"

"I can't have you traipsing aimlessly about the slum alone, prey for any villain who crosses your path. You're too . . . too . . ."

Nell's shoulders tensed, bracing for the inevitable masculine censure. "Helpless?" she supplied. "Naïve? Incapable?"

"Beautiful," he said. "You're too damned beautiful."

The growing indignation in Nell's breast fizzled away like a deflated balloon.

He wasn't the first to call her beautiful. As compliments went, it was the least original she'd encountered. And yet she'd never been called beautiful by him. Other than the arrested stare he'd given her when she'd lifted her veil in his office, he hadn't acknowledged her looks at all.

"Oh," she replied. "That."

"Yes, *that*," he said.

Nell smoothed a nonexistent wrinkle in the fabric of her skirt. "Being beautiful isn't a liability. Not even in the East End."

"No? What would you call it?"

"A weapon," she said.

Miles fixed her with his enigmatic gaze. "So, I was right. You *were* the heavy artillery."

Nell's mouth quirked. She'd forgotten he'd said that. "Not where you were concerned, clearly. My charms—ample as they are—had no apparent effect on you."

"We met for the first time yesterday morning," he said.

"Your point being?"

His expression was dour. "Today we're married."

He was so solemn and grumpy, Nell was tempted to laugh. "That had less to do with my charms and more to do with your cat," she said. "As you're well aware."

"Yet here we are."

"Exactly so." She grew serious again. "And as our train will be stopping in the vicinity, and as I'm more than capable of taking care of myself—"

"If you tell me what it is you're trying to accomplish," he interrupted, "perchance I can assist you."

"Why would you?" she wondered. "The Academy's problems aren't your problems."

"*You're* my problem," he said.

"How romantic," she remarked under her breath.

The two words were an inaudible murmur, lost amid the roaring clang of metal as the train rattled loudly down the track. And yet—

Miles managed to hear them. He gave her a scorching look in reply.

A rush of heat flooded through her in its wake, making her cheeks warm and her toes curl in her sensible half boots. She'd been stared at before. Ogled and admired by everyone from the local village lads to the aged members of the parish council. But no gentleman yet had ever regarded her with such blazing, single-minded intensity.

And Miles wasn't just any man. Not anymore. He was her husband, by heaven.

Her husband.

It didn't mean he was deserving of all of her secrets, but it surely allowed for her to confide in him a little. He had, after all, already proven himself to be an honorable gentleman. One who, in the past, hadn't hesitated to hold another powerful man to account.

She quickly recovered her self-possession, ignoring the lingering effects of the look he'd given her. "Very well," she said. "If you must know, a girl has gone missing and I've been tasked with finding her."

"What girl?" he asked.

"An orphan named Flora Brent. She was en route to the Academy from a workhouse in Surrey. We've traced her as far as Shoreditch. It's one of the reasons I came to London yesterday, and why I booked a room at Mrs. Marigold's."

"You have reason to believe the girl is in Whitechapel?"

Nell nodded. "We suspect she might have fallen victim to one of those unscrupulous madams one reads about. You know the breed—procurers who lure country girls from railway stations with promises of reputable work, only to spirit them to a brothel somewhere where they drug them with adulterated tea and—"

Miles's brows snapped together. His gaze was no longer scorching. It was as sharp as a hunting hawk's. "Brothels?" he repeated, cutting off her speech. "*That's* where you want to go?"

Nell couldn't tell if he was outraged or intrigued. "Not for my own amusement," she said. "It's purely to find out if one of them has taken her. And I won't be 'traipsing aimlessly about the slum' as you so delightfully put it. I have a list of brothels, given to me by a reliable source. I mean to visit each name on it in a perfectly orderly fashion."

"A list of brothels," he repeated without inflection.

Nell recited the names Miss Jean had given her from memory. "Mrs. Pritchard's Gentlemen's Establishment, Mrs. Early's Pleasure Palace, and Mrs. Silkweed's House of Sin."

Miles's eyes narrowed. "And what's this about tea?"

Nell paused to consider. "I suppose it isn't always tea. The madams may drug some other drink. The point is, the girl falls asleep, and once she wakes, she finds herself in a sad state—ruined, alone, virtually a prisoner. Given the choices available . . ." She trailed off.

As she'd been speaking, Miles hadn't been idle. She'd not uttered two sentences before he'd extracted a small notebook and tiny pencil from the inner pocket of his coat and begun scratching away.

"I'm sorry, are you taking *notes*?" she asked him.

"No." His pencil moved rapidly over the page in short strokes. "I'm sketching a portrait."

Nell stared at him, nonplussed. "Of *me*?"

He turned the notebook in her direction for a moment, revealing the rudimentary image of a thin, bushy-haired man with mutton-chop side-whiskers.

Nell leaned forward to see, fascinated in spite of herself. "Who on earth is that?"

"Lawrence Cowgill," Miles said, resuming his drawing.

"And you've chosen this moment to render his likeness because . . . ?"

"I'm going to show it to the employees at the brothels we visit."

We?

"I don't understand," Nell said. "What would be the point—"

"Two points," Miles said. He snapped shut his notebook. "One, Cowgill's death may have had something to do with a story he was writing related to brothels, and this adulterated tea you mention."

Nell let the information sink in, all the possible scenarios racing through her mind at once. She was almost afraid to ask. "And point two?"

Miles held her gaze. "When you disembark at Shoreditch, I'm coming with you."

8

Miles set a protective hand at the small of Nell's back as they departed the front steps of Mrs. Early's Pleasure Palace in Brick Lane. An oversized brute of a man stood outside the house's sagging door watching them go, his coarse features shadowed in the late-afternoon sunlight. He was flanked by a vulgar woman in a shockingly low-cut satin dress.

"Do come again, dearie!" she called to Nell with a mocking laugh. "We'll find work for you!"

Nell faltered a step, her fingers tightening on the carved handle of her cane. She hadn't had it with her when Miles had found her at the Academy, but she had retrieved it before they'd left and had been using it ever since.

"I prefer not to rely on it too heavily when I'm at home," she'd told him.

And this wasn't home. Not here. Not with him. And certainly not in the worst part of one of London's most infamous neighborhoods.

Miles curved his hand around Nell's corseted waist, urging her back down the squalid alleyway from whence they'd come. She didn't flinch at his touch. Perhaps she was becoming used to it? He couldn't begin to count the number of times he'd taken her arm or placed a hand on her back since that fateful moment the vicar had pronounced them husband and wife. As permission went, Miles's right to render her such assistance had been quite literally witnessed and formalized by law. Nell was his now. And he took care of what was his.

"Another dead end," she muttered crossly. "I can't say I'm surprised. When I asked Miss Jean for names, Mrs. Silkweed and Mrs. Early were only afterthoughts. She specifically said to start with Mrs. Pritchard's Gentlemen's Establishment near Lost Hope Yard."

A drunken fellow staggered past them at the intersection of the next street, face ruddy, and trousers poorly fastened. He leered at Nell.

Miles's jaw tightened as he steered her past. Every fiber of his being revolted at escorting his new bride on what amounted to a tour of the slum. It was a gentlemanly response distinctly at war with that other part of him—the barely restrained, bloodhound-like instinct that drove him whenever he was in pursuit of a story.

It was the latter impulse that had compelled him to approach Nell's list in as orderly a fashion as possible. If they were going to do this, and it seemed inevitable that they were, then they may as well do it right.

"Lost Hope Yard is furthest away," he said. "It only made sense to prioritize the names according to location. Otherwise, we'd be doubling back over ourselves."

Nell made a soft sound of disappointment. "Yes, yes, order and method. Yet, where have they got us? All we've learned is that, among the people willing to speak up—or more precisely, willing to accept your coin—no one will admit to having encountered either Miss Brent *or* Mr. Cowgill."

Miles wasn't unsympathetic to her frustration. Investigative dead ends were a common occurrence when pursuing a story. It made them no less exasperating. "Don't let it discourage you," he said. "Not every interview provides answers. It won't stop us asking questions."

Nell's cane clacked sharply along the refuse-strewn ground as they traversed the dark, narrow lanes that intersected the East End. It was hours yet until sunset. The worst of the slum's residents hadn't yet emerged. Among the drunkards staggering the alleyways and prostitutes lurking in the doorways were the hardworking people who called the East End home. Costermongers, washerwomen, and peddlers hawking their wares. Ragged street children ran among them, laughing and shouting, just as Miles had done with his childhood friends in the Rookery.

"I suppose they could have been lying to us," Nell remarked.

"I don't think so," Miles said.

They'd spoken with a handful of bully boys and working girls at the first two brothels. As for the madams, Mrs. Early had been unavailable to them, but Mrs. Silkweed had deigned to come down from her boudoir to answer some of their questions—for a fee. Among them all, most had been suspicious, and many of them sly, but when it came to the point, Miles detected the ring of truth in their words.

"Their establishments are fairly unambitious," he said. "The madams are weary, the premises run-down, and the women faded and—" He stopped short of calling them well used. "Generally older," he supplied instead. "We're looking for someone cold and calculating. Possibly murderous."

Nell cast him an alarmed glance. "You don't suggest that this person might have killed Mr. Cowgill? Or Miss Brent?"

Miles frowned. "I don't know what they might be capable of. Or even if they're the one we're looking for. We haven't much to go on other than a few lines from Cowgill's notes."

In the moments before their train had arrived at the station, Miles had shared those lines with Nell. She wasn't one of his reporters, or even a reporter at all, but she was thoughtful and intelligent. More than that, he had the sense he could trust her.

"Hertfordshire to brothels," she mused. "Presumably meaning country girls come from Hertfordshire? But Miss Brent came from Surrey."

"There mightn't be any connection between the two."

"In which case, we're grasping at straws."

"My instinct tells me no," Miles said.

"Your instinct as a reporter?" Nell replied dubiously.

They turned down an even narrower lane. Cramped buildings teetered in on each other, so close as to temporarily block out the sun. Miles's already heightened senses sharpened with renewed alertness. It was in darkness that the slums of London became truly dangerous. As he escorted Nell through, he didn't let his guard down for a moment.

"I wouldn't dismiss it," he said. "In this business, instinct counts for a lot."

"But it's not fact. It's only hunches and guessing. Even a capable newspaperman—"

"Brilliant, someone called me recently," he reminded her, guiding her into the next street where the sunlight once again shone through. "And fearless. And a champion of truth, and justice, and . . . cats."

Nell flashed him a repressive look. Her heart-shaped face was framed by the fetching tilt of her brown bonnet, its wide black ribbons tied loosely beneath her chin. "This someone sounds like a blithering idiot."

Miles's blood warmed inexplicably as her eyes met his. *How romantic,* she'd muttered on the train. It had been the first she'd mentioned of romance. The first Miles had even thought of it. He'd been struck, in that moment, by what it meant—truly meant—to be married to her. She was no longer a problem to be solved, or an adversary to be bested. She was his wife.

"Actually," he said, "I believe she's rather a clever girl."

Nell didn't appear at all flattered by the compliment. "Rather a clever girl?" she repeated. "You *are* aware I'm not a child to be patted on the head and placated?"

His hand remained at the curve of her waist. Her incredibly shapely waist. Along with the delicate brush of her skirts on his leg and the faint fragrance of her perfume, it was a constant, aggravating reminder of just how womanly she was. "You may rest assured," he said, "that the last thing I would ever mistake you for, Mrs. Quincey, is a child."

A strange expression crossed Nell's face.

Miles belatedly realized that it was the first time he'd addressed her by her married name. *His* name. The warmth in his veins ignited to a disconcerting simmer.

Judging by the color deepening in Nell's cheeks, she felt it, too.

She slowed to a halt at the corner. They stood for a moment, eyes locked, before she finally spoke.

"If we're to do this together," she told him, "we must be equals."

This.

She didn't specify what. It could be their marriage. The search for Flora Brent. The investigation into Cowgill's murder. Or possibly all three.

"But we're not equals," Miles pointed out. "Not in experience."

"You have your experiences and I have mine," she said. "Surely, we can defer to each other's strengths without resorting to condescension."

Miles hadn't been aware that he *had* condescended to her. If so, he certainly hadn't meant to. She was vexing, to be sure, and secretive, and inarguably inconvenient to his life, but he had no doubt that she had other qualities. Finer ones—and fiercer, too. He wasn't repelled by her contradictory distinctions. It was the very quality he admired in cats. Their ferociousness, their daring, and their indomitable independence, all wrapped up with loyalty and affection bestowed on their chosen few.

As he gazed down at Nell, Miles wondered what it might be like to be one of her chosen few.

Or possibly her only.

"Partners, then," he said gruffly.

Nell's eyes brightened at the word. She smiled at him, revealing both her crooked tooth and her beguiling dimples. A brief, but achingly genuine expression, just as she'd given to Shadow in Miles's office in those suspended moments before it had all turned to chaos. "Partners," she agreed.

• • • • •

Nell took Miles's arm for the remaining walk to Lost Hope Yard. This time, it wasn't because she was unsteady on her leg, but because their acquaintance had progressed to a more equitable level. Indeed, as they navigated the narrow alleyways, sinking deeper into the dangerous heart of the slum, she felt rather in harmony with her new husband. And it had nothing to do with any attraction she might feel for him. It was because, she realized, she was beginning to like the dratted man.

Infuriatingly rational as he insisted on being, he wasn't without sparks of kindness and humor. It was just that those characteristics rarely revealed themselves, competing as they did with all that grumpiness.

"You know your way around these parts quite well," she said, as he led her down another short passage. "Have you written many stories about Whitechapel?"

"Several," he said. "But none about the brothels."

"About what, then?"

"Robberies. Murders. Rapes. The odd kidnapping."

Nell blanched. "Heavens."

"Neighborhoods like these aren't generally known as safe places." He drew her to a halt at the top of the next lane, his attention fixing on the filthy, sagging building that stood at the end of it. "There," he said. "I suspect that's it."

Nell followed his gaze. Her pulse quickened. The place matched the description Miss Jean had given her—a crooked house, she'd said, with blackened windows, a newly built set of steps, and a recent coat of white paint to "freshen its face."

Like the previous brothels they'd visited, it had no sign announcing its name. There was only a hulking figure of a man leaning against the door, a cap pulled low over his protruding brow. A bully boy, Nell had learned such men were called. Large, threatening, violent fellows employed to do the brothel keeper's bidding. Down the way from him, a tattered band of ragged children played in the street. Their high-pitched shouts and laughter were an unsettling contrast to the sinister air of the house.

Nell regarded the place with growing apprehension. She didn't have a reporter's instincts. She did, however, possess a healthy amount of feminine intuition. And that intuition told her that this was the brothel they'd been looking for.

Her hand tightened on Miles's arm as they walked toward it.

Seeing them approach, the oversized man straightened from the door. The plaid cloth of his coat strained across the meaty expanse of his heavily muscled shoulders as he came forward to meet them. There was a fresh scratch down the side of his face, red and angry, from his eye to the edge of his mouth.

"Is this Mrs. Pritchard's establishment?" Miles asked him.

The man's menacing gaze flicked from Miles to Nell and back again. His eyes were so dark they appeared black. "Who's asking?"

"We'd like to speak with her," Miles said.

"*We*, is it?" The man's attention returned to Nell, lingering on her face. His lips curled in an oily smile. What teeth he had were discolored with decay. "What's your name, luv?"

Nell felt Miles stiffen beside her. She ignored him. She hadn't been exaggerating when she'd told him that her beauty was a weapon. And while it was true she may not have much experience deploying it in the field, there was a first time for everything.

"Penelope," she answered, instilling a touch of velvet in her reply.

Miles's head jerked sharply in her direction.

"Penelope," the man repeated, devouring her with his black stare. "That suits you." He shot an ominous look at Miles. "And who's this? Your protector?"

Miles took a step forward. Nell pressed his arm, silently urging restraint. At the first two brothels, he'd taken the lead. Now it was her turn.

"Something like that," she said ingenuously. "Do you suppose Mrs. Pritchard might spare me a moment?"

"Oh, I more than suppose, luv," the man said with a chuckle. "Wait here." Turning, he disappeared into the house.

The instant the door swung shut, Miles pulled Nell to face him. He glared down at her, his voice a furious whisper. "What the devil are you playing at?"

"Did you see the scratch down the side of his face?" she whispered back. "Something's happened here, and recently, too."

"Yes, quite. All the more reason for us to be careful."

"I'm being careful. *And* logical. Mrs. Early wouldn't speak with us. We can't afford to risk the same result with Mrs. Pritchard."

"That's no cause to imply that you're—" His jaw visibly clenched. "That I'm—"

"What better cause than a missing girl? Or a dead reporter? If that's not excuse enough to endure such trifling insults, I don't know what is."

A muscle worked in his cheek. "Your protector, by God."

Nell had never seen Miles offended before. She wouldn't have thought he was capable of it. "It's not entirely inaccurate," she said. "A husband is a protector, is he not? Or should be one. In any event, it isn't as if you're really going to sell me to this place."

Miles's face darkened like a thundercloud.

Nell again pressed his arm. "We agreed to respect each other's strengths," she reminded him. "And here, I believe it's mine that will rule the day."

Before he could utter another word, the door creaked open again on its hinges. An older woman emerged, with the large man close behind her. She was tall, and thick about the midsection, with a long face and upswept brown curls liberally streaked with gray. She gave Miles only a cursory glance before fixing her flinty gaze on Nell.

Nell felt the woman's callous scrutiny like an unwelcome touch, moving from the brim of her fanchon bonnet, down the fitted bodice of her brown traveling dress, and all the way to her hem.

"You didn't tell me she was a cripple," the woman said to her henchman.

Anger kindled in Nell's breast. A surge of humiliation followed after it. It wasn't pleasant to be judged like a piece of livestock at a village fair. Certainly not in Miles's presence. And a cripple, for heaven's sake! No one had ever described her in such stark terms before. She found she didn't like it one bit.

But this wasn't the moment for taking umbrage.

If she was to have any hope of finding Flora Brent, she'd have to dispense with her pride. Lifting her chin a fraction, Nell gave the woman an unobstructed view of her face. "Are you Mrs. Pritchard?" she asked.

The woman's eyes took on an acquisitive gleam. "Those accents! Straight out of the Queen's drawing room, aren't you, my fine lady? Yes, I'm Lily Pritchard. Someone sent you to me, did they?"

"Your name was mentioned," Nell said.

"And what's yours, girl? Penelope, Silas told me. But Penelope who?"

"Trewlove," Nell replied.

Miles's arm went rigid under her hand. Nell understood why he might balk at her giving her real name, but the fact remained that no one knew her in London.

And besides, it wasn't her name anymore.

Mrs. Pritchard examined Nell for a fraught moment. "Well, Miss Trewlove," she said at last, "do come into my parlor."

9

Nell's stomach tightened with mingled fear and anticipation. They hadn't been permitted entry into the previous two brothels. Not even for a fee. But Nell's beauty was a different form of currency. She hoped it might prove sufficient to get them the answers they were looking for.

Holding fast to Miles's arm, she accompanied him up the steps and through the front door into a small tiled hall decorated with vulgar plaster statuary. They were met by the overpowering stench of eau de cologne. It permeated the air, a sweet-sickly odor, with a hint of foulness underneath.

"Through here." Mrs. Pritchard motioned for Miles and Nell to precede her through a doorway off the hall. It led into a dimly lit parlor.

Know your surroundings. Know your opponent. Know yourself.

The words echoed in Nell's mind as she swept a discreet glance over the room, taking a careful inventory of the gilded French furnishings, glittering pink crystal lamps, and faux Renaissance paintings (middling reproductions of Venus in all her forms) that adorned the crimson-papered walls. It was so much garish luxury for such a dilapidated place. And yet, there was no carpet on the floor, only a vague rectangular outline on the wood of where a carpet had recently been.

Mrs. Pritchard brushed past them to turn up the oil lamps. She motioned to a red velvet upholstered settee with a sardonic flourish. "Do sit down. We're not used to entertaining the gentry."

Nell watched the woman from beneath her lashes as Miles escorted her to the settee. The gown Mrs. Pritchard wore was made of patterned silk velvet, the seams finished with exceptional skill. It was all of a piece with her coiffure—a lavish style of padded rolls and false curls that Nell suspected could only be attained with the assistance of a lady's maid. Expensive accoutrements for a Whitechapel madam. And ones that hadn't always been available to her, judging by the ravaged lines that etched her face, and the unforgiving slash of her tight-pressed mouth.

"Madams is hard people," Miss Jean had said. And here was surely one of the hardest. Nell had the sense that this woman could order violence at the drop of a hat—or possibly stoop to doing violence herself.

Nell's fingers curled on the handle of her cane as she perched on the edge of the settee. Miles remained standing beside her.

Mrs. Pritchard sat down in the wing chair across from them, while her henchman took up a place by the door. "I won't ask *your* name," she said to Miles. "We're a discerning house, as well as a discreet one. We protect our gentlemen's privacy. As for our girls—we've only the finest and freshest here. If that's what's brought you to my door—"

"That's exactly what's brought me here," Nell said. "I understand you often take girls newly up from the country?"

Mrs. Pritchard's eyes hardened with swift suspicion. "You're not a country lass. Not by the sound of it."

"I was once," Nell said. "I've since made something of myself."

"A striver, are you? I don't discourage it. Though you could do with a bit of help in the way of clothes. You'll catch no men dressed like a dried-up spinster. What you need is black lace and silk chiffon, which I'll provide. That, and lodgings. All to be deducted from your earnings. As for that cane—it will disgust most men even to see it." Mrs. Pritchard flashed a narrow glance at Nell's skirts. "What is it that's wrong with you? Is it your leg? Your hip? Or are your woman's parts at issue?"

A scalding blush rose in Nell's cheeks. "My leg," she said tightly. "And I assure you, it won't be an issue."

"Yet your protector has brought you here to dispose of you," Mrs. Pritchard observed. "Tired of her, are you?" she asked Miles. "Or is it that she's failed to please you in the bedroom?"

Nell was too mortified to breathe. She dared a fleeting glance at Miles. His dark eyes were the coldest she'd ever seen them.

"I have no complaints," he said.

Nell let out the breath she'd been holding. So long as he was willing to play along, they still might hope to get somewhere. "It's nothing of that sort," she said to Mrs. Pritchard. "It's my own entrepreneurial spirit that compels me to strike out on my own."

"A wise decision, while you still have a few good years left," Mrs. Pritchard said.

"More than a few," Nell replied, on her dignity. "I'm but three-and-twenty."

Mrs. Pritchard snorted. "That old?"

"Are your girls so much younger?" Miles asked.

Mrs. Pritchard's thin lips twisted into a parody of a smile. "I give the gentlemen what they want, sir. As for my girls, I keep them close. They're bound to me by contract, just as you'll be, milady." Her attention turned from Nell back to Miles. "I assume you'll be wanting a finder's fee?"

"Let's not get ahead of ourselves, ma'am," Nell said. "I can't commit to an arrangement until I'm confident it will suit me."

"Nothing to say on that score, sir?" Mrs. Pritchard asked Miles.

"It's her decision," Miles said. "I'll not stand in her way."

"I see." Mrs. Pritchard's mouth compressed so tightly it all but disappeared. "You wish to negotiate."

"What I wish," Nell said, "is to speak to some of your girls."

The woman's expression turned dangerous. "Did you hear that, Silas? She wants to speak to the girls."

Silas's broad form filled the doorway. "I heard, missus."

"So," Mrs. Pritchard said to Nell. "It isn't a negotiation you want. It's my secrets." She signaled to her henchman. "You've entered my house under false pretenses."

Nell's blood ran cold. She cast an alarmed glance at Silas as he came forward. "Not at all, but you must see—"

"I see an upstart madam who's looking to open her own establishment," Mrs. Pritchard retorted. "One who wants to steal my trade."

Silas stopped beside Mrs. Pritchard. He cracked his knuckles, awaiting her orders.

Miles set a hand on Nell's shoulder. An outwardly proprietary gesture, but one she recognized at once as silent reassurance. Her growing apprehension eased. He might be a newspaper editor rather than an East End brawler, but he was still a man, and one of intimidating size.

He addressed Mrs. Pritchard with all the formidable authority Nell had heard him use at the offices of the *Courant*. "What you see is a lady unwilling to sign an employment contract without first discovering if the other employees are content in their positions," he said. "I would expect nothing less from a girl of Miss Trewlove's intellect."

"Intellect!" Mrs. Pritchard mocked. "Bless my soul, look at her. As bright as the whist-playing dog at Cremorne, isn't she, Silas?" She stood in a swish of silk velvet. "You may speak to one of my girls. But only one. And you'll do it in my presence. Those are my terms. Take them or leave them."

"I accept them, of course," Nell said. She remained in her seat as Mrs. Pritchard swept out of the room. Silas marched after her.

Miles looked down at Nell. "That took a turn," he said quietly.

"Indeed," Nell replied in equally low tones. "Did you notice the carpet?"

"The lack of it," Miles said. "A strange omission in a room where no expense appears to have been spared."

"A recent omission. There's still dust present along the edges of where it used to be." Nell gave him an anxious look. "I have a bad feeling about this place, Miles."

"You're not alone," he said. "I advise that we go."

"We can't," Nell said. "This is our only chance."

Miles's expression sobered. He must know as well as she did that there would be no coming back to Mrs. Pritchard's after this. Word of their visits to the other brothels would soon reach the madam's ears. She'd learn that they'd been asking a very different sort of questions at those places. Questions accompanied by a sketch of the recently departed Mr. Cowgill.

"It might be," Miles allowed. "But no information is worth putting you at risk."

"I can handle myself," Nell promised him.

Mrs. Pritchard returned before Miles could respond. She was accompanied by a voluptuous young woman in a dyed purple dressing gown. Her pale cheeks were rouged and her hair was colored an unnatural shade of brassy gold.

"Claudine," Mrs. Pritchard said to the girl. "This grand lady is considering joining our establishment if we can prove ourselves up to her high standards. Do put her mind at ease."

"Yes, Mrs. Pritchard." Claudine's voice was thin, her accent decidedly cockney. She sauntered to the settee, flashing a coy smile at Miles before plopping down beside Nell. "What d'you want to know?"

A dozen questions ran through Nell's mind. Was the girl safe?

Was she well treated? Did she truly want to be here, rather than employed at a shop somewhere, or working as a servant in a respectable household?

But Nell wasn't here to save this girl. She was here to save another—one younger and more vulnerable.

She moistened her lips, fully aware that Mrs. Pritchard and her henchman were listening. "How long have you worked here?" she asked.

"Six months," Claudine replied.

"That isn't very long," Nell remarked. "Are most of the girls as new as you are?"

"Some newer," Claudine said.

Mrs. Pritchard gave the girl a warning look.

Claudine shifted in her seat. "Anything else?"

"Do you have your own room?" Nell asked.

"All my girls have their own rooms," Mrs. Pritchard answered.

Nell suppressed a burst of frustration. "And, ah, are you comfortable in it?"

"It's well enough," Claudine said.

"And safe enough, I trust? Despite being in this part of the East End?" Nell searched the girl's face. "What I mean is, you have no exposure to violence of any kind?"

Claudine flashed an uncertain glance at Mrs. Pritchard.

"Silas keeps the door," Mrs. Pritchard replied for her. "Our guests know better than to trifle with him."

It wasn't the answer Nell was looking for. Naturally, a bully boy protected the house from customers who might turn violent. But what of the violence administered from within? Did Mrs. Pritchard ever hurt the girls? Did Silas? The scratch on his face would seem to indicate that he did. And that he'd recently paid the price for it, too.

"If there's nothing else," Mrs. Pritchard said with visible impatience.

"A few more questions, please," Nell begged.

Mrs. Pritchard's lips pressed tighter. She reluctantly motioned for Nell to continue.

Nell cast about for something else she could ask. Something that might reveal more than what she and Miles already knew. At last, she pounced on it.

"What about your days off?" she inquired.

Claudine shrugged. "I get a half day on Wednesdays."

"All my girls do," Mrs. Pritchard informed Nell. "A half day, on alternating days of the week, guaranteed. You'll be granted the same."

Nell ignored her. "What do you do on your days off hereabouts?" she asked Claudine. "You can't go far, with so little time at your disposal."

"Don't need to go far when the Red Lion is right around the corner," Claudine said. "Mr. Drews stands us a pint for brightening up the place. All us girls go there on our afternoons off, excepting the young ones."

Mrs. Pritchard snapped her fingers. "That's enough, Claudine," she said sharply. She pointed to the hall. "Back to your work."

Claudine stood. Her gaze lingered on Nell for a moment before she turned and strolled out of the room.

Exchanging a brief but significant glance with Miles, Nell rose from the settee. She gave her skirts a brisk shake over her wire crinoline. "You have given me much to ponder, ma'am," she said to Mrs. Pritchard. "I shall be in touch as soon as I come to a decision."

Mrs. Pritchard surged to her feet. Fresh suspicion blazed in her eyes. "Wait a moment."

Nell didn't wait. Gripping tight to her cane, she walked purposely from the parlor, Miles at her side.

Mrs. Pritchard and her henchman came after them. "I knew it!" she exclaimed. "This has been some manner of ruse! I see it now. False pretenses, indeed."

Nell's pulse raced. She quickened her step, but the hitch in her gait inevitably slowed her stride.

"Stop, I said. You will answer to me!" Coming up behind Nell, Mrs. Pritchard caught her hard by the arm. She wrenched her around in a painful grip.

Nell spun on the woman in a swirl of skirts and, lifting her cane with a practiced flick of her hand, pressed the tip of it straight against Mrs. Pritchard's heart.

The madam stopped in her tracks with a sharp intake of breath. "Silas!"

The bully boy charged forward to intervene.

Miles deftly moved in front of him, placing himself squarely between the hulking brute and Nell. "Not another step," he warned.

Silas came to a stumbling halt.

Seeing her henchman intercepted, Mrs. Pritchard reached to jerk Nell's cane away from her chest herself.

"I wouldn't," Nell advised her. She brushed a gloved finger over the hidden button beneath the raven's head handle. "There's a mechanism at my fingertip that will release a spring-loaded blade from the end of this stick. I should hate to conclude such a cordial meeting by running you through."

Silas gaped at her. So, too, did Mrs. Pritchard. Possibly Miles as well, though Nell wasn't perfectly sure. Her entire attention was fixed on her adversary.

"We're going to take our leave now," Nell said steadily. "If that's agreeable to all parties?"

Mrs. Pritchard raised both her hands in a show of surrender. Her face was mottled with strangled fury. "Who are you?"

"A schoolteacher," Nell said. She returned the tip of her cane to the floor. Miles was immediately at her side. Slipping her hand through his proffered arm, she turned with him and exited the house.

10

Miles had once observed a dozing cat spring up from its deceptively lazy slumber to effortlessly—and ruthlessly—dispatch an unsuspecting bird. It was the closest thing he had to compare with what he'd witnessed in the entry hall of Mrs. Pritchard's Gentlemen's Establishment. There, his new bride had transformed as instinctively as that feline into . . .

Miles didn't know quite what.

In the moment, he'd had no time to consider it. He had only reacted, putting himself between Nell and what he'd perceived to be the greater danger. But it was Nell—lovely, elegant Nell, with her pronounced limp and her ridiculously large crinoline—whose reflexes had won the day.

A mechanized sword cane, by God.

Miles flashed it a frowning look as he guided her away from the brothel. It appeared no different from any other fashionably made walking stick. But it *was* different. Unless of course . . .

"You weren't bluffing?" he asked her.

"What?" Nell's gray gaze flashed to his, distracted. "No. Not at all."

"Then—"

"We *are* stopping at the Red Lion, I presume?" she interrupted.

His muscles tensed at the prospect. He wasn't some boorish oaf, unable to admit when a woman had had a stroke of genius. Neither was he a careless idiot who would willingly lead a lady into further danger.

"It was clever of you to ask where they spend their half days off," he acknowledged. "In other circumstances, we might be able to pursue the lead, but—"

"There won't *be* any other circumstances. We have little enough time as it is." She directed a look behind them. "I pray Mrs. Pritchard hasn't sent anyone after us."

Miles fully expected the madam would do just that the moment the shock wore off. He'd been on his guard for it ever since they exited the brothel. "Not yet. Not that I've noticed."

"Then we should make the most of it. It's nearly half past six. Providing Claudine was speaking truly, one or more of Mrs. Pritchard' girls should be drinking at the Red Lion right now. If we make haste, we may yet catch one of them."

Miles agreed in principle, though his gentlemanly instincts were all but shouting at him to haul Nell into the next cab that crossed their path and take her straight home to St. James's Square where she would be safe. She wasn't one of his reporters, to be pounding the streets for hours in pursuit of a story. She was his blasted wife.

He nevertheless steered her down the next lane and the next, not back toward Commercial Street, but toward the dissolute public house at the center of the slum.

"Did someone at the Academy teach you to wield a cane that way?" he asked her.

Like him, Nell was busy scanning the streets about them. She seemed to miss nothing, not the unwashed louts staggering across the fetid alleyways, the children shouting as they played, or the shadowy figures lurking between the buildings. "I was trained to wield a sword," she replied absently. "A sword cane isn't very different."

"Trained by whom?"

"Various teachers." She spared him a glance. "Many of our faculty are visiting members. They stay for a time, then move on, imparting what wisdom they can during their tenure."

"Sword fighting," he said flatly.

"Fighting fighting," she said. "Swords are optional." Her gaze met his on a rueful plea. "Please don't let it distract you. We must keep our focus."

He searched her eyes. "Have you any other tricks I should know about?"

"It wasn't a trick. It was a skill. And yes, I daresay I have. But now is hardly the occasion to provide an accounting of them. For one, we haven't the time. For another—"

"As you say," he acknowledged tightly. "We mustn't be distracted." He led her around the next corner. "But this conversation isn't over. Not by a long chalk."

Her eyes narrowed. She looked, for an instant, as though she wanted to say something more. But she didn't. Her attention returned to the cramped street ahead of them.

Miles frowned, his mood worsening by the second. She'd been telling him from the beginning that she could take care of herself. Perchance she had meant it.

He didn't know why the realization should leave him feeling as cross as a bear with a sore head. He respected strength and intelligence in females, far more than any other qualities. It was a woman's strength that had raised him out of the slum and set him on the path to where he was now—independent, successful, practically a gentleman.

Little surprise that he'd never had any use for damsels. He had even less liking for playing the white knight. Still, a man liked to know where he was at with a girl.

"I warn you," he said. "The reaction your face inspired at Mrs. Pritchard's is nothing to the one it will provoke at a public house."

Rather than discouraged, Nell seemed to be heartened by the notion. "Good," she said. "If they're captivated by my face, they won't notice my questions."

"*Your* questions?"

She flashed him a half smile. "You may ask questions, too, of course, if the opportunity arises."

Miles huffed a short laugh. "Generous of you."

"Well," she said, "you *are* the reporter."

And what are you, I wonder? he thought. The unspoken query came with no trace of suspicion or regret. No, Miles realized, with a growing sense of disquiet. It was fascination he was feeling.

The pub was down the next street. Miles had been there before, years ago, when he'd been writing a story on a series of dock robberies. He'd little thought then that he'd return again under such unusual circumstances—on his wedding day, accompanied by his new bride.

In looks, it was much as he remembered. Dark and dismal, with a great wooden beam over the entrance and a patched glass window clouded by grease and soot.

Steeling himself for physical confrontation, he opened the door for Nell. She preceded him into the smoke-filled barroom, her cane clacking on the dirty slatted floor. The scattered wood tables that stood about the place were half-filled with men and women in various stages of inebriation. Several more leaned against the bar, nursing pints of ale and glasses of whiskey and gin.

Nell made straight for the barman. He was wiping down a section of the counter with a soiled rag as he conversed with a red-nosed woman in a stained gray dress.

Miles could have predicted what would happen. Indeed, he *had* predicted it. The moment the man caught sight of Nell, he abandoned the woman in front of him. His face broke into a grin.

"Welcome, miss," he said, not seeming to notice Miles's presence. "What's your pleasure?"

"A glass of gin to start," Nell replied as if she'd been frequenting public houses all of her life. "And a favor."

"A favor, is it?" Still smiling, he set out a glass on the counter and poured out a measure of gin. "What's that, my beauty?"

"I'm looking for a friend of mine from Mrs. Pritchard's," Nell said with a flutter of her lashes. "She comes here on her half days."

Miles watched her work her wiles, his respect for her ingenuity growing by the second. She seemed to call on it effortlessly, as though it were less a practiced art and more a natural, God-given talent. A talent for deception, no less. An excellent thing in a reporter. Less so in a wife.

"You one of Lily's girls?" The barman chuckled. "She's moving up in the world." He finished pouring. "Verity's in the corner, by the window. Only one of Lily's girls here tonight."

Miles and Nell both turned to look. A dark-haired woman in a blue straw bonnet adorned with a bunch of wilted violets sat by herself at a small table, an empty glass mug in front of her. Her eyelids were drooping, and her head resting in her hand.

Finding her, Nell's eyes took on a glint of resolve. "Another gin, if you please," she said to the barkeep. "For my friend, Verity."

The barman poured out a second glass. He pushed them both across the counter to Nell. "That'll be six pence, luv."

Miles thumped the money down on the bar, a fraction harder than was called for. He gave the barkeep a distinct glare of warning.

The barman chuckled again, his smile gone sheepish. "No harm in looking, sir."

Nell collected both glasses in one hand. She moved a few steps away, out of the barman's hearing. Miles followed, remaining close at her side. She sank her voice, her words barely audible over the din of laughter and conversation. "I think it better if I approach her alone."

Miles stood over her, frowning. It went against his every instinct to permit her to ask questions without him being present. She may be clever, but this wasn't a game. Nor was it a classroom at her confounded charity school. A man had been murdered, for God's sake. A young girl very likely taken. There was no room for missteps or amateurish mistakes.

Yet, Nell had acquitted herself admirably at Mrs. Pritchard's. And she wasn't wrong in supposing that she'd have a greater chance of success if she approached the working girl on her own.

Miles resigned himself to the logic of it. "What do you need from me?"

"Money," she said. "And the notebook with the sketch of Mr. Cowgill."

Miles nodded curtly. Her hands were full, so he took the liberty of discreetly slipping the notebook into her reticule, along with five guineas. "I'll be at the bar," he told her. "At the first sign of trouble, I'm taking you out of here."

• • • • •

Nell crossed the crowded floor, conscious of the rough-looking men staring at her as she passed them. As ever, their gazes seemed to flit from her face to her cane and back again. She lifted her chin, refusing to make eye contact with any of them. She couldn't afford for one of them to take it as encouragement. Not when she had so little time in which to cultivate an acquaintance with the dark-haired prostitute in the drooping violet bonnet.

Nell approached the woman's table with single-minded intent.

Miles thought she was enjoying this. She'd seen it in his face. But it wasn't enjoyment she was feeling. It was a frenzied sort of compulsion, driving her to pursue this to the end, even if it should take all day.

Or all night.

For when that night finally came, when she was at last taken back to Miles's house, Nell would finally have to confront the pitiless facts of her new life. Miss Corvus was gone. Nell's students were gone. So was the safety of her little room, and the security of her daily routine. She was cut adrift in a strange sea, and the moment her mission was no longer at the forefront of her mind, the fear and sadness of it would overwhelm her like so many crashing waves threatening to drag her under.

She couldn't face it. And so long as she was here, focusing on what had happened to poor Miss Brent and Mr. Cowgill, she didn't have to.

"Verity? I thought that was you." Nell brazenly took a seat at the woman's table. "I hope you don't mind? I've bought you a glass of gin."

Verity flicked a bleary look between Nell and the glass before taking the gin and downing a swallow. "Do I know you?"

"No, but I should very much like to ask you a few questions." Nell touched her reticule, feeling the shape of the coins Miles had given her. "I'm prepared to make it worth your while."

Verity took another drink. "You're gonna pay me to sit here and drink your gin? And all I have to do is answer a question?" She burst out laughing. "Never heard that before."

"I shall be quick about it, too," Nell promised.

She had little alternative. At any moment, Mrs. Pritchard, her henchman, or some other villain might appear to call Nell and Miles to account. Nell couldn't risk a second altercation. She wasn't confident they could make their escape twice in the same day. Not when she no longer had the element of surprise on her side.

"I understand you work for Mrs. Pritchard?" she said.

The glass stilled halfway to Verity's mouth. She gave another laugh, more cynical this time, before bringing it the rest of the way to her lips. "Aye, I do. What's it to you?"

"I'm looking for a girl," Nell said. "She's fourteen, all of five feet tall, with a slim build, and dark hair and eyes. Just a child, really, but an exceedingly comely one. She'd have arrived at the brothel, possibly on Monday."

"What about her?"

"Did you see such a girl?"

"I might've done. I see all sorts at Mrs. Pritchard's."

"Like what?"

"That depends," Verity drained the glass. She set it back on the table with a hard clink. "How much money are we talking about?"

Nell pushed her untouched glass of gin toward Verity. "Would a gold guinea be sufficient?"

Verity gave a slow double blink. "You're jesting."

"I'm not. I'll give you one guinea to tell me about my missing girl, and another if you'll answer a second question."

Verity snorted. "Well?" She picked up Nell's glass and took a drink. "Let's see them, then."

Nell withdrew two gold guineas from her reticule. She set them on the table before her, out of Verity's reach.

Verity stared at them for several long seconds before giving a slow, almost reflexive, nod. "All right." She lowered her glass. "Happen I did see a girl on Monday. A new girl, what the missus found at the railway station. She were there until yesterday."

Nell's heartbeat quickened. "She's not there anymore?"

"Busted out, didn't she? Let out one of the missus's disinclined guests, too. Caused a right uproar. I saw her myself. The missus was after the man, and Silas was after the girl. She gave him a proper scratch with her nails before she bolted."

Nell stared at Verity, scarcely daring to hope. "She got away?"

"Aye, she did—the stupid little tart. Mrs. Pritchard's ain't all bad, you know. Not if you behave."

Nell slid one of the guinea coins to Verity across the table, keeping the second one in reserve. Relief coursed through her, knowing that Miss Brent had managed to get free, but Nell wasn't done yet. "What do you mean, one of Mrs. Pritchard's disinclined guests?" she asked.

Verity snatched up the first coin. "Some bloke what owed her money. She'd locked him in the attic 'til they could come to terms."

Nell promptly withdrew Miles's notebook from her reticule. Opening it, she discreetly showed the sketch of Mr. Cowgill to Verity. "Is this the gentleman?"

Verity looked at it. She gave another burst of inebriated laughter. "Aye, that's the man. Out of his wits he was. Drunk or something. But I had naught to do with it. I had a punter of me own to deal with. I told the missus to keep it down and I shut me door and that were that."

Nell pushed the second guinea partway across the table, but she didn't relinquish it. Not yet. "What about the man? Did you see him again?"

"Naw," Verity said. "I reckon he paid his tariff and went his merry way. The missus don't let men get the better of her, but she ain't hard-hearted, neither. Once they pay up, she sends them off with her blessing."

I bet she does, Nell thought acidly.

She slid the coin the rest of the way to Verity. "Your mistress won't like to hear that you've answered my questions. If I were you, I'd forget you ever saw me."

Verity took the second guinea. She dropped it along with the first one down the front of her bodice, secreting it in her ample cleavage. "Already forgotten, ma'am. Happy to forget even more if there's another guinea in it."

Nell hesitated for a moment before withdrawing another coin. "Here," she said to the woman. "Take it with my good wishes. And do look after yourself, my dear. It's a treacherous world out there."

11

Nell sat back in the seat of the hired hackney as she and Miles traveled west along the river, leaving the East End firmly behind them. Having shared all of the information she'd learned with him, she no longer had the thrill of the hunt to buoy her battered spirits, nor the joy of discovery, nor even the threat of danger. All that remained was a growing pit of bleak melancholy sunk deep into her stomach, and another feeling—a *worse* feeling—that was something very like the fear she'd experienced as a little girl when those two elderly servants had left her at the gates of the Academy so long ago.

Outside the window of the cab, the sun was slowly setting over the city. With every second that elapsed, they drew closer to Miles's house in St. James's Square.

If Miles sensed Nell's growing apprehension, he didn't show it. He'd fallen into a meditative silence of his own after she had related what she'd learned from Verity. It wasn't until the hackney was passing along the embankment that he finally spoke. "It's illogical," he said.

Nell had spent the past twenty minutes trying and failing to calm her racing pulse. Logic had ceased to matter somewhere between collecting her luggage from the railway porter's office at Shoreditch and sitting down across from Miles in the cab. "What is?" she asked.

"What danger could Cowgill have posed to Mrs. Pritchard?"

Miles asked in return. "Brothel keepers are already known to procure girls. It's common enough knowledge to have brought you to the East End in search of Flora Brent. The practice isn't strictly legal, but neither is it a secret. Not one worth killing over."

"Your point?"

"Why did she lock up Cowgill? What could he possibly have known that would have done a woman like that any actual harm?"

"I don't know," Nell said. "Perhaps there's no reason. Mrs. Pritchard and her bully boy didn't strike me as very reasonable people. I thank God Miss Brent is no longer with them."

"She made a brazen escape for one so young and inexperienced," Miles observed with suspicious nonchalance.

Nell was at once on her guard. "She's a resourceful girl. I only hope her wits enable her to survive the city long enough for me to find her."

"Is that why she was recruited to Miss Corvus's Academy?" he inquired. "Because she's resourceful?"

Nell narrowed her eyes at him. For a man so fond of cats, he did sometimes bear a striking similarity to a dog with a bone. Would he never give up on solving the mysteries of the Academy? Not even now, with Mr. Cowgill presumed dead, Miss Brent missing, and Nell newly his wife?

"Don't be absurd," she replied. "I've never even met Miss Brent."

"Then how is it that she came to be traveling to the Academy?"

Nell lifted one shoulder. "The matron of the workhouse wrote to me."

That much was true. She'd told Nell that Flora Brent was bold, clever, and possessed of a formidable talent for mimicry. A girl with keen intelligence who might benefit from further education.

"I see," Miles said.

Nell ignored his skepticism. "Workhouses provide no opportunities for advancement, but the Academy does. When we hear of promising prospects, as we often do from matrons we're in contact with or from gentlewomen benefactors who minister to the poor, we seek to intervene. That's why the matron in Surrey wrote to us. She hoped we would take Miss Brent in and train her up to be a governess, schoolteacher, or something else of value."

"Something else of value," Miles repeated, lending a wealth of ominous meaning to the statement.

"Indeed," Nell said, growing impatient. "When a person is possessed of natural talent, their prospects necessarily broaden."

"In other words," Miles concluded, "Miss Brent is not like other girls."

"No girls are like other girls," Nell informed him. "We are all of us individuals with our own unique sets of gifts. Sometimes, those gifts are in harmony with the goals of the Academy. Sometimes not." She paused. "Which has absolutely nothing to do with what we're dealing with at present."

"Except that Cowgill and Miss Brent's paths intersected—to Cowgill's detriment."

"That's not Miss Brent's fault. To be sure, it doesn't appear that Mr. Cowgill was there on her behalf at all. Rather, it was *she* who liberated *him*. Perchance, in doing so, she made him an unwitting witness?"

"And they silenced him for it? After she'd already escaped?" Miles shook his head. "Doubtful."

"What else could it be, then? If procuring a defenseless girl isn't crime enough—"

"Something worse. Something that would drive someone to kill a reporter, to ransack his rooms, and to send his tongue to the editor of one of London's most prominent newspapers as a warning."

Nell shivered at the reminder. She'd been surprised with many a lizard, spider, or other creepy crawly hidden in her desk during her tenure at the Academy, but she had never yet seen anything so gruesome as a severed tongue. Not until yesterday.

"What about the other entries Mr. Cowgill had in his notebook?" she asked. "The dates and the names, and something to do with Hertfordshire. It must mean something."

"Exactly so," Miles said. "This encompasses more than an East End brothel. It must. Cowgill didn't report on the poor and downtrodden. He wrote about the upper classes. Lords, ladies, people with money, influence, and pedigree."

"And yet it appears he met his end at a brothel."

"Perhaps that's just it. Perhaps we're viewing this backward. We've begun at the end. But that isn't where this started. Something else happened to set it in motion. Pritchard and Silas are no criminal masterminds. They were an expedient solution to a problem."

"They should be in prison," Nell said.

"They will be," Miles assured her. "Eventually."

She raised her brows. "You're not going to inform the police?"

"I'm not going to tip our hand."

"I suspect we've already tipped it, visiting Mrs. Pritchard's as we did."

"Possibly. However, they didn't ask my name. They didn't seem to know me by sight, either. It was only you who sparked their interest." He smiled slightly. "Penelope Trewlove, renegade schoolteacher."

"Schoolteacher no longer," she reminded him. "I don't know what I am now."

Miles's gaze came to rest on her face. For the first time since they'd departed the railway station, he gave her his complete and undivided attention. "My wife, obviously."

Nell lowered her eyes from his. She didn't want to think about being his wife. Not when she was already near to panicking at the prospect of being married to him. Of taking up residence in his home. Losing her rights, her status, her very purpose in life.

"Nell," he said.

"Tell me about your house," she said abruptly.

Miles was silent for the space of a heartbeat. And then: "There are cats. Four of them—five if you include Shadow. I brought her home last night. She wasn't entirely prepared for it, but it seemed the best thing for her after everything that's happened."

"Five cats," Nell said. "I can little imagine so many."

"I've a housekeeper, too—Mrs. Bright. There are other servants as well, sufficient to keep things in order. Most came with the house."

She glanced up at him in reluctant interest. "The house isn't yours?"

"It belonged to my predecessor, Charles Pelham, the former editor of the *Courant*. He left England two years ago for America. He aims to write a book on their civil war. I took on the lease in his absence."

"What will you do when he comes back?"

"Find somewhere else, I suppose, if Pelham still wants the place. I doubt he will. He's like most inveterate newspapermen. We have no deep attachments."

Nell smoothed a crease in her skirt with unnecessary attention. "Your housekeeper will be shocked that you've come home with a wife."

"It will be no surprise. I wired her from the railway station after we wed. I told her to have all in readiness."

Nell gave him a startled look. "But I thought . . ." She trailed off, realizing her error.

At the time, he'd said he was wiring one of his staff. She'd assumed he meant at the newspaper, not at his home. And certainly not in relation to her or her comfort.

But he'd organized it all, hadn't he? From the special license he'd brought this morning to his visit to the telegraph office, all the way to this moment.

He regarded her steadily from across the hackney. His own thoughts were as unreadable as ever, yet he seemed to fathom hers easily enough. "I won't tell you that you needn't be nervous," he said. "It won't do any good. But trust me a little, won't you? Trust that I'm not careless with the things that are important to me."

Her bruised heart latched on to his gruffly spoken words. Was she important to him now? Simply by virtue of being his wife? Was that how all this worked?

And yet, only a moment ago, he'd owned to having no deep attachments.

It was confusing. Disconcerting. She had no idea of where she stood in this new life of hers. The ground was every second shifting beneath her feet.

"I am nervous," she admitted.

"You're tired. And you've scarcely eaten all day, except for that stale Bath bun you had in the refreshment room at the railway station."

Nell hadn't been aware he'd noticed what she'd eaten. She'd barely noticed it herself. They'd been married but fifteen minutes before, and her mind had been in chaos. She vaguely recalled the bun tasting like sawdust.

Miles's mouth ticked up briefly at one corner in wry acknowledgment of the attention he'd been paying, even when she hadn't been aware of it. "I'm not romantic, as you so aptly noted earlier. But I can see to practical matters. There'll be dinner when we arrive, and Mrs. Bright will have made up a room for you."

Nell gripped her hands together in her lap, suddenly afraid she might cry. "I've lost everything," she whispered.

His analytical expression softened infinitesimally. "I know," he said. "Let me take care of you."

Her eyes welled with tears. She bit her lip to keep them from falling. Turning to stare out the window, she managed a small nod. *Yes. Take care of me. Because I don't know where I'm at or what I'm to do. And I'm so desperately frightened of facing it all on my own.*

• • • • •

Miles didn't know what his house might look like to Nell's eyes. Probably nothing very special. It was, like so many others in the square, four stories of red brick and pristine white stone, with tall glazed windows and black ornamental railings. A once fashionable residence in centuries past. Now it was simply home. A safe place to lodge his cats, and to rest his head between his endless hours in Fleet Street.

Mrs. Bright met them at the door in the waning twilight, her short white hair gleaming like a halo in the glow from the gasolier that hung in the hall. She took one look at Nell's pale face and immediately enfolded her under her ample wing. "Oh, bless me. Is this Mrs. Quincey? Why, you must be exhausted, ma'am. Here, let me take your things."

Miles followed them inside. He dispensed with his hat and coat as his housekeeper divested Nell of her bonnet and gloves. "How is Shadow faring?" he asked. "Not too distressed, I trust."

"The new cat is still in the guest room, Mr. Quincey," Mrs. Bright replied. She paused to address a footman. "Take those bags up to the mistress's chamber, Albert. And tell Gladys to bring up the cans of hot water." She glanced back at Miles as she ushered Nell through the marble-tiled hall. "I've given her fresh food and a clean tray of sand. She showed no interest in either of them. Went straight under the bed, she did."

"Unsurprising." Miles walked after them into the dining room. A cold collation had been laid out on the polished mahogany table—meats, cheeses, fruits, and a loaf of bread, illuminated by two branches of half-melted beeswax candles. Another branch of candles flickered valiantly on the ornate mahogany sideboard that dominated the wall opposite. Unlike the entry hall, the dining room had no gasolier, only an old crystal chandelier that was more trouble than it was worth to light.

Mrs. Bright pressed Nell into a chair. "Horus isn't helping matters. He's been peeping under the door all day."

"That can't be avoided," Miles said. He couldn't isolate Shadow forever. She'd have to get used to the other cats eventually. Knowing Horus, that day would be sooner rather than later.

"Horus is the master's great black cat," Mrs. Bright explained to Nell as she filled a glass for her from a carafe of red wine. "He runs the house. Then there's Smoke, Absalom, and Virgil. And now little Shadow, too. That's five altogether, though you won't see a whisker of any of them until they want you to. They're that good at hiding." She hesitated before returning the carafe to the table, an unsettling thought crossing her plump face. "You *do* like cats?"

"I do," Nell said. "I'm fond of animals."

Miles pulled up a chair next to her. This wasn't the time for sitting a table-length away. Judging from the shadows under Nell's eyes and the uncharacteristic lack of starch in her spine, she was fading quickly. The reality of her new position had seemed to strike her sometime after they'd departed the Red Lion. It had only been a matter of moments before she'd begun to bow under the weight of it.

"There's fond and there's fond," Mrs. Bright said with a trace of censure. She heaped a plate for Nell. "But I don't complain. They're friendly beasts most of the time, and not too much trouble. Though it does put a charge through the ranks whenever Mr. Quincey adds another to the mix. Even the best of them start acting foolish." She reached to put another slice of roast beef on Nell's plate.

"Oh no," Nell protested. "I thank you, Mrs. Bright, but I couldn't eat a fraction of that much."

"I'll help you," Miles said quietly.

Mrs. Bright placed the plate in front of Nell. "You don't want a serving of your own, sir?"

"Perhaps later," he said. He gave her a look.

Mrs. Bright at once understood. "I shall leave you while I see to the mistress's bath," she said. "I'll be back to fetch her when all is in readiness." Bobbing a curtsy, the housekeeper withdrew.

Nell took a half-hearted sip of her wine. "I'm afraid I haven't much of an appetite."

Neither did Miles. He took some bread and meat from her plate anyway, pouring himself a measure of wine and forcing himself to eat and drink as casually as if he and Nell had been dining together in this intimate manner for years.

As he'd intended, seeing him eating prompted her to gradually do the same.

He watched her out of the corner of his eye, assuring himself that she was taking sufficient sustenance.

"What now?" she asked after she'd finished a small portion of her meal.

It was the same thing she'd asked him when they'd sat together beneath the tree in the shadow of Miss Corvus's Academy.

Setting aside his napkin, Miles stood. "A good night's sleep," he said. He offered her his hand. "In the morning, we'll visit the *Courant* to right things with my staff. And then . . . I'll take you to see Mrs. Royce."

Nell's weary gaze flickered with unidentifiable emotion as she set her hand in his. A flare of hope, perhaps. Or possibly relief. "I'd almost forgotten she was returning tomorrow."

Miles hadn't. He had the distinct suspicion that, on learning of Nell's misfortune, Mrs. Royce would attempt to take Nell away from him. The prospect left a surprisingly bitter taste in his mouth, as though the wine he'd just drunk had been laced with poison.

Nell rose from her chair, her hand still in his. "I can't think what she'll say when she learns I've got married. And to you, of all gentlemen."

"I don't know whether to take that as an insult or a compliment," he murmured.

"The former, probably," Nell said. "You may take heart in knowing that Mr. Royce will be equally horrified on learning you've married me."

Miles didn't care what Gabriel thought. He didn't care what anyone thought. Not anymore. The deed was done.

Mrs. Bright materialized in the doorway. "Mrs. Quincey? If you're finished, ma'am, I shall be happy to show you to your room."

Nell relinquished Miles's hand. "Well, I suppose I should retire."

"You better had," Miles said gravely.

Their eyes met and held.

And it seemed to him that something passed between them. Something starkly intimate. Perilously close to tenderness. His chest constricted with the ache of it.

He thought she might say something more, or perhaps *do* something more.

But Nell didn't say anything. Didn't do anything. She simply turned abruptly and, bidding him a civil good night, accompanied the housekeeper out of the room.

12

Nell's heart was beating so heavily she could barely attend to Mrs. Bright's words as the housekeeper gave her a tour of her new rooms.

Good lord. What *was* that? That throb of unnameable longing that had passed between her and Miles in the dining room? Nell had never felt anything like it in her life.

It took her a full five minutes to get her pulse under control. Only then was she able to take in the candlelit grandeur of her new chamber.

And it *was* grand.

Carpeted in pale floral Aubusson and furnished in elegant style, it was easily five times the size of her bedroom at the Academy. An immense curtained four-poster bed stood at the heart of it, flanked by matching mahogany wardrobes. Two overstuffed upholstered armchairs were arrayed in front of a marble fireplace, heavy silk draperies covered the windows (multiple windows!), and in the corner stood a delicately carved dressing table, its surface adorned with a bouquet of white gardenias in a porcelain vase. Similar bouquets of gardenias graced the mantelshelf and the table next to the bed.

Nell bent to smell the ones that stood on the dressing table, inhaling their sweet, sultry fragrance. They were so perfect they didn't look real. "What gorgeous flowers." She glanced up at Mrs. Bright. "Are they from the gardens?"

"Oh no, ma'am. These are shop bought." The housekeeper laid out Nell's prim muslin nightgown and gray flannel dressing gown across the end of the bed. "Mr. Quincey was quite specific. Gardenias, his wire said. I presumed they were your favorite."

Nell slowly straightened from the bouquet, a queer feeling settling in her breast. She didn't know how to reply. Gardenias *were* her favorite flower, but she knew for a fact that she'd never mentioned that to Miles.

Mrs. Bright smiled at Nell's confusion. "The master wanted your room to be comfortable for you. He set it all down to the letter. The rest of us are merely following his instructions, though we are very happy to welcome you home, ma'am."

Home.

Nell traced the waxen leaves of one of the snowy white flowers with her fingertip, thinking of her new room, her new life.

Her new husband.

Mrs. Bright held out her arm. "Come, Mrs. Quincey. The bathing room is this way. Gladys has got the water piping hot in the tub for you."

• • • • •

More than an hour later, after a long soak in the copper tub, Nell was curled up in one of the overstuffed chairs in front of a crackling fire, finishing the final stitches on a sampler, when a knock sounded at her door.

By rights, she should have already retired. She was weary enough for it in body. Yet the wheels of her mind wouldn't stop turning. Her surroundings were too strange and the past two days too full of tumult.

Not to mention that this was her wedding night.

Rather than spend what remained of it staring uselessly into the flames as she waited for her hair to dry, Nell had retrieved her tapestry workbag and begun the painstaking process of sewing a coded message to Miss Corvus. If Nell finished it tonight, she could post it to the Academy first thing in the morning.

"Come in," she called out distractedly, expecting another visit from the maid.

The door opened. It wasn't the maid. It was Miles. He was in his shirtsleeves, his tie loosened, and his hair rumpled as though he'd lately been raking his fingers through it.

Nell's eyes widened and her heart skipped a beat. Despite everything, she hadn't anticipated . . .

But here he was.

He stopped at the threshold, taking in the sight of her unbound hair, uncorseted figure, and bare toes peeping beneath her hem in one comprehensive glance. An odd expression passed across his face. Shock? Alarm? Desire? Nell couldn't tell. It was gone before she could grasp it.

She set aside her sewing. Drawing her dressing gown tighter around herself, she moved to rise.

"Pray don't get up," he said as the door drifted shut behind him. They were the same words he'd uttered yesterday morning in his office.

Yet how much had changed since then.

He clasped his hands behind his back. "I was on my way to my room when I noticed your lights. Are you—That is . . . Do you require anything?"

By some miracle, she kept her countenance. "Nothing at all," she said.

"You're unable to sleep?"

"I haven't tried yet. I'm waiting for my hair to dry from my bath."

A dull flush appeared just above the line of his collar. "Your bath. Of course." He pointedly turned to look about the room, reverting to his usual businesslike manner. "I trust Mrs. Bright has made you comfortable?"

Nell watched him in the glow of the fire. She'd never seen him out of his element before, let alone flustered enough to turn red. Or, rather, *almost* red. He composed himself before her eyes with impressive rapidity, the threat of a blush vanishing from his neck as swiftly as it had appeared.

Such self-control he had. Such unerring command over himself and the world he inhabited.

"She and the maid have been very kind," she answered. "They've already unpacked my cases. And Gladys brought up a hot water bottle."

Nell refrained from describing *that* awkward encounter. The gawky young maid had plainly been perplexed as to why a new bride would require artificial warmth on her wedding night.

"The flowers are beautiful, by the way," Nell added. "However did you know that I liked gardenias?"

Miles walked to the vase on the mantel, examining the bouquet. "Your perfume. It's gardenia, is it not?"

Nell blinked. Goodness. He *had* been paying attention. He must have done to have noted a scent so faint as that. "It's not perfume."

He flashed her a look. "No?"

A peculiar warmth suffused her midsection. He was only an arm's length away, close enough to touch her. And here she sat, naked under the thin layers of her robe and nightgown, with her hair loose about her shoulders, and her bare feet tucked beneath her. She hadn't ever been this vulnerable in the presence of a man before. She'd rarely been this vulnerable with anyone.

It was that very vulnerability that allowed a rare frisson of self-doubt to sneak its way into her soul.

She remembered, all at once, how the men at the Red Lion had looked at her, their attention torn between her face and her limp. The staff at Miles's office had regarded her just the same. So had nearly everyone since she'd arrived in London. Those endless stares, filled with admiration, then bewilderment, and—ultimately—pity.

Nell had told herself that she was bored by it. The identical response over and over again, so dull and predictable. She'd reminded herself that their opinions were no reflection on her. She knew who she was and what she was worth. But that was then. She'd been on her mission, out in the world, crinoline clad and purposeful. While here . . .

She had no defenses.

Mrs. Pritchard's cruel words came back to haunt her. *"As for that cane—it will disgust most men even to see it."*

Most men, the hateful madam had said. A week ago, it wouldn't have mattered to Nell if it was *all* men. But not now. Not in this moment.

She realized, to her vexation, that after a full day spent in his company, one man's opinion was coming to mean something to her.

"It's French bath soap," she informed him. "A gift from Mrs. Royce. She bought it for me when she was last in Paris."

Miles moved the vase of flowers a fraction of an inch to the left, as though its placement had been off. "Bath soap," he repeated with a peculiar lack of inflection. "Of course."

"The teachers at the Academy aren't permitted to wear perfume," she explained. "It would only encourage the girls to want perfume of their own."

"Yes, I see. Quite sensible."

Nell could remain seated no longer. It put her at too much of a disadvantage. She rose from her chair, exquisitely conscious that sections of her hair were still damp, and that she had no corset or crinoline to provide her any armor. "But I do like gardenias very much," she said. "I thank you for them. And . . . And for everything."

Miles turned.

Nell's already surging pulse skittered wildly. She'd thought herself at a disadvantage sitting. It was nothing to meeting him face-to-face. He must be several inches over six feet tall at least. It wasn't as noticeable when she was in her boots and bonnet, but it was painfully obvious now.

"It was done for myself as much as for you," he said.

"Still, you didn't have to be so kind about it all. The special license, the gardenias, the welcome I've received from Mrs. Bright and the other servants. As well as the first-class railway fare. That was all for my benefit, I suppose, though I was too blind to see it at the time."

His brows notched. "I'm not an unfeeling monster, Nell. I'm aware this isn't what you wanted. Being here like this, with me. But . . ." He shook his head. "Since it couldn't be helped . . ."

"Since I ruined you, you mean."

His eyes met hers. The expression in them was solemn. "Perchance we ruined each other."

Butterflies fluttered in Nell's stomach as she returned his gaze. She felt the same bewildering swell of uneasy longing she'd felt in the dining room before they'd bid each other good night. She didn't understand it.

"Perhaps we did," she said. "For better or for worse."

"As the vicar so appropriately put it."

There was an interminable pause.

Nell was the first to break it. "Miles . . ." she began softly. She didn't sound at all like herself.

Miles's throat contracted on a swallow. "Yes?" His own voice was a husky rasp.

"Doesn't it seem strange that . . . that this is our wedding night?" she asked.

"No," he said. "Given that we were married this morning."

"I wasn't talking about the logic of it. I meant—"

"I know what you meant."

"Then—"

"That isn't why I came to your room," he said.

Heat bloomed in her cheeks. "I wasn't implying that it was."

"I truly did just want to check on you. I've been . . . concerned."

She bent her head, recollecting how many times she'd been near tears in his presence today. First in the garden beneath the tower, then during the hackney ride from Whitechapel. He must think her the veriest watering pot. It wasn't her. It never had been. She was as strong as any of her Academy sisters. Stronger.

"You needn't be," she told him.

"Hazard of the job," he said.

She gave him a dubious look. "Newspaper editor?"

"Husband," he replied.

The butterflies' wings beat faster. She felt a trifle breathless. "Are you implying that the mere fact of being married can change how a person feels about another person?"

"It seems to be the case."

"And that's all it is? Some ingrained sense of societal convention?"

"Very likely," he said.

Nell didn't believe it. She wasn't a conventional person. Rather the opposite. "I'm not convinced."

"What else could it be?"

"I don't know," she said. "Perhaps it's simply that we like each other."

Again, he smiled that subtle, dry smile. As though he was amused by her, or by the situation, or perhaps by his own reaction to both. "A remote possibility, surely."

"Don't tease me."

His smile faded. "I don't know what else to do when you're standing in front of me like this. When I—" He broke off, turning his attention to some point over her shoulder. He pushed his fingers through his hair. "It's been a long day. We neither of us are thinking clearly."

"Miles . . ."

His gaze returned to hers. There was no humor in it this time, only the same perilous intensity she'd observed in him on the first occasion they'd met. "What do you want from me, Nell? What do you want me to do?"

"I don't know," she answered honestly. "Something."

He nodded slowly. His jaw hardened, as though he'd come to a decision. "Very well," he said. "Something it is."

• • • • •

Miles was a fool to have come to her room. He had known it from the minute he stopped at her door, from the very instant he'd knocked, even as he'd justified it to himself as gentlemanly concern. The fact was, since that taut moment when they'd parted in the dining room, he hadn't been at all himself. He'd spent the past hours pacing the library, attempting to attend to his correspondence, compiling notes about Cowgill's disappearance, starting an outline of the facts he'd learned thus far about the Academy, even checking on Shadow, all to no avail. He'd been too restless to settle on any task.

Mrs. Bright had said that adding a new cat to the household sent a charge through the ranks. Miles supposed that adding Nell to the house had put a similar charge through him. He couldn't get her out of his head. Couldn't stop imagining what she was doing, what she was thinking. And when he'd entered her room to find her looking so unbearably lovely . . .

His pretense of concern had been laid bare.

Go, his conscience growled as he stood over her in front of the dwindling fire. *Say good night. Take your leave and be done with this madness.*

But he didn't.

He couldn't.

His hand lifted practically of its own accord to cradle her face. Feeling her tremble beneath his touch, his chest constricted on a rush of raw tenderness. How soft she was beneath all that starch. How delicate and unexpectedly vulnerable. The pad of his thumb moved over the silken curve of her cheek in a slow caress. She took an uneven breath.

And there was no resisting her any longer. Bending his head to hers, Miles kissed her very gently on the lips.

Nell's dark lashes fluttered closed. She listed toward him, brow puckered with uncertainty. But there was nothing uncertain about the way her voluptuous mouth yielded to his. She softened to him, lips parting just enough to allow their fractured breath to mingle—hot, quick, mutually unsteady.

Miles had never tasted anything so sweet. Everything within him urged him to take more, to deepen the kiss, to touch her and taste her. She was there for the asking. His very own wife, here in his house, very nearly in his arms. What could be more natural? More logical?

He didn't listen to his impulses. He wasn't focused on himself. He was focused on Nell.

"All of my learning has been theory rather than practice," she'd told him.

She knew what a kiss was, clearly, but Miles doubted she'd ever experienced one. He didn't intend to put her off the business.

His mouth stilled on hers. "There," he murmured. "Was that something enough?"

She huffed a quavery laugh. He felt it as much as heard it. "Yes," she said. "Thank you."

He drew back from her. "Thank *you*."

"How formal we've become."

His hand fell from her cheek. "Forgive me if I—"

"No. Don't apologize." Her face was as pink as a damask rose. "It's just . . . I've never been kissed before."

Miles's heart hammered against his ribs. He'd known that. Of course he had. It made it no less impactful to hear. "No?"

"Wasn't it obvious?" She stepped back from him. Her unbound hair curled in loose waves down her back, the flaxen strands shimmering like moonbeams in the flickering firelight.

Miles wished he'd taken the opportunity to touch it as he'd kissed her. He could only imagine what it would feel like. "Not to me," he said. "But then, I'm somewhat out of practice myself."

She gave him an interested look. "There's no one else that you . . . That is, there hasn't been another . . ."

"No," he said. "Not for a long while." He paused. "And you—?"

"No," she answered. "Never."

He nodded. "Well, that's . . ." But he could think of nothing else to say.

Across the room, the bed loomed in the waning candlelight, the coverlet turned down invitingly.

Miles cleared his throat. He hadn't made it this far in life by abandoning his self-control. "I'll allow you to get some rest," he said. "We have a busy day tomorrow."

She clasped her hands in front of her. "Yes. I should at least try to sleep."

"I should do the same," he said.

"Where is your room?"

"Next door. We're connected through the bathing room. Did Mrs. Bright not mention it?"

Nell's cheeks burned brighter. "Er, no. She didn't say. And I was too weary to ask. But it naturally makes sense. As we're married—"

"Quite," he said. "If you need anything—"

The door creaked open on its hinges. Both he and Nell turned, startled out of their abominable awkwardness, by the sight of Horus pushing his way into her room.

He was the oldest of the strays in residence. An enormous, slightly over-plump, long-haired black cat with wide golden eyes. The undisputed ruler of the house, as Mrs. Bright had described him. He padded across the carpet, making straight for Nell.

Her mouth tipped up. "Horus, I presume."

"Come to inspect you just as he inspected Shadow," Miles said.

Nell sank down, a little clumsily on her injured leg, holding out a hand to the cat in unspoken greeting. Horus approached to sniff the curve of her fingers. He blinked twice before rubbing his cheek against her knuckles. His seal of approval as it were.

"Shall I remove him?" Miles asked.

"Oh no," she replied. "I wouldn't dream of evicting him."

"I warn you, he'll attempt to sleep next to you all night, and possibly steal your pillow."

"I don't mind." Nell scratched Horus's head. "I would appreciate the company."

Miles's muscles tightened, a dozen responses running through his head at once. When it came to the point, he opted for the safest one. "In that case," he said, "I shall bid you both good night."

"Good night, Miles," Nell replied without looking at him. She continued petting the cat. "Sleep well."

Miles hesitated for a moment longer in brooding silence before exiting her bedchamber and heading for his own. He had the bleak premonition that tonight sleep was going to elude him.

13

The following day, at precisely nine o'clock, Nell entered the offices of the *London Courant* on Miles's arm. She had arranged her hair in an unostentatious roll, and dressed with care in her best blue silk day dress, understanding only too well the importance of appearances on this occasion. Her drawstring workbag was looped over her arm in lieu of a reticule. Miles had told her he'd need to remain at his office for an hour or two this morning. It would be the ideal opportunity for Nell to finish the sampler she'd begun last night.

"You should know," Miles said, "my staff will have no reason to suspect ours is a marriage of convenience."

Nell ascended the stairs at his side, cane in hand. Her limp was less evident today owing to yesterday evening's bath and a judiciously applied hot water bottle. She'd even managed to get a few hours of sleep. Horus had kept her company until dawn, a great solid weight against her back, ensuring that she didn't have to spend her first night at St. James's Square completely alone.

"I should think they'd suspect the reverse," she replied frankly. "Given the haste with which we married, most will doubtless believe our match was inspired by some outrageous passion."

Miles showed no sign of discomfiture at her pronouncement. On the contrary, his face might have been carved from granite. He was that controlled. That unemotional. He'd been so since she'd joined him at the breakfast table this morning.

"Very probably," he acknowledged.

Nell paused as he opened the door for her. She supposed he regretted kissing her. Why else would his aspect be even stonier today than it had been when they were strangers to each other?

But they were still strangers, weren't they?

An easy thing to forget when she had taken the man's name and was currently living in his house.

"Would you rather they believe that about us than know the truth?" she asked.

"That we're madly in love?" A frown crossed Miles's brow. "Hopefully, they won't require specifics."

Nell passed ahead of him into the hall. She set her hand back on his arm when he came to join her. "They won't need to, providing you can see your way to regarding me with something marginally warmer than your present state of glacial indifference."

He flashed her a dark glance. "Glacial indifference?"

"I speak as I find." Her skirts brushed against his leg in a soft rustle of silk over starched petticoats as they walked. She felt his muscles tense beneath her fingers.

And she wanted to tell him that he wasn't alone in his regret. She was regretting their kiss, too—though likely not for the same reasons that he was.

No.

She regretted that she hadn't done more. That she'd been so dashed passive instead of kissing him back, touching him back. And now she would never know what lay beyond that soul-quaking moment. She would have to spend the rest of her life imagining it.

"In any event," she said, "it's not my opinion that signifies. It's the employees of the paper we're trying to convince. We must both do our part, mustn't we?"

"The performance will hardly be useful if my staff doesn't recognize me."

"Why wouldn't they?"

"They know me to be a serious man, not a sentimentalist."

She smiled. "Surely, the two aren't mutually exclusive. Not when a gentleman is newly married."

Miles's frown deepened. "Perhaps not."

Nell refused to let his flinty demeanor affect her sense of purpose. Emotion was the enemy of resolve. It prompted one's mind to wander down dead-end roads, ruminating about unfulfilled wedding nights, smoldering looks, and sweetly scorching kisses. Nell had neither the time nor the inclination to indulge such romantic fancies. Not today anyway. She was focused on the task at hand—redeeming both Miles's reputation and her own.

Together, they passed the exact editorial offices she'd walked by two mornings ago, with the same busy newspapermen bustling in and out through the hall. Several stopped with a start, seeing Nell on Miles's arm, her raven's head cane in hand, recognizing her as the mysterious woman in black who had called at the paper on Wednesday.

Nell's fingers curled tighter on Miles's sleeve. She was fairly certain these men had spent the past days gossiping about the fact that she'd been discovered on the floor of their editor's office with her skirts above her knees. And now she was back to face them, this time without the protection of her veil.

But this wasn't the moment to succumb to some misplaced notion of feminine modesty. She kept her head held high, ensuring that her composure didn't slip an inch.

"Mr. Quincey!" A familiar gentleman, with pomaded hair and a pocket watch, cut through the throng to meet them. Mr. Higgins, if Nell recalled correctly. He goggled at her before turning his attention on Miles. "Excellent timing, sir. If you could spare a moment to . . ."

Miles silenced the man by the simple expedient of covering Nell's hand with his. The uncharacteristically affectionate gesture had the effect of bringing both her heart, and all the newspapermen in the hall, to a standstill.

"My dear," Miles said with all the outward sincerity she'd requested of him. "May I present my assistant, Mr. Higgins. And this is Mr. Griffiths, our managing editor; his secretary, Mr. Parker; our news editor, Mr. Cadwallader; assistant editor, Mr. Priest; Mr. Cadwallader's secretary, Mr. Singh; and Higgins's junior, Mr. Flack. Gentlemen, I have the honor of introducing my wife, Mrs. Quincey."

A chorus of astonished murmurs rose up in a mighty conflagration. Some of the men grinned broadly. Others exchanged meaningful looks. Several more appeared distinctly relieved.

"Mrs. Quincey?" Mr. Higgins's face was transformed by a beaming smile. "I say, but this is an agreeable surprise!" He bowed to Nell before reaching to press her hand. "I had little idea when you called on Wednesday that you and Mr. Quincey had an understanding of this sort. Had I known—"

"But we might have guessed, mightn't we?" Mr. Flack said. He clasped Nell's hand in turn. "The only explanation, isn't it? Just as I said to Mrs. Flack, Mr. Quincey would never conduct himself in any way other than with complete dignity and discretion."

"We are pleased, ma'am. Exceedingly pleased," Mr. Cadwallader added. "And may I say, vastly reassured. The *Courant* couldn't have withstood another scandal."

"A joyous occasion," Mr. Griffiths said, talking over the others. He was an older man, gray-haired and portly, with an air of authority. "I heartily congratulate you, ma'am. And you, Quincey. I trust this will finally convince you to take some time off and leave the paper to me."

Nell smiled at each of them in turn with what she hoped was an adequate degree of newlywed demureness—a few blushes, a few flutters of her lashes, and a few shyly murmured words of thanks. It wasn't all contrived. Indeed, standing with Miles, his hand covering hers on his arm as a crowd of well-wishers congratulated them, she might be forgiven for believing it was real. That she was truly Miles's new bride, married out of a surfeit of honest feeling and not out of cold necessity.

"So many editors," she said when all of the gentlemen had finally ceased speaking. "I thought my husband was the only one."

"He's our editor in chief, ma'am," Mr. Griffiths explained. "He bears a responsibility for all of us, and for everything that's printed. But the day-to-day running of the paper falls to me and Mr. Cadwallader."

"Mr. Quincey still keeps a hand in with our most important stories," Mr. Higgins said.

"Quite," Miles agreed brusquely. "Speaking of which, I'm expecting that article on the Lord Mayor of York, Griffiths. And Priest, you owe me a draft of tomorrow's society column. Higgins, Flack, with me."

Uttering a few final words of congratulations, the crowd of newspapermen dispersed. Nell accompanied Miles to his office, with Mr. Higgins and Mr. Flack trotting dutifully behind them.

Miles waited until they were inside, with the door shut and Nell comfortably seated on the fringe-skirted sofa, to drop his affectation of connubial warmth. "I believe Cowgill was murdered at a brothel in Whitechapel," he said.

Both Mr. Higgins and Mr. Flack went ashen at the news. They remained standing in front of Miles, utterly at a loss.

Miles leaned back against the edge of his desk, facing his two underlings. "The boy who brought Cowgill's severed tongue round on Wednesday, he spoke with you, Flack, did he not?"

Mr. Flack recovered himself enough to dart an apprehensive look at Nell, plainly doubting the propriety of uttering the words *brothel* and *severed tongue* in the presence of a lady.

"You may speak freely," Miles told him. "I have no secrets from my wife."

Nell glanced up from removing her sampler from her workbag, meeting her new husband's eyes. Her heart stopped for a beat, just as it had when he'd covered her hand with his. She was sure it was only more playacting. Nevertheless . . .

Partners, he'd said yesterday in Whitechapel.

She had the feeling he meant it.

"Er, yes, sir," Mr. Flack answered.

"What else can you tell me about him?" Miles asked.

"Only that he was a street urchin," Mr. Flack said. "He claimed a beggar woman in Blackfriars gave him a penny to see it delivered to you."

"To me?" Miles asked. "By name?"

"'To him what's the editor in charge of the paper,' I believe the boy said," Flack replied.

Miles nodded. "I thought as much."

Mr. Higgins gave Nell a look similar to the one that Mr. Flack had given her. His disapproval at her remaining in the room to hear such talk was evident. "If you know where he was murdered and by whom," he said to Miles, "then why—"

"I don't know," Miles replied. "I can't prove anything, other than the fact that Cowgill was at the brothel for a time. And for that, we have only the word of an inebriated prostitute who works there. Given the risk to her livelihood, I fully expect her to recant her account if confronted by the police."

Nell threaded her needle as she listened to the gentlemen's discussion. The pattern of her sampler had already been set—a stone house and garden, a jumbled alphabet, and a raven with a white-tipped wing. All that remained was to complete the necessary bit of numerical code that, when solved, would spell out her message to Miss Corvus:

BROTHEL WHITECHAPEL PRITCHARD
SHE ESCAPED
WILL FIND HER

It was Nell who had formulated the idea for using samplers for the Academy's confidential communications. Effie had often ridiculed her for it, calling her a modern-day Madame Defarge. But there was no denying that a woman's post could easily be read, her letters stolen, her secrets unearthed. With a coded sampler, at least, there was little chance of anyone deciphering the message. That is, if they suspected there was a message at all.

"Where are you on the entries in Cowgill's notebook?" Miles asked Mr. Higgins.

"Still trying to place those names, sir," Mr. Higgins answered. "There are any number of people called Innes in London. No Fawn-Purvises, however. But I do have a contact at the post office who—"

"Have you tried *Debrett's Peerage*?" Miles asked. The blank looks on both the men's faces provided his answer. "Fetch me a copy, Flack. I believe there's one in Cowgill's office."

Mr. Flack raced off to do Miles's bidding.

Mr. Higgins remained. "Are you sure Mrs. Quincey wouldn't prefer to wait in my office, sir?" he inquired of Miles. "I would be happy to bring her a cup of tea."

"*Would* you prefer it?" Miles asked Nell.

She continued sewing. "I'm perfectly contented as I am, my love. But I do thank Mr. Higgins for his consideration."

My love.

The words hung in the air for a fraction of a second.

Miles had obviously heard them, and marked them, too. Just as she'd marked his endearment in the hall. His pointed lack of reaction was reaction enough. "My wife is fine where she is," he informed Mr. Higgins. "You may put her and her sensibilities out of your head."

The office door opened again with a clatter. A breathless Mr. Flack entered with a large, leather-bound volume held out in front of him. "*Debrett's Peerage*, sir."

Miles took it. He retreated to the great leather chair behind his desk. Placing the book down in front of him, he purposefully turned through its pages.

Nell's needle stilled on her sampler. She watched Miles in silent expectation.

"Fawn-Purvis," he said at last, with a distinct sound of satisfaction. "Family name of Baron Amstead, age three-and-seventy, of Northwick Hall, Moor Cross, Hertfordshire."

Mr. Higgins and Mr. Flack drew closer to examine the entry. "It mayn't be the same Fawn-Purvis that Mr. Cowgill had in his notebook," Mr. Higgins said.

"It's the only one in the *Peerage*," Miles returned. "And it's in Hertfordshire. If Cowgill wasn't referencing Baron Amstead himself, it might well have been one of his relations."

Nell couldn't imagine what an aged Hertfordshire baron would have to do with the murder of a newspaper reporter in a Whitechapel slum. Then again, if she'd learned anything at the Academy, it was that men were capable of anything. And that went double for men of means and position.

"What else does it say?" she asked.

"His first two wives are deceased," Miles replied, still reading. "But he has issue. A son and heir—Christian—born of his first wife in 1829. And a daughter—Jane—born of his second wife in 1843."

He looked up from the book. "Cowgill was known to attend fashionable house parties. Did he ever attend one at Northwick Hall?"

Mr. Higgins and Mr. Flack murmured their uncertainty.

"He'll have heard something somewhere that set him down this path," Miles said.

"We can send a reporter to Moor Cross," Mr. Higgins suggested. "Ask some questions about the baron and his family."

"No," Miles said. "We remain in London until we know what we're dealing with. Flack, pull all of Cowgill's columns from March. I want to see if anything correlates to the dates he wrote in his notebook. And Higgins, search the newspaper records for mentions of Fawn-Purvis and Innes with those dates in mind—the nineteenth and twenty-eighth of March and the third of September."

"What about the police, sir?" Mr. Flack asked.

"I'll speak with them today," Miles said.

Nell couldn't conceal her surprise. "And tell them everything?"

"No, not everything," Miles said. "But it won't hurt to share some of what we discovered about the events at the brothel. They needn't know how we learned it. As for the Hertfordshire connection . . . We keep it between ourselves for now. No police. No other members of staff. I'll have none of the younger reporters putting themselves at risk in hopes of breaking the story. You saw where that landed Cowgill."

Mr. Higgins and Mr. Flack nodded in solemn agreement.

"I'll pull those columns," Mr. Flack replied.

"I'll search the newspaper records," Mr. Higgins said. "And I can reach out to our contacts at the clubs, and anywhere else the baron or his son might be known."

"Do," Miles said. "And for God's sake, be discreet." With a jerk of his head, he sent the two men on their way.

Mr. Higgins and Mr. Flack promptly obeyed, stopping only long enough to bow to Nell and once again murmur their congratulations, before departing the office and shutting the door behind them.

Miles stood from behind his desk. "You don't approve?"

"I thought we weren't going to tip our hand," Nell said.

"We can't go back to the well with Mrs. Pritchard."

Nell understood that much. People in the slum knew their faces now, and knew who it was they were looking for. "No, but—"

"Let the police find the evidence against her," Miles said. "The *Courant*'s efforts are better spent chasing down the society gossip that precipitated the crime. For that, we must focus our investigations on the beau monde."

"In the form of the Fawn-Purvis family?"

"For a start."

"What about Flora Brent?"

"What about her?"

"She's still missing," Nell reminded him. "She may still be somewhere in the East End."

"I advise you to leave it to the police," Miles said.

Nell traced a pensive pattern over the embroidered raven on her sampler with the pad of her thumb. Naturally, she wasn't going to leave it to the police. What did Scotland Yard care for a penniless orphan girl gone missing in a slum? Miss Brent was no one to them.

But not to Nell.

"In other words," she said, "you suggest I sit back and let the men take charge?"

"I suggest you let the professionals take charge. They can do what we can't for now, at least insofar as the East End is concerned."

"I see. And what will you be doing while the police are investigating Mrs. Pritchard and searching for Miss Brent, and while your employees are scouring the archives for tittle-tattle about the Fawn-Purvis family?"

"Going to Hertfordshire," Miles said as if it were obvious.

Nell set down her sewing with an exasperated breath. She didn't know what irritated her more, the reality of him excluding her or the prospect of him getting himself killed. "How is that any less dangerous for you than it would be for them?"

The corner of Miles's mouth lifted in a brief semblance of a smile. "Fear not, Mrs. Quincey," he said. "Despite appearances, I'm not unaccustomed to a bit of danger."

• • • • •

Miles strolled across his office to join Nell. The closer he came, the less rational he felt. Which was saying something. Rationality had been in short supply since the kiss they'd shared last night. He'd been struggling to regain it all morning. He'd begun to believe he had when—

My love, she'd called him.

He had immediately recognized the endearment for the wifely pantomime that it was. It hadn't stopped his heart from pounding on a throb of longing so intense it had nearly stolen his breath.

And *she* was the cause of it.

She sat there in her modest blue dress, a scrap of needlework in her hands, as well-mannered as you please, when all the while, she was tormenting him to his core.

He'd scarcely slept last night because of her. He'd been . . . Bloody hell. There were no two ways about it. He had been *wretched.* And he had no one but himself to blame. It had been his reckless decision to kiss her. Having done so, it was taking every ounce of his not-insubstantial self-control to keep from doing it again.

"More than a bit of danger, I should think," she said with a touch of asperity. "Unless you consider abduction, murder, and mutilation to be nothing very perilous."

"I haven't spent the whole of my life behind that desk," Miles replied. "Lest you forget, I was raised in the Rookery." He stopped in front of her. "What's this you've been working on so diligently?"

"A sewing sampler," she said.

He paused to examine it. He had a vague idea of how a sampler should look. It was usually the alphabet, wasn't it, with A commencing sensibly to Zed? And numbers, as well, stitched in logical order? But there was nothing terribly orderly about Nell's version. Both the letters and numbers were out of sequence, some of them appearing more than once. And embroidered behind it all, a stone house and garden that bore a suspicious resemblance to Miss Corvus's Academy.

Miles lifted his gaze to Nell's. "Something for the Academy?"

She shrugged one shoulder with studied nonchalance. "An exemplar, merely."

"What does it mean? These numbers and letters, and this raven?" The small black bird was perched atop the gray-thread tower, a single stitch of white on its wing.

"What should it mean?" Nell asked in return. "It's for instructional purposes, that's all. I taught sewing classes at the school—did I not mention it?"

Miles sensed she wasn't being entirely honest with him. Not lying precisely, but keeping her secrets close. Or rather, the Academy's secrets.

It was the latter he'd been determined to uncover at the start of this. But now, as he frowned down at his wife of less than four-and-twenty hours, he felt the disconcerting desire to learn her secrets, too. To find out who she truly was, and what she truly wanted. To discover the things that would make her smile her dimpled smile. That would make her happy with him.

An impossible impulse.

Nothing would make her happy with him. She didn't want to be here. She didn't want to be anywhere but at her blasted charity school.

But here she was just the same.

Her face was tilted up to him, her rolled coiffure shimmering like fairest gold in the sunlight that filtered through his office window. A strand had come loose to curve about her cheek—the same rogue curl that Miles had observed working free on previous occasions. Without thinking, he reached to tuck it back behind her ear. It was silky soft under his fingers just as he'd imagined it would be.

Nell went still under his touch. She took a tremulous breath. "Miles," she began. "About last night . . ."

The door opened again before she could finish.

Higgins popped his head in. "Mr. Quincey?"

Miles turned on his assistant. It took everything within him to keep from biting the man's head off. "What is it this time, Higgins?" he asked tightly.

Higgins gulped. "I'm sorry, sir, but . . . there's a police inspector to see you."

14

Does no one at this paper know how to knock?" Nell inquired after Mr. Higgins had departed to fetch the policeman. She was quite impressed with how polite and disinterested the question sounded given the fact that the entirety of her insides were still trembling from Miles's unexpected touch.

He ran a hand through his thick black hair, looking markedly out of humor. "We've no time for social niceties here. News breaks quickly."

"It's for efficiency, then?"

"That's the idea."

"It doesn't seem very efficient to me, given what occurred when last I was here. Had Mr. Higgins stopped to knock, I'd still be employed as deputy headmistress at Miss Corvus's Academy, and you and I—"

"We wouldn't be married," Miles finished for her. "Quite."

"Something you might wish to take into consideration for the future."

"There's little point in it now that we're wed. You can scarcely ruin me twice."

Nell's lips twitched. But she wouldn't allow herself to smile. Her loss of position was no joking matter. "You may be surprised what I'm capable of, sir, given adequate incentive."

A glimmer of wry humor flickered in Miles's dark eyes. "I believe you capable of anything, ma'am."

The door opened again. Higgins entered in company with a tall, sober-faced blond man in a Melton wool suit. "Inspector Garrick, sir," Higgins introduced the man.

The inspector inclined his head. His close-trimmed beard and mustache added years to his face, but his blue eyes—though weary—were young. He couldn't be that much older than Miles. "Mr. Quincey. Ma'am."

"That will be all, Higgins," Miles said.

"Very good, Mr. Quincey." Mr. Higgins withdrew, shutting the door after him.

Miles remained beside Nell. All sign of humor—good or otherwise—had vanished from his countenance. He was, once again, as inscrutable as stone. "Well, Inspector? I assume you have news about my missing reporter?"

Inspector Garrick hesitated, glancing at Nell. "It's of a delicate nature, sir. It may give offense to ladies."

"My wife is privy to this sad business," Miles said. "I give you leave to continue."

Nell waited anxiously for the inspector to speak. Despite Miles's assurances, the man was still visibly reluctant to discuss the matter in front of a female. It took him a full five seconds to find his voice.

"I'm sorry to report that a body was recovered this morning on the banks of the Thames matching the description you provided of one Mr. Lawrence Cowgill," he said at last. "It's currently being held at the hospital mortuary for identification. If you would be so good as to accompany me there."

"Is this body missing its tongue?" Miles asked.

"It is," the inspector said.

Nell recalled the sight of the severed organ with a private shudder. "Was that the cause of death?"

Again, Inspector Garrick hesitated. "He was stabbed, ma'am. Twice in the chest. The surgeon says the first strike would have killed him."

Nell paled. She looked up at Miles. "Poor Mr. Cowgill."

"Poor Mr. Cowgill, indeed," Miles murmured. He regarded the inspector. "Are you the one tasked with investigating his murder?"

"I have that burden," Inspector Garrick said. "His murder, and countless others. We do our best to solve them, but given our lack of resources, and the daily addition to their numbers . . . I can make no promises."

"We have information that might help you," Miles said.

The inspector stood to attention. "I should be grateful to hear it, sir."

"Excellent." Miles offered Nell his hand to assist her up. "My wife and I can fill you in on the way to the hospital."

• • • • •

One hour later . . .

What is it you were going to say to me before Higgins interrupted us?" Miles asked as their carriage rolled away from the hospital.

Nell fixed him with a frosty glare. He'd included her easily enough on the journey to the mortuary with Inspector Garrick. Together, they had apprised the man of what they'd learned in Whitechapel—about Mrs. Pritchard, Mr. Cowgill's incarceration in the brothel, and even the disappearance of Flora Brent. But when they'd arrived at the hospital, rather than inviting Nell to accompany him in to identify the body, Miles had requested that she remain in the carriage.

No, not requested. *Commanded.*

At the time, Nell had grudgingly agreed. There had been no rational reason for her to go inside. She hadn't known the gossip reporter, after all, and could provide no help with identification. Her presence would have been superfluous. Possibly distracting. Even so, after spending the past twenty minutes languishing inside the cab . . .

She was furious with Miles.

"Partners, you said," she reminded him.

His expression betrayed a flash of bewilderment. "*That's* what you wanted to say to me?"

"No," she replied coolly. "It's what I'm saying to you now."

Miles tossed his hat onto the seat beside him. He loosened his tie. "You're not upset that I prevented you from coming inside?"

"I'm not upset. I'm—"

"A mortuary is a dreadful place, Nell. The bodies are . . ." His forehead creased. "It's not a fit sight for ladies."

The carriage wheels rattled over the road as the horses rejoined the midmorning traffic on the busy thoroughfare. Miles had directed his coachman to take them to the Royces' house in Sloane Street. Effie and her husband were supposed to have returned from Paris earlier this morning. Had things progressed normally, Nell would have been arriving alone to stay with them for a short visit, rather than calling on them in the company of her new husband.

Nell dreaded to think what Effie would make of Nell's reduction in circumstances. For that's what marriage was for her, however much society viewed it as the opposite. Nell hadn't gained anything. She'd only lost. First, her position. Then, her authority. And now her very autonomy.

"That's your mistake," she said. "The same foolish error that prevents men from uttering plain truths in the presence of women. You view us as delicate creatures, too fine and fragile to be dealt with on terms of equality."

Miles's brows sank in a scowl. "I was trying to protect you."

"I don't require your protection."

"You'd rather be exposed to every degradation this city has on offer? Sights that will haunt your dreams? Your waking hours, too?" He shook his head, unrepentant. "No. I won't have it. If I can stand between you and the horrors of the world, I plan to do it. Call it foolish, if you like, but there it is. I won't apologize for it."

Nell's heart stumbled. Drat him and his chivalry. And drat herself for being affected by it. "I don't require an apology," she said, mustering what remained of her indignation. "But I won't be excluded, Miles. Lest you forget, not three days ago, I was the deputy headmistress of a school. Since then—"

"I know."

"And now, for you to presume—"

"I don't presume."

"For Mr. Higgins, Mr. Flack, and Inspector Garrick to treat me as if I were a child—"

"They believed they were treating you with respect," Miles said. "It wasn't meant as an insult. I wouldn't have allowed them to insult you."

Her heart tripped again. It was impossible to be angry with him when he said such things. All the same . . .

She regarded him from her seat across the carriage with burgeoning suspicion. Was he managing her again? The same way he managed his hissing and spitting cats?

A lowering thought.

"I don't wish to be handled with kid gloves," she told him. "I may not have been part of your world these many years, but I'm not ignorant of it. I know what evils are out there. I don't intend to shrink from them. I intend to fight them."

"And to fight them you must see them up close in all their gruesomeness?" Miles looked steadily back at her. His jaw was tight. "You said if this was going to work between us that you and I must defer to each other's strengths. One of mine is shouldering burdens for the people I care about. It wasn't my first visit to a mortuary, but it would have been yours. You've had enough distress to contend with for the past three days. There's no point in you bearing any more of it when I can bear it for both of us."

Nell's breath stopped for an instant. She was one of the people he cared about, was she?

But naturally she was.

He'd admitted as much last night. The mere fact of their marriage had made him care. She had his name now. She was, in law, his possession. He had a responsibility for her.

And perhaps that was truly all it was. Given the facts, it could scarcely be anything else. During the short and tumultuous course of their acquaintance, Miles had never once shown any genuine liking for the *real* her. For Penelope Trewlove—orphan, schoolmistress, radical bluestocking.

Rather the reverse.

Penelope Trewlove had both aggravated and exasperated him.

"You're very considerate," she said. "Still, you take my meaning."

"And I trust you take mine," he said. "I'd not wish the sights I've seen on my worst enemy."

Nell felt a disconcerting twinge of guilt. In all her anger, she hadn't considered that he might have been affected by what he'd seen when he'd gone into the mortuary with Inspector Garrick. "Was it very bad?" she asked.

"No." He grimaced. "Yes."

She exhaled heavily. "Oh, Miles . . ."

"There's no dignity in it. It's just . . . a pitiful end."

"I'm sorry. And here I was selfishly trying to make a point." She searched his face. "Did you know Mr. Cowgill well?"

"No. That's the shame of it. I was brusque with him. Dismissive. I didn't respect his type of reporting, despite how many papers it sold, and I made no effort to hide it. Perhaps that's why he was out there, investigating something serious for a change. He was doubtless trying to prove himself to me."

Nell leaned forward. "Oh no. You can't start blaming yourself. Though, I do understand the impulse. I've been second-guessing my own behavior at every turn since Miss Brent's disappearance. If only I'd gone to fetch her myself. If only—" She stopped herself, hating those two words more than any others in existence. "Do you know," she said, "I find it far easier to forgive myself for the actions I've taken than for the ones I didn't take. It's why, when given a choice, one should always choose the bolder path."

"An interesting philosophy."

"I don't know that it's a philosophy precisely."

If it was, it was mostly an aspirational one. At least where she was concerned. Her fellow teachers took action. So, too, her students. They were the drivers of their own destinies, as Nell had always encouraged them to be. But as for herself . . . From the moment she'd fallen from the tower, events had largely happened *to* her. She'd accepted them. Formed her life around them.

"Did Mr. Cowgill have any family?" she asked.

"None that I'm aware of." Miles raked a hand through his hair. His chest rose and fell on a weary sigh. He looked tired suddenly, as though he hadn't slept very well last night, or possibly at all. "I'll arrange for his burial when I return to the office."

"That's kind of you."

"He was a member of the *Courant*. I would that I could do more."

"You *are* doing more. You're going to bring whoever did this to him to justice, aren't you? That's what's important now. Finding out what brought him to this pass." Nell sat back in her seat. "Did you learn anything else that might be of use?"

"The police surgeon says Cowgill died on Wednesday. He looks to have been in the water two days."

"Then he was already gone when we visited Mrs. Pritchard's," Nell mused. "That's some comfort." Part of her had feared his body might have still been in one of the brothel's upstairs rooms while they'd been questioning the madam below. A frightening thought!

"Garrick is going to begin searching for Flora Brent," Miles said. "He believes she may be a witness. In which case—"

"In which case, she's in danger."

"Exactly."

"I won't give up looking for her myself," Nell said. "Even if the police are involved. I can't abandon her to—"

"I won't ask you to," Miles said. "But . . . I think there might be a better way."

She gave him a doubtful look. "What do you have in mind?"

"Gabriel Royce has a network of spies in houses all over the city. A remnant of his illegal gambling empire. It's possible he might put them to work to find Miss Brent. Failing that, there's an attorney I know in Fleet Street who's something of a miracle worker. He's found people before. We could approach him as well if you're not opposed to the idea."

Nell privately bristled at the implication that she wasn't up to completing her mission on her own. But she wouldn't let her pride get in the way of securing Miss Brent's safety. "I'm not opposed."

In short order, they arrived at the Royces' house in Sloane Street. It was a handsome red brick residence with a black-painted door. Not the sort of place one would envision a man of Mr. Royce's reputation living. It was far too traditional. But Effie had reported that she and her husband were happy there. *"Mr. Royce is dabbling in politics,"* she'd written to Nell. *"For the moment, it serves us to appear respectable."*

"You never did tell me what it was you were about to say in my office," Miles said as their carriage rolled to a halt in front of the stone front steps.

Heat crept into Nell's cheeks. "It will keep."

Fortunately, Miles didn't press her. He descended from the carriage first and turned to hand her down. Together, they walked up the steps to the Royces' front door where Miles applied the brass knocker.

The door was promptly opened by a black gentleman in a plain dark suit. The butler, Nell presumed. Effie had described him and the other servants in her letters.

"Good morning, Kilby," Miles said. "Are Mr. and Mrs. Royce at home?"

"They returned an hour ago, Mr. Quincey." The butler stepped aside to admit them. "I will announce you."

"No need for that, Kilby." Gabriel Royce entered the hall.

Nell had met Effie's husband only once before. Effie had introduced them over dinner at an inn in the neighboring village to the Academy. Then, Nell had thought him a dangerous man—cold and rather wolfish, with his harshly hewn countenance and pale blue eyes. She had also thought him very much in love with Effie. As first impressions went, the latter had far outweighed the former.

"Quincey," Mr. Royce said. "Miss Trewlove." His mouth ticked up with wry amusement as he took in the sight of Nell's gloved hand resting on Miles's arm. "This is a surprise."

Nell slipped her hand free before Effie could see.

The former Euphemia Flite wasn't far behind her husband, looking stunning as ever in a cherry-red caraco jacket and poplin skirt. She wasn't a classic beauty, but she was a singular one, distinguished by glossy ebony hair, dark violet-blue eyes, and olive-tinged ivory skin that bore evidence of her father's reputed lascar pedigree.

An orphan like Nell, Effie had grown up at the Academy. But unlike Nell and Gemma, Effie hadn't remained when she'd come of age. She'd gone abroad at Miss Corvus's command, spending several years as a lady's companion. She'd only returned earlier this year, polished, confident, formidable.

"Nell, dearest." Effie's face lit in a brilliant smile as she crossed the hall to embrace Nell. Her little black poodle, Franc, trotted at her heels. "I wasn't expecting you until later."

Nell hugged Effie tight in return as Franc frisked about their skirts. Emotion welled in her throat. "I couldn't wait."

Effie glanced over Nell's shoulder at Miles. "And what's this?" she asked. "A happy coincidence? Or did you and Mr. Quincey travel together?"

Nell drew back from Effie to look into her eyes. "We *are* together," she said. "Mr. Quincey and I are married."

15

I still don't see why you couldn't have waited until I was back in London," Effie said. "It was only one more day, for heaven's sake. Given the chance, I might have prevented this disaster."

Nell was seated beside her friend on the blue silk-upholstered sofa in the Royces' sunlit drawing room. Effie had seized her hand the moment they'd sat down, holding it tight as Nell related the events that had led to her marriage to Miles. She hadn't let go yet.

Mr. Royce was by the drawing room window, far enough removed to give Effie and Nell the illusion of privacy, but not so far away that he couldn't hear every word. Miles had, meanwhile, paced to the fireplace, where he now stood, facing them, his arms folded across his chest.

"It's done, love," Mr. Royce said to Effie. "Leave it be."

Franc hopped up on the sofa next to his mistress. He pawed at her elbow. Effie put her arm around the little poodle in answer, absently drawing him close. "Can it not be undone?" she asked. "Such things are possible."

"No," Miles said.

Nell's gaze jolted to his. It was one of the few times he'd spoken since they'd retired to the drawing room. Thus far, he'd been content to leave the talking to her. One would think he saw no need to justify their situation to their friends—or to anyone.

Effie's eyes blazed. "And that's to be that, is it?" she demanded of him. "We must just accept—"

"I've accepted it," Nell said. "Truly, I have." She hesitated. "Unless Mr. Quincey—"

"So have I," Miles said resolutely.

Some of the tension in Nell's muscles eased. She had no wish for this visit to devolve into an outpouring of misery and recrimination over a situation that none of them could change. What on earth would be the point?

"There, you see?" She pressed Effie's hand. "I know it's a shock, dearest, but after such a public catastrophe, marriage really was the only solution that would answer."

Effie gave Nell a kindling look. There was plainly much more she wanted to say. It was equally plain that she wasn't at liberty to say it in mixed company. Not if the subject of her ire was Miss Corvus.

Nell returned her friend's gaze, silently promising her that they would speak candidly at the first opportunity. Whatever issues they had with Miss Corvus and the running of the Academy weren't to be aired in public. Not even in front of their husbands.

"I blame Pettiman," Effie said. "The infernal hypocrite. What I wouldn't do if I saw him."

"Likewise," Nell replied. "But we have larger concerns than Reverend Pettiman at the moment." She looked to Miles. "Tell them."

"My gossip columnist, Lawrence Cowgill, disappeared on Monday," Miles said. "At the same time, an orphan named Flora Brent was lured from an East End railway platform by a procurer."

"Miss Brent was on her way to the Academy from a workhouse at my instigation," Nell explained to Effie. "A special girl, I've been told."

Effie looked at Nell intently. She knew very well what that meant. "Is her fate connected to that of Mr. Cowgill?"

"Their paths crossed at a Whitechapel brothel," Miles said. "Miss

Brent escaped. Cowgill was less fortunate. The girl may well have been a witness to his murder."

"We need to find her," Nell said urgently. "And we must find out what Mr. Cowgill knew that led to his death. We're hoping you and Mr. Royce might be able to help us."

"What can we do?" Effie asked. "I'm unfamiliar with Whitechapel, but perhaps Gabriel—?"

Mr. Royce stepped forward from the window. "I know a few people there. I could put the word out about Miss Brent and this reporter of yours."

"For Miss Brent, assuredly," Miles said. "As for Cowgill . . . It's the gentry we're interested in. His murder may have some connection to the Fawn-Purvis family in Hertfordshire."

Effie's ebony brows lifted. "You're not talking about the newly anointed Lord Amstead?"

"What do you mean 'newly anointed'?" Miles asked.

"He's recently ascended to the barony," Effie said. "I heard Lady Belwood mention it."

Nell was familiar with Lady Belwood's name, though she'd never met her in person. Some months ago, Miss Corvus had arranged for her ladyship to sponsor Effie's entrance into society. It had been the first step in the Academy's plan to ruin Lord Compton. Lady Belwood had been an unwitting part of that plan—a useful society figure who owed a mysterious debt to Miss Corvus. She'd had no choice but to help them.

"He's hosting a house party at his country estate next month," Effie went on. "It's well in advance of his year of mourning being over. There are some who find the timing in poor taste."

Nell immediately thought of the third date in Mr. Cowgill's notebook. She exchanged a charged look with Miles. "When next month?"

"I'm not sure," Effie said. "I daresay I could find out." She smiled suddenly. "I know. Why don't you remain here this afternoon? We can call on Lady Belwood together. It will give us ample time to talk."

Nell glanced at Miles. His face was absent expression. "I *would* like to," she admitted, "but I'm not sure—"

"Nonsense," Effie said. "Mr. Quincey can certainly spare you."

Miles straightened from the fireplace. "I do have a great deal of work to attend to at the paper," he said. "If you preferred to remain here until this evening, it wouldn't be inconvenient."

"Not so long as that," Nell objected.

"My days run late," Miles said. "I don't expect I'll be back at St. James's Square until after dinner."

"Splendid." Effie beamed at Nell. "You can dine with us as well."

"We'll see her home in the carriage afterward," Mr. Royce said to Miles. "She'll be safe enough."

"If that's what she wants," Miles said.

Nell could detect no insincerity in his offer. No sign of annoyance or impatience. Even so, she had the oddest feeling that he wasn't entirely pleased by the prospect of leaving her behind.

Nevertheless . . .

"It is," she said.

• • • • •

Miles crossed the drawing room to join Gabriel at the inlaid table by the window. A tray sat upon it, holding a set of cut crystal glasses and a decanter filled with gleaming amber liquid. Brandy, perhaps. Or—knowing Gabriel—more likely whiskey.

The ladies had absented themselves but a moment before. Gone upstairs, ostensibly so that Nell could assist Mrs. Royce with her unpacking. There had been reference to gifts bought in Paris, and something about a new hat. Miles doubted the truth of any of it. Nell and Mrs. Royce had clearly wanted to be private with each other, presumably to discuss Academy business.

Or to discuss the business of Nell and Miles's marriage.

Miles burned at the thought of his private life being laid open for Mrs. Royce to remark upon. But there was no avoiding the indignity. Not when Nell was bosom friends with the woman. Where Nell was concerned, Mrs. Royce's interference was inevitable, just as was the unsolicited commentary of Miles's own childhood best friend.

"Married," Gabriel said as he poured himself a drink. "And to Miss Trewlove of all women."

Miles exhaled. "Yes. I know."

Gabriel poured a second drink for Miles. He passed it to him. "She's an uncommonly attractive specimen."

Miles accepted the glass. "I'm aware."

"And you're—"

"Not." Miles acknowledged the fact with ruthless pragmatism. He knew he wasn't strikingly handsome. Just as he knew he wasn't warm, overtly sentimental, or suavely romantic. Nell knew it, too. She'd said as much on the train after they'd married.

Given the chance, she'd done just as Miles had predicted she'd do yesterday evening. She had chosen to stay with Mrs. Royce rather than remain with him. This time it was just for the day. Next time . . .

Who knew.

Miles downed a swallow of his drink with a grimace. It was whiskey, after all. He didn't normally partake this early in the day, but needs must. "It hardly matters," he said. "We didn't wed because of an attraction on either of our parts."

Gabriel chuckled. "If you say so."

Miles glowered at him. "What are you implying?"

"That you're flesh and blood."

"And have been for many years. I've never succumbed to temptation yet. Not when it went so thoroughly against my own inclinations."

"But this time . . . the temptation was great indeed."

Miles finished the remainder of his whiskey in one swallow. He set down his glass on the tray. "As productive as this conversation is, I'm due back at the paper." He turned to go.

Gabriel's voice sounded at his back. "You should have taken my advice and let the subject of the Academy drop."

Miles stopped where he stood. "This is my fault, is it?"

"Entirely."

Miles turned back to face his friend. "Because once a member of the Academy enters the picture, mortal men don't stand a chance, is that it?"

Gabriel took a drink. "Something like that."

"That may be the case with your wife—"

"Careful," Gabriel said.

Miles ignored the warning. "My own is a different matter."

"I don't doubt it. Unlike mine, yours chose to make the Academy her life. She was in a position of power. If you imagine you can file her away in a corner while you go on as if nothing has changed, you're in for a rude awakening."

Miles stiffened at the charge. It was too uncomfortably close to what he'd originally intended to do. "What do you know of the Academy? Or about my wife's role there?"

"I know some of the locals in the neighboring village call it the Crinoline Academy. An apt description, I thought—all the ladies girded in steel. Other than that . . ." Gabriel shrugged. "I know nothing more than you do yourself."

The Crinoline Academy.

It was indeed an apt description. But as information went, it was nothing like the sort Miles was interested in.

"What has your wife told you about the place?" he asked.

Gabriel leaned back against the windowsill. He swirled his whiskey in his glass. It sparkled like melted gold in the sunlight. "Precious little."

"Nothing about their curriculum?"

"Ah."

"Then you *do* know."

Gabriel raised his glass to his lips. "I know they can defend themselves."

Miles recalled Nell raising her cane to Mrs. Pritchard's chest with a practiced flick of her wrist. "And that's all?"

"What else? I've not yet met Miss Corvus. I've never even been permitted inside the gates."

"No?" Miles's mouth tipped in a humorless smile. "Perhaps my wife *does* have more power than yours."

Gabriel's pale gaze sparked with immediate interest. "You went inside?"

"I did."

"To the manor house?"

"I was allowed no further than the gardens. It's where I proposed."

"With the charity school looming behind you? And Miss Corvus herself somewhere inside?" Gabriel gave a derisive snort. "I'm amazed you could maintain your focus on Miss Trewlove with an unfinished story to tempt you."

"I told you, I'm not a slave to temptation."

"There's temptation and there's temptation," Gabriel said. "So long as you have your priorities straight."

Miles's smile took on an edge. "You're lecturing me about priorities?"

"From a place of experience. Not three months ago, I was ready to sacrifice everything to solidify my position in the Rookery. And look at me now."

Miles didn't require a reminder. He'd witnessed his friend's transformation firsthand. Gabriel had given up his underworld throne in order to marry the woman he loved. He no longer ran the

Rookery, not in any official capacity. He now had a completely respectable position on the St. Giles District Board of Works. A wife, a home, a future in politics. A future, full stop. And all because he'd lost his heart to a complicated, vexing, and wholly unsuitable female.

"You can't compare my marriage to yours," Miles said. "You proposed to your wife out of love. I proposed to mine out of necessity."

"Very gentlemanly of you, making such a sacrifice."

"I was thinking of my reputation at the paper."

"Naturally, you were." Gabriel finished his drink. "What was Miss Trewlove thinking of, I wonder?"

"She was more reluctant to accept than I was to ask," Miles answered him. "If that doesn't explain our relationship, I don't know what does."

Gabriel's mocking smile dimmed with understanding. "So, it's like that, is it?"

Miles didn't answer. He ran a hand over the back of his neck, weary of the conversation. "I must get back to the office. I've been out since Wednesday. It's inexcusable at any time, let alone with a reporter just murdered." Again, he turned to leave. This time, he didn't stop until he reached the hall, and only then to retrieve his hat and coat from Kilby.

Gabriel followed Miles to the door. "Surely, the owners of the *Courant* make allowances for a honeymoon? You're a newly married man."

"And have spent all of yesterday exploring Whitechapel brothels with my new bride." Miles settled his hat on his head. "The honeymoon is over. I've a paper to run." He glanced back at Gabriel as Kilby opened the door for him. "See that my wife doesn't venture into the slum without me, would you? And if you could exert yourself to finding Miss Brent before anyone else gets themselves killed?"

Gabriel bowed. "I shall do my utmost."

16

I blame myself," Effie declared as she rummaged through the steamer trunk that sat on a bench at the end of her carved four-poster bed. "Come to London, I said. Go to the theater and the symphony. Visit the dressmaker. Kiss a handsome fellow."

Nell was perched on the edge of Effie's mattress, her cane lying on the embroidered coverlet next to her. She well recalled the advice Effie had issued several months ago. She'd urged Nell to see a little of the world, to experience something of life, before committing herself to the Academy for the remainder of her days.

"It wasn't that," Nell began.

"But Mr. Quincey of all men!" Effie uttered.

Nell winced. It was proving a greater challenge to assuage her friend's outrage than she'd anticipated. Effie had been fuming since they'd entered the vast upstairs bedchamber. Her own, judging by her scattered luggage and the perfume bottles and plated hairbrush that sat on the dainty little silk-skirted dressing table. But not hers alone. There was evidence of her husband's presence in the shaving implements on the washstand and the pocket watch and pair of onyx cuff links that lay atop the low mahogany bureau.

They shared a bedroom, Nell realized. Yet more proof of the closeness Effie enjoyed with her new husband. Was it any wonder she looked askance at Nell's marriage to Mr. Quincey?

"Effie, really," Nell said. "Mr. Quincey isn't *that* bad."

"Oh no. Only stern, disapproving, and completely lacking in sentiment. And he dislikes dogs, did I mention?"

Franc raised his head from the tufted satin pillow where he lay curled up on the bed.

Nell gave the poodle a reassuring pet. "I'm sure he doesn't," she said. "Just because he's fond of cats—"

"Obsessed with cats, more like. And with his paper. And with his own consequence." Having located the item she was searching for (a flat green velvet box), Effie slammed shut the lid of her trunk. "He's a thoroughly unpleasant gentleman."

Nell understood why Effie might think so. During her pursuit of Lord Compton, Effie had called on Miles at the *Courant* with Franc in tow, unaware that there would be cats present in his office. And Franc didn't care for cats. The result had been pure pandemonium. Add to that, the fact that Effie had been lying about her identity, misrepresenting her intentions, and generally creating chaos wherever she went, and it was no mystery why she and Miles hadn't got on.

Effie didn't value order and method. While Miles had too much respect for them to ever appreciate chaos as a strategy. And if one didn't appreciate chaos, one couldn't wholly appreciate Effie.

"Don't be ridiculous," Nell said. "Mr. Quincey has many redeeming qualities."

Effie came around the edge of the bed to join Nell, the velvet box in her hands. "Very well," she said. "If that's true, then name his best one."

Nell could think of half a dozen of Miles's good qualities at once. His loyalty. His sense of honor. His kindness to animals.

The way he kissed.

But that wouldn't serve. Not as a defense to Effie's ill opinion of him.

And it wasn't his best quality in any case. That was something else. Something unique to him—as vexing as it was impressive.

"Regrettably," she said, "his best quality is also his worst one."

Effie elevated her brows in question.

Nell grimaced. "He pays attention."

Effie studied Nell for a moment in silence. "I see."

Heat rose in Nell's cheeks.

Effie smiled. "Is that a blush, Miss Trewlove?"

"It is not," Nell said.

Effie sank down beside her. The mattress dipped beneath her weight. "There's much to be said for a man who pays attention."

Nell met her friend's eyes with a flash of rueful humor. "There were three separate bouquets of gardenias in my new bedroom when I arrived."

"So," Effie mused, "the dour Mr. Quincey isn't, after all, lacking in sentiment."

"No," Nell said. "Which is nothing to the point. Ours is a marriage of convenience."

"In truth?"

"Of course. What else could it be?"

Effie searched Nell's face. "And your wedding night . . . ?"

The heat in Nell's cheeks deepened. "Was spent alone. Or rather, with one of Mr. Quincey's cats."

"Good heavens," Effie said. "You poor dear."

"Not at all," Nell replied, a trifle defensive. "I slept extraordinarily well."

"You do know that you're welcome to stay here?"

"That's very generous of you but—"

"I would insist upon it if I thought you would heed me. But you won't, will you? You'll honor this marriage out of some foolish sense of duty to the Academy, when all the while your heart is breaking."

"It isn't breaking."

"Nell—"

"I won't say I haven't shed any tears, because I have. I didn't wish to leave my position. The Academy is my home. It's where I still long to be." Nell huffed a sad little laugh at how pathetic she must sound. "I'm afraid I've not entirely come to terms with being cut adrift."

Effie rested a consoling hand on hers. "Miss Corvus should never have asked you to go. She should have stood by you, come what may. Even if—"

"Even if her loyalty to me damaged the prospects of every other girl at the Academy? If it affected the teachers? If it ruined the school? No." Nell shook her head. "You understand as well as I do why Miss Corvus acted as she did. We'd have done no differently in her place."

"Perhaps not," Effie admitted grudgingly. "That doesn't mean I have to be happy about it."

"If it helps, she's indicated that I might eventually be permitted to return."

"When?"

"Someday. When enough time has passed and the gossip has died down. She says I might teach again. Possibly even live there."

Effie considered the prospect with a frown. "And Mr. Quincey doesn't object."

"No," Nell said.

It wasn't exactly true. She'd only asked Miles about the first part. The teaching part. She'd said nothing to him about returning to the Academy to live.

"Then all that's left is to wait," Effie said. "While you do . . ." She passed Nell the velvet box. "Perhaps this might cheer you."

Nell opened the hinged lid. Inside, two gilded hairpins lay on a bed of green velvet. They were made in the shape of delicate golden butterflies. She caught her breath. "Oh, goodness."

"I bought them for you at the same shop that made my dragonfly hairpins," Effie said. "And look—" She removed one from the box, pressing a fingertip to the sturdy metal wires to illustrate their strength. "They're perfect for lock-picking."

"They *are* perfect," Nell said. "Simply perfect." She embraced Effie. "Thank you, my dear. You are too good."

"Nonsense. It's you who's the good one. And with these, you shall be even better." Effie squeezed her tight before releasing her. "No door will ever be locked to you again."

"I shall wear them always," Nell vowed.

"You can begin now." Effie placed them in Nell's hair for her, securing them in the roll at her nape. "Lady Belwood notices outward appearances. If we're to call on her, yours must be *comme il faut*."

"I wasn't aware you were still in contact with her ladyship," Nell remarked.

Effie drew back after securing the final pin in Nell's tresses. "I don't claim she likes me very much, but . . . I do make a point of nurturing the connection. She knows everyone worth knowing in London, and since many people still believe I was something like her ward, I've seen no useful reason to dispel the fiction."

"Does Miss Corvus know?"

"Should she?"

Nell gave her friend a speaking look. Effie was notorious for not following the rules. But Miss Corvus made those rules for a reason. It didn't matter if those reasons were sometimes a mystery. "She was the one who provided the introduction. She might not have intended the acquaintance to last any longer than our business lasted with Lord Compton."

"If you're worried that Lady Belwood will speak out of turn, you needn't be," Effie said. "She can't even bring herself to mention Miss Corvus's name."

"Which should be sufficient to warn you," Nell replied. "Miss

Corvus often has plans within plans, the purpose of which only she can discern. By ignoring her commands, you could very well be disturbing a hornet's nest."

"Lady Belwood? A hornet?" Effie scoffed. "Come now. She's a manageable creature. It can surely do no harm to keep in contact with her."

"Effie . . ."

"Besides," Effie added, undaunted, "her ladyship and I still occasionally travel in the same circles. I can hardly pretend I don't know her, can I?"

Nell privately acknowledged her point. "Will she help us?"

"Reluctantly, but yes. Whatever power Miss Corvus holds over her hasn't diminished. Lady Belwood is still wary of anything to do with the Academy. She'll oblige us, if only to get us out the door the sooner." Effie stood. "Shall we go?"

"By all means." Nell rose, retrieving her cane.

Effie cast it a glance. She was unable to disguise the flash of guilt in her eyes.

Nell didn't give her a chance to indulge it. She'd wasted enough time on her injury in this life. All those months recovering under the care of questionable physicians, and all the regret-filled years that followed. It was in the past now, and they were here, firmly in the present, with far more important things to occupy their minds.

"Do you mind if we stop at the post office first?" Nell asked. "I've a sampler to send to Miss Corvus."

"If you like." Effie collected her black silk parasol. It was as stylish as it was lethal, boasting a tip constructed of razor-sharp steel. "Is it about Miss Brent?"

"It is."

"You said she was special?"

"Unusually intelligent, the matron at the workhouse tells me. As well as being a talented mimic." Nell followed Effie to the bedroom door. "The matron claims Miss Brent can duplicate any accent she hears to flawless effect."

"Intriguing."

"I thought so. And she's proved resourceful, too. She escaped from the brothel on her own, and scratched the bully boy on the way out. He'll bear a scar."

Effie's mouth curved with satisfaction as she set her hand on the doorknob. "Striking a blow for all womankind. I like this Miss Brent already."

"Do you think Mr. Royce will be able to locate her?"

"If he can't," Effie said, "then no one can."

• • • • •

The Belwoods' tall, white stucco town house in Brook Street was at the heart of fashionable Mayfair. On Nell and Effie's arrival, a liveried footman admitted them into a lavish drawing room decorated in shades of apple-green silk and antique gold brocade. Massive gilt-framed portraits of generations of grand-looking lords and ladies in powdered wigs and lace adorned the walls, an oil-and-canvas testament to the Belwoods' esteemed pedigree.

They had not been waiting long when Lady Belwood swept into the room. She was a handsome blond woman of passing middle age, attractively plump and impeccably dressed in a striped-silk afternoon gown with a box-pleated hem. An anxious line marred her fair brow as she crossed the thick carpet. "Mrs. Royce," she said. "I was not expecting you."

Nell stood, along with Effie, from the velvet-tufted settee. She stared at Lady Belwood, feeling the oddest sense of recognition. Nell had never met the woman before. Of that she was certain. Yet, there was something strangely familiar about her. The austere beauty in the turn of her countenance, perhaps. Or the peculiar way she had of swishing her skirts behind her as she came to meet them. The twinge in Nell's breast told her that she'd seen it before. That she knew that face. That figure. That impatiently sashaying walk.

"Lady Belwood," Effie said, dropping a flawless curtsy. "May I present my friend, Mrs. Quincey?"

Lady Belwood turned her attention to Nell for the first time. She gave her a civil nod. "Mrs. Quincey."

"My lady." Nell curtsied as elegantly as she'd been taught to do in the deportment classes she'd taken at the Academy as a girl.

"Mrs. Quincey is the wife of Mr. Miles Quincey, editor of the *London Courant*," Effie said. "You're familiar with their gossip column, I presume?"

Lady Belwood motioned for them to resume their seats. "I read it on occasion," she said, taking a chair across from them. She arranged the folds of her skirt. "You will forgive me, Mrs. Quincey, but you have caught me unaware. As Mrs. Royce knows, my receiving hours don't begin until one o'clock."

"I thought it best not to risk involving any of your other callers in the business we've come to discuss," Effie said.

Lady Belwood tensed. "Business? What business?"

Effie smiled. "We were hoping you might tell us more about Lord Amstead's house party next month."

"What about it?" Lady Belwood asked.

"When it takes place, for one," Effie said.

"Saturday next," Lady Belwood replied. "The third of September."

Nell's heartbeat quickened. It was the same date mentioned in Mr. Cowgill's notebook.

"It's a shooting party more than a house party," Lady Belwood said. "Country parties during the first weeks of September generally are."

"Will you be going?" Effie asked.

"I will," Lady Belwood said. "I confess, I am not well acquainted with the new baron. His family rarely emerges from Hertfordshire and they keep no house in town. However, my husband, Sir Walter, was a longtime correspondent of Lord Amstead's late father. They shared a passion for genealogy through the post." She looked to Nell. "My husband is an invalid, Mrs. Quincey, with a formidable ancestry. He's presently working on a lengthy family history."

Effie's eyes lit with interest. "Sir Walter is attending the house party with you?"

"Certainly not," Lady Belwood said. "His health won't allow the journey. He's asked me to attend in his place. Which is convenient for Lord Amstead. I understand his party is short of ladies, many of his gentlemen friends being bachelors."

Nell seized on the fact. "Is that so? You encourage me to ask a favor of you, my lady."

Lady Belwood regarded Nell down the length of her perfectly sculpted nose. "You presume a good deal on so brief an acquaintance, ma'am."

"It's in a good cause, I assure you," Nell said.

She knew full well that this way lay danger. But she couldn't think of that now. And she couldn't think about whether or not Miles would approve. The house party was but a week away. Time was too precious to let such an opportunity pass.

"Would it be within your power to secure an invitation to the party for me?" she asked Lady Belwood. "Seeing as how Lord Amstead is short of ladies, my presence is sure to be welcome."

Lady Belwood was incredulous. "Do you know his lordship?"

"Not yet," Nell said. "Perchance you can provide an introduction?"

Her ladyship turned a frosty look on Effie. "I cannot begin to imagine why you and your friend would think that I should ever allow myself to be imposed upon—"

"Mrs. Quincey is one of my sisters from Miss Corvus's Academy," Effie interrupted. "Did I not mention it?"

The color drained out of Lady Belwood's face. Her gaze jerked to Nell's. *"You?"*

Nell gave her an apologetic smile. "Until yesterday, I had the honor of being deputy headmistress."

"A teacher? That's all?" Lady Belwood's rigid features relaxed a fraction, as though the information was some little relief to her. "And now you're married to a newspaperman?"

"He will, of course, be accompanying me to the house party," Nell said.

"Will he indeed," Lady Belwood replied acidly. "And just how will that help the balance of ladies to gentlemen?"

"It may not," Nell conceded. "But I will still be there. And my husband's presence is essential to me. Though I'd prefer we leave any mention of his occupation out of it."

The villains who had murdered Mr. Cowgill had sent his tongue to the editor of the *Courant*. Nell didn't intend to risk anyone at the house party learning that that gentleman was Miles. Not if she could help it.

"You might simply say that Mr. and Mrs. Quincey are family friends," Effie suggested helpfully. "That you require Mrs. Quincey's companionship in order to attend. Ladies are left alone all day during shooting parties, are they not? You wouldn't wish to be bored."

Lady Belwood's bosom swelled with indignation. She surged up from her chair. "Will the demands of this *woman* never cease?"

"Miss Corvus," Effie whispered to Nell in explanation as the two of them rose from the settee.

Nell understood. She stepped forward to Lady Belwood, setting a gentle hand on her silk-clad arm. "Not a demand," she said. "A request. And it's me making it, not Miss Corvus."

Lady Belwood glared at her. "The last time I sponsored one of your number, I was made party to the ruination of a good and decent gentleman."

Effie gave an indelicate snort. "Lord Compton was neither good nor decent."

"And now I must trust that you won't embroil me in some further scandal?" Lady Belwood lifted her chin. "If I do this, I must have your word that it will be an end to whatever imagined debt I owe that woman."

"It's not within my power to discharge your debt to Miss Corvus," Effie told her.

"No," Nell said. "But it's within mine."

She may not be deputy headmistress any longer, but she flattered herself that she still held some influence at the Academy. Surely, Miss Corvus would respect the bargain Nell was making.

She pressed Lady Belwood's arm. "See that my husband and I are invited, and you may consider your debt repaid."

Lady Belwood held Nell's gaze. After a pointed moment, she nodded. "I shall send Lord Amstead a note." She turned in a swish of silk to go to the gilded writing desk in the corner. The action stirred up a cloud of her ladyship's perfume—a singularly unique blend of jasmine, tuberose, and honey.

Nell remained frozen where she stood as Lady Belwood walked away from her. She had the sensation that time had stopped. No, not stopped. Rather, it was running in reverse. Taking her away from London, all the way back to that little house in the country with the two aged servants. The house where the perfumed lady had visited her one final time eighteen years ago.

It was the last occasion Nell had smelled that fragrance.

Until today.

17

By the time Miles returned home, night had fallen and St. James's Square was sunk into darkness. It stretched between the inadequate glow of the scattered streetlamps, an oppressive, heavy gloom made worse by the unrelenting fog, smoke, and grit of the city to which not even fashionable Mayfair stood immune.

His driver set him down in front of the silent town house. The carriage pulled away immediately after, the clatter of wheels and the ring of steel-shod hooves fading as the coachman headed for the mews.

Miles hadn't intended to work so late, but despite what Griffiths would have Nell believe—that Miles's position as editor in chief was one of more general than specific responsibility—he still had a paper to get out.

There had been important articles to review, advertising revenue to discuss, and several meetings to attend with his subordinate editors. Add to that, poring over old issues of the *Courant* and reading all of Cowgill's previous columns published in the month of March, and Miles's day had been long indeed. He'd been obliged to stay until the very end.

It had nothing to do with any reluctance he might feel about returning home to his new wife. On the contrary, there had been several moments during his workday when he'd found himself foolishly anticipating sharing something with Nell. And yet . . .

He'd stayed away until he was almost certain she had retired.

It wasn't because he didn't want to see her. No. It was because he was beginning to want her too much.

A troubling state of affairs, finding himself physically attracted to the woman who had married him under duress. The same woman who had never left the confines of Miss Corvus's Academy until two days ago. Who had only yesterday admitted to him tearfully that she'd lost everything.

Miles would be the worst sort of conscienceless brute to take advantage of her in her time of vulnerability. And, after the kiss they'd shared last evening . . .

He didn't entirely trust himself not to.

Recognizing the impulse was the first step to overcoming it—or so he told himself. It helped that Nell had preferred to be out of his company today. Perhaps she would choose to do the same tomorrow and the next day, too. Given enough time apart, Miles may yet conquer this.

He used his latchkey to let himself in. The gasolier had been left on for him. It was turned down low, giving only enough light for him to see through the hall. He was mounting the stairs, a bundle of various documents he'd taken from the office tucked under his arm, when he noticed a strip of light flickering under the wood-paneled doors to his library. He stopped on the bottom step, his chest heavy with indecision.

After a long moment, he descended back to the hall. Setting his shoulders, he entered the library. It was a masculine space—the walls lined with dark mahogany bookcases, the furnishings oversized and heavy, and the years-old residue of pipe smoke lingering in the air.

Nell was seated in one of the large oxblood leather chairs in front of the fireplace. Her head was bent over a scrap of embroidery, her fingers moving steadily as she deftly plied her needle. She hadn't changed for bed yet. She was still in the same blue silk dress she'd worn to his office this morning. Two of his cats, Absalom and Virgil, were stretched out on the hearth rug in front of her, dozing in the warmth of the crackling flames.

"You're still awake," Miles said.

Nell glanced up. Shadows danced over her face, lending a brittle cast to her countenance. It was surely a trick of the firelight, but . . . she appeared unusually fragile. As though she were crafted of too-fine porcelain that might crack at any moment. "I am."

Miles went to her, the heaviness in his chest transformed by swift concern. He retrieved the tinderbox from the mantel and lit the branch of candles that stood beside it. "You'll ruin your eyes sewing in this dim light."

"I can see well enough," she said.

He doubted the truth of her statement. She was doing detailed work. Another sampler, it seemed, this one characterized by a border of tiny blue flowers. Equally tiny butterflies flitted among the blooms. There was a small raven, too, with a stitch of white on its wing, just as Miles had observed in the sampler she'd been working on at the *Courant*.

"Have you eaten?" he asked.

"I dined with Mr. and Mrs. Royce," she said. "And you?"

"I had something at my office."

Flack had brought in a box of questionable meat pies he'd procured from a street seller.

Miles's gaze fell to Absalom and Virgil. The former was a long-haired white cat with only one eye—the remnant of an injury he'd suffered during his days as a brawling tom in Fleet Street. The latter was a short-haired gray with a wise, owllike little face. "I see you've made new friends in my absence."

"I wouldn't go that far," Nell replied. "I believe it's the fire that's drawn them here, not me. Though they have permitted me to pet them."

"A triumph," Miles said. Like all his rescued cats, Absalom and Virgil didn't trust humans easily.

"I looked in on Shadow as well," she told him. "She accepted a dish of cream, but she still won't allow me to touch her."

"Give it another week," Miles said. He had seen it often enough with street cats. They needed to gain confidence in their surroundings. To trust that they'd be safe. Until they did, the best thing for them was quiet and consistency.

Miles hoped it would prove the same for Nell. Whatever had prompted their marriage, he wanted her to feel at home here.

"What time did you return from the Royces'?" he asked.

"Their carriage set me down an hour ago."

"And you came in here rather than retire?" He studied her face. "I trust you weren't waiting for me."

Nell's busy needle finally stilled. A troubled line etched her brow. "I didn't realize it then, but . . . perhaps I was."

Miles's heart thumped heavily. He went to the sideboard on the opposite side of the room. It was, like most of the furniture in the house, large, dark, and more functional than fashionable. Yet more evidence of Charles Pelham's tenure. The former editor in chief had been an unrepentant bachelor.

Setting down his stack of papers, Miles lifted one of the decanters. The documents slid to the polished surface of the sideboard in a disorganized heap, revealing Cowgill's notebooks, along with multiple old issues of the *Courant* that Miles had brought home for further study. "Would you like a glass of brandy?" he asked.

"No, thank you."

He promptly returned the decanter to its place. If she wasn't going to have a drink, then neither would he.

She rose from her chair behind him, the rustle of her petticoats and crinoline as recognizable to him now as the velvet-edged tones of her voice. "I learned several things today," she said.

He turned. "So did I."

She looked at him expectantly, her shapely figure silhouetted in the glow of the firelight.

Miles leaned back against the sideboard. Given his unruly feelings, it was wiser to keep a bit of distance from her. He could think clearer then. Just. "I went through the death notices in the paper. I discovered that the late Lord Amstead died on the nineteenth of March."

Her brows lifted. "The first date recorded in Mr. Cowgill's notebook?"

"Exactly."

"And the second date?"

Miles shook his head. "I read all of Cowgill's columns from March. The second date has no relation to any of them as far as I can tell. There's no evidence he was ever at Northwick Hall. The only party he attended in Hertfordshire this year was at a place called Bricket Lodge, owned by a wealthy tradesman by the name of Jefford." He paused, adding, "Cowgill did mention Lord Amstead, however. It was in his column the week after Amstead's father died." He reached into the half-spilled stack of papers and extracted the copy of the *Courant* that contained the column. He crossed the well-worn red-and-gold carpet to give it to her. "It's here."

Nell stepped forward. Her bare fingers brushed his as she took the paper. Miles's pulse surged dangerously. If Nell was similarly affected, she didn't show it. She skimmed Cowgill's column in the candlelight, reading the relevant passage aloud. *"A Hertfordshire lord is on the ascent, and not before time. Your humble correspondent hears that the vertically inclined gentleman was growing impatient to assume the title."* Her eyes lifted to his in question. "Vertically inclined?"

"Ambitious. Eager. Possibly something more."

She handed the paper back to him. "The late baron was three-and-seventy. I suppose his son had been waiting a long time to inherit."

"Impatiently waiting, according to Cowgill."

Nell frowned. "Do we know how his father died?"

Miles returned the paper to the stack of documents on the sideboard, his blood still thrumming with heat. He ruthlessly refocused his attention on the matter at hand. "Succumbed in his sleep, apparently, after a decades-long battle with heart trouble."

"So, his demise was not unexpected."

"Not that I'm aware." He turned back to her. "What about you? Any luck at Lady Belwood's chasing down the third date?"

Nell was silent for several seconds. And then: "It's a shooting party," she said. "It takes place on the third of September."

Miles felt a flare of satisfaction at her discovery. Their investigations were making progress. "So," he said. "We have the date of the late baron's death, the date of the new baron's shooting party, and one unaccounted for date in between. Another day in March, not long after the late Lord Amstead died."

"What could it be in reference to?" Nell wondered. "And what could any of it have to do with brothels and adulterated tea?"

"And five thousand pounds," Miles reminded her. "It's a princely sum. More than most people see in a lifetime."

"Mrs. Pritchard's brothel *did* shows signs of recent prosperity."

"You presume she was the recipient of the money?"

"It seems likely," Nell said.

Miles ran a hand over the side of his jaw. The coarse scrape of stubble abraded his palm. He was clean-shaven, but his beard always came in late in the evening. It had never mattered before. He'd lived alone. But now . . .

It occurred to him that, with Nell in residence, he might have to start shaving twice a day.

He pushed the thought out of his head.

"I must go to Hertfordshire," he said brusquely. "I'll need to speak to the locals. Try and find out the significance of that second date."

"As to that," Nell said, "Lady Belwood was able to provide some assistance."

"What manner of assistance?"

"She's arranging for us to receive an invitation to the shooting party."

His hand fell from his face. "What?"

"I took the liberty of asking her to act on our behalf," Nell said. "She wrote a note to Lord Amstead while Mrs. Royce and I waited, telling him that you and I were friends of hers and she required my companionship in order to—"

"*Your* companionship?" Miles took a reflexive step toward her. He stopped himself before going any further. "Are you telling me that this invitation includes you?"

"Naturally, it does. Lord Amstead's party is short of ladies. My presence is the impetus for him to extend us an invitation. 'My exceptionally beautiful and vivacious young friend,' Lady Belwood wrote in her note. What gentleman could refuse such a temptation?"

If Miles didn't know better, he'd think Nell was baiting him. She had only this morning reminded him that they were supposed to be partners. Perhaps this was a test?

"Are you serious?" he asked.

"Is it such an outlandish proposition?" she returned with deceptive calm.

Miles didn't answer. Not directly. "Has it not occurred to you that they'll know exactly who we are?"

Nell paced back to the fireplace. She was without her cane. A hitch in her left leg marred her gait. "It did occur to me," she acknowledged. "Except that they don't know you by name. And the only ones who know our faces are Verity, Claudine, Mrs. Pritchard, and Silas. The chances that any of them will be at an aristocratic shooting party in Hertfordshire are surely slim to none."

"They know *your* name," Miles said. "If Lord Amstead is involved, they'll likely have shared it with him, along with descriptions of both of us. Once he discovers I'm affiliated with the *Courant*—"

"The party is but three days in length. We'll be gone in a blink. But once we're there . . ." She looked at him over her shoulder. "We'll be perfectly placed to search for clues. Not to mention, we'll be able to talk with Lord Amstead, *and* his servants. Perhaps we'll even find out who Innes is."

Miles stifled the urge to utter an oath. He admired her initiative. Her intelligence, too. But a fellow had his limits. "A man has been murdered, Nell. The danger involved—"

"Isn't it better to draw that danger out than to sit idle waiting for the next blow to strike at random?" she asked. "To face it head-on?"

"I commend your courage, but . . . no." He shook his head. "There's a fine line between daring and recklessness."

Nell spun around to face him. "Not daring," she said in a burst of impatience. "Action. I've spent too long allowing things to simply happen to me. My life at the Academy. Our marriage. Your kiss last night."

Miles froze. "What about my—"

"I don't care about courage. It's control I want." Closing the distance between them, she came to a halt in front of him, so close that her wide skirts bowed against his legs. She set her hands flat on his chest.

Miles's breath lost its rhythm. Her touch was so light, so soft. He nevertheless felt the weight of it all the way through the layers of his shirt and waistcoat.

He didn't let it distract him.

Indeed, staring down at her, he was possessed by the same suspicion he'd had when he'd first entered the library. That unsettling sense that something wasn't right. She was too pale. Her gray eyes too fever bright. Raw vulnerability trembled beneath her every word.

His voice deepened. "Nell—"

She slid her hands up to his shoulders, beneath the fabric of his coat. "Miles," she said.

And she kissed him.

18

Nell had to stand up on the toes of her half boots to reach Miles's mouth. He didn't make it easy for her. Not at first. Not until she curved a hand around his neck and tugged him down to her.

She was being impulsive. Nonsensical. A victim to the roiling emotions inspired by the last several days of heartbreak and upheaval. Until today she'd thought she was managing it. But she wasn't.

She couldn't.

Not any longer.

Miles bent his head to hers, a frown furrowing his brow. His lips were firm and unyielding. Until suddenly they weren't. The change came over him in a delirious instant. One moment he was rigid and resisting, the next his arms were around her in a crushing embrace and his mouth was claiming hers—fiercely, hungrily.

Nell clung to him, breathless. This—this is what she needed. To be wanted beyond sense. Beyond logic or reason. Her fingers tangled in the thick hair at his nape as she kissed him back with half-parted lips.

They were closer than they'd ever been—locked in each other's arms, her bosom pressed to his broad chest and her skirts tangled precariously about his legs. It still wasn't close enough. She pulled at him restlessly.

Miles's arms tightened about her waist in response. The bones of her corset creaked in protest. His voice was a harsh rasp against her lips. "I fear I'm crushing you."

"I want you to," she whispered back. "I want more."

He gave it to her, pressing hot kisses to her cheek, her jaw, her throat. The scratch of his stubble grazed her skin in the most delicious fashion.

Nell's fingers clenched in his hair. Her heart was beating in triple time. There was no room for anything but sensation. It felt good to be wanted. To be desired. To know that, despite whatever it was that had made him resist her initially, he couldn't resist her in the end. In that, at least, she had power.

"Easy," he murmured as she brought his mouth back to hers. "Easy, sweetheart."

"I'm so restless."

"I know." His hand splayed at her back—a large, heavy weight, holding her steady. "There's no rush."

Heat crept into her face. She feared he was rejecting her. "You'd rather we stop?"

"No," he said. "No. It's just . . . this is unexpected."

"You hadn't thought that I—that we—"

He huffed. "I've been trying like the devil not to."

She stared up at him, painfully conscious of her own inexperience. "Then you *do* want me?"

Miles's gaze softened. His hand came to cradle her cheek. "Desperately," he assured her.

A surge of emotion constricted Nell's throat. Perhaps she'd been wrong to kiss him. Perhaps she was using him shamelessly.

But no.

That would imply that anyone would have done. Any man. Any friend. Anyone who might help to keep the storm of emotion at bay. But it hadn't been just anyone she'd wanted as she'd departed Lady Belwood's house this afternoon. It had been Miles.

She turned her face into the curve of his palm. "I want you, too," she told him. "I'm sorry I was so clumsy about it."

"Not clumsy," he said. "Wonderful."

Her mouth lifted in a tremulous smile. "After all but mauling you in your library?"

"Mauling me," he repeated with a trace of husky amusement. "Is that what you did?"

"I fear I did."

He stroked her cheek with the pad of his thumb. His expression grew serious. "What I don't understand is why."

"Must there be a reason?"

"No, but I suspect there is one." He smoothed a lock of her hair from her face. "What happened today, Nell?"

Nell's eyes burned with the threat of tears. She slowly pulled away from him. He made no effort to stop her. His hand dropped from her cheek and his arm loosened at her waist. She took a limping step back. She was at once colder. More alone. Just as she'd been when she'd stood in Lady Belwood's drawing room, staring at her ladyship's retreating figure in stunned silence.

A tremor went through Nell to recall it. Her voice cracked. "The silliest thing," she said. "I believe I met my mother."

• • • • •

Miles settled Nell back in her chair by the waning fire. He pressed a snifter of brandy into her hand. "Lady Belwood?" he said. "Are you certain?"

"As certain as I can be." Nell's slim fingers curled around the bowl of the glass. "I don't resemble her. Not enough that anyone would notice. But I know that perfume. And she *was* familiar. It's the only explanation—"

"Drink," he urged her.

Nell took a grudging sip. She grimaced as she lowered the snifter. "I'm not distraught," she said. "Only unsettled."

"I should say so," Miles replied.

He was rather unsettled himself. Not five minutes ago, he'd been kissing her like a madman. His body was still coiled tight, his blood still surging in a dangerous simmer.

It shouldn't have happened. Not any of it. But it had, to his amazement. *She'd* kissed *him*. And just like that, he'd abandoned his reason, cast aside restraint, and given in to the impulses he'd been battling since the moment they'd met. There had been no more room for logical argument. There had only been Nell. Her soft mouth and body, and the feel of her fingers twining insistently in his hair.

She was, indeed, the heavy artillery. Once she'd turned her sights on him, Miles hadn't stood a chance.

"Lady Belwood sponsored Mrs. Royce's entrance into society, did she not?" he asked.

"She did."

"Then she's a connection of hers?"

"Not of hers, no. Of Miss Corvus's. It was she who provided Effie with an introduction to Lady Belwood."

Effie. The former Euphemia Flite. Now Euphemia Royce.

Miles had always suspected the woman was trouble. And if she was, the mysterious Miss Corvus must be doubly so. It was she who had sent Mrs. Royce to London to ruin Lord Compton. She who had directed Nell to come to Miles's office to put his questions about the Academy to rest.

A woman who was recruiting girls with natural talent. Girls who grew into formidable ladies like Nell and Mrs. Royce and God knew how many others that were even now embedded in fashionable households, well-to-do schools, and perhaps even married to powerful men.

"I don't believe I was ever supposed to meet her," Nell said. "If Effie had severed the contact, I never would have done. But now . . . I can't simply pretend I didn't see her. That I don't know who she is."

"Of course not," Miles said. "What about her? Lady Belwood? Did she show any sign of recognition?"

"No. Though . . . she did appear distressed to hear I was affiliated with the Academy, but she rallied when she discovered I was a teacher. I daresay she assumed it meant I wasn't an orphan."

"She's afraid of encountering the child she gave up," Miles concluded.

"I suppose she has reason." Nell took another grimacing sip of brandy. "She's very rich, I believe. Or rather, her husband is. He's consumed by the consequence of his family pedigree, apparently. I didn't ask when they married, but if it was eighteen years ago, it would explain why she gave me away."

Miles sank down onto one knee beside her. At the moment, the empty chair opposite her seemed too far away. "Eighteen years? Do you mean that . . . she kept you for a time?"

"Not personally, no. Two servants had charge of me in a little house outside a village somewhere—I don't know which one. Lady Belwood sometimes came to visit. She used to bring me sweets, and pinch my cheeks. She called me her bonnie girl. It was the only name I knew until Miss Corvus christened me Penelope. I had a little toy loom, you see, like Odysseus's wife. I was permitted to bring it with me when I came to the Academy."

"Lady Belwood surrendered you there?"

"Not her. She hadn't the courage to do it herself. She simply stopped coming. It was the servants who took me to the Academy. I can only presume Lady Belwood had arranged it with Miss Corvus ahead of time."

He studied Nell's pale face. "Miss Corvus never told you?"

Nell's mouth was set in a bleak line. "Miss Corvus is not a great believer in looking backward. She sees no utility in the past."

"What about Mrs. Royce?"

"She doesn't know. If she did, she'd never have taken me there. Effie's not cruel like that."

"I didn't expect she was," Miles said. "I only thought that, if you confided in her, she might have offered you some comfort."

Nell stared into her glass. "I didn't tell her."

"Why not?"

"It's complicated." She paused. "Mothers are a sore subject with some of us."

"I'm beginning to see that."

"Was your relationship with your mother—?"

"Complicated? No. It was brutally straightforward."

She looked at him in question.

"My mother had me out of wedlock," Miles said. "She lost her position as a result. She had been a governess." He didn't know for whom. He'd never managed to find out. "She had nothing and no one. Only me. She poured all of her learning and all of her ambition into me. The moment she could manage it, she sent me away—to save me, she said. She died while I was serving my apprenticeship. Caught a putrid fever in the Rookery and was gone in two days. I learned about it in a letter from Gabriel."

Nell's face contorted with sympathy. "Oh, Miles. That's dreadful."

"It was, rather."

The last of the fire crackled and popped, embers floating up the chimney from the grate. Absalom and Virgil stretched idly on the hearthrug, completely unconcerned about revelations from the past. They were creatures of the moment. And this moment was warm and safe, despite the presence of two increasingly melancholy humans.

Nell searched Miles's gaze. "At the Academy, you told me that taking up your apprenticeship meant leaving the one person you loved. Was it her you meant?"

"It was."

Her soft gray eyes shimmered in the firelight. "I'm so sorry."

"It was a long time ago," Miles said. "In any case, she's not forgotten. I honor her in everything I do. I daresay it's why I made such a bother over my ruined reputation. She sacrificed everything for me to become the gentleman I am today."

"You're a splendid gentleman," Nell said. "She would be proud of you."

His mouth hitched briefly. "Splendid," he murmured. "I shall add that to the list I'm compiling, along with brilliant, fearless, and a champion of truth, and justice, and cats."

"Do," she told him. "I don't mind."

The way she looked at him, so tender and sincere. It had a perilous effect on his heartbeat. Indeed, since entering the library, it was beginning to seem to Miles as though he'd lost control over the basic rhythms of his own body. His pulse was too heavy. His temperature too hot. And his muscles in a perpetual taut state of readiness.

His gaze fell to the lush curve of her lips. He wanted to kiss her again. But the timing wasn't right. Not now when she was upset, and when they were both talking about their mothers, for God's sake.

He stood. Plucking the half-empty snifter of brandy from her fingers, he returned it to the sideboard. "Lady Belwood is attending Lord Amstead's shooting party?"

"She is."

"If we attend—"

"*When* we attend," Nell corrected him.

He came back to her. "You'll be in company with her for three days."

"I'm aware."

"What do you propose to do about it?"

"I don't know," Nell said. "Perhaps nothing. It's only three days as you said. My attentions will be focused on discovering the link between Lord Amstead and Mr. Cowgill's death. I doubt there'll be time to spare for any personal concerns."

Miles nodded, resigning himself to their course. She was right. However dangerous, it was the best way to find out whatever it was that had led to Cowgill's death. They'd be foolish not to seize the opportunity.

"The third of September is right around the corner," he said. "I'll have to arrange for my absence at the *Courant*. And you—"

"I shall need some new gowns if I'm to play my part," Nell told him. "If you wouldn't mind standing the expense?"

It wasn't the most passionate of marital intimacies. But it was an intimacy all the same. At the moment, Miles would take it.

"Naturally," he said. "You're my wife."

19

Nell followed Effie into the gaslit shop in Conduit Street. The door opened into an elegant showroom furnished with several comfortable chairs, a gleaming trifold mirror, and luxuriant displays of colorful fabrics and trimmings. A tall counter of polished mahogany stood at the back. There was a curtained door behind, presumably leading to the workrooms.

Nell's gaze drifted over the shimmering silks, rich velvets, and exquisitely printed muslins. She had never been to a dressmaker's establishment before. From the earliest age she was able, she'd been making her own clothes. An easy enough task for one skilled in needlework. Especially one who wasn't obliged to design anything more intricate than the plain dresses that made up a schoolmistress's wardrobe.

"Mr. Malik was recommended to me shortly after Mr. Royce and I married," Effie said. "His designs are much lauded at the moment. The best one can get outside of Paris. He's even made dresses for the Queen's ladies-in-waiting."

Nell lowered her voice. "He must be dreadfully expensive."

"You needn't trouble yourself on that account," Effie said. "Not if Mr. Quincey is paying the bill."

Nell frowned. She had no intention of taking advantage of Miles's generosity. The two of them were only just beginning to grow closer. And last night . . .

Well.

They had kissed, of course. And embraced each other passionately. But it wasn't that which made the thought of him settle so warmly inside her heart this morning. Her growing feelings couldn't be reduced to mere physical attraction.

No.

Miles had been kind. Caring. He'd looked after her at her lowest point.

One of her many lowest points these past several days.

And he'd done so with no discernable gain in sight. He hadn't used the opportunity to wrest information out of her about the Academy. He hadn't even demanded another kiss—or more. Before leaving the library, he'd summoned the maid to make up a hot brick for Nell's leg, and then gently, but firmly, commanded that she retire.

Nell hadn't seen him since. He'd gone to his chamber and she'd gone to hers. By the time she'd come down to breakfast this morning, he'd already left for the paper. And on a Saturday, no less.

"The master always goes in on Saturdays," Mrs. Bright had explained as she'd poured Nell's tea. "Sundays, too, since that business with Viscount Compton. He's keen to find a story that will restore the *Courant*'s fortunes." The housekeeper had given Nell a sympathetic look. "I confess, I did hope he'd adjust his habits now he's a married gentleman, but you know what the paper means to him."

More than Nell meant to him, obviously. He'd been wedded to the paper far longer than he'd been wedded to her. And now, she'd gone and complicated things between them even further.

Looking back on it, she supposed she should regret her behavior. She hadn't only thrown herself at him. She'd shared something with him that she hadn't even shared with her Academy sisters. It had seemed right at the time. Unlike Effie or Gemma or Miss Corvus herself, Miles wasn't part of the collective effort. He belonged to Nell alone. Her very own person, to kiss, to confide in.

And Nell had never had anyone of her own before.

She said to Effie, "I do wish the two of you were on better terms."

"Nonsense," Effie replied. "We're in perfect accord. We both want to see you looking your best."

A young Indian lady in an impeccably tailored wool dress emerged from the curtained back room. She inclined her head to Effie in recognition. "Mrs. Royce. Good afternoon."

"Mrs. Jones," Effie said, approaching the counter. "I do hope you can help us. My dear friend, Mrs. Quincey, is urgently in need of several dresses for a shooting party next Saturday. I don't suppose Mr. Malik can fit her in for a rush order?"

Mrs. Jones swept an assessing gaze over Nell. A smile curled her lips. "He might be persuaded."

"Excellent," Effie said. She addressed Nell. "Mr. Malik used to be a tailor. The beauty of his creations is in the cut." She turned back to Mrs. Jones. "Mrs. Quincey requires no extra adornment, as you see. Only a suitable frame to enhance her already formidable attributes."

"Just so." Mrs. Jones gestured to the back room. "If you will allow me to take your measurements, madam?"

Nell walked toward the curtained door. Effie didn't accompany her. Nell paused. "You're not coming?"

"You don't require me for this part," Effie said. "And we've little enough time to spare before you leave for Hertfordshire. I shall take the opportunity to visit the milliner and draper on your behalf, and to pay a visit to a clockmaker's shop I know of in Oxford Street."

"A clockmaker?" Nell echoed dubiously.

"I've business with his assistant," Effie explained. "I'll be back before you've finalized your order."

"But how will I know what's most suitable?" Nell asked.

"Leave it with Mrs. Jones and Mr. Malik," Effie said. "They won't steer you wrong."

Nell spent the next two hours in her underclothes, standing atop a raised platform in one of the fitting rooms, being measured, marked, and swathed with beautiful fabrics.

Mr. Malik was indeed a visionary. A tall, bronze-skinned gentleman with a studious set to his brow, he took no liberties and engaged in no idle conversation, but somewhere along the way—as he diligently draped and pinned—he conjured an effortless variety of magic.

Nell learned that shades of maize and gold could turn her skin from a flat porcelain to a rich, luminous cream, and that delicate blues and greens could make the gray in her eyes dazzle with the incandescent shine of a moonstone. Colors mattered, it seemed. So did textures, and strategically placed darts and seams.

By the time Effie returned later that afternoon, Nell had ordered several gowns, two sets of blouses and skirts, and a smart little caraco jacket—all of it billed to her new husband.

"It was always Miss Corvus's dream to see you outfitted in fashionable style," Effie remarked as the Royces' carriage departed Conduit Street.

Nell sat back in her seat across from her friend, her hip aching from spending so much time standing immobile. "Perhaps once," she acknowledged.

"Pity she won't see it." Effie's eyes took on a pensive expression. "Pity about all of it."

Nell knew what her friend was referencing. And it wasn't Nell's recent expulsion from the Academy. It was about the day Nell had fallen from the roof.

Effie was terrified of heights. After climbing up to the top of the

Academy tower as a girl, she'd found herself too frozen with fear to get down. Nell had been obliged to go after her. That Nell had slipped in the process had been entirely an accident.

Which made no difference to Effie's conscience. She'd always blamed herself for snuffing out Nell's early potential.

But Nell didn't blame her. Perhaps she had once, in the direct aftermath, when she'd been laid up, recovering from her injuries, during all those interminable visits from incompetent local doctors. But that was a long time past, and best forgotten. She loved Effie too well to dwell on it. And she understood. She truly understood.

"Never mind that," Nell said, gently changing the subject. "What did you buy at the milliner's and draper's shops?"

"Three fetching little hats, four pairs of gloves, a lace parasol, and various other odds and ends."

Nell inwardly recoiled at the undoubted expense. "And the clockmaker's establishment? You never said why you were going there."

The carriage slowed amid the traffic of the busy street. It was an overcast day, but still a dry one, and the storekeepers were doing a steady trade. Gleaming coaches jockeyed for position in the road as well-to-do ladies and gentlemen in fine clothes were assisted in and out of their vehicles by liveried footmen.

"Ah, that," Effie said. "I ordered a new cane for you."

"You *what*?"

"The one you already have is too recognizable. You'll require another for Hertfordshire. Something plain and unobtrusive."

Nell's eyes narrowed. "And useless?"

"Far from it. The clockmaker's assistant, Miss Peele, is rather talented with mechanized wheels and coils. She's fitting it up with a spring-loaded blade just as your previous one had. It will still serve if you get into trouble. Which I trust you won't with Mr. Quincey there to protect you."

"Is Mr. Royce always there to protect you now you're married?"

Effie smiled at the mention of her husband. "He tries to be, poor man. But he has his work to attend to. He can't forever be chasing after me."

A hollowness formed in Nell's chest. She'd never had anyone who loved her so particularly. Who would be willing to chase her to the ends of the earth in order to save her, protect her. Not a sweetheart. Not a mother. Not even a friend. When it came to the point, Nell had always been sacrificed. Lady Belwood had given her up for selfish gain. Miss Corvus for the greater good. The end result had been the same.

And Nell wondered, is that what she would have done? Had she a daughter, a protégé, someone who relied on her, would she have set them aside? Abandoned them? Or would she have risked everything to assure their safety and happiness?

She gazed out the carriage window at the passing storefronts, a pensive frown notching her brow. The well-to-do ladies and gentleman with their fine clothes and their fine servants were far removed from the wretchedness that lay in the less fashionable parts of the city. Looking at them, one could almost believe that the slums of London didn't exist. That there weren't people there, even now, subsisting in the worst circumstances, struggling for their very survival.

"Would he object if we went to Whitechapel?" she asked abruptly.

"Unequivocally," Effie said. "What did you have in mind?"

Nell turned back to her. "This will be the fourth night that Flora Brent has been on her own, somewhere out there, at the mercy of heaven knows what or whom."

"We're exhausting every effort to find her. Mr. Royce has already sent two of his men to make inquiries. And you and Mr. Quincey haven't been idle."

"I want to do more," Nell said. "I've been thinking about where she might have gone after she fled the brothel. All she's known is the workhouse. There are few places she would naturally trust. A church, perhaps? Or possibly she tried to find her way back to the railway station? Or what if . . ." A thought occurred to her. "Could she have sought out another workhouse? Whichever one there is in Whitechapel?"

"Not unless she's possessed of no spirit at all," Effie said. "What sort of girl longs to return to the workhouse?"

"A frightened one. One seeking sanctuary."

"But Miss Brent is resourceful. If it were me, I'd be retracing my steps. Attempting to course correct."

"So, back to the railway station?"

"She'd need fare first," Effie said. "And there are few ways for a girl her age to earn it in a slum."

Nell's spirits sank at the implication. "She could be begging."

"She could be," Effie allowed, but she didn't sound convinced.

"I can't in good conscience depart for Hertfordshire without making another attempt to find her," Nell said. "And something else. There's a seamstress near Commercial Street. I spoke with her the day I arrived in town, but I left her no way to reach me. I'd like to see her again before I go."

"What seamstress?" Effie asked.

Nell told her about Miss Jean. Effie listened with interest. It wasn't often either of them encountered someone who had been able to withstand Miss Corvus's maneuverings.

"You mean to say Miss Corvus tried to recruit this woman as a teacher?" Effie asked. "And she refused?" Her forehead creased. "I wonder what her special skill might be?"

"Sewing, I daresay."

"In other words, she's you."

"If she is, she's needed," Nell said with ruthless pragmatism. "The girls can't afford to be without a sewing instructor. And they will be until I'm able to return. None of the other teachers has a passion for stitchery."

"Well, that's that, then." Lifting her black parasol, Effie rapped once with it on the ceiling. The carriage slowed to a halt. A young footman jumped down from the box and came to the window. "We're going to Whitechapel," she informed him. "Commercial Street."

The footman's eyes widened. "But Mrs. Royce, the master wouldn't—"

A coachman behind them called over him: "Get a move on, guv!"

"You're blocking the road!" another driver shouted.

"Quickly," Effie said to her footman. "We haven't got all day."

Face set with resignation, the young servant returned to his perch. The carriage rolled on.

"Mr. Royce is ridiculously overprotective of me," Effie explained to Nell. "As are the servants by extension. One would think I couldn't take care of myself."

"You're fortunate to have someone who cares for you so deeply," Nell said.

Effie's expression softened. "Yes. I still sometimes can't believe it. I do wonder if I deserve it."

"You deserve to be happy."

"So do you," Effie said. "Even if it *is* with Mr. Quincey."

Nell managed a faint smile. It didn't last. She couldn't think about Miles right now. Not when she was on the verge of returning to the slum. He would be furious with her when he found out. And it wasn't because he was overprotective of her, or because he was anything like being in love with her. It was because he'd asked her to leave it to Mr. Royce and she'd agreed.

But really, Nell told herself, it hardly mattered. They'd be back before nightfall.

So long as they didn't encounter any difficulties.

• • • • •

Entering Whitechapel Road some forty minutes later, they were but two turnings away from their destination when the Royces' carriage slowed to a crawl. Makeshift stalls lined the street where yesterday there had been none, selling everything from meat, fish, and greens to crockery, carpets, and furniture. Noisy crowds gathered round them—women bartering with salesmen and men loading carts with newly purchased items that were too cumbersome to carry.

"The Saturday market," Effie said. "We shall have to get out and walk if you can manage it."

Nell peered out the carriage window in dismay. "There are so many people."

"Saturday is payday," Effie explained. "People are anxious to make their earnings last the week. It benefits them to get their goods as cheaply as possible."

"Hence the street market?"

"They pop up all over the city." Effie rapped on the ceiling. The carriage stopped. This time, there was no one to object to them blocking traffic. It was already obstructed by the teeming crowds.

The footman opened the carriage door for her.

"We shall be stepping out here," she told him. "You may pull along the roadway and wait for us."

The footman was unhappy but obedient. "Yes, Mrs. Royce. Shall I accompany you?"

"No need." Effie allowed him to assist her down.

Nell descended after her. Though her hip was aching, she left her cane behind. Effie was right. It was too recognizable, particularly here in Whitechapel.

Effie tucked her parasol under one arm. She offered Nell her other.

Nell took it gratefully. Together, they stepped into the road, Effie in her blue figured silk jacket and skirt and Nell in her simply cut gray carriage gown. They weren't the only well-dressed ladies among the shoppers. Women of every sort were patronizing the stalls.

"Miss Jean's lodgings are in a lane off of Commercial Street," Nell said. "It shouldn't be far from here."

"Are you certain you're able—"

"I can manage." The walk would do Nell good. Her leg benefited from use. Too much stillness inevitably made the pain worse.

"You'll have to direct me," Effie said. "I'm not as familiar with Whitechapel as I am with the Rookery."

Nell steered her friend through the raucous throng. Their wide skirts brushed against the crush of people who were positioning themselves to obtain the best prices at the various stalls. Determined customers shouted out to the butcher, the fishmonger, and the bootmaker. Among them were rough-looking men and rouge-cheeked ladies in satin gowns. Children, too, though not of the neat and orderly variety. The dirty-faced youngsters ran through the crowds, fleet as ferrets. Some of them pickpockets, Nell suspected.

"The people of the neighborhood are out in force," she remarked to Effie. "What are the odds that Miss Brent is among them?"

Effie slowed her footsteps. "I hadn't considered, but . . . you're right. She could very well be here now."

Nell scanned the faces of the women and girls they passed, looking for any who matched the description given in Flora Brent's health records.

"What should we do?" Effie asked.

"We should shop," Nell said decisively.

Effie smiled. "An excellent idea."

They walked to a fruit stand with a large selection of shiny red apples and bright yellow lemons. From there, to the vegetable stand (where a man was loudly proclaiming the quality of his cauliflowers), and on to the stalls of a flower seller and a butcher. At each stop, as they perused the seller's wares, Nell and Effie discreetly examined the faces of the other customers and those of the people lingering nearby.

Most appeared to be humble working folk—women with raw hands and men with perspiration-stained collars. They talked loudly among one another, uninhibited by the presence of strangers.

While Effie dutifully purchased apples, a head of cauliflower, a bunch of roses, and a cut of meat, Nell listened to whatever fragmented scraps of conversation floated her way.

"—new mangle would cut my washing work—"

"—enough to buy a nice roast for Sunday dinner—"

"—could grow them myself if I had a proper garden—"

"—drank his wages again, the useless sod—"

"—not fit for a dog, I told him, but what choice had I—"

It wasn't until Nell and Effie ventured to a baker's stall that their efforts finally paid off.

Two stout older women carrying baskets were conversing together as a gray-bearded man in an apron readied their order.

"She's a good Christian soul, is Mrs. Davenant," one of the women said to the other. "Taking a girl in off the street, what might cut her throat in her sleep."

"The girl ain't that sort," the other replied. "I've seen her myself. She's a highborn little lady."

The first woman gave a scornful cackle. "A highborn little lady working as a scullery maid in Whitechapel Road?"

"Fallen on hard times, hasn't she? A love affair gone wrong, so's I heard. The girl's parents cast her out."

The first woman accepted three loaves of bread from the baker. "Haven't we got enough of our own seeking work without paying wages to gentlemen's daughters?"

"That's old widow Davenant for you. Mark my words, she'll train the girl up as a proper parlor maid. Lend her a bit of countenance, won't it? Having a maid announce callers what sounds like the Princess Royal."

The two ladies burst into laughter as they departed the stall.

Nell stared after them. Old widow Davenant in Whitechapel Road. Could it be possible? "A new scullery maid with accents like the Princess Royal," she murmured just loud enough for Effie to hear. "Do you suppose . . . ?"

"Do I suppose what?"

"That rather than hiding, Miss Brent has found herself a job?"

Effie looked back at Nell intently. "Resourceful, indeed," she said. "It's worth investigating."

"How many loaves, ma'am?" the baker demanded impatiently.

"We'll take one," Effie replied. "Thank you." She extracted a coin from her reticule to pay for the item. The baker took it, counting out her change.

"I beg your pardon," Nell said. "Could you point us to Mrs. Davenant's residence? It's very near here, I believe."

"Old lady Davenant?" The baker handed Effie the loaf of bread. "Her what lives in the big house on the corner?"

"Which corner would that be?" Effie asked as she tucked the bread into her bag along with her other purchases.

The baker's eyes darkened with suspicion. "You acquainted with the lady?"

"Mrs. Davenant is expecting us," Nell answered him with all the no-nonsense starch of her former position. "So, if you would be so good as to direct us, sir."

The baker pursed his mouth for a moment before gesturing to the left. "That way," he said. "The brick house with the white pediments on the windows."

Nell thanked him for his trouble.

Effie casually gave her food-laden shopping bag to a beggar woman as she and Nell headed off down the road. "Mrs. Davenant is expecting us, is she?" she inquired of Nell with soft amusement.

Nell gave her friend a resolute look. "If she's harboring an Academy girl, she certainly should be."

20

The house with the white pediments lay but two streets away on the corner of Whitechapel Road and a narrow, unmarked lane. On applying at the front door, Nell and Effie were greeted by an imperious-looking housekeeper.

"Mrs. Davenant, if you please," Nell said.

The housekeeper's cool gaze skimmed over them. "Whom should I say is calling, madam?"

"Miss Trewlove and Miss Flite," Nell promptly replied. They weren't here in their personal capacities. They were here on behalf of the school. Their husbands' names needn't enter into it. "We have a charitable matter to discuss with your mistress."

The housekeeper didn't appear impressed by this information. She left them standing on the front step while she inquired within "as to whether Mrs. Davenant was at home." Returning a moment later, she conducted them into a small parlor where a silk-clad lady with a lace cap pinned atop her iron-gray curls was seated on a chintz sofa.

"Miss Trewlove and Miss Flite, ma'am," the housekeeper announced.

Mrs. Davenant rose. "Ladies."

"Mrs. Davenant," Nell said. "How do you do? I am Miss Trewlove, and this is Miss Flite."

"Ma'am." Effie inclined her head.

Mrs. Davenant returned the perfunctory salute. She motioned for them to sit. "My housekeeper tells me you wished to speak to me about a charitable endeavor. If it's donations you're seeking—"

"It is not," Nell said. She and Effie remained standing. "We've come about another matter."

Nell didn't mince words. She couldn't afford to. Not when the housekeeper might, even now, be carrying word of Nell and Effie's arrival to the other servants. They couldn't risk Miss Brent bolting.

"Miss Flite and I are affiliated with a charitable school near the Epping Forest," she said. "An orphan girl lost her way when traveling to join us on Monday. We've been at pains to find her."

"I am sorry for your troubles," Mrs. Davenant said. "But I know of no such girl."

"We understand you've recently employed a young scullery maid," Nell said.

Mrs. Davenant gave them a bemused look. "Little Louise? But she's not an orphan child. She's a girl of excellent family."

"Might we inquire as to when she entered your employ?" Effie asked.

"On Wednesday evening," Mrs. Davenant said.

"And how—?" Nell began.

"My cook found her in desperate circumstances near St. Mary's Church," Mrs. Davenant supplied with a hint of impatience. "Her family had cast her out, and she was in need of respectable employment. I considered it my Christian duty to offer her a position. She's a hard worker, and far too refined to have been left to roam the streets."

Perhaps it was true. Perhaps this Louise was truly a runaway from a genteel household. But Nell didn't think so. "Might we speak with her?" she asked.

"I hardly think it necessary," Mrs. Davenant said. "As I've told you—"

"Is she in the scullery now?" Effie interrupted.

"Why yes," Mrs. Davenant replied. "But—"

"I'd be grateful for a word with her," Nell said. "I promise I won't take any more of her time than necessary."

Mrs. Davenant's lips flattened. "If you insist." She crossed to the bellpull by the coal fireplace and gave it a firm tug. "I'll have my housekeeper fetch the girl."

"I'd far rather your housekeeper took me to her," Nell said.

A frown puckered Mrs. Davenant's wrinkled brow. "You begin to alarm me, Miss Trewlove. Is this orphan you're looking for a dangerous child?"

"Only a frightened one," Nell said. "I've no desire to startle her. If you'd permit me to accompany your housekeeper to the kitchen, I'm certain we can resolve the matter with a minimum of distress."

The housekeeper materialized in the doorway of the parlor.

"Take these ladies down to the kitchen, Mrs. Simpson," Mrs. Davenant said. "They desire a word with Louise."

"Yes, ma'am." The housekeeper looked to Nell and Effie. "This way, ladies."

"I shall go," Nell said. She shot Effie a weighted glance. "Miss Flite, I'm sure, has other business to attend to."

Effie's mouth tipped with understanding. "Quite so. I shall meet you outside when you're finished."

Nell nodded. If it *was* Miss Brent working in the scullery, they must take every precaution. The poor girl had already been tricked once by a woman posing as a helpful friend in the form of Mrs. Pritchard. Given the chance, Miss Brent would likely flee rather than trust her fate to another stranger.

Moving a little slowly on account of the stiffness in her leg, Nell accompanied the housekeeper back into the hall and down a narrow flight of stone stairs to a smoke-filled kitchen. A heavyset woman in an apron was toiling over the stove. A similarly apron-clad servant girl—dark of hair and slight of figure—was seated at a long plank table busily chopping potatoes and carrots for the pot.

Nell's pulse leapt. If it wasn't Flora Brent, it was a girl who bore an uncanny resemblance to Miss Brent's description.

"Beg pardon," the housekeeper said. "This lady requires a word with Louise."

The dark-haired girl was up from the table in a flash. She gawked at Nell, her pretty face gone white as bleached linen.

The cook cast a sharp look behind her as she stirred one of the bubbling pots on the stove. "She'll have to be quick about it. I've got the evening meal to see to, and those vegetables won't prepare themselves."

"It won't take but a minute," Nell said. "If Louise can spare it?"

Miss Brent retreated from the table. "I should be pleased to speak with you, ma'am," she said in accents as polished as any Mayfair debutante. "If you would but give me a moment to rinse my hands at the pump."

Before Nell could reply, Miss Brent darted to the back door of the kitchen. She flung it open, preparing to make her escape, only to come to a stumbling and very astonished halt.

Effie stood on the opposite side of the door, barring the way. "Miss Brent," she said. "You weren't leaving, I trust?"

Miss Brent raised her hands to push Effie aside—or possibly to give her the same brutal treatment she'd given to Silas at the brothel.

Nell came up behind the girl before she could inflict any harm. "I am Miss Trewlove," she said. "Deputy headmistress of Miss Corvus's Benevolent Academy for the Betterment of Young Ladies. The matron at the workhouse will have told you my name. It was me you were meant to meet on Monday at Waltham Station."

Miss Brent spun around to face Nell. Her eyes were wide. She stared at her for a moment. And then—

Her lower lip wobbled. "Miss Trewlove? Is it really you?" The elegant accents were gone. In their place was a voice that was exceedingly young and unmistakably working-class.

The housekeeper and cook gaped at the girl with twin expressions of incredulity.

"It is." Nell set a reassuring hand on Miss Brent's thin shoulder. She gave it gentle squeeze. "I've been looking for you for several days, my dear."

Miss Brent's face cracked. "I didn't have any fare to take the train. A woman at the station took my pocket money and my ticket, and she—"

"We know," Nell said. "You have been exceptionally brave, and done so well on your own. But you're not alone any longer. Miss Flite and I will take care of you now."

Effie entered the kitchen, closing the door behind her. "The sooner we can get you out of Whitechapel the better," she said. "It's not safe for you here."

Miss Brent instinctively drew closer to Nell. "Are you taking me to the charity school?"

Nell slipped a protective arm around her. "We are," she promised. "But first you must speak with the police and tell them what happened with the woman at the railway station."

"The police!" the housekeeper exclaimed in tones of horror.

"I was ever so hungry," Miss Brent said. "And she had tea and cake from the refreshment stand. I didn't see as how it would do any harm to—"

"We'll speak about it later," Nell said. "For now, Miss Flite is correct. We must go. But before we do—" She addressed the housekeeper. "I assume this young lady is owed three days' wages?"

The housekeeper went rigid. "This person appears to be no young lady at all."

"Yet she was working diligently enough when I entered the kitchen," Nell said.

"I wouldn't know," the housekeeper sniffed. "You shall have to speak to the mistress about it."

"We will." Nell urged Miss Brent to the kitchen stairs. She'd been working here under false pretenses, it was true, but she'd still been working. Whatever she'd earned was hers to keep.

The cook scowled. "This is all very well, but what about supper?"

"I'll send Polly down," the housekeeper replied tersely. She followed Nell, Miss Brent, and Effie back up to the parlor where a shocked and appalled Mrs. Davenant made a tremendous show of doling out Miss Brent's wages from her strongbox.

"An orphan girl," she muttered as she counted the coins. "Upon my word."

"I'm sorry I lied to you," Miss Brent said, looking suitably chastened.

"And well you should be," Mrs. Davenant retorted, handing her what she was owed. "Preying on my charitable instincts with a false name and a false history? Taking advantage of my kindness? For shame, child."

Nell didn't allow Miss Brent to linger, either to apologize again or to explain. It was already approaching six o'clock. Nell needed to get the girl to St. James's Square. With a final word of thanks to Mrs. Davenant, Nell and Effie shepherded Miss Brent out the front door.

The sky was darker than the hour merited, storm clouds gathering to block out the sinking sun. Rain was imminent. Nell could smell the dampness of it saturating the crisp evening air as she headed down the street with Miss Brent.

Effie walked a length ahead of them. "Where is the dratted carriage?" she complained under her breath.

Nell searched for it along with her, scanning the crowded roadway.

There were even more people out than there had been when they'd entered Mrs. Davenant's house. Street markets, it seemed, grew busier in the evenings. Some of the sellers were already setting out their naphtha lamps.

Nell continued on, Miss Brent safe under her arm and Effie several steps ahead. They were so focused on finding the carriage that none of them noticed the hulking brute of a man emerging from the shadowy alleyway until it was too late.

"If it isn't my little hellcat," he said. "Thought you could scratch me and get away with it, did you?"

Nell's stomach dropped. Good lord. It was Silas!

He stepped in front of Nell and Miss Brent, as enormous a figure as Nell remembered him being at the brothel. The same angry scratch marred his brutal features.

Miss Brent recoiled in fear. "Miss Trewlove!"

Nell pushed the girl behind her. "Stay back," she commanded. "I'll handle this."

Silas's black gaze leapt to Nell's face. He gave a visible start. *"You."* Dawning understanding registered in his eyes. "You're a friend of hers?"

"I am," Nell said. "So, you'd better take care what you say next."

The noise of the market rose up around them. Shoppers were gathered at the stalls further down the way, too busy with their bartering to notice the altercation taking place at the mouth of the alleyway.

"Or else what?" Silas slid a look to Nell's empty hands. "Don't have no cane this time, do you?"

Nell drew herself up in preparation for a fight. "I don't require one."

As they spoke, Effie circled around Silas, her parasol in hand.

The bully boy didn't mark her. His gaze was riveted on Nell and Miss Brent. Effie had been too far ahead of them to attract his notice. "Mrs. Pritchard's looking for this one," he said, dipping his chin at the girl. "Hand her over and you can go on your way. It's more than you deserve."

"Why don't *you* go on *your* way?" Nell returned. "While you're still able to walk?"

Silas barked a scornful laugh. "You reckon I can't take on a couple of troublesome females? What d'you think I do all day and night long? The two of you ain't nothing."

"The three of us," Nell said.

Effie jabbed the sharpened steel tip of her parasol between the bully boy's shoulder blades. "You overlooked me," she said. "A stupid error. But then, you're not a very bright man, are you?"

Silas froze. It was only for an instant. Pivoting with extraordinary speed for such a large man, he grabbed the silk stalk of the parasol and yanked it with all his might, pulling Effie nearly off her feet.

Rather than submit to falling toward him, Effie released her grip. Silas staggered back, unchecked, propelled by his own momentum.

Nell leapt aside, dragging Miss Brent with her into the alley, before he could tumble straight into them.

Silas dropped the parasol as he struggled to keep his balance. It clattered to the ground. "Bloody women," he cursed, narrowly preventing himself from falling. "More trouble than any of you are worth." Regaining his footing, he again turned on Nell. Whatever tissue of patience he'd had was gone. His expression held all the subtlety of an enraged bull. "I'll have that girl now if I have to bust all your heads in the effort."

Behind him, Effie strode to retrieve her parasol.

Silas lunged for Miss Brent.

The girl let out a startled cry.

Alerting Nell with a short whistle, Effie tossed her parasol over Silas's head.

Nell's hand shot up to catch it. She flicked the parasol round as if it were a fencing foil and, with the same precision with which she wielded a needle, dashed the razor-sharp tip across Silas's brow. A line of blood sprang up in its wake, falling straight into the man's eyes.

His hands flew to his face. A stream of oaths followed.

Nell's heart raced. She'd practiced fighting for years, with every manner of weapon, but she'd never before drawn blood. Well. Not to this degree anyway. "The carriage!" she called to Effie.

"It's there," Effie called back. "This way!"

Nell grasped Miss Brent's arm. "Hurry."

Silas lunged at them again blindly as they passed. This time he wasn't reaching to retrieve Miss Brent. It was violence he was after. His fingers were closed into a fist.

Nell moved to push Miss Brent out of the way. The action put Nell briefly in Silas's path. Only a split second, but it was long enough. His fist connected with Nell's shoulder with all the power of a steam locomotive.

Pain tore through Nell. She fell back against Miss Brent.

"Nell!" Effie ran to her.

Silas continued his advance with murderous intent. Blood streaked his face. "I'll teach you," he snarled. "You upstart, meddlesome b—" His words died away on an inarticulate grunt. Then his eyes rolled up and he crumpled into a heap on the ground.

Behind him, Miss Jean stood, a cloth shopping bag clutched in her upraised hand. It sagged under the weight of something heavy inside. "Are you mad?" she asked them, her breath coming fast. "Do you know who that is? It's Mrs. Pritchard's bully, for God's sake!"

"Miss Jean." Nell gave the woman a weak smile. Her right shoulder and upper arm were throbbing. Her head, too, for some odd reason. She had the vague notion that she was about to faint.

Miss Brent's thin arms were tight about Nell's waist, supporting her. "Miss Trewlove," she sobbed.

Effie and Miss Jean hurried to assist the girl. Effie's arm curved around Nell in an iron-fast grip. Miss Jean's arm came, too, holding Nell up from the opposite side. Their skirts were crushed against one another in a profusion of petticoats and wire crinolines.

"Don't you dare swoon, Penelope Trewlove," Miss Jean commanded her.

"I never swoon." Nell's knees sagged beneath her. All three ladies caught her up, preventing her from collapsing right there in the alley.

"What the devil do you have in that bag?" Effie asked Miss Jean as they conveyed Nell toward the street.

"My new iron," Miss Jean said. "Just bought it at the market, too. That lummox's head better not have put a dent in it."

Miss Brent cast a terrified look back at Silas. "Did you kill him?"

"He's not dead, luv," Miss Jean said. "He'll come round soon enough. The three of you best be gone when he does."

"What about you?" Effie asked.

"I'll be fine," Miss Jean said. "He didn't see me. And if he did—"

"The school," Nell murmured. "Sewing teacher."

Miss Jean gave her a dubious look. "What? Me?"

"Safe there," Nell said. "Girls need you."

Miss Jean scoffed. "Don't be daft. You know I can't read."

"Doesn't matter. Tell her, Effie—" Nell broke off, overcome by a wave of nausea. She was vaguely aware of the ladies holding her tighter, bearing more of her weight. Miss Brent was weeping.

The carriage rolled up in front of them. Effie's servants took in the scene with swift alarm. The footman jumped from his perch and sprinted to join them.

"Mrs. Quincey is a trifle lightheaded," Effie informed him. "Help me get her into the carriage."

"I'm perfectly all right," Nell insisted.

And then she fainted.

21

Miles stood beside the fireplace in the drawing room as Flora Brent gave an account of her abduction to Inspector Garrick. In other circumstances, Miles would be listening to her tale as avidly as the policeman was. But not on this occasion.

No.

His attention was entirely fixed on Nell.

He'd returned home early from the office today, after a brief stop at a jeweler's shop in Bond Street, to find his alarmingly pale wife seated with unnatural stiffness on the drawing room sofa. She hadn't been alone. Mrs. Royce was with her, along with Gabriel, Inspector Garrick, and (to Miles's astonishment) the formerly missing Miss Brent.

"She was on the railway platform at Shoreditch Station," the girl said from her place beside Nell. "A lady in a fine dress. She came up to me all friendly like while I waited to change trains. She asked where I was going and who my people were."

Inspector Garrick's pencil paused over the notepad where he'd been recording Miss Brent's words. "This was Mrs. Pritchard?"

Like Miles and Gabriel, the policeman remained on his feet. Miles suspected it was a consequence of the profound inadequacy they were all feeling. The three of them, poised for action to no avail. It was the ladies who had faced danger today, not them. In the aftermath, the men were powerless. They could do nothing but loom, and pace, and question.

Nothing but try their damnedest not to explode with anger at the risk the women had taken.

Even famously self-controlled Gabriel appeared as though he was a hair's breadth away from losing his composure. He stood beside his wife as she perched on a chair near Nell, his arms folded and a muscle ticking rhythmically in his cheek.

"That's her name," Miss Brent said. "Mrs. Pritchard. Though I didn't know it 'til later."

"And you told her who you were?" Garrick asked.

"I told the truth—that I was an orphan traveling to a charity school. I thought that would put her off me seeing as how I wasn't nobody important, but she was even kinder then. She brought me a cup of tea and a piece of cake from the refreshment stand. I drank the tea and . . . I came over all faint-like." Miss Brent's lip quivered. "She said I needed to lie down, and I was too poorly to say different. The next thing I knew, I was in a room by myself with a locked door and no windows. I thought it must be at the railway station, but it wasn't. It was in a house."

"Was this the same day?" Garrick asked. "When you woke up?"

"The next, I reckon, or the day after. My mouth was all dry and my head hurt. I'd been sleeping a long while. And I think she'd been nursing me. I dreamed she came and gave me more tea to drink."

Miles frowned. Adulterated tea, just as Cowgill had reported. He met Nell's eyes, expecting her to exchange a knowing glance with him—to signal that their thoughts were tending in the same direction, as they so often had during their investigations. But she didn't. Her gray gaze was oddly unfocused.

A growing sense of disquiet took root in his chest. Something wasn't right.

"What happened next?" Garrick asked, his pencil poised.

"Mrs. Pritchard came the next morning," Miss Brent said. "She told me . . ." The girl's face flushed red. "She . . . She said I'd have a gentleman caller in the evening. That I was to behave if I knew what was good for me."

Mrs. Royce's eyes kindled with fury. Gabriel set a hand on her shoulder.

"It's all right," Nell said to Miss Brent, so softly Miles could scarcely hear her. "You're safe now."

Miss Brent took a deep breath. "I knew I had to get away or else something bad was going to happen to me. I tried the door, but it was still locked. I called for help and no one answered. Except . . . I heard someone else calling for help, too. A man."

Miles regarded the girl with sharp attention.

"What did you do then?" Garrick asked.

Miss Brent flashed a questioning look at Nell and Mrs. Royce. "I don't rightly know . . ."

"Tell the inspector everything," Mrs. Royce said. "You won't be in any trouble."

Miss Brent worried her lip in her teeth for several seconds before making her answer. "I used my hairpins to unlock the door from the inside."

"Clever girl," Mrs. Royce said approvingly.

Miss Brent sat up a little taller, bolstered by the praise. "I crept out of the room into a dark hall. I was in the attic, I think. There was another door there. I heard the man's voice behind one of them. 'Help me! Please help me!' he said. So, I unlocked his door, too." A glimmer of annoyance passed over her face. "I wish I hadn't," she added uncharitably. "He burst out, making such a racket, shouting and stumbling all over as we went down the stairs. Mrs. Pritchard and her man, Silas, came straightaway. Mrs. Pritchard went after the man and Silas tried to grab me. I scratched his face. And then—" She shrugged. "I ran out of the house."

Miles opened his own notebook to the sketch of Lawrence Cowgill. He crossed the room to Miss Brent to show it to her. "Is this the man you set free from the room at Mrs. Pritchard's?"

Miss Brent bobbed her head up and down. "That's him."

Miles met Garrick's eyes. "Lawrence Cowgill."

Garrick gave a somber nod. "Did you see what happened to this man?" he asked Miss Brent.

"Mrs. Pritchard chased him into a room off of the hall," she replied. "I heard a crash. I reckon he tripped, but I couldn't stop to help him."

Garrick's pencil scratched steadily in his notebook.

"Will that be all, Inspector?" Mrs. Royce inquired.

"One more question." Garrick addressed Miss Brent. "Do you mind telling me where you've been since Wednesday?"

"I got a job working as a scullery maid," Miss Brent said as if it were the most rational thing in the world.

"A job?" Garrick queried, puzzled. "Where?"

"At Mrs. Davenant's house in Whitechapel Road," Miss Brent said. "Mrs. Pritchard stole my railway ticket and pocket money. I had to earn enough to pay the fare to Miss Corvus's Academy."

Garrick stilled. "*That's* the charity school you were destined for?"

Miles gave the inspector an alert glance. Unless he was very much mistaken, that was recognition in the man's eyes. "Do you know the place?"

"I have a passing acquaintance with it," Garrick said.

"That's interesting," Mrs. Royce observed. "I don't recall the Academy having had any business with Scotland Yard."

"It wasn't in my professional capacity." Garrick paused. "I grew up in the neighboring village."

"Did you, indeed," Mrs. Royce said. "I do hope you weren't one of those annoying lads who used to hang about the gates of the school."

A dull flush crept up Garrick's neck. He cleared his throat. "It was a long time ago," he said brusquely. He turned back to Miss Brent. "You remained working as a scullery maid for how long?"

"Until today, sir," Miss Brent replied. "When Miss Trewlove and Miss Flite came to rescue me."

Miss Trewlove and Miss Flite?

Miles and Gabriel exchanged a dark glance.

"Mrs. Davenant paid me my wages and we left," Miss Brent continued. "But Silas set upon us in an alleyway before we could reach the carriage."

An ominous silence fell over the room. Nell's gaze dropped to her lap, and Mrs. Royce pointedly didn't look at her husband. The air vibrated with unspoken tension. Miles didn't know which of them was more in danger of losing their composure, him or Gabriel.

Gabriel broke first. *"Set upon you?"* he repeated in a tone of perilous calm. "What might that mean?"

"He tried to take me back to Mrs. Pritchard's," Miss Brent explained. "Miss Flite fought him with her parasol. Then she threw her parasol to Miss Trewlove and Miss Trewlove cut him over his eyes. But Silas didn't stop. He came at us again, and he hit Miss Trewlove ever so hard with his fist—"

Miles surged forward. *"What?"*

"We brought her here in the carriage," Miss Brent continued haltingly. "Miss Flite used smelling salts to bring her round." She looked between Nell and Mrs. Royce. "Did I do wrong? Should I not have said—"

"It's fine," Nell assured her. Her words were just as faint as they had been before, with a breathless quality to them, as though she was speaking with enormous effort.

Miles's gaze raked over her. "He hit you?" She wasn't only pale, he realized, she appeared a trifle green. A fine mist of perspiration had gathered on her brow. "Where?"

"It's nothing," she said in the same weak voice. "I don't wish to alarm the girl."

Mrs. Royce stood abruptly. "Given the circumstances, I believe it would be best if my husband and I took Miss Brent back to Sloane Street. She can stay the night. I'll take her to the Academy myself in the morning."

"*We'll* take her," Gabriel said.

Mrs. Royce smiled. "A fine idea. If you're quite finished, Inspector Garrick?"

"I have all I require for now." Garrick closed his notebook. "I may have more questions in the days to come. Until then . . ." He gave a warning look to Miles and Gabriel. "I want no retaliation against this Silas fellow. I still need to speak with the man. If he's beaten or God forbid killed in the meanwhile, the case may collapse altogether, and there will be no justice for Miss Brent or Mr. Cowgill."

Miles was only half listening to the inspector's words. He was too busy examining every visible inch of his wife for signs of injury. Kill Silas? It sounded like a fine idea. At the moment, Miles would be quite happy to take the man apart with his bare hands.

"Leave Pritchard and Silas to the law," Garrick ordered them. "If I can prove they murdered Cowgill, they'll hang for it. Let that be enough."

"Then prove it," Gabriel said. "Before I lose my patience and deal with the man myself."

"That's hardly helpful, my love," his wife said to him. She moved to fetch Miss Brent. "Shall we go, dear, and leave Miss Trewlove to rest?"

"I want to stay with you," Miss Brent said to Nell, touching her right arm in entreaty.

Nell sucked in a sharp breath.

The girl jerked back her hand. "I'm sorry! I didn't mean to hurt you."

"It's all right." Mrs. Royce drew the girl up from her seat. "Miss

Trewlove will be fine. She only needs some peace and quiet." She gave Miles a pointed look. "And a doctor wouldn't go amiss."

Miles's stomach lurched with apprehension. He waited until everyone had departed the drawing room before sinking down on his haunches in front of Nell. "Did he hit your arm?"

"My shoulder," she said.

He moved to rise. "I'll summon the doctor."

"No!" she objected sharply. "I don't want a doctor."

"Want has nothing to do with it. If you've broken a bone—"

"I won't see one, Miles. I *hate* doctors. Ever since . . ." She trailed off, closing her eyes. Her breath came in soft, shallow gasps. "I only need a cold compress. And . . . perhaps a sip of laudanum."

Miles had never heard such patent absurdity. "Have you lost what's left of your good sense?" he growled at her. "First to have gone to Whitechapel when I explicitly told you—"

"I know."

"To fight a man who has already committed murder—"

"I *know*."

"And then to let that infernal friend of yours prop you up on the sofa like a broken doll, all the while you're suffering agonies—"

"Not agonies." Nell exhaled another labored breath. "Though very near, I confess."

Miles glared at her. "If you won't permit a doctor to examine you, I'll do it."

Her lashes lifted a fraction. "You?"

"I know enough to tell if anything's broken. And if it is," he added sternly, "I'm calling the doctor, with no arguments from you. Agreed?"

A frown creased her brow. "Agreed," she said at length. "But first . . . I'd like to lie down in my bed."

Miles didn't need to be told twice. Scooping her up carefully in his arms, he carried her from the drawing room.

Mrs. Bright and several of the other servants were hovering outside the door. The housekeeper approached as Miles crossed the hall with Nell. "I knew something was amiss," she said. "I'd have rung for the doctor myself if I didn't fear it would be taken as impertinence."

"Never mind it," Miles replied curtly. "Do you have any laudanum in the medicine cupboard?"

"Yes, Mr. Quincey," Mrs. Bright said as he mounted the staircase. "I'll bring it up directly."

Miles continued up the stairs to Nell's bedchamber, cradling her safely in his arms. It might have been romantic if she wasn't grimacing with his every step.

All the while, his chest was so tight with conflicted emotion he could hardly breathe himself. He wanted to scold her. To rake her so thoroughly over the coals that she'd never do something so bloody stupid again.

And he wanted to hold her closer. To comfort and protect her. To keep her safe and never let her go.

Most of all, he wanted to howl with rage. To go out and find Silas and systematically tear the villain limb from limb. That such a man—that *any* man—should cause Nell even one moment of pain.

It was too much—all these blasted feelings. How was Miles to endure it? How could anyone?

Steeling himself against the chaos within him, Miles placed Nell down gently in the center of her four-poster bed. He drew back from her, exerting all of his not insubstantial will toward addressing the task at hand. "How attached are you to this dress?"

Nell's eyes were closed again. She no longer had the look of a sleepy tigress waiting to pounce. She looked young and heart-wrenchingly defenseless. "Not very," she answered with an effort. Her countenance was waxen. "You bought several more for me today. They're much prettier."

His chest constricted tighter. "I'm pleased to hear it." He examined the set of her sleeve. "I'll have to cut it off."

"My arm?" she asked with a disturbing lack of concern.

"Your bodice."

Nell didn't reply.

Miles feared she may have slipped into another faint. It was a mercy, really, given what was to come.

He cast about her bedchamber for her ubiquitous sewing bag. He found it wedged in the cushion of a chair by the fireplace. Rifling through its contents, he located a pair of sewing scissors.

And that wasn't all.

The workbag held at least four unfinished samplers, all of which appeared to contain the same jumbled letters and the same curious black raven with the white-tipped wing he'd observed in the samplers Nell had lately been sewing.

Miles examined them with an arrested frown.

And it struck him, so suddenly he was amazed he hadn't recognized it before. They weren't sewing samplers at all, were they?

They were ciphers.

22

Nell came awake again at the feeling of cold steel brushing over the naked flesh of her arm. A jolt of pain shot from her shoulder all the way down to her fingers. *"Oh!"*

Miles loomed over her on the bed, her dainty sewing scissors dwarfed in his large hand. "Sorry," he muttered. "I didn't mean to jostle you."

"What are you—"

"It's your blasted corset cover. It will have to go, too."

"My what—?" She peered downward. Heat surged into her face. Her bodice was gone. All that remained was her corset and cambric corset cover and her thin muslin chemise beneath. It was nudity, practically. Or as close to it as she'd been in his presence. "But why?"

"I believe I know what the problem is." He continued cutting. His face was set with concentration. "When Silas hit you, he may have dislocated your shoulder."

Another wave of nausea swept over her. She briefly closed her eyes, feeling her corset cover fall away. Cool air whispered over her bare arms and the exposed expanse of her bosom that swelled over the top of her tightly laced corset. "Which means—?"

But Nell knew what it meant. There was only one way to mend a dislocated limb. She'd seen it years ago at the Academy when a girl had injured her arm in a cart accident.

"I can repair it," Miles said. "Unless you've decided you're ready for the doctor?"

"No." Nell shook her head. "No doctors."

Miles fell silent.

She cracked open an eye to find him studying her uncovered shoulder. A deep frown notched his brows. "Is it very bad?" she asked.

"It's as I suspected," he said. "I won't lie to you, this is going to hurt."

Her stomach knotted with dread. As if she wasn't hurting enough already.

"Mr. Quincey?" Mrs. Bright entered the room. She was accompanied by the housemaid. "I've found a half bottle of laudanum left over from when Cook had a toothache. And Gladys has brought hot water, bandages, salves, and a pot of tea for the mistress."

"Laudanum first," Miles commanded. He met Nell's eyes. "Once it takes effect, I'll reset your shoulder."

Nell gave a tense nod in reply. It was the only way. A dislocated limb couldn't heal on its own.

Mrs. Bright crossed the bedchamber with the brown bottle of laudanum in hand. Miles took it from her. It was he who administered it to Nell. Cradling her head with extraordinary gentleness, he tipped her up to take a small quantity of the bitter, reddish-brown liquid.

Nell didn't confine herself to a single sip. All things considered, she'd rather not feel it when Miles wrenched her arm back into place, even if that meant briefly losing control of her faculties. She took a second drink, and might have foolishly swallowed more had Miles not removed the bottle from her lips.

He lowered her back to her pillow, pausing just long enough to smooth the damp hair from her brow. "Almost over," he said.

She gazed up at him. "You've done this before?"

"A few times."

"Recall that I'm not a man," she said.

His mouth quirked wryly. "I don't need reminding."

"Adjust your strength accordingly. I rather like my arm."

"I'll be gentle," Miles promised. He smoothed her hair again. "Trust me."

"I do trust you, but . . ." A surge of panic closed Nell's throat. Memories of the month she'd spent in the infirmary after her fall from the Academy's roof flooded back. "I don't like the sickroom. And I hate doctors. I don't want—"

"Shh," he murmured. His touch on her brow was soothing. "No doctors, sweetheart. Just me."

Mrs. Bright hovered anxiously nearby. "Would you like me to remove the rest of her clothes, Mr. Quincey? She'll be more comfortable without those wire underpinnings."

"Leave it," Miles said. "I'll undress her afterward. It will be less painful once her shoulder is set."

Nell's head was becoming too fuzzy for her to fully register the implications of the exchange. He was going to undress her? He couldn't. She never let anyone see her injured leg. It was too private. Too humiliating.

Mrs. Pritchard's evil words echoed in her head in an endless loop. *"It will disgust most men even to see it."* She'd been speaking about Nell's cane, not her leg, but in her present state, Nell could make no differentiation.

"I drank too much laudanum," she whispered. "But you can't—"

Miles's voice sounded as though from a great distance away. "If you'll hold her, Mrs. Bright. I need her as still as possible."

"Miles," Nell said. Or perhaps she only thought it.

He took hold of her wrist and elbow in a firm grip.

She cried out, "No, wait—!"

One sharp, forceful jerk upward, a decided scrape and crunch, and then—

Darkness closed over her.

• • • • •

When next Nell awoke, her pain was largely gone. Night had fallen, and her bedchamber was lit by a low fire and the soft glow from a distant branch of candles. Rain drummed against the windowpanes. She couldn't tell how late the hour. She only knew that she was warm and safe in her bed, with Miles keeping vigil in a chair beside her.

She was also in her chemise and drawers.

At some point, it seemed, he had undressed her. Or someone had. But not all the way. Her drawers were knee-length. The injured part of her thigh was still well covered.

Strangely, the fact wasn't at the forefront of her mind. Indeed, except for the lingering soreness in her shoulder, she felt wonderfully relaxed. It was as though the laudanum had been a magic elixir, muffling not only her pain, but a great many of her inhibitions as well.

"Where did you learn to do that?" she asked softly.

Miles straightened in his chair. His hair was rumpled, and he was absent his coat and cravat. She belatedly realized that there had been a cat sleeping in his lap. A small, short-haired black one Nell hadn't seen before. Smoke, she presumed. He jumped down as Miles leaned toward her, disappearing out of her sight line. "You're awake," Miles said.

"Where?" she asked again.

"One of the skills I picked up during my years as a foreign correspondent. There were a great many brawls in Marseille, and more than a few dislocated limbs." Miles took her hand in both of his. His voice deepened, his eyes searching hers. "How do you feel?"

"Better," she said.

Some of the tension in his face eased. "Good." He raised her hand to his lips and pressed a kiss to her knuckles. "Excellent."

She brushed his cheek with the edge of her finger. "I'm muddled."

"The laudanum," he said. "You'll be clearer headed tomorrow."

She gazed into his eyes. "Did you undress me?"

He looked steadily back at her. "I did."

She touched his cheek again, feeling oddly unconstrained by self-consciousness or doubt. "You didn't cut away my crinoline, I hope."

His mouth tipped briefly. "Very nearly. It's a confounding article."

"I'm a confounding article," she informed him.

His smiled lingered. "You're lucky you're not in your right mind at the moment. I'd planned to scold you afterward."

"Hmm." Somehow, the notion didn't trouble her. "You should congratulate me."

"Should I?"

"I saved her."

Miles's expression reverted to solemn lines. "You did," he acknowledged. "At great peril to yourself."

Nell made an effort to marshal her thoughts. They were drifting like vapor in every direction. "She isn't our daughter," she told him.

He gave her a look that was hard to read. "No. She isn't."

"We haven't a daughter. But if we did . . . no peril would be too great."

"Is that why you went back to Whitechapel in search of Miss Brent?" he asked. "You wanted to prove something to yourself?"

Nell didn't know. She couldn't recall what she'd been thinking of when she'd returned to Whitechapel so impulsively, except that it had had something to do with Lady Belwood.

"Nobody came for me," Nell said. "But I came for her."

Miles's black brows dipped with sudden fierceness. "*I* would have come for you. Had I known what you intended, nothing on earth could have stopped me."

Her gaze fell away. "You say that—"

"I don't say things I don't mean." He held her hand to his lips. A note of gruffness entered his voice. "We're partners, aren't we? A fact you seem to forget when it suits you."

"I don't forget."

"After last night, I thought we—" He didn't finish.

Nell brought her eyes back to his. Last night she had kissed him. *Passionately* kissed him.

Their gazes held for an aching moment. Outside, the rain continued to fall in an endless drumbeat. Along with the crackling of the fire, it was, for those few taut seconds, the only sound in the room save the uneven thump of her heart.

Miles abruptly released her hand. His coat was draped over the back of his chair. He retrieved something from the pocket. Turning back to her, the candlelight glinted across the item in his fingers. It was a gold ring.

No. Not a ring. A wedding band.

"I bought it today in Bond Street." He picked up her hand again with exquisite care, as though she were a fine, delicate lady for whom he cherished some tender affection and not the troublesome creature he'd married out of duty. "If I may?"

A lump formed in Nell's throat. The day they'd wed, he had promised to purchase her a ring at the first opportunity. It was a purely practical matter. Which did nothing to explain why her hand quaked as he slipped it onto her finger.

His hand was unsteady, too. Or so she thought. She couldn't be completely sure. Her perception was off. It felt as though she'd stepped into a hazy painting—the colors indistinct and the edges all blurred.

"It fits," he said huskily.

"Yes." Her heart beat hard.

It was only a piece of jewelry. It didn't mean anything. And yet, an undoubted feeling came with it. She belonged to him now.

An unsettling proposition.

Women weren't property. They were free and independent beings, whatever the law might say. And Nell valued her freedom. Even so . . .

There was something powerful in belonging to a person, and in knowing that they belonged to you in turn.

The effects of the laudanum loosened her tongue, making her sound like a smitten girl. "I'm glad it's you," she said. She impulsively reached to cup his cheek. "I do like you so much."

Miles's solemn countenance softened. "I gathered that."

"And do you—"

"I'm mad for you," he said gravely.

Mad.

It wasn't liking. It wasn't love. To be mad was to be bewitched, bedeviled, irrational. Qualities that were the antithesis of all Miles represented. But Nell had no ability to analyze the distinction in her present state. It slipped away before she could grasp it. All she cared about was the look in his eyes and the feel of his stubble-shadowed jaw in the curve of her hand.

She drew him to her and kissed him.

A groan emerged from Miles's chest as their lips met. He braced himself over her on one forearm, mindful not to touch her right shoulder. And he kissed her back—deeply, sweetly. But not carefully. His mouth captured hers with a scorching heat.

Had Nell not already been lying down, she felt certain her knees would have buckled beneath her.

He kissed her as though he'd been thinking of nothing else since they'd parted last night. As though the recollection of the embrace they'd shared in the library had worked on him, hour by hour, until his adamantine restraint had reached its breaking point. All Nell had done was unwittingly provide a spark to the tinder.

Mad for her, he'd said.

She felt a little mad, too. Overwarm and restless, her blood thrumming wildly.

Her lips parted for him without conscious thought. There was no awkwardness. No hesitation. He'd already learned the soft shape of her. He angled his mouth over hers with perfect symmetry, touching her, tasting her, drinking in her little gasps and sighs.

Nell curled her hand around the back of his neck. She vaguely realized that she was in over her head. Perhaps she had been from the moment they'd met. He was bigger than she was. Older. More experienced.

Her mouth briefly slid from his. "You said you were out of practice."

"Did I?" He kissed her again.

"Must one?" she asked breathlessly.

"Must one what?"

"Practice?"

His lips stilled on hers. He was breathing heavily. "Kissing, do you mean?"

"We could," she said.

Miles drew back to look in her eyes. His color was high.

"Unless you're entirely opposed to the idea," she said.

"Of practicing?" he questioned hoarsely. "With you?"

Her fingers played in the hair at his nape. "It needn't mean anything. Only it seems a waste to be married and to like each other tolerably well enough and to not at least—"

"More than tolerably well," Miles said. "And I'm not opposed to the idea." He huffed an unsteady laugh. "Though I'd prefer we didn't practice while you're under the influence of laudanum."

"I'm not—" She stopped herself. Because she was. She *was*. Why else would this feel so wonderfully unreal? "Well." She smiled at him dreamily. "Perhaps I am."

"Your head is going to be aching in the morning," he said.

"Mmm."

"Your shoulder as well. I'll make a sling for your arm tomorrow. You mustn't move it for the next several days."

"Mustn't I?"

He gave her a severe look. "No sewing samplers," he said portentously.

It sounded as though he was admonishing her. An odd thing given their present positions.

"Do you have something against samplers?" she asked.

"It's rest you require, not needlework," he said. "Remain in bed tomorrow. The next day, too."

She stroked the back of his neck. His skin was hot to the touch. "Like this?"

Another short, husky laugh. "No. Not quite like this." He pulled back from her slowly.

Nell's hand slipped from his neck. She didn't protest his withdrawal. Her lids were heavy. Her limbs, too. She turned her head into her pillow with a sigh.

Somewhere through the fog that addled her brain, she felt Miles gently removing the pins from her tightly plaited coiffure. He loosened the bound coils of her hair with caressing fingers, easing the sharp pressure on her scalp. It was deliciously soothing.

The last pin dropped to the bedside table with a soft clink. Warmth engulfed her as Miles tucked the coverlet around her. "Sleep," he said.

And she did.

23

The next morning, for the first time in memory, Miles didn't go into the office. Instead, after a night spent in the chair beside Nell's bed, he rose at dawn to wash and dress. He laid a fresh fire in Nell's room, attended to Shadow (who was gradually beginning to warm to her new surroundings), and—when the hour was passing reasonable—went down to the kitchens and personally requested his wife's breakfast.

Mrs. Bright hurried in as Gladys and Cook assembled the tea, toast, sausage, eggs, and porridge. "Mr. Quincey! You needn't have come yourself. You'd only to ring and I'd have sent Gladys to the mistress's room with a tray."

"I'll take Mrs. Quincey's tray to her," Miles said. He was in his shirtsleeves, his jaw freshly shaven.

Mrs. Bright and Cook traded glances, and Gladys disguised a smile.

"Strawberry jam or marmalade, sir?" the maid asked, holding up two small pots for his perusal.

Miles frowned. He didn't know which jam Nell favored. In truth, he knew little about her likes and dislikes. "Both," he said. "And some of those honey cakes, too. And an orange, a plate of smoked herring, bread rolls, and a pot of cocoa."

When the tray was heaped high with anything he thought might tempt Nell, he carried it up to her room. She was still snuggled beneath the counterpane of her four-poster bed, just as he had left her when he'd finally departed her room. Except now, Horus was curled up at her side.

Miles pushed the door shut behind him as he entered. The soft click was enough to make Nell stir.

She emerged from beneath the coverlet with a groan of protest, her uninjured arm flung over her eyes. "What time is it?" she asked.

His gaze traveled over her as he approached the bed. Warmth ignited in his veins despite his best efforts to contain it. Last night he'd removed all but the final layer of her clothes. He'd taken down her thick, silken hair. And he'd kissed her with all the restraint of a starving man who had inexplicably found a feast laid before him.

For that's what Nell was—a feast, a banquet, a beautiful, decadent meal made up of lush curves, sultry sweetness, and unapologetic cleverness and daring. He'd wanted to devour her whole. To make her his in the truest sense of the word. And she had, for those brief heated moments, seemed to want him just as furiously. It had been evident in the way she'd touched him, the way she'd kissed him back, if not precisely in her words.

"I do like you so much," she'd said to him.

Like.

Like.

Not *I want you desperately*. Not *I'm mad for you*. Not any of the passionate nonsense he'd uttered to her over the last two days. But *like*.

Yet, she'd spoken of their kissing again. Or rather, of their *practicing* kissing.

Miles would be a fool to believe any of it. She'd been suffering the aftereffects of a painful ordeal, both physically and emotionally. Not to mention the fact that she'd taken a generous dose of laudanum.

If she remembered even half of what she'd said—or what they'd done—he'd be amazed.

"It's early," he said. "How's your shoulder?"

"Sore."

"And your head?"

She squinted at him from beneath her bare arm. "Splitting."

"That's to be expected." He set the heavy tray down on the mattress beside her. "It's the laudanum. You'll feel better once you've had breakfast."

Horus rose from his place beside her with a languorous stretch. He sharpened his claws on the counterpane.

Nell turned her face back into her pillow. "I couldn't eat a morsel."

"You will," Miles assured. He nudged the shapely curve of her hip. "Can you sit up?"

Another groan. "Miles . . ."

"Cook's gone to tremendous effort. I'd hate to return your tray untouched."

Nell made a soft sound of complaint. "Oh, very well," she grumbled. "For Cook's sake."

Folding her right arm protectively against her bosom, she struggled to a sitting position. The coverlet slid to her waist. Her long-lashed eyes were sleepy, and her unbound hair adorably rumpled. The short sleeves of her muslin chemise drooped low, exposing a tantalizing expanse of creamy porcelain skin.

But it wasn't that which commanded Miles's attention. It was the enormous bruise blooming where Silas's fist had struck her.

Miles's muscles tightened with cold fury to see it.

Garrick had warned him not to act. That to exact any form of vengeance on Silas would impede justice for Cowgill and Miss Brent. But in that moment, Miles didn't care about his late gossip reporter, or even about the little orphan girl.

Turning abruptly, he strode out of Nell's room through the

connecting door to the bathing room and from there into his own darkened bedchamber. Absalom and Virgil were sleeping soundly on his bed. Miles passed them without a word, heading for his wardrobe.

He extracted one of his plain white linen shirts from inside. Twisting it into a semblance of a sling, he knotted the ends of it. Mrs. Bright would have likely come up with a more elegant solution, but Miles had no interest in involving the servants any more than was necessary. It was doubtless counterproductive given the circumstances, and very probably ill-advised, but he felt a fierce possessiveness toward Nell. If anyone was going to look after her while she recovered, it was going to be him.

Returning to her room, he found her nibbling a morsel of one of the honey cakes, her hair tumbling about her shoulders in a chaos of flaxen waves. Horus stood over her breakfast tray, tail twitching as he presumptuously sniffed the plate of smoked herring. Nell made no move to discourage him.

Miles picked up the cat and unceremoniously dropped him onto the floor. Horus stalked off across the carpet with offended dignity. "You shouldn't permit his impudence."

"I daren't do otherwise," Nell replied as she popped a crumb of cake into her mouth. "He's been in residence far longer than I have."

"You're mistress here now," Miles said. "It's your home, as well as his." He lifted the makeshift sling. "If I may?"

She gave it a dubious look. "Is that one of your shirts?"

"It is."

An endless pause. "Well," she said. "I expect it will do."

She held herself still as a statue while he placed it over her neck, wincing only once as he carefully settled her bent arm in the cradle of the sling.

"There," he said. "How's that?"

She exhaled a breath he hadn't been aware she'd been holding. "Much improved, thank you."

A stab of tenderness took him unaware. She was more self-contained than she let on. Despite her recent confidences. Despite her kisses. Her true feelings ran deep—her discomfort, her disappointment, her sadness. He suspected she'd had years of practice concealing them.

"Most of the pain you're feeling is from the swelling at the joint," he said. "It will go down in a day or two. Until then, ice will help. I'll have Mrs. Bright bring some up after you've eaten."

Nell broke off another morsel of cake. "Have you eaten?"

"Not yet," he said.

"There's plenty here."

"Yes. For you."

"You might at least have some tea. There are two cups."

"The other is for your cocoa."

"Tea *and* cocoa?" Her dimple appeared to the right of her mouth. "You must think me ravenous."

He ran a hand over the back of his neck, sheepishly admitting, "I didn't know which you'd prefer."

"Tea," she said.

"What about jam?" he wondered. "Strawberry? Marmalade?"

"Strawberry. And no herring," she added. "I dislike fish intensely."

"Noted." Miles committed her preferences to memory.

"And you?" she asked.

"Given a choice? Tea, strawberry, no herring. Otherwise . . ." He shrugged. "When I'm busy working, I eat whatever one of the clerks bring me."

"Then you won't mind eating some of this," she said. "I'll never finish it all on my own." She gestured to an empty spot on the bed. "You can sit there if you like. There's room now your cat has gone."

Miles hesitated but a moment before succumbing to the temptation. He wasn't, after all, made of stone. The mattress dipped beneath his weight as he sank down across from her. The breakfast tray stood between them. He watched with solemn attention as Nell poured him out a cup of tea from the small silver pot. It was . . .

Wifely.

"As you see, I'm not entirely incapable without use of my right hand," she said. "I can even sew with my left if I'm pressed."

"No sewing," Miles said as she passed him his teacup.

Her brows lifted. "You don't mean to say you were serious about that?"

Ah.

So, she *did* remember last night.

"Given the amount of laudanum you took, I assumed you had forgotten our conversation," he said.

A hint of color pinkened her cheeks. "I wouldn't call it much of a conversation."

An answering heat crept up Miles's neck. "No," he said a little gruffly. "I don't suppose it was."

She raised the silver teapot to fill her own cup. Her gold wedding band glinted on her finger. "In any case, you may as well attempt to prohibit me from breathing."

It took Miles a moment to recall what they'd been discussing. Her sewing, hadn't it been? Her secrets, more like. "It's that important to you? Those samplers you've been sewing night and day?"

"Samplers, plain work, fancy work. Any sort of sewing." She added a dash of milk to her cup. Miles made a mental note of it—tea with milk, no sugar. "When I was recovering after my fall," she said, "I'd have lost my sanity if I hadn't had a needle and thread in my hand."

"You sewed to pass the time?"

"There was a great deal of it to pass." She raised her teacup to her lips. "I'm rather good, you know. At sewing." She flashed him a roguish smile over the brim of her cup. "So, if you have any missing buttons that need attention . . ."

Wifely, he thought again. It shouldn't be so attractive to him, these glimpses of domesticity. But it was. Because it was *her* pouring his tea and offering to mend his clothes. And because he hadn't been lying last night. He *was* mad for her.

"Mrs. Bright does the mending. But you may take over if you like." He frowned at her, adding, "Once you're recovered."

She returned her cup to the tray. Scooping up a portion of jam with a knife, she awkwardly attempted to spread it over an uncooperative piece of toast.

Miles took hold of the crust without a word, keeping it steady for her.

"How would you feel if you were prohibited from doing what you loved best?" she asked as she finished spreading the jam. She glanced at him, curious. "What *do* you love best, by the way?" She picked up her toast. "And I don't mean the newspaper. That's work."

"You're speaking of hobbies."

"If you like."

He dusted the crumbs from his fingers. "I don't have any."

The toast stopped halfway to Nell's mouth. "None? Not riding or chess or gambling? Or whatever else London gentlemen do?"

"I don't ride," he said. "I rarely play chess. And I never gamble."

"Cats, then," she said, biting into her toast.

He gave her a bewildered look. "Cats?"

She nodded as she chewed. "You do have five of them."

"They're not a hobby," he said. "They're a . . . I suppose they're a necessity of life."

"You've always had them?"

"No. Not until I went away for my apprenticeship." Miles recalled those bleak early days in the West Country, away from the Rookery for the first time in his life, cut adrift from everyone and everything he knew. "I was lonely," he said. "I started feeding a tomcat who used to frequent the alley behind the printing shop. I made a pet of him. That's how it started."

Nell's expression softened with understanding. "They were your friends."

"They were," he acknowledged. "They still are."

"But you're not still lonely, are you?"

His mouth quirked dryly. "Less so recently."

A hint of a smile touched her lips in reply. "Do you truly have nothing you enjoy doing outside of work?"

He drank more of his tea before finally confessing, "I frequent a boxing saloon in Lambeth."

Her eyes glimmered with interest. "Boxing," she repeated. She took another bite of her toast, crunching thoughtfully.

"You don't approve?" he inquired as she chewed.

She covered her mouth with her hand while she swallowed. "On the contrary. I box a little myself."

Miles stilled.

Her dimple emerged again. "Have I shocked you?"

"You can box?" he asked. "In addition to sword fighting?"

"Granted, I'm not as good at it as I am at fencing. Not in terms of pure power. But . . . I do have what you might call good science."

Miles's brows lowered. He was beginning to suspect she was quizzing him. "I'm to believe you're an expert pugilist?"

"I've read the *Oracle of the Ring*." She offered him what remained of her jam-covered toast.

Miles accepted it, absently taking a bite. He was familiar with the name of the old boxing text. "Is this another of your skills that's more theory than practice?"

"Oh no." She reached for her teacup again. "I've practiced."

"I know they can defend themselves," Gabriel had said.

And they could, apparently. With sword-canes, with razor-tipped parasols, with their fists.

Miles's gaze dropped to Nell's bare hand. It was pale and dainty, her slim fingers curled around her painted porcelain cup. It was decidedly *not* a hand meant for boxing.

"At the Academy?" Miles asked with studied casualness.

"Naturally." She sipped her tea. "We prepare our girls for everything they might face in the real world."

Miles temporarily ignored the *we* and the *our* in her statement. "You anticipate your graduates engaging in fisticuffs?"

"We'd be foolish to discount the possibility." Nell lowered her cup. Her tone took on an edge. "Why? Do you imagine that females aren't familiar with violence? That it doesn't come our way regardless of our rank in society?"

Miles's frown deepened. "No," he said. "I'm aware how some men treat women."

"What do you propose women do about it?" she asked. "Wait for a gentleman to rescue them? In many cases, it's the gentlemen who are doing the offending."

Miles knew that, too. Indeed, he'd long believed that his mother's employer had been her seducer. Or possibly her ravisher. Why else would she have refused to tell Miles for whom she'd been working as a governess at the time she'd fallen pregnant with him?

"What I'd rather," he said levelly, "is that my wife not court violence by venturing into the slum. Particularly after we'd already agreed that it was too dangerous."

"I won't apologize. Not when the result was the recovery of Miss Brent." Nell picked up the orange.

Miles plucked it from her fingers. He peeled it for her. The sweet fragrance of fresh citrus permeated the air. "The end justifies the means, does it?"

"In this instance, yes. Besides," she added, "I did tell you I wouldn't give up looking for her."

"You did."

"And you said you wouldn't ask me to."

"I recall."

"Anyway, it's done now. Mr. and Mrs. Royce will be taking Miss Brent to the Academy today. She'll be safe there."

"What she'll be is Miss Corvus's responsibility." Miles sectioned the orange. "And you're mine. If you expect us to leave for the house party on Saturday, you'll do as I say and rest for the next several days. *And* you'll stay out of trouble. If anything were to happen to you . . ." The very possibility of her coming to further harm instantly darkened his mood.

Her mouth curved softly. "Are you growing fond of me?" she asked. "Is that it?"

He scowled at her. "If you don't know the answer to that by now, you haven't been paying attention."

Nell's smile reached her eyes. She beckoned him closer with a crook of her finger. Miles dutifully leaned toward her across the breakfast tray. His blood pumped furiously. She was going to kiss him, he knew, despite his scolding, despite his scowls. She wasn't at all put off by him. It seemed a miracle somehow, that a creature like her should find him at all appealing.

But she did.

This time, he didn't wait for her to press her lips to his. He closed the remaining distance between them and pressed his to hers. A firm, claiming kiss, as brief as it was decisive.

"Now that's settled," he said gruffly.

A faint blush stained Nell's face, but her tired eyes were still shining. "Yes," she agreed.

Affection tugged at his heart. His mouth tilted in a lopsided smile. He felt like grinning. Drawing back, he handed her a section of orange. She popped it into her mouth.

He took one of the sections for himself, the two of them eating in companionable silence. It occurred to him that this was what lovers did, breakfasted together in bed in a state of comfortable dishabille. But she wasn't his lover. She was his wife.

And more.

Somewhere between the moment he'd entered his office to find her sitting there, black-veiled and mysterious, and this moment now, the two of them had become friends. Intimate friends. He would pull down the moon for her if she asked him to.

But she never would, would she? Not when she was convinced she could pull it down for herself.

The fact both annoyed him and made him admire her all the more.

"I have something you can do to occupy your time while you're on the mend," he said.

She wiped her sticky hand on a cloth napkin from the tray. "Besides sewing? Or leaving the house? Or doing anything else remotely interesting?"

"Quite." Miles rose from the bed. Once again, he disappeared through the connecting door and into his bedroom. He promptly returned with the armful of documents he'd brought home from the office on Friday. "Cowgill's old columns," he explained in answer to her questioning look. "Along with his notebooks, and some articles Higgins pulled about the Fawn-Purvis family. I've gone through them once in a cursory fashion, but . . ."

Nell sat up taller in bed. "You'd like me to go through them again?"

"If your aching head will permit it."

Beaming at him, she held out her left hand. "You may leave them with me."

24

Nell couldn't recall when she'd ever been so spoiled and looked after in her life. Miles tended to her all day, by turns doting and dictatorial. He brought her trays of food, ice for her shoulder, and hot bricks and water bottles to ease the ache in her hip and leg. He might even have overseen her bath that evening if she had permitted it.

Which she hadn't, of course.

She wasn't ready for *that* level of intimacy.

Instead, Gladys and Mrs. Bright assisted Nell, helping her bathe and dressing her in a fresh nightgown, and brushing out her hair.

"The master has been beside himself," Mrs. Bright was emboldened to remark as she plaited Nell's tresses. "He stayed up all night in that chair by your bed."

"Did he?" Nell asked, surprised. She hadn't known that. She'd assumed he'd retired after she'd fallen asleep.

"I couldn't move him," the housekeeper said. "He was that concerned about you. And he's been no easier today. Downstairs at dawn, pacing and growling, and sending out for all sorts to tempt you."

Of that, Nell *was* aware. Fresh bouquets of gardenias adorned her bedchamber, a box of cream-filled Swiss chocolates had appeared on her luncheon tray, and at dinner, Miles had surprised her with the first volume of Mr. Trollope's new novel, *Can You Forgive Her?*—a book Nell had offhandedly admitted to desiring to read, and one that wasn't due to be published for another week.

"But how?" she'd asked Miles in amazement. "It isn't out until September."

Miles had shrugged, as if he hadn't just given her something as precious as a diamond. "I know one of the editors at Trollope's publisher, Chapman & Hall. He owed me a favor."

Nell's insides warmed to recall it. "He's a dear," she said to Mrs. Bright.

Gladys giggled as she made up the bed.

Mrs. Bright shot a repressive look at her. "That's enough."

Nell smiled slightly. She didn't imagine anyone had ever called the stern Miles Quincey a dear before. Not in the servants' hearing. She didn't wonder that the young maid was entertained by it. "He's worrying quite unnecessarily," she said.

"That may be so, ma'am," Mrs. Bright replied as she tied off Nell's plait with a satin ribbon. "But may I say what a pleasure it is to see him so well occupied."

Nell settled back in her chair by the fire, her injured arm tucked safely in the sling Miles had made for her. He wasn't the only one who had been well occupied today. Nell had spent hours reading every scrap of paper he'd given her about Mr. Cowgill and the Fawn-Purvis family. It had been exhausting work in her condition. Though her head was vastly improved from this morning, her shoulder and hip were paining her dreadfully.

She reflected that she shouldn't have spent so much time in bed today. She should have got up and walked around her room, if only enough to keep her leg from cramping. But the very thing that helped her old injury seemed to aggravate her new one—and vice versa. It was exceedingly frustrating.

Mrs. Bright set a tray down on the table by Nell's chair. It held a small porcelain pot and cup. "I've brewed some willow bark tea for you, ma'am. It will help the pain. And Cook's preparing a bran poultice for your shoulder."

Nell was vaguely disappointed that it wasn't Miles who had brought the tea. She hadn't seen him since she'd withdrawn for her bath. "Has Mr. Quincey already retired?"

"Retired? Heavens no. He's gone to the *Courant*." Mrs. Bright poured the tea, oblivious to the effect of her words.

Nell stared at her. "At this time of night? Whatever for?"

"I expect he realized he'd left something unfinished."

A shiver of apprehension traced down Nell's spine. Standing abruptly from her chair, she limped to one of her bedroom windows. She drew back the heavy curtain to peer down toward the street. It was pitch black out, save for the faint glow of the too-few street lamps that dotted St. James's Square. A dense fog was visible, swirling around the lampposts and clinging to the black iron fence along the green.

And Nell asked herself: What unfinished business could Miles possibly have to attend to that was important enough to draw him away from her side on a dark and moonless night?

She could think of only one answer. And it had nothing to do with journalism.

• • • • •

Miles didn't mind the darkness. He'd spent most of his childhood in the shadows. Indeed, on this occasion, he was far more concerned with someone seeing him than he was with his own ability to see.

He'd dressed for invisibility, all in black, with his hat pulled low over his brow, and the collar of his heavy overcoat standing up to shield the lower half of his face. No one meddled with him as he strode through the narrow, fogbound lanes of the Whitechapel slum.

He carried himself as if he belonged here. As if he'd spent his life on these streets, with these people. The few who dared look at him askance cast him a wide berth. He was too big. Too intimidating. Too bloody furious.

It radiated off of him in menacing waves, all the rage he'd bottled up throughout the day every time he'd looked at the darkening bruise on Nell's shoulder. Every time he'd seen her grimace with pain, exhale a trembling breath, or hold her arm to her breast like an injured dove.

Miles had known what he was going to do from the moment Flora Brent had revealed that Silas had struck Nell. It mattered little that Inspector Garrick had warned Miles and Gabriel against retaliation. This wasn't vengeance. It was justice.

Up ahead, Mrs. Pritchard's Gentlemen's Establishment stood amid the billowing fog, its entrance illuminated by a string of lanterns. Silas towered in front of the door. He was talking to a shifty-faced gentleman in a poorly fitting suit. A customer, presumably. Silas stepped aside for the man, admitting him into the house. As he turned, the light shone over his face, casting the jagged red scratch on his cheek, and the new one across his brow, in harsh relief.

Miles's muscles tightened on a fresh surge of anger. Miss Brent had said that Nell had cut Silas over the eyes with the tip of a parasol, and here was the evidence of it. A flesh-and-blood reminder of how Silas had threatened Nell, and of what she'd been obliged to do to defend herself.

She shouldn't have had to. Miles should have been here to protect her. That he hadn't been was, objectively, no fault of his own. Even so, he couldn't forgive himself.

Steering clear of the lantern glow, Miles took up a position in the shadows of a urine-soaked alleyway that ran alongside the entrance to the brothel, and he waited.

And waited.

He'd been there nearly an hour before Silas at last abandoned his post and ducked into the unlit alley to relieve himself.

Miles remained concealed by the dark and fog until the bully boy was rebuttoning his trousers. Only then did Miles emerge, as silently as a phantom, to grab the man by his wilted neckcloth.

Silas grunted in surprise. "Who the—?"

Miles hit him square across the jaw. There was a satisfying crunch of shattering teeth.

Silas let out a howl of pain. He lunged at Miles with upraised fists.

Miles evaded him, using the darkness to his advantage.

"Show yourself!" Silas snarled, swinging wildly. He was a huge brute of a man. All brawny muscles and raw power. A true brothel bully who could effortlessly subdue disobedient working girls and unruly customers.

But Miles wasn't as easy an opponent. Nor was he untutored in the ways of violence. He hit Silas again, and again. Punishing blows to the face and stomach.

Silas continued to strike out into the swirling fog, never making full contact. All he did was further exhaust himself. The metallic smell of his blood soon warred with the stench of urine.

Miles's own blood ran cold. He may have abandoned his rationality in coming here, but he hadn't dispensed with it when delivering the much-deserved thrashing. He was strategic. Efficient. Good science, Nell would have called it.

The thought of her inspired a final blow to Silas's chin. The bully staggered back from it, hitting the filthy wall of the alleyway. He slid down to the ground, his head lolling forward.

Miles marked the rise and fall of the man's chest.

Not dead.

He'd only been beaten severely, just as any number of villains in the slum were beaten on any given night. The case against him was in no way imperiled. Garrick could still ask his questions, bring his charges, have his hanging. And no one would be the wiser. Silas may as well have fought a shadow.

Miles briefly emerged from the darkness to stand over the man's unconscious figure. "Come near my wife again," he said, "and I'll kill you."

25

It was well past midnight by the time Miles returned to St. James's Square. The house was dark except for the dimmed gasolier Mrs. Bright had left on for him in the hall.

He climbed the stairs to his room. He had to wash and change to rid himself of the stench of the slum. And then—

He wanted to see Nell. He *needed* to see her, even if it was only to catch a glimpse of her sleeping form beneath the covers of her bed. He wouldn't be able to calm himself otherwise.

It had been years since Miles had engaged in a fight. He was no longer used to the aftereffects. The cold sweat. The delayed exhaustion. The ache in his hands and the sudden bursts of pain wherever Silas's fists had managed to deal him a glancing blow. Blows Miles hadn't even felt at the time—he'd been too full of rage to feel anything but his own blood lust.

He passed the door to Nell's bedchamber on the way to his own. No light shone from beneath it. She would have gone to sleep hours ago. Mrs. Bright had mentioned something about a poultice and a special tea.

Exhaling heavily, Miles opened the door to his own unlit bedroom. He entered, shutting the door behind him. He shed his hat, coat, and gloves, and was in the process of unknotting his cravat when he heard the strike of a friction match.

A flame blazed forth, illuminating Nell in the darkness. She was seated in the upholstered wing chair beside his bed.

Miles froze where he stood.

Nell lit a taper candle on the small table beside her before wafting out the match. Her countenance was inscrutable. "Good morning," she said.

Miles swallowed hard. "Good morning."

Nell didn't rise from the chair. She was in her dressing gown, her hair disposed in a plait over her shoulder, and her right arm still in its makeshift sling. A quilted blanket was draped across her legs.

"What are you doing in here?" he asked.

"Waiting for you." She motioned to a collection of medicinal implements on the table. "I have a jar of salve and a roll of bandages. There was a can of hot water, too, but it's gone cold by now. I've been waiting for some time."

"Nell—"

"He's not dead, I trust?"

"No."

"And he didn't see you?"

"No."

"Well, then." Her rigid expression relaxed a fraction. "Come here, if you please. I would come to you, but my leg is being uncooperative after sitting for hours in this chair."

A sharp twinge of guilt constricted Miles's chest. He crossed the room to Nell. Rather than remain standing, he sank down on his knees in front of her, bringing their eyes level. "How did you know?"

"I've been a teacher for many years. I have a sixth sense when mischief is afoot."

"Mischief?" He gave a hollow laugh. "You do have a way of taking the heroism out of it."

Nell lifted her hand to smooth the rumpled hair from his brow. Her fingertips were cool and gentle. Infinitely soothing. "I didn't need you to be heroic," she informed him. "But I understand the impulse."

Miles bowed his head to her touch. Some of the tension went out of him. "Do you?"

"I was responsible for Miss Brent," she said. "And you—well, I daresay you feel you're responsible for me."

"I *am* responsible for you."

"Because I'm your wife."

"Yes."

But that wasn't all. It wasn't even the largest part of it. His overpowering sense of protectiveness for her had nothing to do with any antiquated notions about ownership, duty, or property. It was something dearer. More important.

"And because you're my friend," he said.

Nell's gray eyes were solemn in the candlelight. She wasn't angry, but otherwise . . . it was impossible to tell what she was thinking. "Friendship is a powerful thing."

"It seems so," he said.

Powerful enough that he'd do anything to keep her safe. To make her happy. Powerful enough that he was beginning to have difficulty imagining his life without her.

She dropped a glance downward. "Let me see your hands."

He reluctantly presented them to her. He'd been wearing gloves when he'd pummeled Silas, but they'd had no padding in them. His knuckles were raw, and a few of them bleeding.

Nell examined them in the candlelight, unflinching. "You must soak them before I apply the salve and bandages," she said. "If you don't mind cold water. I'd hate to trouble the servants for another can of hot."

"I don't mind," Miles said. But he didn't move to the basin. Too weary to consider the wisdom of it, he leaned forward and rested his head in her lap.

Nell stiffened beneath him in surprise. But only for an instant. In the next, she was relaxed again, her body wondrously soft against his cheek beneath the layers of her blanket, and her voluminous nightgown and robe.

Miles breathed her in. The scent of candle flame and clean linen, and a fragrance that was distinctly hers—some heavenly combination of gardenias, warm skin, and woman. Peace followed with it. He didn't know what tomorrow or the next day would bring. But right here, right now, he knew beyond all doubt that this was where he belonged.

Nell's fingers threaded through his hair. Her voice was pure velvet—husky and soft. "Mrs. Bright says you didn't sleep last night."

"I slept."

"In a chair by my bed?"

"No place I'd rather have been," he murmured.

She continued stroking his hair. "Must I do the same tonight? Keep vigil over you?"

"On no account." In a moment, he would get up and carry her to her own room. She didn't need to remain here to treat his trifling wounds. She had her own injuries to contend with. She required rest. Still . . .

He couldn't bring himself to move.

"I finished reading all of the documents you gave me," she told him. "Mr. Cowgill's columns, the whole of both his notebooks, and the articles on the Fawn-Purvis family. There was nothing to indicate the significance of that second date. And absolutely nothing mentioning anyone named Innes. I did, however, learn that Mr. Cowgill attended a great many house parties."

"He did," Miles acknowledged.

"Is that where he gathered his society gossip?"

"That was the rumor."

"And another thing," she said. "Did you notice that Baron

Amstead's ancestral estate, Northwick Hall, was designed by Sir Robert Taylor?"

"Mmm." Miles had seen the brief mention of the man's name in one of the articles.

"He was an architect of some repute, I believe. Highly sought-after for a time. He designed many great houses."

Miles didn't know. He couldn't think presently. Not about that or about anything else. The feel of her fingers was turning his brain to melted treacle.

No one in his life had ever touched him so soothingly. Not even his mother. Rose Quincey had been a hard woman, full of fierce determination. She hadn't allowed for any softness. To her, it was equivalent to weakness. Miles hadn't felt the lack of it. He'd known no different. But this . . .

To be petted and caressed by the lady he was coming to care for . . .

It was a pleasure beyond anything.

"Miles," Nell said. "Did you hear me?"

"Yes," he replied gruffly. "What did you say?"

Her fingers tightened in his locks in gentle reproof. "I asked if you were going into the office today."

"Mmm."

"Is that a yes?"

"Yes. Tomorrow."

"Today *is* tomorrow," she said with a hint of impatience.

Miles suppressed a grimace. She was right. He needed to get up. To take her to bed, and then to take himself to bed, if only for the few remaining hours until dawn. If he didn't, he'd get no proper sleep.

"When you go in to work," Nell said, "I wonder if you might do something for me?"

"Anything," he said.

"Do you suppose the *Courant* has access to the architectural plans for Northwick Hall? They must be available somewhere, given Sir Robert's reputation."

The question was provoking enough that Miles finally raised his head. "Why would you require plans for Amstead's house?"

"Common sense." She removed her hand from his hair. "We'd be foolish to travel to Hertfordshire blindly. If we had a floor plan to consult, it would give us an idea of where the different rooms are located, and where the exits might be in case we need to make use of them."

Miles slowly sat up. The delicious fog that had temporarily numbed his brain receded. A burgeoning suspicion came in its place. "Have you done this sort of thing before?"

Nell lifted her uninjured shoulder in a casual shrug. "Knowing one's surroundings is the first step of any successful endeavor."

His brows lowered. "Is this more wisdom from the Academy?"

She smiled. "Wisdom to live by."

• • • • •

Nell was in the library the next day, snuggled in a chair in front of the fire reading her advance copy of *Can You Forgive Her?*, when Effie came to call.

"Reading rather than sewing?" Effie observed as she entered. "This is a change."

Nell put away her book. She rose from her chair to greet her friend. "Mr. Quincey has forbidden me from sewing while my arm heals."

Effie closed the distance between them, the velvet-trimmed skirts of her amethyst silk carriage gown rustling in an elegant swish of expensive fabric. "Forbidden? Has he?" Rather than embracing Nell, Effie gently clasped her left hand.

Nell pressed Effie's fingers in return. "Out of an excess of concern."

It was the only reason Nell had acquiesced. However trying his commands, she'd known Miles had her best interests at heart. His every action had attested to the fact, from the nightlong vigil he'd kept at her bedside to the beating he'd administered to Silas.

She shouldn't be moved by any of it. Certainly not the violent aspects. But it was difficult not to be. Nell had never had anyone behave so protectively toward her before.

Effie's gaze skimmed over Nell's right arm. It was still cradled in Miles's makeshift sling. "How are you faring?"

"My shoulder was dislocated," Nell said. "But it's on the mend now. I hardly notice the pain."

She wasn't being entirely dishonest. Her shoulder did feel much better today. Even so, she'd refrained from putting on her corset or crinoline, and had instead dressed in a loose-flowing wool day dress and soft slippers. A shawl was draped about her shoulders in a concession to the weather. Outside, the air was damp, and the sky was dark with clouds. A storm was coming soon.

"Did he end up summoning a doctor?" Effie inquired.

Nell gave her a speaking look. "What do you think?"

Effie frowned. She recalled as well as Nell the medical miseries that Nell had gone through in the aftermath of falling from the roof. The bleedings. The purgatives. The barbaric surgeries and painful manipulations of her joints. It had been a variety of hell.

"What then?" Effie asked. "Did his housekeeper reset your arm, or—"

"It wasn't our housekeeper," Nell said. "It was Mr. Quincey himself. He's been taking care of me."

Effie's mouth curled into a slow smile. "I see."

Nell willed herself not to blush. "Enough of that," she remonstrated. She drew Effie to the fireplace. "Come. Tell me what happened with Miss Brent."

Effie sat down across from Nell in one of the large oxblood leather chairs. "First, you tell *me* something. When Mr. Quincey came to the Academy, you didn't, perchance, allow him inside the gates, did you?"

"Why do you ask?"

"Because Mr. Royce insisted that *he* be let inside the gates. As though he had a God-given right to wait in the garden. I immediately deduced it was because your husband had been in the garden first. Was he?"

"He was," Nell admitted.

Effie snorted. "Men."

Nell smiled, amused in spite of herself. "They're competitive, I suppose."

"When it comes to the Academy, definitely. My husband wouldn't like your husband to be granted any privileges that have been denied to him."

"A brief spell in the garden can hardly be called a privilege."

"More of one than being exiled outside the gates," Effie said. "In any event—"

"Miss Brent," Nell supplied.

"Miss Brent, yes." Effie grew serious. "You'll be pleased to know that Mr. Royce and I conveyed her to the Academy without incident. Miss Corvus welcomed her there, and promptly surrendered her into Gemma's charge."

Nell exhaled a relieved breath. Gemma may not be the most tenderhearted of the Academy's teachers, but she was certainly one of its fiercest. No harm would ever come to one of her charges. "And how did Miss Brent find her new surroundings?"

"She was curious above anything else. Her eyes were as wide as they could possibly be, taking it all in. She barely blinked once from the moment we entered the grounds. Fortunately, the Academy appeared to be to her satisfaction. I parted with her after a short time, confident that all would be well." Effie paused. "It was then Miss Corvus summoned me to her study for a private word."

A rogue quiver of anxiety went through Nell. She immediately thought of the sampler she'd posted to Miss Corvus two days before. The delicate pattern, bordered with butterflies and tiny blue flowers, and featuring the requisite raven with its white-tipped wing, had contained a coded message consisting of only two words: **Lady Belwood**.

Nell had sent it, not as a challenge, but as a courtesy. A simple message informing Miss Corvus that Nell had discovered the identity of the woman who had given birth to her and surrendered her to the Academy. She hadn't anticipated a reply. One hadn't seemed necessary. There was surely nothing Miss Corvus could reveal about the past that Nell hadn't already ascertained herself.

"Did she?" she asked with forced unconcern.

"I shan't beat about the bush," Effie said. "It involves that odious Reverend Pettiman."

Nell stared at her friend. "*Pettiman?* What about him?"

"It seems that, since your contretemps in Mr. Quincey's office, the reverend has not been idle. He's written to a handful of the school's benefactors, *and* he's expressed his concerns to the other members of the council. Miss Corvus has assured him that you and Mr. Quincey are married now, but for some reason he questions the legitimacy of the union."

"What?" Nell was stunned. "But . . . why would he doubt it?"

"I believe it has to do with the banns not being called."

"We married by special license. The banns weren't necessary."

"*And* with the lack of a marriage announcement being published in the papers," Effie added.

Nell fell silent. No. There had been no announcement. And there could be none now. Not after Nell had given her full name to Mrs.

Pritchard. Not without revealing to everyone that Penelope Trewlove, former schoolteacher, had married Mr. Miles Quincey, editor in chief of the *London Courant.*

"Could Mr. Quincey not print something?" Effie asked. "A sort of belated—"

"No." Nell shook her head. "It's impossible. We're traveling to Hertfordshire in four days' time to attend Lord Amstead's shooting party. He can't learn that Mr. Quincey is editor of the *Courant.* And he mustn't find out that my maiden name is Trewlove. If he did . . ."

"Yes, I see. It's too dangerous." Effie's expression was grim. "Which leads me to an alternative solution. Mind you, it was Miss Corvus who proposed it, so don't bite my head off."

Nell's lips compressed. "Go on."

"Write to Pettiman directly. Invite him to come here. Perhaps even to stay with you for a day or two as an honored guest—"

"Are you insane?" Nell interrupted, aghast.

"Not I," Effie objected.

"That I should permit that offensive, sanctimonious prig to come here and stay under my roof when all the while—"

"Then don't," Effie said. "Invite him for dinner. Or—even better—for tea. An hour's visit at most, and you'll be rid of him. Surely, it's a small sacrifice given the magnitude of his power in relation to the Academy. And only think, the sooner the scandal dies away the sooner you can return to your teaching post."

Nell lapsed into guilty silence. It had been several days since she'd thought of returning to the Academy. She'd been too busy settling into her new life with Miles. *Enjoying* her new life. She'd all but forgotten that it was supposed to be temporary.

The reminder brought with it a pang of anguish.

It wasn't like her to be selfish. For the past eighteen years of her life, the needs of the Academy had always come first.

"Is that what you would do?" she asked.

"After I considered strangling the man and discreetly disposing of his wretched body?" Effie sighed. "I wouldn't like it," she said, "but yes. If I thought it would do the trick."

Nell resented the obligation to her core. But resentment was a useless emotion. Academy girls were meant to keep their eyes on the future. Nell knew that better than most. These petty insults and offenses were nothing in comparison to the good that the school was doing. That it must *keep* doing.

"Very well." Standing all at once, Nell limped to Miles's desk. It stood on the opposite side of the library, a great carved mahogany monstrosity with a green leather blotter covering its surface. "If I must do it, I may as well get it over with." She opened the topmost drawer, searching out paper, ink, and a steel-nibbed pen.

The latter two implements were readily to hand, but the paper was harder to come by. She had to look through two drawers before she found a stack of it. But it wasn't blank. It was covered with Miles's handwriting. An article he was writing, Nell supposed. She gave it the veriest glance as she moved to flip through the pages, seeking a fresh sheet. And then—

Her attention was arrested by a familiar name.

Miss Corvus's Benevolent Academy for the Betterment of Young Ladies

It was the heading on what appeared to be a vast outline of facts about the charity school. Nell scanned the pages, her blood running cold. There were details about Miss Corvus, names and employment information about several of the Academy's graduates, and notes about the charity school's special curriculum—self-defense, swordplay, and coded samplers. And something else, too. A final line, recently added:

Rule No. 1—Know your surroundings.

26

Miles returned early from the office on Monday evening, in possession of the architectural plans for Northwick Hall. He was eager to present them to Nell. She'd been at the forefront of his mind all day, while he'd sat through dreary meetings about dwindling sales and loss of advertising, while he'd argued with the other editors about who was best qualified to take over Cowgill's column, and while he'd revised a lengthy article one of his reporters had written on the rumors of war brewing in Japan's Shimonoseki Straits.

But when Miles looked for his wife, first in the drawing room and the library, then upstairs in her room, she was nowhere to be found.

He exited her bedchamber, frowning, the portfolio that held the plans still tucked under his arm.

Gladys was scurrying down the hall with an armful of linens. She stopped when she saw him, dropping a curtsy. "Mr. Quincey, sir."

"Has Mrs. Quincey gone out?" he asked.

"No, sir," Gladys replied. "She's in the guest room, with the new cat."

Miles felt an unmistakable surge of relief. For a moment—

Stupid.

Nell wouldn't have left him. They were growing closer every day. Even after Miles had dealt with Silas, she had—by some miracle—

understood. She had stroked his hair, and bandaged his bleeding knuckles. He'd carried her to her bed afterward, kissing her softly before retiring to his own. It had seemed to him that they'd parted on the best of terms.

He walked down the hall to the door of the guest room where Shadow had been safely ensconced since last week. He entered quietly.

It was a modestly sized chamber, furnished with a canopied bed, a chest of drawers, a small walnut secretary desk, and several comfortable chairs. Nell was seated in one of them, her arm still in its sling. She wore a loose-fitting brown dress.

Miles's mouth hitched. "Making progress?" he asked as he closed the door behind him.

Nell didn't smile in return. "Remarkably so."

"Let me guess," he said. "Shadow darted beneath the bed the instant she heard me open the door?"

"She did."

"Sorry for that. I'm afraid I couldn't wait. I have something for you." He lifted the portfolio. "The architectural plans for Northwick Hall. As requested."

Nell gave him an unfathomable look. "I have something for you as well."

Rising from her seat, she went to the secretary. He belatedly registered that the writing surface had been opened on its hinges. Papers were laid out across it.

"Do you recognize these?" she asked.

Miles set aside the portfolio and joined her at the secretary. His heart stopped as he skimmed the pages. They were his notes about Miss Corvus's Academy. "You went into my desk."

It was the absolute wrong thing to say.

Nell's gray eyes hardened to flint. "I wasn't prying into your affairs, if that's what you mean."

"It isn't—"

"I was searching for paper to write a note to Reverend Pettiman—"

"What?"

"To invite him to visit us."

"Why the devil—?"

"Mrs. Royce called this morning. She told me that Pettiman's been stoking the scandal over our marriage, because the banns weren't called and because there was no formal announcement in the papers. Miss Corvus suggests we invite him here in hopes of finally putting his concerns to rest. Which we must do somehow or else I'll never be permitted to return home."

Miles froze. It seemed for a moment that the ground shifted beneath his feet. "What do you mean *return home*?"

"To my life at the Academy," Nell said hotly. "To teach. To live. To be with the people who actually care about me."

His stomach sank. She'd mentioned something of the sort when he'd proposed to her. Of resuming her duties as a teacher once the scandal died down. But she'd said nothing about returning to the Academy to live.

Is this what she'd been planning all along? To abandon him at the first opportunity?

The realization turned Miles's blood to ice.

"*That's* why I went into your desk," she said. "Imagine my surprise when I chanced upon your treatise about Miss Corvus, our graduates, our curriculum, and everything else that you've been—"

"It's not what you think," he said.

"Oh, isn't it?" There was an alarming quaver in her voice. "Then you aren't writing a story about the Academy?"

Miles took a step toward her. Any distress he felt on his own behalf was at once overshadowed by concern. "I'm not. I swear I'm not."

"It appears you are."

"I take notes," he said. "When there's a story—even one I'm not going to publish—I have to organize it so that—"

"By writing down things I've told you in confidence?"

"What things?"

"Coded samplers," she said, furiously tapping the word on the page with her fingertip.

Miles shook his head. "You didn't tell me anything about them. I merely deduced it."

Her cheeks flushed with anger. "How dare you? To be spying on me and making your deductions? I thought—"

He caught her arm to stop her retreating from him any further. His voice deepened. "If you would have been honest with me from the start, I wouldn't have had to deduce anything."

"Honest? Why? So you can add it to your rough draft?" She gestured to the page again with an angry flourish. "And what about that? That was this morning, Miles!"

He shot a glance back to his notes. To the line he'd added before departing for the office. *Know your surroundings.* He suppressed a flinch. "It was stupid of me to record it," he said. "But it struck me as being important."

She wrenched free of his grasp. "What a fool you must think me."

"Nell—"

"Every conversation. Every secret. You made me forget—"

"Stop. Listen to me."

She turned her back to him. "I came to London to prevent you writing about the school. And all I've done is given you fuel to compose your most damning article yet."

He came up behind her. "Is that what you think of me?"

"I think you love the *Courant*," she said. "That you'd do anything to save it. It's why you married me, isn't it? To save the paper from another scandal? If you'll go that far, I must suppose that no length would be too great."

"I do want to save the paper," he acknowledged. "But—"

"Mrs. Bright said you were anxious to find a story that would restore the *Courant*'s fortunes." Nell's words thickened with emotion. "What better than a tale about a school full of upstart women attempting to reform the world on their own idiotic terms? It will be both titillating and hilarious to your gentlemen readers, I daresay."

Miles's chest tightened. He feared she might be weeping. "You wrong me."

She folded her uninjured arm over her injured one. Her head bowed, revealing the vulnerable curve of her neck.

Miles had to clench his hand at his side to keep from reaching out to her. "If I *am* guilty," he said, "it's only in the method of my mind. It requires order to such a degree that if I don't set the facts of a situation down on paper, I can't make sense of them. That's all those are. My attempts to make sense of the Academy—and of you."

She flashed him a narrow glance over her shoulder. *"Me?"*

He was relieved to see she hadn't shed any tears. "You're still nine tenths a mystery to me."

She scoffed.

"You are," he said. "I don't believe you even belong to me. You're still *hers*. Still *theirs*."

"I belong to no one."

"Your loyalty does."

Nell turned back to him. Her arms were still folded protectively in front of her. "And what about *your* loyalty?"

"You have it," Miles said without hesitation. This time he couldn't refrain from touching her. He lifted his hand to her face. Blessedly, she didn't pull away from him. She remained there, still as a trembling kitten, uncertain yet whether it would permit the impertinence or whether it would dash off and disappear.

And he felt so much for her.

It coiled tight within him. A vital, palpable thing. Friendship, he'd thought. A mad, desperate attraction. But it was something else, wasn't it? Something far more perilous to his heart.

She was right. He did love the *Courant*. Until she had come into his life, it had been all he'd loved.

But not anymore.

He held her gaze. "You've grown up hearing about how Miss Corvus was betrayed by the blackguard she was meant to marry. She's raised you to distrust all men as a result. With good reason, I don't doubt. But you can trust me, Nell. You can trust *me*. I would never hurt you. Not on purpose."

Her mouth trembled.

"And I'm not going to publish that story," he said. "Not for any reason. Not even if you left me tomorrow and never came back." He swallowed against the lump in his throat. "But . . . please don't do that."

• • • • •

Nell's hurt and anger were already beginning to fade. At Miles's husky plea, they disintegrated further.

It occurred to her that she may have been unfair.

No. Not unfair. *Unreasonable.*

She'd assumed the worst of him on the flimsiest evidence. And not based on his own actions, but on the actions of men so unconnected with him—with either of them—as to not matter at all.

But when she'd seen his notes . . .

The feeling of betrayal had been so stark and sudden. Like a slap to the face, but worse. And it wasn't her anger at Miles that had pierced her to her soul. It was her anger at herself.

She'd let down her guard with him. Had lowered her defenses and allowed him into her confidence, her bedchamber, her heart, by heaven. And like any skillful thief he'd taken everything she'd offered—and several things she hadn't.

"Regrettably, his best quality is also his worst one," Nell recalled telling Effie. *"He pays attention."*

Isn't that what he'd been doing ever since they'd met? Noticing everything? Cataloging it and organizing it, setting it down on paper like the analytical madman he was?

It wasn't malice, she realized. It was simply Miles.

Some of the starch went out of her spine. At length, she covered his hand with her own.

A spasm of relief crossed his face.

Nell hadn't imagined she could feel any worse. "I'm sorry if I—"

"Don't apologize," he said. "I won't hear it. It was I who—"

"Yes, but I do understand. I should have—"

"Why would you? You don't know me well enough yet to realize that I'm a man of my word."

Nell inwardly winced. He was being unduly generous. She may not have experience with the strength of his word, but she *did* know that he was a man of principle. One willing to take any number of risks to do the right thing. It was the whole reason the *Courant* was in its present predicament, because Miles had risked public support for the paper in order to expose the corruption and hypocrisy of a powerful man.

She dropped her hand from his. Folding her arms again, she walked to the recessed window on the opposite side of the room. The curtains were drawn back, revealing the low, cushioned seat. Outside, rain clouds filled the evening sky, blocking out the setting sun. A soft drizzle fell against the glass.

"It's easy to forget how short a time it is since first we met," she said.

Miles came to stand beside her. "We've been in each other's company's a great deal since then."

"Yes." Nell had marked every second of it on her heart.

"It's unusual," he said. "Most couples meet only a handful of times before they marry."

"At a ball or a concert, I imagine. Everything formal and proper."

"And brief. They don't spend hours together on trains, or traversing the London slums."

She gave him a fleeting half smile. "But that was after we married," she said. "You might call it our honeymoon."

The muscle at the corner of his mouth twitched. "A singular honeymoon."

"An exciting one," Nell said. "Yet for all that . . . you're right." She sat down on the window seat. The rain-beaded glass was cold at her back. "We don't know each other as well as we ought, do we?"

Miles sank down at her side. His body was very close to hers. Tall and broad-shouldered and impossibly warm. "We know that we like each other tolerably well."

Nell recognized the words she'd uttered to him two nights ago. The same ones she'd said when she'd proposed that they practice kissing. A disconcerting heat pooled low in her belly. "More than tolerably well, surely," she returned, echoing the reply he'd given her then.

Miles was provoked into another wry smile. It didn't last. His face reverted to solemn lines. "*Are* you returning to the Academy?" he asked.

Nell's stomach trembled, recalling the things she'd said to him at the height of her distress. She'd never intended . . .

But it was too late now.

"I had planned to, when you first proposed," she admitted.

Miles's gaze was unflinching. "Had," he repeated. "Past tense?"

Nell was ashamed to confess it. Too long had she prided herself on her dedication to the Academy. It had defined the last eighteen years of her life.

"What does that say about me?" she asked. "That I've devoted my life to teaching those girls, only to abandon the cause the moment I'm comfortably ensconced somewhere with a gentleman?"

"Not just any gentleman," Miles said. "Your husband. And you've hardly abandoned the cause since we wed."

"No," Nell allowed. "I suppose not." She subsided into silence, caught in a moment of aching indecision. For all their closeness, the weight of her secrets still remained between them.

And not only hers. The secrets of the Academy.

Nell didn't want them there. Not anymore. Not if it meant being divided from the man she was coming to care for above anyone else in this world.

"As to the cause," she said slowly, "it's not what you think."

Miles's already rapt attention sharpened with journalistic awareness.

"Miss Corvus has no interest in grooming lady spies or female revolutionaries," Nell told him. "Her first and best concern has always been in instilling us with an unfettered sense of our own strength. *That's* the mission of the Academy. We're encouraged to be self-sufficient in every regard. To think for ourselves, and to defend ourselves."

Nell was rather proud of that fact, both as a teacher and as a former student.

"Society makes a prison of women's bodies and minds," she said. "It's how they control us, by diminishing us. Academy girls are aware of such limitations, but we are none of us bound by them. We're taught to navigate the confines of social restriction—to utilize our natural talents to advance the cause of women *and* to rectify wrongs when we can."

"Such as the wrongs perpetrated by Viscount Compton?" Miles asked.

"His crimes were outside of the common way, but yes," Nell acknowledged. "We have special classes for the most promising of our girls. The majority of them are never called on to use their skills, but given the chance . . . there's little they're not prepared to do."

Girls like Nell, Effie, and Gemma. And Flora Brent, too, Nell endeavored to hope.

"The parish council doesn't object to Miss Corvus's curriculum?" Miles asked. "But I suppose they don't know about it, do they?"

"No one does. At least, no one who might interfere. That's why we couldn't allow you to write about the Academy. We daren't risk the scrutiny."

"Understandable," he said. "You wouldn't want the rest of the world to know that Miss Corvus is in the business of forging weapons."

"And now you've married one of them," Nell said. A quiver of uncertainty entered her voice. "It can't be what you wanted."

"Having you here with me?" Miles brushed a lock of hair from her cheek. His touch was infinitely tender. "It's all I want."

Her vision blurred. She blinked rapidly to clear it.

He searched her tear-damp eyes. "What do you want, Nell?"

Nell's throat tightened. She hated to make herself vulnerable, to him or to anyone, but there was no denying the truth. Not anymore. "To be with you," she said softly.

The words sent a visible tremor through Miles's frame. He took her in his arms. She caught a glimpse of his face as he pulled her close. His solemn expression had fractured.

"There," he said, his voice gone gruff. "That wasn't too painful, was it?"

Nell burrowed into his embrace. His arms were strong around her, his body hot as a furnace. And still she wanted more. More of his strength, his heat, his reassurance. She exhaled a ragged breath. "It's been a dreadful day since I found those papers."

"I know, sweetheart."

"And all because of that wretched Pettiman."

Miles's cheek was pressed to her temple. She felt him smile. "You weren't really going to invite him for tea?"

"I *did* invite him," Nell said. "I suggested a date next week, after we return from Hertfordshire. I'll be better equipped to deal with him then."

"I suppose it's preferable to having him as a houseguest."

"The lesser of two evils, certainly." Nell hesitated. "Miles?"

"Yes, my dear?"

She slowly drew back to meet his eyes. "How did you know about the samplers?"

Miles didn't answer immediately. He only looked at her. "The lack of order," he said at last.

Her brows notched. "Is that all? Not all samplers are orderly."

"Do all samplers include a raven with a white-tipped wing?"

She started.

"You did ask," he said apologetically.

"It's not *that*. It's just—" She gave a disgruntled huff. "I tell the girls that no one looks that carefully at our samplers. And if they do, they're only examining the quality of our workmanship. How well we stitch our numbers and letters and so forth."

But she hadn't reckoned for Miles Quincey. He noticed everything. Or perhaps just everything about her.

"What I wonder," he said, "is why the Academy uses them at all."

Nell's chin lifted with a trace of pride. "It was my idea."

Miles's eyes softened with an unidentifiable emotion. "I gathered that. But why are they necessary? Why not simply write letters?"

"Miss Corvus wrote letters all those years ago when she was engaged to Lord Compton. Her brother meddled with her post. Her letters were surveilled, opened, and read, sometimes destroyed. It was another way of manipulating and controlling her."

"And you and the others at the Academy worry that the same might happen to you?"

"It easily could," Nell said. "Women have little privacy in this world, not in our correspondence, our bank books, not even our own bodies. And legal rights are largely denied us. In most circumstances, we're considered little more than property, dependent for our kind treatment on the better natures of our brothers, fathers, and husbands. If they should fail us—"

"Quite," Miles said grimly. "I don't wonder that you think so ill of my sex."

"I don't," Nell replied. Not all of them, anyway. "At the same time . . . my own sex would be woefully remiss if it didn't endeavor to acquire power of its own."

"Power comes in many forms."

"It does," she agreed. "Knowledge is the ultimate power."

"To know your surroundings," he murmured.

She smiled briefly. "Essential for any female entering a new situation."

Shadow chose that moment to creep out from under the bed. She padded across the woven rug, step by cautious step. She'd been eating well since coming to live in St. James's Square. Her coat was glossy and her stomach was much rounder than it had been when Nell had first met her in Miles's office.

"Look, Miles," Nell whispered.

Miles's gaze followed hers, watching the little tabby approach. He didn't speak. Didn't move a muscle.

"You wait for them to come to you, don't you?" Nell inquired softly. "Not me. I'm far too impatient." Slipping from his arms, she descended to the carpet in a pool of her poplin skirts. Her left leg twinged in protest.

Shadow hesitated but a moment before resuming her course. She came straight to Nell, slowly, carefully, tail upraised and whiskers quivering with alertness. When Nell stretched out her left hand, the cat advanced to delicately bump it with her nose.

She'd let Nell touch her this way before Miles had entered the room, but now, she permitted a further intimacy. Rubbing her cheek against Nell's fingers, she allowed Nell to pet her—first her head, then the curve of her small back, and even her tail.

Nell glowed with pleasure. She cast a beaming glance up at Miles. "Do you see how friendly she is?"

But Miles wasn't looking at Shadow. He was looking at Nell, an expression in his eyes that made her heart skip a beat.

And Nell knew, as suddenly as she'd known anything, just why it had hurt so much to think he'd betrayed her. And it wasn't because of her pride, or her history with her mother, or any loyalty she owed to Miss Corvus and the Academy.

It was because Nell was falling in love with him.

27

The following days unfolded in a heady mix of quiet moments interspersed with a furious haste. Nell was consumed with preparations for their departure to Hertfordshire. When she wasn't treating her shoulder injury, applying ice and poultices and praying that her bruises would fade as quickly as possible, she was studying the plans for Northwick House, perfecting her lock-picking skills, and practicing using the new sword-cane that Effie had delivered to her on Tuesday.

Miles was equally busy. He continued going into the *Courant* each morning, though his days were nowhere near as long. He returned home in the afternoons, often bringing Nell articles he'd discovered in the paper's archives on the history of the Fawn-Purvis family, or reports of various people named Innes residing in and around London.

They spent their evenings discussing their findings over long, candlelit dinners in the dining room. There, seated intimately together at one end of the table, they strategized about how they would proceed with their investigations when they arrived at the shooting party, and what they would say about themselves if anyone presumed to question them.

"I've already told Lady Belwood she's not to share your connection to the paper," Nell said. "Which means, if someone should ask, we'll have to come up with another occupation for you."

"There's no need to invent an entirely new identity," Miles replied logically. "I'll simply say I'm a gentleman of leisure. It's an easy enough fiction to maintain."

Nell nodded her approval, lamenting that she hadn't thought of such an easy solution herself. "You're right, of course. The best fabrications are often the least elaborate."

Miles gave her a measuring look as he drank his wine. "You have some experience with fabricating stories?"

"I was a schoolteacher," she said. "We hear half-truths all day long. You may believe I've become an expert in them."

• • • • •

As the days passed in rapid succession, they were both of them so focused on the shooting party, and on Mr. Cowgill, Mrs. Pritchard, Lord Amstead, and the mysterious Innes, that there was little time remaining to address any other concerns.

There was, however, always time for kisses.

Miles kissed her before leaving for Fleet Street each morning, and he kissed her again on returning—sometimes in full view of the servants.

And he kissed her at night.

Or rather, *she* kissed *him*.

Slow, languorous kisses in the dining room, the drawing room, and in front of the fire in Nell's bedchamber. Miles let her set the pace of them. He never pressed or demanded, or crushed her to him in that fierce way he had that night in the library. But Nell was in no doubt of how much he wanted her—or of how much control he exerted not to take their embraces further.

Indeed, as she clung to him in the evenings, feeling his muscles taut under her questing hands, she had the sense that she was kissing a dangerous beast that could, at any moment, seize her in its grip and—

Well.

It was excessively exciting. A little frightening, too. Despite the warm feelings he kindled within her, she wasn't ready for further intimacies. Her body was still too much her own. To share it—truly share it—would mean making herself vulnerable in a way she'd never been vulnerable before.

And she couldn't bring herself to do it. Not when there was a chance it might ruin everything.

None of the servants seemed to notice that their master and mistress's marriage was still unconsummated. They treated Nell as if she was in every way Miles's wife. She was consulted on household matters—the lighting of fires, the order of candles, and the schedule for changing the linens, to name but a few. On Thursday morning, Mrs. Bright even went so far as presenting Nell with menus for the following week and broaching the subject of dinner parties.

"Does Mr. Quincey often entertain?" Nell asked in bewilderment as she perused the proposed courses for next week's meals. She was seated on the drawing room sofa, absent her sling for the first time since her shoulder injury.

Mrs. Bright stood across from her. "Not as yet, ma'am, but the wives of the married editors do often give dinners. With Mr. Quincey being the most senior gentleman at the paper, I did presume he would do the same now he's wed."

Nell doubted Miles would want to. He wasn't the most socially inclined of gentlemen. Then again, he did value his reputation. And if a formal dinner would help to burnish it, Nell would be a poor wife indeed not to host one for him.

How difficult could it be? She'd practically run the Academy. Planning a dinner party could surely be nothing in comparison. If she was strategic, she might even turn the chore to the Academy's advantage. She could invite the school's largest benefactors, Lady

Summers, Mrs. Crookshanks, and Mrs. Weaving. Reverend Pettiman, too, since having him for tea was no longer an option.

Nell had received the man's response to her invitation only yesterday. A patronizing refusal, referencing fallen women, Christian forbearance, and some self-important nonsense about "treating with sinners." Tea, it seemed, was too private an affair to suit his elevated opinion of himself. He wanted his good opinion to be courted in front of witnesses.

"Of course," she said decisively. "We must plan something for when we return from Hertfordshire."

Mrs. Bright beamed her approval. "Very good, Mrs. Quincey."

.....

The next day, Nell's dress order was delivered from Mr. Malik's shop. The elegant merino and muslin delaine blouses, colorful poplin skirts, and silk and velvet gowns were carefully folded within more than a dozen tissue paper–lined dress boxes. She was upstairs unpacking them, with Gladys's assistance, when Albert, the footman, materialized at the door of her bedchamber.

"I beg your pardon, Mrs. Quincey," he said, "but there's an Inspector Garrick to see you."

Nell straightened to attention. Inspector Garrick had come? He must have news about the investigation. "You may put him in the library, Albert," she said. "I'll be down directly."

Straightening her woolen day dress and smoothing her hair back into its chignon, Nell made her way downstairs. She was entering the hall when Miles walked through the front door.

She came to a surprised halt. Her mouth curved into a smile. "You're home early."

Miles's dark eyes gleamed to find her standing there. Removing his hat, he shut the door behind him and, without faltering, crossed the marble-tiled floor to take her in his arms. "I thought I'd better. We've an early train to catch tomorrow."

Nell set her hand on his chest as he bent his head to kiss her. His lips were warm and firm, making her pulse flutter madly.

And she wondered if she'd ever get used to it. The strength of his embrace. The way he held her, kissed her, made her feel wanted and protected, even as her knees quivered and her blood heated to a dangerous simmer.

Her fingers curled in the fabric of his black waistcoat. "Miles," she murmured against his mouth.

"Yes, love?"

"Inspector Garrick is in the library."

Miles went still. He drew back a fraction to meet her gaze. There was a question in his own.

"I was just going to see him," she said. "If you'd like to accompany me? I'm sure he'd prefer to speak to us both."

Miles composed himself before her eyes—reverting all at once from an affectionate husband into a single-minded reporter determined to get his story. He was still in his black wool overcoat and gloves. He made no move to divest himself of them. Wordlessly, he offered her his arm.

She took it gratefully.

"Where is your sling?" he asked as he led her to the library.

"I'm practicing going without it," she answered. "In preparation for the shooting party."

"And is it—?"

"It's bearable," she said. "So long as I don't move my right arm overmuch."

Her shoulder joint was still too swollen for her to raise her arm above her head or to lift anything even remotely heavy without pain. As for her new sword-cane, though she was getting better at flourishing it with her left hand, Nell couldn't manage it at all with her right. It made the cane all but useless as a practical accessory. She sincerely hoped she wouldn't need to lean on it during their time in Hertfordshire.

Entering the library, Nell and Miles found Inspector Garrick at the hearth, warming his hands in front of the fire. He came to attention when he saw them. "Mr. Quincey. Mrs. Quincey." He bowed. "Good afternoon."

"Inspector." Miles escorted Nell to a leather chair by the fireplace. He waited for her to sit before turning to address the policeman. "You have news?"

"I do, sir," Garrick replied. "Not all of it favorable."

Miles remained standing by Nell's chair. "Go on."

"We arrested Silas Davidson yesterday morning," Garrick said.

Nell hadn't been aware of Silas's surname.

"On what grounds?" Miles asked.

"Not murder," the inspector said. "I've yet to prove that particular charge. Mr. Davidson was arrested for the abduction and unlawful imprisonment of Flora Brent. He attempted to flee, but was in no fit state to do so. You may or may not be aware that he was recently beaten by an unknown assailant."

"Was he?" Nell affected an expression of concern. "How dreadful." She paused, unable to resist adding, "Though I'm sure it was no less than he deserved."

Miles was inscrutable. "Unknown, you said?"

"These things happen in that part of the city," Garrick replied. "It won't impact our bringing him to justice. The assault doesn't appear to have anything to do with his abduction of Miss Brent or his alleged involvement in the murder of Mr. Cowgill."

"I'm confident you're right," Miles said.

Nell didn't trust herself to look at her husband. She knew full well why Silas had been beaten. And it wasn't because of what he'd done to Miss Brent or Mr. Cowgill. It was because of what he'd done to her. "What about Mrs. Pritchard?" she asked.

"I trust you've arrested her as well," Miles said. "She's as guilty as he is."

"Guiltier," Nell said. "It was she who drugged Miss Brent and took her from the railway platform."

"Quite right." Inspector Garrick's mouth set in a bleak line. "That's the bad news I alluded to. On arriving at the brothel yesterday with my officers, we discovered that Mrs. Pritchard had already fled. Our subsequent efforts at finding her have so far proved fruitless. She's either very well hidden, or . . ."

"Or what?" Miles asked.

Garrick gave them an apologetic grimace. "Or she's no longer in London."

• • • • •

Miles paced the hall, stopping intermittently to check the time on his pocket watch. Their bags had already been packed and secured atop the carriage. All that was missing was Nell.

It wasn't like her to be late. As a former schoolteacher, she was typically a pattern card of promptness. Miles would have expected her to be even more so today. Their train was leaving Euston Station at half past ten. They had to be on it if they were to reach Northwick Hall before one.

He was about to go to her room to see what was taking her so long when Nell appeared at the top of the stairs.

At least, he believed it was Nell.

Miles stared up at her, rendered temporarily speechless.

She looked very different from her usual self. And her usual self was quite breathtakingly lovely. The heavy artillery, he'd called her when she was wearing lusterless black bombazine. But this . . .

This was an entirely different degree of lethalness.

She stood on the landing, clad in a golden-yellow carriage dress that had been cut with an elegance that bordered on the divine. The close-fitting bodice hugged her figure, accentuating every voluptuous dip and curve, and the full skirts swept over her hips in a swell of voluminous fabric that terminated in a delicately pleated hem.

The ensemble was completed by crisp muslin undersleeves, a slim belt with a gilded buckle, and a little scrap of a straw hat with an upturned brim.

Miles swallowed, and swallowed again. His mouth seemed to have gone completely dry.

Nell straightened her skirts, settling the folds gracefully over her crinoline. The gown's color lent a striking luminance to her complexion. The effect was aided by the golden net that bound her fair hair. "Well?" she asked.

"I don't know what to say," he replied.

"But you do like it?"

He cleared his throat. "*Like* seems an inadequate word in the circumstances."

Her mouth tipped at one corner. "It was you who purchased it for me," she said. "And this is only a day dress. Wait until you see my evening gowns."

"If they enhance your charms any more effectively than this one," Miles replied gravely, "I fear my constitution may not be up to the experience."

Her dimple appeared. She slowly began to descend the steps, a pronounced hitch in her gait. She wasn't using her cane. She wasn't yet strong enough to wield it with her right hand.

Miles bounded up the stairs to offer her his arm. When she took it, he felt, rather foolishly, like the luckiest man in the world. It was boyish. Ridiculous. She was his wife, not some untouchable stranger. All the same . . .

His heart thudded heavily.

"You must lean on me in the absence of your cane," he said.

Her smile softened. "You may believe that I shall."

Miles gazed down at her, his chest gone tight. "I'd have it no other way."

• • • • •

They arrived at Euston Station a short while later, with just enough time left to entrust their luggage to a porter before their train was due to arrive. After a hurried walk through the crowded terminus and a brief stop at the ticket office, Miles and Nell joined the other passengers on the platform.

It wasn't the busiest time of day at Euston, but Euston was, at any hour, one of the busier stations in London. Ladies and gentlemen with their families and servants milled about amid the smoke and steam, along with less salubrious individuals traveling alone. It was noisy and chaotic, with people calling out to each other, and porters racing by with their luggage carts.

Miles kept Nell close at his side. He couldn't fail to notice the reactions she engendered. The pointed, and sometimes stunned, looks from men and women alike. It provoked a fierce protectiveness in him.

"You don't enjoy traveling?" Nell asked him.

He flashed her a distracted glance. "Don't I?"

"You're scowling dreadfully," she said.

Miles inwardly grimaced. Was it that obvious? "They're staring at you," he said.

"Are they?" She sounded entirely unaware. "It's my gown, I daresay."

"It's not the gown," he grumbled. "It's you in it."

"That's very flattering. But wouldn't our time here be better spent looking out for Mrs. Pritchard rather than glaring at admiring strangers?"

"I'm capable of both."

A faint smile touched Nell's lips. She was amused by his primitive behavior, he didn't doubt. "Do you think she might be here?" she asked.

"If she's smart, she'll have gone to France," Miles answered.

"And leave behind the empire she was building?"

Miles made a derisive sound. "An empire, was it? That foul establishment of hers in Whitechapel?"

"From her perspective. She had five thousand pounds to refurbish her premises, and was offering the prettiest girls, newly luxurious surroundings, and absolute discretion for her gentlemen clientele. She was plainly on her way to having the most prestigious brothel in town. I don't see her giving that up to go on the run."

"It was either that or meet the hangman."

"But would she have been hanged? Inspector Garrick hasn't yet been able to prove that she and Silas murdered Mr. Cowgill. As yet, they're only being charged with the abduction of Miss Brent."

"They could still face the noose," Miles said. "More likely, they'll be transported. Either way, Mrs. Pritchard was wise to run."

Nell's expression sobered. "Perhaps she has. Still . . . I can't rid myself of the uneasy feeling that she's here somewhere, watching us. Plotting her revenge." She scanned the platform as she spoke, as though she might find the runaway madam among the gathering crowd.

When her hand tightened spasmodically on his arm, Miles feared for an instant that she had. But when he followed Nell's frozen stare through the billowing smoke from the arriving train, it wasn't Mrs. Pritchard he beheld waiting on the platform with her maid and footman in attendance.

It was Lady Belwood.

28

The train to Hertfordshire departed Euston Station with a gust of steam and a heave of grinding metal. Nell sat across from Lady Belwood in their shared first-class compartment. Miles was in the upholstered seat beside Nell, examining the railway timetable with undue attention. She supposed it was his way of recusing himself from any prospect of conversation. He'd taken refuge in silence ever since she'd invited Lady Belwood to join them.

He didn't approve, that much was obvious. He thought Nell impulsive. Unwise. Perhaps even self-destructive. As for his opinion of Lady Belwood . . .

From the moment they'd encountered her on the platform, Miles had regarded the woman with an edge of cool disdain.

Nell was touched by his show of protectiveness. Doubtless he'd rather Nell had limited contact with her ladyship, thereby sparing herself any additional hurt.

But despite the queasiness in her stomach and the uneven flutter of her pulse, Nell couldn't regret her suggestion that they travel together. She told herself she was being practical. Thinking of the shooting party. It had nothing at all to do with the fact that Lady Belwood was her mother. That she had abandoned Nell to an orphanage eighteen years ago in exchange for a life of wealth and privilege.

"Have you no maid with you?" Lady Belwood asked when they were underway. Her own servants had been relegated to a lower-class carriage at the back of the train. She wasn't diminished by the lack of them. She sat straight and proud, the picture of elegance in her rose-pink silk-and-velvet traveling gown.

"I don't keep a lady's maid," Nell replied.

Miss Corvus believed that self-sufficiency began with one's toilette. Both Nell's old gowns and her new ones were made with front fastenings as a consequence, allowing her to dress and undress herself. Nell would have it no other way.

"You and Mrs. Royce are singular ladies in that regard," Lady Belwood said. Her disapproval was evident. She was a woman who took pride in her appearance.

"I expect we are," Nell said. "We have both been used to shifting for ourselves from a young age."

If Lady Belwood registered the significance of Nell's statement, she didn't show it. "I shall lend you the services of my own maid while we're at Northwick Hall."

Nell acknowledged the offer with an inclination of her head. "You are very generous."

Lady Belwood gave a dismissive wave of her kid-gloved hand. "I have a reputation as a lady of fashion. My friends must necessarily be as faultless in their dress as I am."

Outside the window of their compartment, the hectic London scenery whipped by at an ever-increasing pace. It was but thirty miles to their stop in Hertfordshire. A negligible distance by train.

"I hope we *shall* be friends," Nell said. "Despite our difference in age."

Her ladyship's eyes hardened with swift censure. "We do not speak of age, Mrs. Quincey. It is an indelicate subject."

Nell affected a chastened expression. "Forgive my ignorance, ma'am. I hadn't a mother to advise me."

Miles flashed Nell a frowning look.

Nell ignored it. She was too busy observing Lady Belwood's reaction.

Her ladyship's countenance had gone oddly flat. She withdrew a perfumed handkerchief from her cord-trimmed sleeve. The scent of jasmine, tuberose, and honey stirred in the air.

Nell breathed in the familiar fragrance. With it came a barrage of memory. The little country house. The two aged servants. The fine, perfumed lady who pinched her cheek with such seeming affection.

Lady Belwood raised the handkerchief to her nose. "I cannot abide railway smoke," she complained. But she wasn't coughing or sniffing. She was studying Nell. "Your mother . . . She died, I presume?"

"It was a long time ago," Nell said vaguely.

"After which you decided to become a teacher at a charity school? With your natural endowments, you could surely have embarked on a more auspicious path."

"You will have noticed my limp, ma'am," Nell said.

Lady Belwood dropped a look at Nell's skirts as though she could see the injury beneath. She gave a faint moue of distaste. "I had thought it a temporary affliction."

"It is a permanent one," Nell informed her. "A fall when I was a girl was the cause of it. It damaged my prospects."

"But your face—"

"Small compensation for my broken body."

Lady Belwood flinched. "You are too severe, Mrs. Quincey."

"Not at all," Nell said. "I simply prefer facing unpleasant facts. To do otherwise is to live in a fantasy world. A dangerous course, don't you agree?"

"I don't quite—"

"Unpleasantness doesn't disappear merely because we don't acknowledge it. On the contrary, I find that it has a way of rearing its head at the most inconvenient times."

Miles thrust the railway timetable in front of Nell. "Perhaps reading would be preferable to conversation, my dear?"

Nell took the timetable from him with a cool glare. Did he think her conversation ill-advised? Cruel, perhaps?

And perchance it was.

Nell hadn't planned it to be. None of this had been planned. It was only now that Lady Belwood was seated across from her, looking so rich and superior, with her fine clothes and aristocratic airs, that Nell realized the ugly truth of her own feelings.

She wasn't just hurt by her mother's abandonment of her. She was *angry*.

Certainly, Miles could see it, even if Lady Belwood could not. He was coming to know Nell too well.

"Not very riveting reading, you'll agree," Nell said as she set aside the timetable. "I should have brought a book." She was mortified to hear a catch in her voice.

Miles gently took hold of her hand.

Nell's throat tightened.

It seemed he did know what she was feeling. And he was making an effort not to silence her, but to reassure her. To show her that, whatever she faced, she wasn't facing it alone.

The anger in Nell's heart dissipated. It was no match for the affection she felt for Miles Quincey in that moment.

Her fingers curled around his in reply. She didn't look at him. She didn't dare. Given her unruly emotions, she feared she'd burst into tears.

She stared out the window. She'd been a fool to believe she could endure Lady Belwood's company unaffected. Even Miles had seen it. But it was too late now to rectify the mistake. They had the remainder of the journey to endure, and the whole of the shooting party, too. Three interminable days.

Nell wondered how on earth she was going to make it through.

• • • • •

The train rolled up to the platform halt at Moor Cross in Hertfordshire at a quarter to noon precisely. From there, a hired carriage conveyed them the remaining five miles, along an uneven muddy track, to the Fawn-Purvis family's remote ancestral estate.

Gusts of wind buffeted the body of the coach, making it shudder and shake. Nell didn't envy Lady Belwood's maid and footman, who had been obliged to ride outside. Rain looked to start any moment. If the color of the sky didn't tell her so, the bone-deep ache in her hip and leg certainly would. Her shoulder, too. It had lately seemed to pain her whenever the temperature dropped. She folded her right arm in front of her, bracing it as the wheels of the carriage struck every pothole.

Lady Belwood clutched at the strap on the door to prevent herself from being bounced out of her seat. "Dreadful road," she muttered. "I shall speak to Lord Amstead about it when we arrive."

Miles's hand was firmly at Nell's waist, holding her steady against the worst of the jostling. He looked out the window. "That must be Northwick Hall."

Nell leaned past him to see for herself. A large Palladian mansion loomed ahead. It was made of a pale whitish-gray stone that perfectly suited the bleakness of the landscape. A long elm-lined gravel drive led to the massive front doors. It was there the driver took them, bringing the carriage to a halt in the selfsame moment the doors of the house swung open and several liveried servants emerged.

One of them assisted Lady Belwood from the carriage, while the others attended to the baggage strapped to the roof. Miles descended next so that he might hand Nell down himself.

Nell held on to his arm as she surveyed the premises. Wind whipped at her skirts and at the ribbons that trimmed her stylish straw hat. There was as yet no sign of anyone who looked important enough to be Baron Amstead. The closest she saw was an older gentleman with a thickening midsection and a balding brown pate who carried himself with an immense and formal dignity that immediately identified him as his lordship's butler.

He bowed to them and, after a brief word with one of the footmen, invited them to accompany him into the house's vast entrance hall. A fire was burning at the end of it in a cavernous hearth, hot enough to take the chill from the air. Portraits adorned the walls—ancient oils of an antiquity even greater than the ones Nell had observed in Lady Belwood's house. This was the home of a gentleman who had valued his ancestry. Or rather, the former home of one who had.

The man who now came to greet them was not the aged Baron Amstead who had corresponded for so many years with the elderly Sir Walter Belwood. It was a comparatively younger man in a loose-fitting flannel suit. He was sandy-haired and hearty, with a conspicuous ease of manner.

"Lady Belwood," he drawled, bowing over her hand. "I am charmed."

"Lord Amstead," Lady Belwood acknowledged him.

His lordship turned to Nell. A smile spread over his face. "And this vision must be your much-praised friend, Mrs. Quincey." He flourished another bow. "Your servant, ma'am." On straightening, he at last addressed Miles. "Mr. Quincey? A privilege. I hope you're fond of shooting. We're a bloodthirsty lot here at Northwick."

"I can hold my own," Miles said.

"Sir Walter sends his regrets, my lord," Lady Belwood said. "He has bid me do my utmost to enliven your party."

"Your gracious presence is my recompense, my lady. And the

presence of this lovely creature." Lord Amstead's speculative gaze lingered on Nell. He smiled again with quicksilver rapidity. "But I get ahead of myself. You must be tired from your journey. I shall let you refresh yourselves. When you're ready, you may join me and my other guests in the drawing room for cake and sherry."

"Are we the last to arrive?" Miles asked.

"There are one or two more stragglers," Lord Amstead said. "But we won't let their tardiness affect our pleasure." He motioned to the butler. "Innes? Do show my guests to their rooms."

Nell's breath stopped. It was all she could do not to stare at the butler. She'd noticed him when he'd appeared outside, of course, but she hadn't really looked at him. Not until this moment.

Yet, *he* was Innes!

She flashed a glance at Miles. He returned her gaze, his expression inscrutable.

"This way, if you please," Innes said in a colorless voice.

The entry hall opened into a circular stair hall where winding, cantilevered steps rose to the floors above in a dramatic display of architectural splendor. Nell had noted the feature when she'd studied the house plans. It was one of Sir Robert Taylor's signature designs.

Innes preceded them up the stairs. Lady Belwood came after him, along with her lady's maid—a superior sort of woman in a black stuff dress, who held her ladyship's jewel case in her arms as protectively as a mother might hold a newborn child.

Nell and Miles followed. They'd gone no more than a few steps when Lord Amstead called out from behind them.

"What's this, Mrs. Quincey?" he questioned in a tone of surprised concern. "You haven't injured yourself during the journey?"

Nell stilled beside Miles. Much as she leaned on her husband, there was no disguising her limp. Not completely.

Exchanging another weighted glance with Miles, she pivoted on the steps to bestow his lordship with a rueful smile. "A trifling thing," she said. "I'm afraid I twisted my ankle when I stepped onto the train at Euston."

"Did you, indeed? Poor lamb." Lord Amstead was all sympathy. "Shall I summon my physician?"

"That won't be necessary," Miles said. "I'll see to my wife myself."

Lord Amstead inclined his head. "As you wish."

Nell's fingers clenched tighter on Miles's arm as they resumed their progress up the stairs. Innes was far ahead, with Lady Belwood and her maid. Reaching the third floor, they entered a long, carpeted hall. All the while, Nell was running over the facts from Mr. Cowgill's two notebooks in her mind. The three dates from the first one, and the broken lines from the second.

19th March, 28th March, 3rd September.
Fawn-Purvis, Innes
From Hertfordshire to Brothel
Depot
Sleep/Tea
5000 pounds.

She had thought Innes might be another nobleman. Or possibly a villain in the fashion of Silas and Mrs. Pritchard. But he was neither. He was a servant. A butler. And not just any butler. He belonged to Lord Amstead.

After installing Lady Belwood and her maid in one of the rooms that lined the hall, Innes turned his attention to Nell and Miles. "Lord Amstead has put you in the gold room," he said, opening a door several doors down from Lady Belwood's. "It possesses a pleasant view of the duck pond."

Nell entered ahead of Miles, doing her utmost to conceal her limp. It had already drawn far too much attention. She let her gaze drift over the bedchamber, hardly noticing the furnishings. All she wanted was a moment alone with her husband.

"A lovely room," she said, though she'd taken in none of it. "We're obliged to Lord Amstead for his consideration."

Innes bowed. "A maid will return in half an hour's time to escort you to the drawing room."

Nell waited until the butler had withdrawn and his footsteps faded down the hall before turning to Miles. "The mysterious Innes!" she whispered.

Miles's mouth was set in a grim line. "Amstead's butler, of all people."

"Is that why Mr. Cowgill grouped them in his notebook? Because they were working together to achieve some nefarious purpose?"

"It seems likely."

"But what purpose?" she asked. "Something to do with young women and brothels, presumably."

"And with something that happened on the twenty-eighth of March," Miles said. "Nine days after the late baron's death."

Nell frowned in thought. "If this were a gothic novel, it would be connected to a murder and a forged will."

Miles removed his hat, gloves, and overcoat. He tossed them over the back of a chintz armchair near the bedroom's small fireplace. "But the late Lord Amstead wasn't murdered. He was verifiably ill. And his son is a hereditary peer. No alteration to a will could have prevented him from inheriting the estate."

Nell attempted to take off her own hat, but with only her left hand to aid her, the knot in the ribbons eluded her. "It might have stopped him from inheriting any money that wasn't entailed," she said, struggling.

Coming forward, Miles gently brushed aside her hand and untied the ribbons himself. "His finances aren't public knowledge. Nor was the will."

Nell ignored the tremor of warmth that went through her as his bare fingers brushed her skin. "In a house of this size, with dozens of servants, and a small village nearby, *everything* is public knowledge."

Miles removed her hat. Her gloves came next, one careful tug at a time. "Meaning?"

"There's always gossip, isn't there? We've only to listen for it, and we're sure to learn something. Mr. Cowgill must have done the same at all those house parties he attended. Unless he was such a clever reporter as to employ a more effective method—one that even you don't know about."

"He wasn't." Miles placed Nell's things in the chair along with his own. "If I had to guess, I'd say he was tactless. Possibly bumbling. It's how he ended up in the Thames."

Nell shivered at the reminder.

Miles didn't fail to notice it. "It's not too late to take our leave. If you've changed your mind—"

"I haven't," she said quickly. "And you needn't worry. We'll be much more careful than poor Mr. Cowgill was."

Miles didn't seem reassured. He went to the mahogany washstand in the corner. It had been prepared with a ewer of water and a stack of fluffy white cloths. "I don't like it," he replied as he filled the basin. "The house is too remote. The weather pestilential. And if Amstead is in league with his butler—"

Nell came up behind him. "There are other guests here," she reminded. "Lady Belwood, and heaven knows how many others. We'll be safe enough."

"Silas has already been arrested," Miles said. "If Amstead is involved, he may well be frightened. Desperate. And desperation makes a man reckless."

Nell didn't know anything about desperate men. Indeed, she knew little about men at all. Everything she'd learned since coming to London had been in relation to Miles. And he wasn't like the men she'd heard about all her life at the Academy. The ones who took advantage of women. Who condescended to them, exploited them, betrayed them.

No.

Miles Quincey was honorable, decent, and true.

And he wasn't opposed to taking action when the occasion called for it—a fact she was reminded of whenever she caught a glimpse of the abrasions on his knuckles.

She looked at them now, remembering how he'd returned to the house after his altercation with Silas. The way he'd knelt before her and rested his head in her lap.

"Would you like to wash first?" he asked her.

Recollecting herself, Nell gave a dismissive wave of her hand. "Go ahead."

Rail travel was a grimy business. It was impossible to have gone any distance by train without accumulating a layer of grit and soot. They would both need to wash their face and hands, and to brush off their clothes, before appearing in the drawing room.

But she wasn't ready yet. She needed to stretch her legs to alleviate the ache in her hip. Folding her arms at her waist, she walked the length of the room. This time she looked at it. Really looked at it.

At St. James's Square, she and Miles had connecting rooms. Most fashionable couples did, to her knowledge—Effie and Mr. Royce notwithstanding. But this wasn't a master and mistress's suite. It was a guest chamber, consisting of only one room.

Only one bed.

A flush of heat swept through Nell as she was struck by the logical ramifications of this fact.

Amid all their strategy sessions by candlelight, all their studying architectural plans and discussing the shooting party, she and Miles had never once addressed the possibility that they'd be sleeping together during their three days at Northwick Hall.

Pacing to the window, she twitched back the curtain with an agitated hand. A great expanse of lawn stretched out below, leading to a serene, tree-shrouded pond. It was a pretty enough prospect, yet all she noticed was the hazy reflection of the bed in the glass. It was a smallish four-poster. Even smaller than the one she occupied alone in St. James's Square.

"Is your leg paining you?" Miles asked.

Nell stifled a flinch. The last thing she wanted to be thinking about right now was her leg. "It's no matter," she said dismissively.

"And your shoulder—"

"It's fine." She let the curtain fall closed.

Miles straightened from the basin. He dried his damp face with a towel. "There's time enough before we're due downstairs. You might lie down on the bed—"

"No," she said. She closed her eyes briefly, hearing the note of shrillness in her voice. Taking a steadying breath, she moderated her tone. "Thank you. I don't need to rest. I need to move. I've been still far too long."

Miles regarded her from across the room, a thoughtful frown at the back of his gaze.

Ignoring his scrutiny, Nell put action to word, walking from the window back to the fireplace, and then to the wardrobe. But wherever she went, the bed was still there in the corner of her eye, making her pulse skip with anxiety.

It was hours yet until it would be time to retire. She had the sinking feeling that she'd be counting every minute of them.

29

Miles stood in front of the drawing room fire with two of the other guests, Mr. Pargeter and Mr. Radford. They were sportsmen in broadcloth and tweeds, talking loudly about the chances of favorable weather for hunting in the morning, and about which guns they'd brought, and how many birds they hoped to bag. Miles responded to them in turn, all the while keeping a diligent eye on his wife.

Nell was seated on one of the matching damask sofas that flanked the fireplace, along with Lady Belwood and a fashionably clad older lady by the name of Mrs. Thompson. They were sipping tea and conversing. Lord Amstead perched in an armchair beside them, his gaze riveted to Nell's face.

Miles's fingers clenched on the stem of his sherry glass. He'd marked Lord Amstead's reaction to Nell when they'd first arrived. The man had been thunderstruck by her.

The gentlemen guests in the drawing room had behaved in a similar fashion when Nell had entered on Miles's arm. They'd all ceased speaking, leaping to their feet so abruptly one might be forgiven for thinking that an old sergeant major of theirs had surreptitiously entered the room and commanded them all to attention.

There were seven gentlemen altogether, including Miles and

Lord Amstead, but only four ladies. Of those four, Nell was the youngest, and by far the most beautiful. It was a recipe for disaster. And bloody inconvenient besides. Miles was meant to be investigating Cowgill's murder, not spending the whole of the next three days guarding his wife from a pack of amorous, aristocratic jackals.

Nell was partially to blame. She insisted on viewing her beauty as a weapon. Even now, with so many gentlemen openly staring at her, she gave no sign that she appreciated the potential for danger. On the contrary, rather than discouraging Lord Amstead's attention, she was encouraging it with veiled looks and smiles, and all the confidence of an experienced flirt.

It was a dramatic difference from how she'd been behaving in their room not fifteen minutes earlier. One that Miles recognized as being entirely inspired by the change in location. The drawing room was not, after all, a bedroom possessed of only one bed.

For that had surely been the cause of her discomfiture. Miles hadn't needed to be a mind reader to discern it. He'd observed the initial anxious glance she'd given the bed. Had seen the way she'd avoided looking at it thereafter.

The irony of the situation wasn't lost on him.

Nell had plainly never considered that the two of them would be obliged to sleep together during their stay at Northwick Hall. While, for the past week . . .

Miles had been thinking of little else.

"It's Monday evening's dance that concerns me, Mrs. Quincey," Lord Amstead was saying to Nell. "You see our lamentably uneven numbers. I blame Calverley, Pargeter, and Radford. They're long overdue to marry."

"Speak for yourself, Amstead," Pargeter called out with a laugh.

"It's you who must get yourself to the altar," Mr. Calverley added from his place on the sofa across from Nell and the other ladies. He was a ruddy-faced country gentleman, slightly older than Pargeter and Radford.

"Too right, sir," Amstead replied gamely. "I require a lady wife to act as my hostess. In the absence of one, perhaps I might steal yours, Quincey?"

Miles forced his fingers to relax on his sherry glass. It was either that or break the stem in two. "If my wife doesn't object," he said.

Amstead directed a coaxing smile at Nell. "Well, ma'am?"

Nell took his cajoling with good humor. It was only her eyes that betrayed a certain calculation. That familiar, sleepy tigress look. Miles recognized it, even if no one else did. She was studying the baron as intently as any great cat, searching for clues, weaknesses. "You may borrow me, certainly," she said. "Though I warn you, my lord, I am not at my best."

Lord Amstead patted her hand. "It's the weather. Cold as the dickens this morning. Makes every ailment seem worse. My late lamented father would have been crying out for his hot water bottles and rugs, God rest his soul."

"Sir Walter and I were saddened to hear of your loss," Lady Belwood said.

"As were we all." Lord Amstead heaved a dramatic sigh. "But life must go on. I consider this party a celebration of my dear father. One that has been too long delayed."

"An excellent notion," Mrs. Thompson said. "These inflexible rules of mourning are too restrictive on the present generation. Why adhere to them for another six months as a matter of form when your father's life should be celebrated?"

"Well said, madam," the heavily bewhiskered Mr. Thompson concurred. He sat across from his wife, a teacup balanced on his beefy knee.

"He had over seventy long years, did he not?" Lady Belwood inquired.

Amstead's lips thinned as he drank his sherry. "Three-and-seventy, my lady. Very nearly four-and-seventy."

"Do you shoot, Quincey?" Mr. Radford asked.

"I do," Miles said.

"Do you prefer a ten bore or a twelve bore?"

"It depends on the game," Miles said. "I trust Amstead will provide what's necessary."

"Oh, he'll outfit you with guns and a loader, all right. Though I far prefer bringing my own. You should, too, next time you come. Bag more birds that way."

"Do you often shoot here at Northwick?"

"Not as frequently as I'd have liked," Radford replied. "Amstead's father wasn't keen on hosting guests. He kept himself to himself, and his children under lock and key."

Overhearing them, Amstead broke off his conversation with the ladies. "Not quite under lock and key," he retorted. "My father wasn't a tyrant."

Radford lowered his voice for Miles's ears alone. "Pretty near to one, if you ask me."

"His children, you said," Miles remarked quietly in reply. "He had a daughter, I believe?"

Miles recalled seeing her name in the peerage. She'd been the child of the late baron's second wife, born more than ten years after his first wife had given birth to a son. There had been no further mention of her, neither in *Debrett's*, nor during the course of Miles's and Nell's research into the family.

"Fair Jane," Radford said.

"Are you talking of m'sister?" Amstead demanded with a flash of irritation. "Not a pretty subject, mind you. Not suitable for company."

Radford winced. "Apologies. Forgot myself."

Nell briefly caught Miles's gaze. A silent question passed between them. Just what had happened to make Jane Fawn-Purvis's name unsuitable for company?

Miles resolved to find out.

"I'd rather discuss the lady in front of me," Amstead said. He leaned toward Nell. "Tell me, Mrs. Quincey, how is it that you came to be so indispensable to Lady Belwood? She would have it that she couldn't attend my party without you."

Nell lowered her teacup back to its saucer, returning her attention to her host. "Before my marriage, I often acted as companion to her ladyship," she said. "We've come to rely on each other's company."

"Is your marriage of a recent vintage?" Amstead asked with interest.

Nell smiled. "Very recent," she said. "We are newlyweds."

Amstead's brows elevated. "Is that so?" He looked from Nell to Miles and back again. "Why, that's charming. And illuminating as well. It explains why your presence must include that of your husband. Newlyweds are reluctant to be parted, I'm told."

Nell affected an air of swift concern. "It wasn't too great an inconvenience to include us, I hope?"

Amstead waved the suggestion away. "The only inconvenience arises from your twisted ankle, ma'am. In allowing you to come, I'd intended you to dance."

"An unfortunate complication, to be sure," Nell said. "For me as well." She paused, adding earnestly, "I do so love dancing."

Miles took a stiff sip of his sherry, watching with equal amounts of pride and vexation as Nell twined the baron around her finger. She was almost too good at this. The deliberate half-truths and seemingly ingenuous flirtation. Miles had first observed it in Whitechapel when she'd effortlessly charmed her way into Mrs. Pritchard's brothel.

"We must endeavor to get you well, then, mustn't we?" Amstead said. "You will have all the cushions, compresses, and cups of tea you require. I shall make it my mission to see you recovered in time to dance the opening set with me."

"My husband might have something to say about that," Nell replied. "I have promised most of my dances to him."

Lord Amstead snorted. "Nonsense. We adhere to town rules here at Northwick. No dancing with one's spouse more than three times at the same soiree. You don't desire us to think you countrified, do you?"

A dour elderly woman who had been introduced as the baron's near neighbor, Lady Upshott, telegraphed her disapproval from a nearby chair. "Your teasing is in poor taste, Amstead. You hardly know the woman."

"Another mission of mine," Amstead said to Nell. "To get to know you. For the next three days, I will be entirely at your disposal."

"At the risk of neglecting your other guests? I wouldn't dream of it." Nell raised her teacup back to her lips. "Though, I do have one request to make of you, my lord."

"Name it," Amstead said.

"I would appreciate if your housekeeper could take me through the long gallery during my stay. I'd love to hear the history of all the portraits."

Miles's attention sharpened. This was something he and Nell had discussed during their preparations for the party. One of the many possibilities for gaining more information about the Fawn-Purvis family.

Amstead's gaze became intent. "You've heard of my long gallery?"

"Your house is famous hereabouts," Nell said. "It was designed by Sir Robert Taylor, was it not?"

"It was. The Fawn-Purvis family has a long and distinguished history in this part of Hertfordshire. But as to my housekeeper conducting a tour . . ." Amstead shook his head. "I'm afraid it's impossible. She knows nothing of the history of the portraits. She only came in the summer."

"I see," Nell said. "Another servant, then? Someone of longer tenure? There must be one who knows the history of the house."

"Sadly not," Amstead replied. "There was a great turnover in the staff after my dear Papa died. Had to put many of the old retainers out to pasture. It was a mercy. My father was an excellent fellow, but he kept some of the servants too long at their posts. They were ready to be pensioned off."

"A hard task, but a kind one," Lady Upshott pronounced. "Though I wouldn't have been without Mrs. Virtue for the world if I were you. Housekeepers like her are worth their weight in gold. Her talents are wasted at Bricket Lodge. And your father's butler! Gone to some grand house in Derbyshire, I heard. Well, they will be lucky to have him. As for you—you just see that the house doesn't fall to rack and ruin in their absence."

Miles exchanged a glance with Nell. Cowgill had attended a house party at Bricket Lodge in the spring. It was the only one he'd attended all year. Was it there that he'd heard something? Seen something?

Lord Amstead downed the remainder of his sherry. "No one is indispensable."

"A good servant can be," Lady Belwood said. "My own housekeeper has been with me since I married Sir Walter. A full eighteen years. I should be lost if she left me."

Nell's gaze came to rest on her ladyship's face. A trace of brittleness entered Nell's expression. "Eighteen years is a good long while, ma'am," she said.

"Household affairs," Pargeter muttered. "Tedious."

"Only four ladies present and it's still the primary topic of conversation," Radford commiserated under his breath.

Nell's attention didn't linger on her mother. A deliberate choice, Miles suspected. When dealing with the woman, Nell had difficulty controlling her emotions. And if they were to succeed in getting to the bottom of Cowgill's murder during their stay, both Nell and Miles would have to keep their emotions under close control.

"About the gallery, my lord," Nell said, turning back to Amstead. "If no one else can offer a tour, perhaps I might apply to Mr. Innes?"

"No use there, either," Radford said. "Innes was only recently elevated to butler, wasn't he, Amstead?" Radford addressed Miles with a chuckle. "Used to be his valet."

Miles looked at Nell again. Was she thinking what he was thinking? Every other servant had been dismissed. All except for Innes, who had been promoted from valet to butler. An extraordinary elevation, and one that might well be due to some nefarious service he'd performed for Lord Amstead.

"Don't be absurd, Mrs. Quincey," Amstead said. "I shall take you through the gallery myself. Tomorrow afternoon, say, when the gentlemen and I return from shooting?"

Nell smiled. "That would be perfect, my lord."

"And quite informative, I'm sure," Miles said. "My wife and I have a mutual fascination with historical paintings. We shall look forward to your tour."

Nell's dimple made a brief appearance. Whether it was on account of Miles's blatant possessiveness or Lord Amstead's obvious irritation at the same was difficult to tell.

Miles wished he could find humor in the situation, but he assuredly could not.

A man had been murdered. And the crime very well may have originated with someone in this house. If not Baron Amstead or Innes, then one of the others.

Miles was taking no chances. Not where his wife was concerned.

However ridiculous he must make himself, however much he must play the jealous, overbearing husband, he privately vowed that, for the remainder of the party, Nell wouldn't spend a moment alone with any of the men in attendance.

Excepting himself.

30

Nell had sometimes observed a local farmer near the Academy using a clever collie to cut a sheep from his flock. It was in just such an effortless manner that Lord Amstead singled Nell out from his small herd of guests, placing her next to him at tea, then at dinner, and then again as they gathered in the drawing room afterward for cards. It was he who commanded her smiles and her conversation, he who refilled her wineglass (three times altogether!), and he who partnered her at whist.

The other gentlemen had only stared. So, too, had Lady Belwood. Nell had caught the woman stealing anxious glances at her all evening. As for Miles . . .

There had been no opportunity for Nell to speak with him alone. Not even when they returned to their room to change for dinner. Lady Belwood's maid had been there, waiting to assist with Nell's evening toilette.

Miles had politely withdrawn. He hadn't returned until the maid had buttoned the final jet button on Nell's blue grosgrain silk bodice and placed the last pin in her gracefully rolled coiffure. Even then, Nell had been denied a chance for a quiet word with her husband, for Lord Amstead had been close at Miles's heels.

"You've promised to act as my hostess," Amstead had reminded, offering Nell his arm. "Isn't that right, Quincey? And a charming one she'll make. I shall be the envy of every man at the table."

Miles hadn't given his permission. Neither had he objected. He knew as well as Nell did that they must exploit any chance at getting close to Lord Amstead. It didn't mean Miles liked the idea. Quite the reverse. As Nell had taken the baron's arm, she'd caught a glimpse of a muscle working in Miles's jaw.

He was displeased. Possibly angry.

Or possibly something else.

Nell endeavored not to dwell on it. Indeed, as the evening progressed, she was too focused on gathering information from Lord Amstead and his guests to think very much about Miles at all. When she did, it wasn't to fret over his potential jealousy, but to long for a moment alone with him so she might share what she'd learned.

An uncomfortable dilemma.

The only place she and Miles could have any semblance of privacy was their room. And there was that dratted bed to consider.

But there was no avoiding it forever. Inevitably, the hour finally arrived when it was time to retire.

Miles accompanied Nell upstairs to their bedchamber in brooding silence. The lamps had been lit for them and the bed turned down. A fire was kindled in the hearth, bathing the room in a flickering glow.

Nell turned to face him the instant he shut and locked the door. "Bricket Lodge," she said.

Miles regarded her with a frown.

Nell was undeterred. He obviously understood what she was referencing. They'd exchanged a significant look when Lady Upshott had mentioned the place during tea.

"Mr. Cowgill was there earlier this year," she reminded him. "What if he encountered Lord Amstead's former housekeeper, Mrs. Virtue, during his stay? What if, in the course of attempting to glean some gossip for his society column, he heard something damaging about the Fawn-Purvis family?"

"I suspect he did," Miles said.

"Which would explain why Lord Amstead got rid of all of the servants. He didn't want them sharing whatever it is they knew." Folding her arms, Nell walked to the fireplace. "If his lordship has something to hide—" She broke off, coming to a halt on the hearthrug. "And that's another thing. What do you suppose happened with his sister, Jane?"

Miles slowly crossed the room to join her in front of the fire. The shadows from the flames danced over his solemn countenance. "A scandal of some sort. I shall find out more tomorrow. If Amstead won't discuss it, you can be certain that one of his sporting friends will."

"And at least one of the ladies," Nell said. "Lady Upshott seems the most likely to traffic in gossip. She's well enough acquainted with the family to know the names of the old butler and housekeeper. Doubtless she knows about the sister, too."

"You can question her and the others tomorrow when I go out shooting with the men. I'll talk to Radford if I can get him alone long enough. As for Amstead—"

"Amstead, exactly," Nell repeated the name with dramatic emphasis. "*Amstead*."

Miles's brow creased.

"That's what he's called now," Nell explained. "Not Mr. Fawn-Purvis. The moment he ascended to the title, he became Baron Amstead. Lord Amstead. Or just Amstead, as his friends call him. Do you see? It only came to me this evening during all those hours in the wretched man's company. Mr. Cowgill's notebook didn't mention Amstead at all. It mentioned Fawn-Purvis and Innes."

Understanding registered on Miles's face. Astonishment followed with it. "By God, you're right."

In her excitement, Nell instinctively moved closer to him. She sank her voice. "What if he wasn't referencing the baron? What if it was another family member entirely?"

"Jane Fawn-Purvis?" Miles suggested.

"It must be," Nell said. "Something about her and Innes."

"You think they were—?"

"No." Nell wrinkled her nose at the thought. "Heavens, no. According to the peerage, Jane is a girl in her twenties. While Innes must be past fifty at least."

"It's not unheard of."

"Possibly not. But really, Miles. Innes? He's no Sir Galahad."

"Not to you, perhaps."

"Or to any young girl, I should think. Even if he was . . . what has that to do with Whitechapel and five thousand pounds? And if he *did* debauch Amstead's sister, why is he still here? Why wasn't he dismissed along with the rest of the servants?"

"We'll find out soon enough," Miles said. "If not from our efforts tomorrow, then from Mrs. Virtue herself."

Nell's eyes widened. "You propose that we visit Bricket Lodge? But how? We can't ask Lord Amstead's coachman to drive us there."

"No. But we can borrow a gig and drive there ourselves."

"On what pretense?"

"The most obvious one."

She looked at him blankly.

Miles remained unsmiling. "That I require time alone with my wife."

Her heartbeat quickened.

"It's the only rational response to recent events," he said. "Amstead has commandeered you since our arrival. No husband worth his salt would stand idly by without demanding equal time."

Nell could think of nothing suitable to say in reply. She'd suspected Miles wasn't happy with her having spent so many hours out of his company this evening. It seemed she hadn't been wrong.

Unless he *was* simply offering the most likely excuse.

How was she to guess? Her new husband was difficult to read at the best of times, but since entering their bedchamber he'd betrayed scarcely any emotion at all. He'd been silent and still, watching her with a peculiarly measuring look. As though he were a very large predator determining the most efficient way to dispatch its prey.

Nell tightened her arms around herself. She was suddenly conscious of the closeness of the room. *And* of the presence of the bed. A quiver went through her that had nothing to do with the sinking temperature outside.

"Yes, well . . . That sounds like an excellent plan," she said.

With that, she abruptly went to the small dressing table near the window. She took a seat on the padded bench in front of it.

Miles didn't follow her. He went to the end of the bed. She couldn't tell what he was doing there. Undressing, very probably. There was the sound of fabric brushing fabric as he removed his jacket, and the whisper of cloth as he unknotted his cravat. He'd worn an elegant black evening suit for dinner. It was the handsomest she'd ever seen him.

She began withdrawing the hairpins that secured the thick roll at her nape, dropping them one by one into the porcelain pin jar on the table. Her hand wasn't as steady as she'd like. "You're not really bothered about Lord Amstead insisting on my company, are you?" she asked at last.

"Irritated," Miles said. "I've had to spend half the day watching him salivate over you, and seeing you smile at him in reply."

Nell half turned in her seat, forcing herself to look at him. He was in his shirtsleeves, his cravat loose at his neck and his coat tossed over the end of the bed. "They weren't genuine smiles," she informed him.

"I know they weren't," he said.

Her brows lifted in question.

"Your mouth was closed," he said. "When you mean it, you show your teeth."

A surge of embarrassment went through her. That he should notice *that*!

She turned back to the dressing table, grateful that the only looking glass was a minuscule one on a small silver stand. She had no desire to see how fiercely she was blushing. "My teeth aren't my best feature," she said stiffly.

"According to whom?" he asked.

Nell removed another pin from her hair. "Anyone with eyes."

She'd damaged them when she fallen from the tower. Her front tooth was only crooked, but she had lost some at the back. They'd been shattered when she hit the ground, along with her hip and thigh.

"You have a beautiful smile when you mean it," Miles said.

Her hand stilled as she loosened her rolled coiffure.

"When you don't, as well," he added. "But I prefer your genuine smiles."

She huffed. "I don't know why."

"Because they're real," he said. "And because they're mine."

The words provoked a strange trembling in the pit of Nell's stomach. She gave him an uncertain glance.

His mouth ticked up briefly at one corner. "But not only mine, sadly. It was Shadow who received the first of them."

Nell remembered. It had been in Miles's office, the day they'd met, a mere moment before the little tabby had plunged beneath Nell's skirts. "I didn't think to guard myself," she said. "I wasn't trying to beguile you at the time."

"Weren't you?" Miles crossed the room to join her.

Nell's blood warmed as he came to stand beside her. He removed his cuff links one at a time, placing them down on the dressing table.

It was all too much. Too intimate. Her poor heart couldn't handle it.

She moistened her lips. "Miles . . ."

"Yes, my dear?"

She summoned her courage. "What were you thinking of doing about our sleeping arrangements?"

"What would you like to do?" he asked.

She set her hands in her lap to stop their trembling. "I don't know. I—"

Miles sank down in front of her. He took her hands in his, engulfing them in warmth. "What is it that you're afraid of, sweetheart?" He searched her face. "It's not me, is it?"

"No."

"Isn't it?"

"It's not you." She pressed his hands in return. "It's . . . me." She hesitated, hating that she must give voice to her insecurities. "Everything has been so lovely between us. I don't want to ruin it."

"How could you?"

"By disappointing you."

He scoffed.

"I'm not perfect," she said.

"Nor am I," he replied. "Far from it."

"You know what I mean. I . . ." She swallowed hard. "It's my leg, you see. The sight of it—"

"I've seen your legs."

"You haven't." Her voice fell to a mortified whisper. "Not without my drawers."

Miles's expression softened. He brought her hands to his lips. "There is no part of you I wouldn't find beautiful."

Nell's heart swelled with yearning. She wished she could believe it. "But what if—"

"No more what-ifs." Miles stood, drawing Nell gently to her feet along with him. He gazed down at her intently, his hands still holding hers. "Tell me, are you expecting Lady Belwood's maid any moment?"

"No," Nell said. "I . . . I told her she wasn't needed."

"Good," Miles said. "Shall I help you undress?"

Heat flooded through her. She wondered, vaguely, if it was possible to blush all over? If so, she was surely doing so.

But she refused to be a coward.

Miles wasn't a stranger any longer. He was her friend. Her partner. Her husband. All of which paled beside the fact that she'd been falling in love with him for days.

But no longer. She *was* in love with him. His integrity. His loyalty. His kindness. And not only that. She loved the way he held her and kissed her. The way he looked at her as if she were the single most important thing in the world.

She wanted more of it.

She wanted *all* of it.

"Yes," she whispered.

31

Nell's eyes fell closed as Miles took her in his arms and kissed her. His mouth was a searing brand—hot and fierce. It sparked an answering heat within her, melting her from the inside out. As she listed against him, half-parted lips yielding eagerly to his, she had the vague thought that this was why some ladies swooned. Not because of maidenly shock at the intimacy of such a kiss, but because the pure pleasure of it made one's limbs turn to treacle.

It was overwhelming in the best way. *He* was overwhelming. Strong and warm, and powerful in his restraint. He wanted her; that was evident. But he didn't lose control. Despite the tautness of his muscles and the thrilling smolder in his eyes, he was, as ever, a gentleman of method.

She felt him reach to the back of her dinner dress, searching for the fastenings. "They're in the front," she murmured against his lips.

Miles exhaled an unsteady laugh. It was the only sign he was in any way affected by their embrace. That and the heavy beating of his heart. It thudded hard against Nell's breast as he held her, giving her an exhilarating sense of her own power.

She drew back just enough for him to access the tiny buttons that ran down her tight-fitting bodice. He made quick work of them, despite her bosom rising and falling rapidly beneath his fingers. It was impossible to remain calm. Her pulse had already been racing before he'd begun, and what equanimity she had remaining was rapidly stripped away by the kisses and caresses he bestowed on her as he divested her of first her dinner dress, then her corset, crinoline, petticoats, and stockings.

Were Nell in a more coherent frame of mind, she'd have been impressed with the ease with which he removed her garments. It was doubtless owing to his childhood in the Rookery. He was as deft as any pickpocket. Before she knew it, she was standing in front of him in nothing but her thin muslin chemise and drawers.

A rush of anxiety went through her then. A moment of soul-quaking doubt.

Miles gave her no opportunity to indulge it. Rather than dispensing with the last of her clothing, he swept her up in his arms and carried her to the bed. He set her down on the soft mattress. She'd scarcely time to catch her breath before he came down over her. He was careful of her injuries, mindful of her right shoulder and her left hip, even as he bore her down into the feather pillows. His mouth captured hers again with a scorching intensity.

Nell's doubts scattered. So did the remainder of her inhibitions. She slid her left arm around his neck, kissing him back. A full day away from the *Courant*, and he still smelled like newspaper print. It was mingled with the scent of fresh linen, polished leather, and the lemon verbena of his shaving soap. A familiar fragrance, and one that had lately become as dear to her as the deep pitch of his voice and the wry curve of his smile.

Her fingers curled tight in his hair. Her own hair was tumbling wildly about her bare shoulders. He'd tugged it free from its remaining pins at some point. Nell didn't know when. She was in no fit state to take an inventory of everywhere he'd touched her.

And she wondered—was this all there would be tonight? Just kisses?

Hot, gorgeous kisses. Each dissolving into the other, the next one beginning before the last had properly come to an end.

But no.

Eventually, inevitably, Miles pulled back to look at her. His face was flushed, his gaze dark with passion. His mouth quirked in a fleeting smile. "Now that I've rid you of most of your armor."

"What about your armor?" Nell asked breathlessly.

A serious expression came over him. "You've already taken it from me."

"Not all of it." She tugged at his waistcoat.

Miles wordlessly conceded her point. His waistcoat was disposed of over the side of the bed. His boots were next. And then his shirt. He pulled it off over his head, consigning it to the same fate.

Nell stared at his naked torso. Heat suffused her midsection. His broad shoulders, strong arms, and well-muscled chest were as hard as chiseled stone, every plane and groove defined as clearly as a classical sculpture.

This was the body of a man used to exertion. A man for whom physical strength was as much a weapon as the steel-nibbed pen he wielded.

A frequently used weapon, by the looks of it.

Along with a handful of bruises from his recent altercation with Silas, several old scars marked Miles's skin. Were they from his early years in the Rookery? Or were they another souvenir of the time he'd spent as a foreign correspondent?

Miles's color heightened under her unflinching regard. He returned to her without removing his trousers, still half-dressed just as she was. Accessible, but not entirely exposed. It was a deliberate choice. As if to illustrate to her that they hadn't yet gone too far. That this could still stop at any time. He gathered her into his arms.

"It's not too late to change your mind," he said.

She nestled against him. "Have I given you the impression that I want to?"

His lips grazed over her cheek and her temple. "You had three glasses of wine at dinner. Some might argue that I'm taking advantage."

"You can drink three glasses as well," Nell suggested. "It would put us on an equal footing."

Miles searched her gaze. Whatever he saw there seemed to settle his doubts. A solemn resolve entered his eyes. "No," he said. "For this, I want to have all my wits about me."

Nell managed a faint smile, even as a flood of warmth crept into her face. She wanted this, and she wanted it with him. It didn't mean she wasn't apprehensive about what was going to happen next.

He stroked her heated cheek. "How much do you know, sweetheart?"

"Everything," she said with schoolmistress matter-of-factness. "I read books."

Unlike most of fashionable society, Miss Corvus didn't believe in keeping girls in ignorance. It was one of the tenets of the Academy. A necessary part of knowing oneself. Academy girls were taught all aspects of human biology.

Miles's hand drifted to Nell's waist. He pressed a lingering kiss to the curve of her throat, distracting her. "Outside of books."

Her heartbeat quickened. "My body isn't a mystery to me." She inhaled sharply as he slipped his hand inside her chemise. *"Oh."*

"You're so soft," he said gruffly. His hand slid over her frame in gentle passes, shaping itself to every dip and swell. "Let me—"

"Yes," she answered. "Yes."

She didn't fully know what she was agreeing to, only that she wanted him closer. *Needed* him closer. Her own shyness didn't matter. Until—

He murmured a husky question in her ear.

Nell closed her eyes against a swell of embarrassment. She gave an infinitesimal nod.

Miles didn't prolong her discomfort. He rid her of her muslin drawers as efficiently as he'd rid her of everything else.

Nell was left in nothing but her chemise. It covered her to her hips, still preserving some of her modesty. But it wasn't modesty that concerned her now. Burning with self-consciousness, she dropped a reluctant look at her exposed left thigh. The muscle had withered over time, making it markedly smaller than her right one.

And that wasn't the worst of it.

Two thick, ugly scars crisscrossed her pale flesh—evidence of the brutal procedure she'd suffered through when an overzealous surgeon had attempted to repair the damage incurred from her fall.

A troubled frown darkened Miles's gaze.

"I did warn you," she said. "It's ghastly."

"Hush," he replied. He lifted the hem of her chemise, exposing the full length of her old wounds. He touched them gently, sending a convulsive shiver through her. "How did you—?"

"I broke several bones when I fell. The village doctor brought in a local surgeon to try and repair them. He was rather ham-fisted."

Miles muttered an oath.

Nell swallowed hard as his hand curved around her naked thigh. He didn't appear at all disgusted by the sight and feel of her injury. It was tender concern that marred his brow, not revulsion.

"Does this hurt?" he asked. "When I touch you like this?"

"No," she whispered.

"But it does hurt you sometimes?"

"It aches when the weather is cold. Or when I've been still too long. Or when I move too much." She took a trembling breath. "It's temperamental at the best of times. So are most injuries of this sort, I'm told."

"I wish I could take the pain away for you," he said.

Her heart turned over. "It's nothing I can't manage. Indeed, I rarely think of it except . . ." She winced. "I confess, I did fear it would put you off."

He flashed her a scorching glance. "Do I look like I'm put off?"

Nell blushed to the roots of her hair. "Well . . . As to that . . ."

Miles silenced her virginal stammering with another kiss.

And she forgot about the past. About her pain, and her imagined imperfections. They all faded away. Only the present mattered, here, in the arms of the man she loved.

The fire in the hearth was still blazing, the lamp on the dressing table still lit. There was no hiding under cover of darkness. They could see each other clearly. Shyness intermittently assailed her, most noticeably when he helped her out of her chemise, and then again when he removed his trousers. But it didn't last. It couldn't. Not when Miles was caressing her and praising her, whispering that she was beautiful, perfect, that he adored every inch of her.

He was endlessly gentle, endlessly patient, seeming to know just where to touch her. Just how to move.

She soon felt the same exquisite restlessness she'd felt when they had embraced that night in the library. It coiled tight within her, making her pull at him with unladylike insistence. This time, rather than calm her wildness, Miles encouraged it with gruff words and coaxing touches.

Nell had imagined, when the moment finally arrived, she would overthink it. That instinct would be overcome by maidenish insecurity. Academy girls were taught to prize self-control over everything else. To lose one's composure was to lose one's dignity. It was a weakness. One to be avoided at all costs.

But when Miles came to her, there was no indignity in her response to him. No insecurity or weakness. They were equals. Partners. Even the fleeting glimmer of pain Nell experienced at the ultimate moment was nothing compared to the infinite closeness.

Miles gazed down at her then, his face taut and his eyes brilliant with heat. "Are you all right?" he asked hoarsely.

She touched the hard line of his jaw. "Are you?"

His breath was ragged. "No," he said. "But I soon will be, so long as you keep holding me."

After that, there were no more words. There was only heated gasps and urgency.

And pleasure. So much pleasure.

Nell didn't know how to catalog it. She had never examined her individual wants or needs. Never succumbed to selfish desire. For as long as she could remember, she had been a part of the whole. The needs of the Academy had always come first. Her mentors. Her sisters. Her students. But not now. In this, she came to him alone. Fully alone.

And he came to her—only her.

Nell kissed him and held him, and she thought *mine, mine, mine.*

She hadn't realized she'd given voice to the sentiment until Miles's deep voice breathed a husky promise in her ear.

"Yours," he said. "Always."

• • • • •

Miles held Nell in the dwindling firelight. She was warm and pliant in his arms, snuggled against him, skin to skin, deep beneath the heavy blankets that covered the bed. He'd drawn them up over them at some point. He couldn't recall when. His brain wasn't yet functioning at its full capacity.

Nell idly traced his bare chest. "Where did you get these?"

Miles's muscles jumped under her questing fingertips. Even now, after all the intimacies they'd shared, her touch still made his breath quake. "The bruises are courtesy of Silas."

"Not the bruises." She found an old scar under his breastbone. "This."

"A memento from the Rookery. Another lad stabbed me when I was twelve."

Nell flicked him an appalled glance. "Why on earth would he do that?"

"He was a young villain trying to make a name for himself. He came for Gabriel one day in an alleyway and I got in the way of his knife."

"Heavens."

"It looks worse than it was," Miles said.

"Was the boy arrested?"

"No. At the time, Rookery disputes were settled within the Rookery." Miles refrained from describing the punishment Gabriel had meted out to the lad. Even Miles hadn't known about it until later.

Nell's fingers slid to the even bigger scar on his abdomen. "What about this one?"

Miles's blood simmered with renewed heat. He stopped her hand before she could delve further. "A stabbing incident in a tavern brawl in Marseille."

She met his eyes with wry humor. "You got in the way of another knife?"

He smiled briefly. "Something like that."

"What was the story about?" she asked. "I assume you were working on one."

"I was."

"And?"

"It was about smuggling." Lifting her hand to his lips, Miles pressed a kiss to her fingertips.

"I never knew reporting could be so dangerous."

"I've been telling you."

"Yes, but . . ." She trailed off as he kissed the palm of her hand. Her fingers curled against his cheek in response, gently cradling his face.

Miles's heart thumped hard. It had been the biggest surprise. How sweet she was. How tender. She had so much affection in her. An untapped reservoir of it. And she had given it all to him, freely, generously, with an innocent abandon that had altered the very alchemy of his soul.

"I'm tempted to leave tomorrow," he said abruptly.

She started. *"What?"* Her hand tightened on his cheek. "But why? We've hardly begun."

"You're more important to me than any story."

Her gray eyes softened. "That's kind of you to say, but . . . I don't see why you must choose between the two."

Miles didn't hesitate to answer. Never mind that it made him vulnerable. Never mind that she might not feel the same. A fact was a fact. "Because I love you."

Nell stared at him. Her throat worked on a swallow. "Miles—"

"I love you," he said again. "There's no story in the world that's worth risking your safety. No newspaper either. I'd give up the *Courant* tomorrow if I thought—"

She gripped his face. "I'd never ask you to! Why would you think—"

"I'd do anything to keep you safe. Anything to keep you full stop. All I want in exchange," he finished gravely, "is to be with you."

"You *are* with me. I thought that much was evident."

"I want more," he said. "I want this—you—all the time. Forever."

"You have me," she said. "So long as I have you in return."

Miles scowled. "I told you that I'm yours. That I love you. How much plainer—"

"But I love you, too," she said.

It was his turn to stare. He suspected he'd misheard her.

Nell's mouth tipped in a tremulous smile. "I can't believe you haven't noticed. You notice everything else."

Miles slowly shook his head. He felt a trifle dazed. "I didn't think . . ." He stopped, his mouth gone dry. "I knew you liked me, but—"

"Of course I like you! You're the best man I've ever known. The smartest. The bravest. The most considerate. A champion of truth, and justice—"

"And cats," he finished for her. "Don't forget the cats."

"We have five of them," she replied dryly. "I could hardly do so."

We not *you*.

Miles didn't fail to catch the distinction. They were their cats now, not his alone. Indeed, he wasn't alone anymore at all. Gathering Nell close, he kissed her softly, deeply, telling her again that he loved her. That he was mad for her. That he was never going to let her go.

Tomorrow, when he returned from shooting, they would tour the portrait gallery, and the next day they would contrive to visit Bricket Lodge. The sooner they did, the sooner they could discover whatever it was Cowgill had learned there. And then they could return home and start the rest of their lives together.

All that remained was to get through the next two days without getting themselves killed.

32

Nell descended the circular stairs, a shawl around her shoulders and her tapestry workbag in hand. The cold light of morning filtered through the high windows in the entry hall. It was half past ten. Miles had gone shooting with the other gentlemen. She hadn't witnessed him leave. He'd departed their bed when she was still sleeping. A deep, boneless slumber. Indeed, she couldn't recall when she'd ever slept so peacefully.

It wasn't entirely owing to pleasure. It was because she hadn't been alone. Miles had remained with her through the night—a great, warm presence in her bed. She'd let her guard down with him. Had trusted him to take care of her. To watch over her. And he had.

But of course he had. He loved her.

He loved her.

The knowledge of it had not only lifted Nell's spirits, it had lightened the weight of responsibility on her shoulders. A weight she had carried from a very young age. The Academy had taught her vigilance, but last night she'd set that vigilance aside. She had been safe with him. It was that which had enabled her to sleep so deeply.

She'd awakened several hours later when a housemaid had brought in her breakfast tray. Married ladies were granted the privilege of taking their morning meal in bed. And since all four ladies at the party were of the married variety, it was trays all around.

As she advanced into the hall, Nell couldn't be sure that the others weren't still in their rooms. Since emerging from her own chamber, she'd seen no one but servants about. It gave her the perfect excuse to explore a little.

She'd start with the library. Lord Amstead may well keep a desk there that she could search. And if it should be locked—well. That's what the butterfly hairpins securing her chignon were for.

According to the architectural plans, the library was located in the east wing of the house. Nell was just crossing the hall toward it when Innes stepped into her path.

She came to a startled halt.

"Good morning, Mrs. Quincey," he said. "If I may be of assistance?"

Nell swiftly took his measure. Except for the dignity with which he held himself, he was unremarkable in appearance. His suit was a dull black, his long face absent any obvious sign of malice. Yet he was a big man—taller than her, and physically stronger, presumably, despite his thickening middle. A man who might very well be capable of violence.

"I was on my way to his lordship's library," Nell answered. "It's this way, isn't it?"

"You might prefer the morning room," Innes said. "A fire has been lit and there are writing implements available. If madam would permit me to show her there?"

Nell privately cursed her luck. If the morning room was where he wanted her, there could be nothing of interest there. She was tempted to tell him no. That she'd prefer the library. As for an escort, given her knowledge of the house plans, one was wholly unnecessary.

But it was early yet in her stay to be making trouble. For now, she would do better to play the biddable guest.

"That would be kind of you," she said.

Innes gestured toward the east wing. "This way, if you please."

Nell followed alongside him down the corridor. As they walked, she discreetly examined his profile. A frown knit her brow. Perhaps it was only her imagination, spurred on by the fact that Mr. Cowgill had mentioned Innes by name in his notebook, but . . .

A strange suspicion began to take hold of her. The vague idea that she'd seen him before. Either that, or someone very like him. To be sure, there was something oddly familiar in his face. Nell couldn't quite put her finger on it.

"Is it true that you were formerly Lord Amstead's valet?" she asked.

Innes's mouth flattened. "That is correct, ma'am."

"I congratulate you on your promotion. There aren't many servants who could make such a leap. Not in a great country house such as this. A vast knowledge must be necessary to keep things running smoothly."

Innes replied with cold formality. "I am honored by his lordship's faith in me." He motioned to an arched doorway. "The morning room, madam."

Nell preceded him inside the prettily furnished room. It wasn't empty. A lone figure in a green taffeta day dress sat in one of the tufted chairs by the cherrywood fireplace, her fair head bowed over a white square of embroidery.

It was Lady Belwood.

She looked up as Nell entered. Her needle stilled. "Mrs. Quincey."

Nell suppressed a rogue surge of emotion. "Lady Belwood," she said. "May I join you?"

Her ladyship straightened in her seat. Her face was peculiarly colorless. "By all means. You have brought your sewing, I see."

Nell touched her workbag. "I've a sampler to finish."

Innes silently withdrew. Nell cast a final glance after him. She'd met several gentlemen during her time in London. The villains in Whitechapel, the staff at Miles's office, the men at the fashionable shops. Even a police inspector. She ran over their faces in her mind, trying to find a match for Innes's, with no success.

"Do sit down," Lady Belwood said.

Nell crossed the thick carpet. With every limping step, she was conscious of Lady Belwood's regard. Her ladyship had looked at her in just such an anxious way yesterday evening during dinner and cards. An odd look—as though she were struggling to place Nell's face, just as Nell had been struggling to place Innes's.

It was Nell's own fault. During the journey from London, she'd admitted to not having a mother. Naturally, Lady Belwood was fearful that Nell might be the child she'd given away. It was the very reason Nell had made the ill-advised admission—to provoke the woman's fear and guilt.

Not Nell's finest moment. Nor her wisest, either. The last thing she and Miles needed while investigating Mr. Cowgill's death was another complication.

Sitting down in the chair opposite her ladyship, Nell withdrew a half-finished sampler from her workbag.

Lady Belwood resumed sewing. "Sir Walter is very fond of my embroidery," she said. "He insists I be the one to initial all of his handkerchiefs, and all of the household linens." She tipped the scrap of white fabric in her hand so Nell might see her work.

Nell didn't have to pretend to be impressed. The delicate pattern, with its swirling letters and subtle floral motif, was one of the finest examples of stitchery she had ever seen. "It's beautiful," she said. "You have an exceedingly elegant hand."

"I've often been praised for it," Lady Belwood acknowledged with no trace of humility. She craned her head to see Nell's work. "May I?"

Nell held her sampler out for her ladyship's perusal. It wasn't her best effort, but it was still rather formidable, all things considered.

Lady Belwood's eyes shone with frank appreciation. "You're very talented."

"Thank you," Nell said. "I confess, I do enjoy needlework."

"May I ask how you learned it?" her ladyship inquired. "Was it a governess who taught you? I recall you mentioning that you had no mother."

Nell quietly threaded her needle. She hadn't expected Lady Belwood to broach the subject. She hadn't thought her bold enough.

Then again, they *were* alone. And for the first time, too. During their previous meetings, there had always been at least one other person present—Effie, Miles, the guests at the shooting party. Someone to distract, to mediate, to set a guard on Nell's tongue.

But not now.

Nell could say anything.

She finished threading her needle. "Everyone has a mother."

Lady Belwood's gaze intensified. This time it wasn't fixed on Nell's needlework. It was fixed on her face. "Did I misunderstand you?" she asked. "What you said on the train—"

"I did have a mother," Nell informed her.

Lady Belwood's countenance betrayed a flicker of relief.

It didn't last.

Nell stabbed her needle into the coarse cloth of her sampler. "She left me when I was very young."

Lady Belwood lost what remained of her color. "I see." Her gaze dropped back to her handkerchief. She smoothed the embroidered letters with her thumb. "May I ask . . . under what circumstances?"

"I was too young to know them," Nell said. "The woman who bore me surrendered me to Miss Corvus's Benevolent Academy when I was but five years of age. I was left there, with my meager belongings—a few scraps of clothing and a little toy loom."

A moan escaped Lady Belwood's lips.

Nell forced herself to look at her. Hurt and compassion warred within her breast. "Why did you do it?" she asked.

"Is it you?" Lady Belwood asked in return, her voice the veriest whisper. "Is it *really* you?"

Nell didn't deny it. "I recognized your perfume when I called on you with Mrs. Royce," she said. "I still remember it. And that isn't all."

Lady Belwood had gone white about the mouth. She was clenching hard to her embroidery.

"I remember that you stopped coming," Nell said. "That the servants left me at the gates of the Academy without explanation. Without so much as a name. I deserved neither, I suppose. I was nothing to you."

Lady Belwood's unfocused gaze fell to the handkerchief in her clenched hand. Blood was seeping into the white fabric. She loosened her hold on it, revealing the distressing sight of her sewing needle sunk partway into her thumb. She stared at it blankly. "Oh dear," she said in a queer, hollow voice. "I seem to have pricked myself."

Nell sprang up in alarm. Tearing a scrap of muslin from one of the squares of fabric in her workbag, she hastened to Lady Belwood's side. She carefully removed the needle from her ladyship's thumb and used the makeshift bandage to bind the wound.

All the while, Lady Belwood sat quiet, betraying no sign of pain. Nell wondered if the revelations about the past had sent the woman into shock.

"It happens often in the workroom at the Academy," Nell remarked for lack of anything better to say. "A result of handling needles too cavalierly. You must rinse the wound at the first opportunity. And some carbolic wouldn't go amiss if you—"

"I have thought of you every day for the last eighteen years," Lady Belwood whispered.

Nell's lungs squeezed. For an instant, she couldn't breathe. She briskly tied off the bandage. Smoothing her skirts, she withdrew back to her chair, grateful to restore the distance between them. "You were afraid, for every one of them, I daresay, lest I reappear and spoil your happy life."

"I *was* afraid," Lady Belwood admitted. "Afraid of being found out. Afraid I had done wrong by you."

Nell sat down. "One fear necessarily outweighed the other."

"I was but nineteen," Lady Belwood said. "The man—your father . . . We were in love. He had promised to marry me."

"But he didn't. Obviously."

"He died."

Nell's blood rushed in her ears. It occurred to her that Lady Belwood may not be the only one of them experiencing some degree of shock. "What?" she asked softly.

"It was typhoid fever," Lady Belwood said. "He went so quickly. He never knew I was in trouble. I was left to deal with it on my own, with only my guardian to counsel me—an aged maiden aunt, without an ounce of compassion for my predicament. She made arrangements for you to go to a farmer's wife in Shropshire. The woman had a dozen children already. You'd have been a drudge."

"Is that why you kept me for a time?" Nell said.

"I couldn't part with you. Not when—" Lady Belwood stopped. She continued with an effort. "Your father was the love of my life, you see. You must understand what that means to a girl. Yours is a love match, is it not?"

Nell blinked. "How do you—"

"I've observed you together," Lady Belwood said. "You appear to deal with each other with a good deal of tenderness."

Nell briefly dropped her gaze, thinking of her husband. One wouldn't know it to look at him, but yes. Miles could be excessively tender. He had been so last night. Rather fiercely so.

"I love you," he'd said to her.

The memory of it made Nell's heart contract. "It is," she acknowledged. "That is . . . we do."

"Then you *do* understand," Lady Belwood said.

Nell would rather she didn't. She didn't want to think of Miles catching a fever and dying. The very idea of it was enough to depress her spirits.

Lady Belwood slowly folded her bloodstained handkerchief. "I thought, if I kept you somewhere . . ."

"That you could pay me discreet visits until I came of age?"

"I don't know what I imagined the future would hold for you. I was only a child myself."

"You were nineteen," Nell said. "The Academy produces teachers younger than that. I was one of them. At seventeen, I already had charge of dozens of girls."

"I was not brought up in such a way," Lady Belwood said. "I was raised to make a suitable marriage. Which became unlikelier by the day after you arrived. I lost my bloom. And there was gossip in the village. My guardian sent me away to London to quell it. It was there I met Sir Walter."

Nell didn't need to be told what had happened next. She was already aware of the weight Sir Walter put on his pedigree. The consequence of such an obsession was all too obvious.

"It was not a love match," Lady Belwood said, "but he was a good man. Respectable."

"Wealthy."

"A necessary quality in a husband. He'd never have tolerated an illegitimate child. The very notion would have been abhorrent to him. I was obliged to make a decision. As I say, I was but a young woman."

"Four-and-twenty by that point. Older than I am now."

"There was no way to keep you indefinitely. I soon realized I had been stupid to keep you at all. That woman—Miss Corvus—

promised a good life for you. You would be fed and housed, and brought up to a respectable trade." Lady Belwood paused. "It appears she was right. You have grown into something like a lady. And married, as well. A girl of your birth couldn't ask for better."

"Every girl can ask for better," Nell said. "And well she should."

Lady Belwood's eyes flickered with immediate suspicion. "Is that what this is about? You want something from me? Money, I assume. Or is it an introduction into society like I provided for your friend, Mrs. Royce?"

A flare of anger took Nell unaware. The nerve of the woman! To suggest that Nell was motivated by some base desire, rather than the simple urge to learn the truth about her origins.

But that's what Lady Belwood was, wasn't she? A person driven by her own desires. The desire for wealth, comfort, respectability, even at the cost of her own child. Naturally, she would assume that Nell was the same.

"I want nothing from you," Nell said.

"You mean to punish me," Lady Belwood concluded. "To plague me with the threat of exposure."

"Don't be absurd. I have no desire to expose you."

"No? Tell me, then. Who else knows who you are? Mrs. Royce? If she does, then my secret will never be safe. That woman is a—"

"Mrs. Royce doesn't know. No one does, excepting myself, Miss Corvus, and my husband."

"Your *husband*?" Lady Belwood's pale face flushed with outrage. "And you call that no one? Your husband publishes the city's most widely read gossip column. If that isn't a threat—"

"When I threaten you, ma'am, you'll know it," Nell said sharply. "And I shan't require my husband or anyone else to execute that threat."

Lady Belwood gaped at her.

Nell moderated her tone. "I meant it when I said I want nothing from you. All I required was knowledge of my own circumstances."

"I've told you all I can," Lady Belwood said. "Any further discussion on the subject would risk a scandal."

Before Nell could make her reply, the door swung open and Lady Upshott swept into the room.

"What's this about a scandal?" she asked.

Nell and Lady Belwood stared at her with varying degrees of dismay. Good gracious. How much had the old woman overheard?

Lady Upshott gave an amused snort. "Amstead won't thank you for dredging all that up again." She came to join them, with a spryness that belied her age. A lace morning cap was arranged over her silver hair. "His sister is a sore subject with him."

Lady Belwood opened her mouth to disabuse Lady Upshott of her misapprehensions.

Nell didn't allow her to. The misunderstanding was too fortuitous not to exploit. *This* was why Nell had come here. Not to confront her mother or to hold her to account, but to find out what had led to Mr. Cowgill's murder. It was that which was important at the moment. Her past would have to wait.

Setting her feelings about Lady Belwood aside, Nell addressed Lady Upshott. "We meant no offense, ma'am," she said. "Still . . . one can't help but wonder about poor Miss Fawn-Purvis's fate."

"The same fate as meets many a silly lass." Lady Upshott sat down on the morning room settee. Like Nell and Lady Belwood, she had brought her workbag with her. "Surprising, I'll allow, but not extraordinary."

"Why surprising?" Nell asked.

Lady Upshott withdrew her needlework from her bag. "I thought her too sensible to be taken in by a man. She was a young gal but not a stupid one. Used to have the running of the place when the old baron was ill."

"Some gentlemen can be very persuasive," Nell said.

"Expect he was." Lady Upshott gave another snort. "I never met him. No one did. Jane Fawn-Purvis kept her secrets close. I'd have said she was a confirmed spinster right up until the day she eloped with the fella."

"An elopement," Lady Belwood murmured. "That is a scandal, indeed."

Nell deliberately avoided looking at her. Their conversation had left her emotions too raw. Too confused. She couldn't afford to be distracted. "Not an insurmountable one, surely," she said.

"It is if the man's a wrong 'un," Lady Upshott replied. "Not one of our class, according to Amstead. Some rogue in London with no money or prospects. Miss Fawn-Purvis cast her lot with him, and ruined her good name in the bargain. Amstead was obliged to wash his hands of her."

"A sad tale," Nell said. "Was Lord Amstead the one who told it to you?"

Lady Upshott commenced her sewing. "Miss Fawn-Purvis could hardly do so. She'd up and went, hadn't she? Less than a fortnight after her father died. And without a word to anyone, the sly cat."

Nell collected her own needle and sampler to resume her work. Her mouth curved in a pensive frown. Could it be that this was the significance of the second date in Mr. Cowgill's notebook? That it was the date of Miss Fawn-Purvis's infamous elopement?

But they had only Lord Amstead's word that it *was* an elopement.

What it if hadn't been? What if it had, in fact, been something far more sinister?

33

The long gallery on the third floor of Northwick Hall ran the length of both wings, with a line of silk-draped windows on one side and a row of aged, gilt-framed paintings on the other.

Nell strolled at Miles's side down the narrow, red-patterned carpet, her hand tucked in his arm, as Lord Amstead gave an abridged history of the most important of his noble ancestors. The gentlemen had only returned from shooting at five, and with dinner at seven they had little time for more than a cursory tour.

In other circumstances, Nell would have lamented the missed opportunity to gather more information about the Fawn-Purvis family, but not today. She hadn't been alone with Miles since he'd got back and was anxious to tell him what she'd learned from Lady Upshott—*and* about the conversation she'd had with Lady Belwood.

"My great-grandfather, Alfred," Baron Amstead said. "It was he who rebuilt the east wing after the fire and laid out the plans for the formal rose gardens. A true visionary." He glanced at Nell. "But you must see it up close, Mrs. Quincey." He offered his arm. "If your husband will permit."

Miles made no objection.

Reluctantly releasing his arm, Nell moved forward to take Lord Amstead's.

The baron covered her hand with his. "The portrait was painted by Sir Joshua Reynolds," he said, drawing Nell up to the frame. "It was he who recommended my great-grandfather wear a red coat with gold buttons. It gives the pose a martial air, does it not?"

Nell murmured her approval. "All of the portraits we've seen thus far are of distant ancestors," she said as he drew her on to the next painting. "Do you have none of more recent generations?"

"Of myself, do you mean?" Lord Amstead chuckled. "Is that what you'd like to see, ma'am? A portrait of me?" He flashed a grin back at Miles. "Your wife flatters me, Quincey."

Miles kept pace behind them, his hands clasped at his back. His face was absent humor. "Doubtless she'd like to see your parents."

"Or perchance your sister," Nell said. "Is her portrait here?"

Lord Amstead's arm stiffened under Nell's hand.

"I do appreciate the way the artists depict a woman's clothing," Nell continued, with what she hoped was creditable guilelessness. "The prevailing styles and the texture of the fabrics. It's an art in and of itself." She glanced at Miles. "Is it not, my love?"

"As you've often remarked," Miles replied.

Lord Amstead tugged Nell forward. "My parents are further on," he said. "As for my sister . . . a middling painter took her likeness as an infant. The result is nothing worth your notice. It's stored somewhere in the attics, I believe. This next portrait, however—"

"Lord Amstead!" Innes's voice echoed down the length of the gallery.

Lord Amstead came to a halt, and Nell and Miles along with him.

Innes strode toward them. His face was set in tense lines. "Beg your pardon, my lord, but—"

"What is it, Innes?" Lord Amstead demanded impatiently.

Innes stopped in front of them. Perspiration dotted his brow. "An urgent matter has arisen that requires your immediate attention."

"It will have to wait," Lord Amstead replied. "I'm entertaining my guests, as you see. Mrs. Quincey and I—"

"It cannot wait, my lord," Innes said.

Lord Amstead locked eyes with his butler for a fraught moment. Something seemed to pass between them.

"Very well," Lord Amstead said abruptly. He smiled again, looking to Nell and Miles with an air of forced jovialness. "A host's work is never done, is it? I might have known when I decided to give a shooting party that I'd be run off my feet. Another hazard of being without a wife." He lifted Nell's hand to his lips, pressing a kiss to her knuckles. "Until dinner, ma'am." With that, he departed the gallery with Innes, leaving Nell and Miles staring after them.

"Something's happened," Miles said.

"Yes, but what?" Nell settled her hand back on her husband's arm. Together, they continued down the length of the gallery.

"We'll likely find out at dinner," Miles said.

Imposing portraits of gentlemen loomed ahead. Nell had little interest in seeing them. It was Jane Fawn-Purvis's likeness she'd hoped to view.

"Shall we sit?" Miles asked. The tall windows opposite the paintings were deeply set. Cushions lined the stone ledges, offering an inviting place to rest.

"If you don't mind." Nell's leg had been paining her today. She expected Miles had noticed. The care with which he assisted her to the window embrasure confirmed her suspicions. He kept a supportive hand at her waist, not relinquishing his hold until she was comfortably settled on the cushioned seat.

"I shall be glad when this business is over," he said, sinking down next to her. "I've had my fill of watching that blackguard handle you."

"Handle me? Hardly. In any event, it's all in a good cause."

"We've learned nothing from him."

"No," she conceded. "But I did learn something from Lady Upshott today. She shared a bit of gossip about Jane Fawn-Purvis."

Miles listened intently as she related everything the elderly lady had told her. "I heard much the same from Radford," he said when she'd finished. "Almost verbatim."

"You don't believe it was the truth?"

"I believe that Radford *thought* it was true. That doesn't make it so."

"I came to the same conclusion with Lady Upshott. She had the details of Miss Fawn-Purvis's elopement from Lord Amstead. There's only his word that it happened at all."

"Yet Miss Fawn-Purvis isn't here. And hasn't been since early March, apparently. Possibly from the exact day mentioned in Cowgill's journal."

"If it *was* Miss Fawn-Purvis's disappearance he was referencing," Nell said, "we must consider the possibility that something worse befell her than a ruined reputation. Something involving the railway depot, adulterated tea, and brothels."

Miles frowned. "If that's the case, Amstead would have to be far more ruthless than he appears."

"He well could be," Nell replied. "You never know what a man is truly capable of until he's backed into a corner. If Amstead's sister possessed some information that could be used against him—if she'd seen or heard something damaging—"

"It would have had to be damaging indeed for him to resort to such a dastardly plot."

"Do you suppose she's dead?" Nell asked.

"I think it's a distinct possibility," Miles said.

Nell suppressed a shiver. That would make it two deaths. One a sheltered young lady, and the other a gossip columnist who had had the misfortune of stumbling upon the mystery of her disappearance. Had Mrs. Pritchard and Silas killed them both? Or had Amstead or Innes stooped to getting their hands dirty?

"We'll know more tomorrow," Miles said. "I've laid the groundwork for us to strike out on our own."

She perked up. "To visit Bricket Lodge?"

"I told Amstead that I was impatient to spend time alone with you. I mentioned taking you for a drive. There's an old mill on the river about four miles from here that's considered a spot of great local beauty. I suggested we might go there."

"Pity it won't really be a pleasure trip."

Miles looked at her steadily. "Everything's a pleasure when you're with me."

Nell's pensive expression softened. "What a lovely thing to say."

"It's the truth." He reached to brush a stray lock of hair from her temple. His touch was gentle. Careful. He searched her face with uncommon seriousness. "How are you?"

"Very well." She gave him a quizzical smile. "Shouldn't I be?"

"You seem not quite yourself."

"Don't I?" Nell's smile faded. "I daresay it's because I spoke with Lady Belwood this morning. We had a rather candid discussion about her reasons for giving me up."

Miles's brows lifted. "You told her she was your mother?"

"It all tumbled out," Nell said. She recounted the conversation to him, ending on a weary sigh. "I don't know what I was thinking. I might have known it wouldn't make me feel any better."

"You're still angry with her," Miles concluded.

Nell opened her mouth to admit that she was, only to realize it was no longer entirely true. She may not like the choices Lady Belwood had made, but—as a woman—she could understand them. Not everyone had a Miss Corvus in their life, or formidable sisters like Effie and Gemma, encouraging them to be bold and fearless.

"I thought I was," Nell said slowly. "In truth . . . I believe I feel sorry for her. She was alone and faced with an impossible situation. Many ladies would have done the same—or worse."

"You take a generous view."

"An honest view. It doesn't mean I wish to have her in my life.

Indeed, when we return to London, I hope I won't be obliged to see her overmuch."

"I'm sorry you had to see her at all," Miles said. "That you had to face any of this unpleasantness."

"Don't be," Nell replied. "It doesn't change anything. I know who I am."

He stroked her cheek. "Is that all that's been troubling you today?"

"What else?"

"After last night . . ." His voice deepened. "I hope you're not too . . . that I wasn't unduly . . ."

Heat crept into Nell's face. "I'm not," she said quickly. "And you weren't. You were perfect. The things you said—"

"I meant every word."

"So did I," she assured him.

His fingers curved around the back of her neck. He brought his brow to rest against hers. "I have been thinking about you all day," he confessed. "Missing you. Wanting you. Worrying that I seduced you into doing something you'll regret."

Butterflies swarmed in Nell's stomach. *Heavens*. The way he looked at her. The way he spoke—so husky and fierce. She could easily forget that they were in a public place. "Miles—"

His lips found hers in a soft kiss. "I love you, Nell," he said. "Tell me again that you love me."

"I do love you." She nuzzled his nose. "And I shall tell you something else as well. A secret."

Miles stilled.

"I didn't need any help undressing last night," she said. "I could have done it all myself. That's why my clothes fasten in the front."

He was surprised into a hoarse laugh. "Do you mean to say that—"

"*I* seduced *you*," she informed him.

Miles's chest rumbled on another low chuckle. "Did you indeed, my darling?"

Nell kissed him, smiling, her words a velvet whisper against his mouth. "And I'd do it again."

• • • • •

Dinner that evening was very different from the previous evening's meal. Instead of demanding that Nell join him at the head of the table, Amstead enlisted Lady Belwood to act as his hostess. It was she who sat beside him, and she who received the bulk of his attention.

Such that it was.

From what Miles could see, her ladyship enjoyed none of the warmth Nell had received from their host, and less than half the amount of his smiles. Baron Amstead's mood had altered considerably since returning from whatever business he'd had with his butler. His eyes were harder, his spine stiffer, and his demeanor lacking its characteristic bonhomie.

On more than one occasion, Miles observed him looking down the table at Nell. She'd been placed beside Miles this evening, to his great relief. A seating arrangement that wouldn't have occurred at a larger house party. Husbands and wives never sat next to each other as a rule. But here, with only four women at table, exceptions to that rule had been allowed.

"It's bad news, I assume," Nell murmured to him as she speared a roasted potato with her fork.

Miles turned to look at her. His heart briefly lost its rhythm, just as it had when she'd emerged from their room in her evening finery. He couldn't blame Amstead for staring. In her elegant blue silk dinner dress, her flaxen hair arranged in a rolled bandeau, Nell somehow managed to look even more beautiful than she'd been yesterday or the day before.

Or perhaps it was only his view of her that had changed. He was no longer merely mad for her. No longer smitten and desperate. He was a man in love.

"Probably," he said.

"He's been flashing looks at me all evening," Nell whispered. "Do you suppose he's heard that I've been engaging in gossip about his sister?"

"Let's not jump to conclusions," Miles replied quietly. "It may be nothing."

Amstead narrowed in on them from the top of the table. "I won't have it," he announced. "All of us bachelors present, and Quincey flaunting his newlywed bliss in our faces." His words were edged with a good-natured humor that didn't meet his eyes. "For God's sake, man. Haven't you the decency to pretend indifference to your own wife?"

The other gentlemen at the table laughed, and the ladies tittered. Teasing newlyweds was a time-honored tradition in fashionable society.

"Impossible," Miles said.

"As it would be for any man," Radford chimed in gallantly. "Given the inducement."

"Mr. and Mrs. Quincey are abandoning us all tomorrow to go for an intimate drive to Fairbend Mill," Amstead said. "They desire to be alone."

More titters and laughter.

Miles held Amstead's gaze. There was something ominous under the man's show of affability.

"Were I a miserable old cur like my father, I would object," Amstead said. "Fortunately for the pair of you, I'm a romantic." He stood abruptly, raising his glass. "To true love!"

The others obediently lifted their glasses, echoing his toast. "To true love!"

Nell's shoulders tensed. Miles tensed, too, recalling that fateful moment at Mrs. Pritchard's Gentlemen's Establishment when Nell had brazenly introduced herself as Penelope Trewlove.

Perchance Amstead's toast was a coincidence. Many a married couple had surely been feted with the same two words.

But Miles had been a reporter too long to trust coincidence. When it came to discerning the truth of a situation, his gut was a far more reliable indicator. And in that instant, his gut told him that, sometime between the moment Amstead had left them in the gallery and the moment they found themselves in now, their host had discovered exactly who they were.

34

Nell entered their bedchamber ahead of Miles, her blood still simmering with apprehension. Lord Amstead had been all politeness to them for the rest of their meal and during the tense game of whist that followed. He'd instigated no quarrels and made no outright accusations. Even so . . .

Miles closed the door after her. "Pack your things," he said. "We're leaving."

Nell didn't need to inquire as to why. She'd understood as well as he had what the baron's toast could have meant. "We can't," she replied. "We still have to speak to Mrs. Virtue."

"To the devil with Mrs. Virtue. It's too dangerous. If Amstead knows who we are—"

"Even if he does, he can scarcely admit it, can he? Not without revealing his connection to Mrs. Pritchard." Nell limped to the fireplace, brow furrowed in thought. "He must have received an express from London. Either that, or Innes did. Something from Mrs. Pritchard, presumably, giving him my name and description."

"Which is exactly why we're going," Miles said. *"Now."*

"We can go tomorrow. After we visit Bricket Lodge."

"Nell—"

"One more night won't make a difference," she said. "And consider, this may be our last chance to speak to Mrs. Virtue, and to find out whatever it was she told Mr. Cowgill. We can't let the opportunity pass."

Miles uttered a blistering oath.

"You know I'm right," Nell told him.

He glared at her as ferociously as a baited bear.

She held her breath, waiting for him to issue some high-handed husbandly decree.

But he didn't. He was far too sensible.

"Very well," he said at last. "But after we talk to her, we're on the next train to London."

She exhaled. "Of course."

"I want your word, Nell."

"You have it," she said.

Miles was unmollified. Stalking to the wardrobe, he stripped off his coat and tore loose his neckcloth, casting both over a chair.

He was all scowls and grumbles until they retired to bed. It was only then that his mood seemed to improve. He held her and loved her with such reverence, such tender care, that Nell quickly realized it wasn't anger that had made him so cross. It was his overwhelming sense of protectiveness toward her. He was afraid she'd be hurt. That he would lose her somehow.

A remote possibility, but one that was obviously still plaguing him the following morning when they set out after breakfast in their borrowed one-horse gig.

Miles stared ahead in stony silence as he drove over the remote country road. He wasn't happy; that much was clear. Had it been up to him, they'd be heading to the platform halt instead of to Bricket Lodge.

"Have I shown you the spring mechanism on my new cane?" Nell asked when the silence between them had stretched on for nearly a mile. She lifted the sleek black walking stick from the seat beside her. It was narrower than her raven's head cane, with a plain, curved handle. "I need only press the inset button thusly and . . . voilà!" A blade shot out from the bottom of the cane. "Look how sharp it is."

"If you're attempting to reassure me," Miles said, still staring straight ahead, "you're doing a poor job of it."

"What could be more reassuring than a spring-loaded blade?"

He flashed her a repressive glance. "This may come as a shock, but the thought of you fighting some villain with that cane does absolutely nothing to ease my mind."

"I'm not inept, you know."

"As I've observed. May I remind you that you're also injured."

She flushed. "I'm accustomed to my leg being—"

"I'm not talking about your leg. I'm talking about your shoulder."

Nell fell quiet. He did have a point. "It doesn't matter in any case," she said at length. Retracting the blade, she set her cane back down on the seat. "In a few short hours, we shall be safely back in London."

"Yes," he said firmly. "We will."

Bricket Lodge was situated on the edge of the river. A sprawling mansion of fairly new construction in comparison to grand estates like Northwick Hall. The gaudy fretwork and excessive embellishments marked it as the residence of a wealthy tradesman rather than the ancestral home of a member of the gentry.

Miles bypassed the front of the house in favor of the kitchen yard at the back. A young groom in his shirtsleeves was washing his face at the pump. He sprang up when he saw them drive in and trotted forward to take hold of the horse's bridle.

"Are you stopping, sir?" he asked Miles. "Shall I water your horse?"

"That depends," Miles said. "Is Mrs. Virtue at home today?"

"She is, sir," the lad replied.

"Excellent." Miles jumped down from the gig. Coming around

to the other side of it, he lifted Nell out of her seat, setting her feet gently on the ground.

Warmth radiated through her at his touch. But this wasn't the time to indulge the sensation. Marshaling her thoughts, she collected her cane. She couldn't put her weight on it yet, but it bolstered her confidence to have it with her.

Miles offered his arm and Nell took it, accompanying him to the back door. A scullery maid answered their knock. She admitted them into the warm kitchen and, on learning the purpose of their errand, immediately hared off to fetch Mrs. Virtue.

Nell and Miles were left standing there, amid the smoke from the fire and the steam from the pots boiling on the stove, subjected to the curious stares of the cook, the kitchen maid, and a stray footman enjoying a cup of tea at the work table.

The housekeeper appeared in short order. She was an older lady. Approaching sixty, if Nell had to guess. Her gray hair was tucked under a cap, and her black stuff dress was neat as a pin. She looked them over with an air of reserved civility. "Ma'am. Sir. How may I help you?"

"My husband and I are visiting from London," Nell said. "We have a private matter to discuss with you. If you might spare us a moment alone?"

Mrs. Virtue pursed her lips. She was too well-mannered of a servant to question them about their business here in the kitchen, with the other members of staff craning to hear. "Indeed," she said. She gestured to the slate-tiled hall. "My apartment is through here."

Nell and Miles followed her into the housekeeper's room. It contained a small table, an iron bedstead, and two horsehair chairs. The starkness of the furnishings was softened by a lace tablecloth and a vase of fresh flowers.

"I don't know what this is in regard to," Mrs. Virtue began after shutting the door. "But—"

"I am Miles Quincey, editor in chief of the *London Courant*," Miles said without preamble. "I have reason to believe that you spoke to a reporter of mine some months ago. A man by the name of Lawrence Cowgill. He was a guest here at the time."

Mrs. Virtue's face betrayed a flash of alarm. "I'm sorry but I—"

"He paid you, I presume," Miles said.

The housekeeper blanched. For a servant to sell secrets about their employer was a betrayal of the worst kind. "You can't be saying that, sir."

"No one knows but my wife and me," Miles said. "We'd prefer to keep it that way."

Nell stepped forward. "All we ask," she said, "is that you tell us exactly what you told Mr. Cowgill."

"Why don't you ask *him*?" Mrs. Virtue returned. "I'd have thought he'd have printed it by now anyway. I looked for it in his column for two months straight. If he—"

"Cowgill is dead," Miles said bluntly. "He was murdered."

Mrs. Virtue's jaw went slack. She staggered backward, sinking into one of the horsehair chairs. "Murdered?" she breathed. "Heaven help me."

Nell perched on the edge of the chair opposite her. "You had suspicions about something, was that it? Something that happened at Northwick Hall?"

Mrs. Virtue nodded mutely.

"Did it involve Miss Fawn-Purvis's elopement?" Miles asked, coming to stand beside Nell.

"She didn't elope," Mrs. Virtue replied sharply. "She had no one to elope with. She was going to London to see a solicitor."

Nell pulse quickened. "For what purpose?"

"Something had upset her," Mrs. Virtue said. "She told me she needed to speak to someone impartial, but quiet-like, without anyone else knowing. She'd written to him, she said."

Nell leaned toward her. "Do you know why she—"

"All I know is she left on the train," Mrs. Virtue said. "Wouldn't take any servants with her. She was afraid someone might report back to her brother. It were simple enough, she told me, to travel straight to London. She planned to hire a cab at the railway station when she arrived to take her to the solicitor's office."

Nell's stomach sank. She thought of what had happened to Flora Brent at the railway station. Is that what had happened to Jane Fawn-Purvis? Had she arrived alone and vulnerable only to be intercepted by Mrs. Pritchard?

"Did she tell you why she wanted to keep her appointment from her brother?" Miles asked. "Was it because she suspected him of something?"

"I know nothing of what she suspected," Mrs. Virtue answered. "Naturally, I have my own suspicions, but I'll not give voice to them. I have no intention of finding myself jailed for slander, or libel, or whatever it would be."

"If what you have to say is the truth, no one can prosecute you for making it known," Miles said.

The housekeeper shook her head. Her mouth was set in a mulish line. "It's a small world in this part of Hertfordshire, and I have my livelihood to think of. I'll not be caught maligning the new baron or that good-for-nothing valet of his, no matter what they might have done."

"You believe they did something to Miss Fawn-Purvis?" Nell asked.

"Someone must have, mustn't they?" Mrs. Virtue retorted. "Jane Fawn-Purvis left on that train for London. But she never came back, did she? And no lawyer ever came down here after her. It's only her brother who claims to know what happened to her. And how could he, I ask?"

"How could he, indeed," Nell replied grimly.

• • • • •

Miles and Nell returned to Northwick Hall in the early hours of the afternoon. Their journey back was largely made in silence, both of them privately pondering the implications of what they'd learned from Mrs. Virtue.

It was only as they rolled up the drive to the stone stable block at the hall that Nell finally spoke. "I suppose we must hand it all over to Inspector Garrick," she said in a tone of defeat.

Miles liked it no better than she did. Every fiber of his being was urging him to continue chasing the story. To keep going until he'd run Amstead, Innes, and Mrs. Pritchard to ground and held them to account for whatever they'd done to Cowgill and Miss Fawn-Purvis. Not to mention Miss Brent.

But there was more at stake here than his desire for a story. He had Nell to think of now. Her safety eclipsed every other concern.

"It would be the wisest course," he said. "Someone will have to question Amstead, and he's not likely to provide answers if that questioner is a newspaperman."

Nell clutched to the padded bench seat as the gig bounced over the gravel. "It's too dreadful. To think that he might have done this to his own sister. To have gotten rid of her so callously. And working with the likes of Mrs. Pritchard, too. How on earth would a gentleman of his stature even have come into contact with such a person?"

"You forget that, until recently, Mrs. Pritchard was the proprietor of a gentlemen's establishment."

"I know *that*. My point is, Lord Amstead never goes to London. He'd have had no opportunity to avail himself of her offerings. If he does know her, they'd have had to meet some other way."

"We shall have to leave it to Garrick," Miles said.

He guided the horse to the entrance of the stables, bringing the gig to a halt. No groom emerged to meet them. Most of the outdoor staff were off on the shoot with Lord Amstead and the other gentlemen. But not all of them. There had been a lone lad present this morning when Miles and Nell had departed. It was he who had hitched up the gig for them.

"What is it?" Nell asked.

"No groom," Miles said.

"He's probably in the kitchen having a cup of tea."

Miles gazed up at the main house, frowning. "Possibly."

"I can go up and fetch him if you like," Nell suggested. "I could use the exercise."

"You're not going anywhere on this property on your own," Miles said. "I'll put the horse away myself. We can walk back together."

Tying off the reins, he jumped from the gig and came around to assist her down. He set her lightly on the ground. She stood back, holding her cane loosely in her hand, while he unhitched the horse from the gig. When he'd finished, she walked alongside him as he led the horse into the stables.

The interior was dark, save for the shafts of sunlight that shone through the doors. Some of the horses knickered in greeting to their returning friend as Miles settled him into an empty loose box. It was the work of a moment. A few seconds, merely, during which Miles's back was turned.

It was long enough.

He was just securing the door when a noise sounded behind him. He spun around in the same instant a figure sprang from the shadows and grabbed Nell by her throat.

It was Mrs. Pritchard.

35

Nell's cane fell from her hand as Mrs. Pritchard dragged her backward. It clattered to the hay-strewn floor, completely out of reach. She inhaled a choking gasp. The woman smelled of eau de cologne and acrid perspiration. A foul stench, as though she hadn't washed in days.

Her right arm was tight around Nell's neck, squeezing her throat. And in her other hand—

Nell emitted a reflexive squeak of protest as the blade of a straight razor pressed to her jugular.

"Don't make a sound, my fine lady," Mrs. Pritchard said. "And you!" she snarled at Miles. "Move a muscle and I'll slit her throat."

Miles stood frozen across from them. He didn't move. Indeed, he didn't appear to breathe. His attention was focused on Nell with hawklike intensity.

"Or maybe I'll slit her throat anyway," Mrs. Pritchard said. "It'd be no more than she deserves after destroying my business and sending the law after me."

"It won't solve anything," Nell said.

Mrs. Pritchard poked her with the razor's edge. "I said shut up, you. I've had enough of your false tongue."

Nell felt a drop of blood roll down her throat. She swallowed hard.

Miles's fists clenched at his sides. "You haven't thought this through."

"What's to think about? I've no business because of her. No good name." Mrs. Pritchard squeezed Nell's neck tighter, briefly cutting off her supply of air. "I've had to go on the run like a dog."

Nell coughed and choked. She pulled at Mrs. Pritchard's arm to no avail.

A spasm of anguish crossed Miles's face. It was gone in a flash, replaced by a look of murderous resolve. "If you had thought it through," he continued, "you'd realize that the instant you hurt her, I'll kill you myself."

Mrs. Pritchard uttered a rasping laugh. "I'm dead either way, my fine fellow. All that remains is to decide how many of you I'll take with me."

Nell's eyes watered as she struggled to breathe. "It was Amstead."

Mrs. Pritchard nicked her again with the razor. Another drop of blood sprang out in its wake.

Miles took a reflexive step forward.

"Stay back!" Mrs. Pritchard commanded. "Do you think I won't do it?"

"Amstead used you," Nell said. "And now he's discarding you like rubbish."

Mrs. Pritchard stilled. Her foul breath gusted on Nell's cheek. "What did you say?"

"It benefits him for the Crown to hang you," Nell answered. "If you're executed for killing Mr. Cowgill, Amstead's secret will die with you."

"She's right," Miles said.

"Don't listen to them, Lily." A man's voice sounded at the door of the stables. He stepped inside. It was Innes. "They're liars, the both of them. They'll talk you in circles 'til they have you thinking black is white."

"It's too late, Jeb," Mrs. Pritchard said. "Amstead's not going to give me any more money. He told me so when I arrived yesterday."

"Shut up, Lily," Innes warned, coming closer.

"All that business about sending me to France," Mrs. Pritchard went on. "It was for your benefit. I saw it in his face. He means to summon the magistrate. To see me hanged. Your own sister!"

Sister?

Nell stared at Innes. She saw it clearly, then. He and Mrs. Pritchard had the same tall build, long face, and thickening midsection. The same merciless eyes. She was amazed she hadn't noticed the resemblance before.

So, this was the link between Lord Amstead and the brothel. The madam was his valet's sister. A conscienceless woman with lofty aspirations, happy to commit all manner of crimes if the payout was large enough.

"It's just like I said," Nell rasped. "You're rubbish to him. So are all women. You know it to be true. Only think of what he did to his sister."

Innes sneered at Nell. "How does a schoolteacher know anything about it?"

Nell tugged at Mrs. Pritchard's arm, forcing her to loosen her grip a fraction. She drew a quavering breath. "Schoolteachers are experts on human nature. We see the best and the worst of it every day in our students."

"Children," Innes scoffed.

Miles crept closer. "What is Amstead if not a child?" he asked. "Think on his crimes. He's a selfish man who cares nothing for other people. My wife is right. You're disposable to him."

"What do you know of his crimes?" Mrs. Pritchard demanded. "How could you know anything?"

"Of course I know," Miles said. "Did you not think I'd make it my business to find out after you sent me Cowgill's tongue?"

Mrs. Pritchard gasped. "*You're* the editor at that paper of his?"

"I am," Miles said. "Cowgill was my reporter. I have all the evidence he gathered at my disposal. Whatever happens here, it's going to press."

Innes confronted his sister, his face mottled with outrage. "You sent that man's tongue to the bleeding newspaper?"

"As a warning," Mrs. Pritchard said.

"You bloody stupid b—"

"Do you see?" Nell whispered to the madam. "How easily they abuse and dismiss you? You have but one chance left to ensure they get what's coming to them."

"What chance?" Mrs. Pritchard asked.

"Tell us your story," Nell said. "The whole truth before they can silence you. My husband will see it's printed. It's the only way to bring down Amstead."

Mrs. Pritchard fell quiet. She was breathing heavily.

"Don't do it, Lily," Innes said. "Don't dare even think on it. If you do, I'll not be responsible—"

"Amstead poisoned his father," Mrs. Pritchard blurted out. "Tripled his tonic one night. Gave him so much morphia he dropped off his twig, and the sister knew it. She was going to see a solicitor about it in London. Amstead knew when and where. He'd intercepted her letter."

Nell met Miles's gaze. She had never felt more validated in her decision to use samplers for the Academy's secret communications.

"God help you, Lily," Innes said. "You're a dead woman."

Mrs. Pritchard kept on, the words pouring out of her in a vile stream. "Innes came to me. Said there was five thousand pounds in it if I could dispose of the girl. I met her on the platform. I offered her some tea. Silas helped me get her back to the brothel. He wanted to keep her. Thought she could be turned into a good little earner. But I was that set on honoring the agreement with Amstead. 'Oh no,' I said. 'It's the Thames for her.' And that's where we put her."

Nell shuddered. She had known it was a possibility. That didn't stop her heart from breaking for Jane Fawn-Purvis. The poor, well-meaning girl. A sheltered young lady setting out on her own, in a righteous cause, only to have met these base, bloodthirsty villains.

"And Cowgill?" Miles asked, taking another silent step forward.

"He was sniffing around asking questions," Mrs. Pritchard said. "First in Hertfordshire, then in Lost Hope Yard. He came to the brothel. Said he was a reporter at the *London Courant*. 'I've a story due to my editor,' he says. 'About Lord Amstead's sister and her connection to this place.' Didn't have any choice, did I?"

"You drugged him, too," Miles said. "But you didn't kill him. Not outright."

"We couldn't be sure what he knew," Mrs. Pritchard said. "We might have let him go eventually, had that girl of yours not set him free. He made a run for it, the stupid sod, and tripped on the parlor carpet."

"You stabbed him there," Nell said. It was why the carpet had been missing when she and Miles had visited the brothel. It had doubtless been covered in blood.

Mrs. Pritchard poked her razor into Nell's throat in reply. "Well, he was struggling, wasn't he?"

Nell gulped. She had no cane with which to defend herself. No parasol. And her hairpins were out of reach. The only weapon she had was her own ingenuity.

It was a formidable weapon, if she said so herself.

"Should we be writing this down, my love?" she queried her husband.

Miles looked as though he was about to lose what remained of his composure. His fists were still clenched and a muscle was flexing spasmodically in his jaw. "No need, dearest," he said. "I've committed it to memory."

"I have only one final question," Nell said to the madam.

"What's that, then?" Mrs. Pritchard asked.

"Why did you take Miss Brent? With a lady at the bottom of the Thames and a reporter drugged in your attic, it seems an unholy risk."

"Taking risks is half the game in my business," Mrs. Pritchard said. "She was an uncommonly pretty lass. Elegant-like. That's why I did it. She'd have made me money." The razor traced Nell's throat. "So would you have done. There's a fortune to be made in a face like yours. Even if you are a crippled schoolteacher."

"Not only a schoolteacher." Nell met Miles's eyes across the distance. She dropped him a wink. "I'm the heavy artillery."

With that, she went limp in Mrs. Pritchard's hold. The madam instantly attempted to pull her backward—just as Nell had intended her to do. It was a maneuver Nell had practiced countless times in the Academy's athletic room with Gemma Sparrow. One Nell had long perfected. She tucked her left shoulder and bent her left leg and, with a duck of her head and a half spin under Mrs. Pritchard's arm, she freed herself from the foul woman's grasp.

It was a fleeting victory. No sooner had Nell broken loose than Mrs. Pritchard came for her, the straight razor brandished in her upraised hand.

Miles charged forward to put himself between Nell and her attacker. Innes charged, too. The two men met in a fearsome exchange of blows.

Amidst the tumult, Mrs. Pritchard lunged at Nell.

Nell sidestepped the attack, the fingers of her left hand curling over her thumb. There was no time to retrieve her cane. Nor even a hairpin. Dropping her weight onto her back foot, she drew back her fist and punched the woman square in the nose.

Mrs. Pritchard screamed as blood spurted from her nostrils.

Nell hit her again, and again, calculated self-defense giving way to blind fury.

This was the woman who had abducted Miss Brent. Who had

murdered Miss Fawn-Purvis and Mr. Cowgill. And now she wanted to hurt Nell, and possibly Miles, too.

Nell wouldn't have it. She wouldn't let her. Anger flooded her senses. She wasn't aware the fight was over until a strong arm encircled her waist, pulling her back against the warmth of an equally strong body.

"You're all right," Miles said gruffly. "It's over."

Nell turned in his grasp. As he enfolded her in his embrace, it was all she could do not to burst into tears. "What about Innes?" she managed to ask.

Miles held her fast against him. "Out cold," he said. "Just like his sister."

Nell shot a glance back at the madam. The woman had slumped down in an unconscious heap against the wall, her face a bloody mess. Innes was nearby on the floor of the stable. His countenance was in a similar state. "I didn't get to see you fight him," she said.

"You were occupied."

"I was, rather." She hugged him fiercely. "Oh, Miles. It's too dreadful."

Miles's arms tightened around her in a painful grip. "I thought she was going to—"

"She didn't."

"Your throat is bleeding."

"It's nothing, I promise."

"If I had lost you—"

"I was in no danger," she said. "Not really."

"Good God. Must I thank Miss Corvus for that maneuver of yours? And those levelers you delivered to Pritchard. Was that your version of good science?"

"I confess, I wasn't thinking of good science at the time," Nell said. "For a moment, I let my emotions get the better of me."

He kissed her temple. "I've aged ten years since we entered this stable."

"We're not done yet." She drew back to meet his eyes. "Shouldn't we . . ."

"What, love?" he asked.

"Tie them up?" she suggested.

Miles's mouth quirked. "A brilliant idea, per usual. We can use those lead ropes."

Together they secured Innes and Mrs. Pritchard. Miles was just finishing tying the butler's ankles together when a shadow darkened the door.

It was the young groom.

"Beg your pardon, sir, but . . ." The boy's eyes goggled at the scene before him. "I say, is that Mr. Innes?"

"Excellent timing." Miles straightened. "What's your name, lad?"

"Vernon," the boy answered.

"Listen closely, Vernon," Miles said. "I need you to go back to the house and fetch me the housekeeper, and two of the largest footmen you can find. Tell them a serious crime has been committed and we require the magistrate."

"Yes sir," the boy stammered. "Right away, sir." He took off like a shot.

Nell smoothed her rumpled carriage gown. "What about Amstead?"

"He and the others won't be back from shooting for another several hours," Miles said. "I'll deal with Innes and Pritchard in the meanwhile. We need to hand them over to the magistrate so he can secure them, and their testimony. If this goes to trial, it's going to be their word against Amstead's."

Nell had half imagined that she and Miles would confront Amstead themselves. She'd have liked to see the man squirm. But she recognized the futility in such a plan. The baron had kept himself far enough removed from the actual crimes to retain some degree of plausible deniability. He would undoubtedly plead ignorance to the accusations. "He *will* be held responsible, won't he?"

"He will," Miles vowed.

• • • • •

Later that day . . .

Nell snuggled against Miles inside the baron's luxurious black-lacquered carriage as it rolled away from Northwick Hall. It was Lady Belwood who had commandeered the vehicle for them. Amid all the chaos with the magistrate, and all the accusations flying between Mrs. Pritchard, Innes, and Lord Amstead, Nell's mother had stepped forward, taking on an air of imperious authority.

"This is an outrage!" she'd declared to the magistrate. "Can you not see that Mrs. Quincey is grievously injured? Only look at the blood on her throat! A carriage must be ordered at once to convey her back to London. I fear for her safety in Hertfordshire with such villains about as these."

Mrs. Pritchard (who had been exponentially worse off in terms of blood and bruises) had struggled against the burly footman holding her. "*Her* fear *us*?" she'd shrieked. "That woman's a menace! Look at what she did to me—"

"Enough!" the elderly magistrate had boomed. "Take her away, lad," he'd directed the footman. "And the butler, too. But separately, mind. I'll not have them rehearsing their stories together."

Innes and Mrs. Pritchard had been unceremoniously hauled outside by their respective jailers.

Lord Amstead had watched them go, his face pale and perspiration dotting his brow. Unlike Mrs. Pritchard and Innes, he had not been restrained. "It's a grievous misunderstanding, I tell you," he'd insisted. "A man can't be held responsible for what his servant and his servant's relations get up to. Had I any inkling of what they claim to have done to my sister—"

"You will of course wish to summon your solicitor, my lord," the magistrate had said severely. "These are serious charges. As for you—" He'd addressed Miles and Nell, his attention lingering on the marks from the razor that marred Nell's throat. "Her ladyship is quite right, Mr. Quincey. You must see your wife home. But you are to keep yourselves available for further questioning."

"My wife and I remain at your disposal," Miles had said. "And at the disposal of the investigating officers in London."

The magistrate's already dour expression had become grimmer still at the reference to Scotland Yard. "A terrible business," he'd muttered. "The late baron was a dear friend of mine. To think he mightn't have met his end by natural means—"

"You won't object to summoning your carriage for Mr. and Mrs. Quincey, will you, Amstead?" Lady Belwood had interjected. "Whatever the outcome of this unseemly affair, you're still the host of this party. Your guests are your responsibility."

Amstead had glared at Nell and Miles with unvarnished hatred. "Even those guests who have obtained entry by false pretenses? By all means. Let them be conveyed back to London in high style."

A shiver went through Nell as she recalled the way he'd looked at them. She nestled closer to Miles. "For a moment I thought he might leap straight for us," she confessed. "He was so angry."

Miles's arm tightened around her. "He wouldn't have hurt you. I wouldn't have let him. Lady Belwood wouldn't have either, come to that. Did you mark how she positioned herself?"

Nell *had* marked it. Lady Belwood had stood on Nell's side, not on the side of the gentry, protecting Nell the only way she'd known how, by demanding an elegant carriage for her and prompt passage home. Nell had been oddly touched by the gesture. "She did seem rather solicitous of my welfare, didn't she?"

"A welcome change, given what's passed."

Nell wasn't concerned with the past at the moment. It was the future that troubled her. "Indeed," she said as the carriage continued over the well-rutted stretch of road that led to the platform halt at Moor Cross. "But what about Amstead, Miles? If he does manage to foist all of the blame on Innes and Mrs. Pritchard—"

"It won't matter."

She felt a flicker of doubt. Despite the accusations against him, Lord Amstead was still a gentleman of wealth and title. And well-to-do men were notorious for getting away with things. "You're that certain he'll be held to account for his crimes?"

"If not by the law," Miles said, "then certainly in the court of public opinion."

Nell drew back. Searching her husband's eyes, she saw the same peculiar gleam of journalistic intensity she'd observed in his office the first time they'd met. "You don't mean what I think you mean?"

"I do." He framed her face with his hands. His voice deepened with resolve. "This is the story that's going to restore the *Courant*'s fortunes. All I have to do is write it." Bending his head, his mouth captured hers. "Let's go home, sweetheart."

Her pulse fluttered wildly. "So you can begin your article?" she asked against his lips.

"The article can keep for another day or two," Miles said. He smiled. "You and I have our own story to attend to."

Nell beamed up at him. "A love story," she said. And she kissed him back with all her heart.

EPILOGUE

One month later . . .

"A fine meal, Mrs. Quincey, and a welcome, if somewhat belated, introduction to your home," Reverend Pettiman said as Nell escorted him into the gaslit hall.

Miles followed, with Lady Summers on his arm. A stately widow in beaded gray silk, she was one of the Academy's chief benefactresses.

She and the reverend were the last of the dinner guests to take their leave. The others had already departed into the night.

Nell signaled for Mrs. Bright to fetch the stragglers' things, all the while maintaining the same demure but gracious smile she'd been wearing since the evening had commenced. She refused to let it falter, no matter that her face was aching from the strain of it. Tonight had been too important to let her pride take precedence. It was her and Miles's first dinner party as husband and wife. Not only had Pettiman and Lady Summers been in attendance, but several of Miles's colleagues from the *Courant*, too.

It had been a delicate juggling act, presiding over such a gathering. Nell had been fretting over it for weeks, planning the event down to its very last detail. Now it was over, she owned to a distinct feeling of success. Not one of them could accuse her of having failed in her duty as hostess. She'd wined and dined the lot of them, deferring to Miles through the whole of it like the modest, obedient—yet still elegant—society wife she was purporting to be.

"My husband and I have been honored by your presence," she said to Reverend Pettiman. "My only regret is that it's taken so long to set your mind at ease."

Mrs. Bright approached with the reverend's hat and overcoat.

"Indeed," Pettiman said as the housekeeper assisted him into his things. "However, given what I'd witnessed, and the sinful inclinations of many females, you will agree that my concerns were amply justified."

Nell most assuredly did *not* agree. She limped forward, urging her guests to the door. The full skirts of her velvet dinner dress rustled softly over her petticoats and crinoline. "I trust we can put it behind us now, for the sake of the charity school."

"Quite so, quite so." Pettiman's florid cheeks were redder than usual—a result of the many glasses of wine he'd imbibed at dinner. It had been an expensive vintage, and one he hadn't refrained from enjoying to the fullest. "Marriage and family are a cure for every ill. As I told Miss Corvus when last we met, 'Miss Trewlove may have strayed from the path, but she appears to have found her way back to it again through the sanctity of matrimony. We must let her be an example to the girls.'"

"My wife is an example to all women," Miles said gallantly, coming to join them.

Nell's smile curved with genuine warmth as she met her husband's eyes. He was strikingly handsome in his black dinner suit, with its cream silk waistcoat and matching cravat. She'd delighted in looking at him this evening, and in listening to him as he'd talked with the other newspapermen.

He'd been in his element. So knowledgeable. So confident. And very much in the good graces of the paper's senior editors and advertisers since writing his shocking series of articles on Baron Amstead.

Following publication of the first installment, the *Courant*'s circulation had nearly doubled.

As for Amstead, after a protracted investigation, he had only this week been arrested and charged with murder and conspiracy. It was largely owing to the public outcry from the articles, *and* to the dogged efforts of Inspector Garrick. According to him, there was every reason to believe that the baron would be brought to trial.

"Mrs. Quincey is certainly an exemplary hostess," Lady Summers agreed. She permitted Mrs. Bright to assist her with her cloak. "If this evening's entertainment was an illustration of how expertly she ran her classroom, I cannot wonder that Miss Corvus was so grieved to lose her."

"Miss Corvus hasn't lost me, ma'am," Nell said. "She never could."

Artemisia Corvus had been a mother to Nell in her own way. And more than a mother. She'd been a mentor, a guide, sparking the very fire that now burned within Nell's breast, encouraging her to think, to plan, to dare.

There was no forgetting that. And no distancing herself from it, either. Nell and Miss Corvus were still in regular communication. She kept Nell informed about the school, its most promising students, and the continuing progress of Flora Brent, who was, by all reports, thriving in her new environment.

Nell's relationship with her real mother was a different matter. She only saw Lady Belwood occasionally in passing. They exchanged civil nods in Bond Street and wordless salutes in Hyde Park. Silent but meaningful gestures, typified by their emotional restraint. *I see you,* they seemed to say. *I know you.*

It was enough for now.

"And there's nothing to grieve, is there?" Pettiman said. "Not when Mrs. Quincey has been so admirably replaced in the form of the new sewing teacher, Miss Jean."

"Ah yes, Miss Jean!" Lady Summers agreed. "Now, *she* is an exemplar. So modest and unassuming. So exceedingly proper."

Nell exchanged a speaking glance with Miles. Miss Jean was nothing of the sort. She was a stubborn cockney minx, who—when called upon—could wield an iron as capably as a needle. She'd only agreed to come to the Academy as a means of securing her safety in the aftermath of her assault on Silas. But once there, Miss Jean had lingered. Nell hoped she'd ultimately decide to stay.

"The school is fortunate to have her," Nell said.

Albert, the footman, opened the front door, letting in a gust of cold air. Lady Summers's carriage awaited her in the street amid the swirling fog, with Pettiman's hired coach queued close behind it.

Miles came to stand beside Nell as they bid their guests a final good night. Nell tucked her hand in his arm, grateful to be near him again. They'd been obliged to sit at opposite ends of the table at dinner. It was the fashionable way of things.

"You can stop now," Miles said after Pettiman and Lady Summers had departed and the door was shut firmly behind them.

Mrs. Bright and Albert withdrew, leaving Miles and Nell alone in the hall.

"Stop what?" Nell asked, turning to face her husband.

"Smiling," Miles said dryly.

Nell was surprised into a rueful laugh. "Were my efforts that obvious?"

"To me? Yes." His hand lifted to cradle her face. "I know every shade of your smiles."

Warmth pooled in her belly. She turned her face into his touch. "I daresay you do."

He stroked the curve of her cheek with infinite tenderness. "I don't require it, you know."

"Require what?" Nell was losing the thread of the conversation. How could she not when he caressed her like this?

"Obedience," he said. "Blind agreement. Whatever it was you were aiming for at dinner."

She leaned into him. "I was endeavoring for perfection."

"Ah. Now, that you already have."

"Foolish. I've told you I'm not perfect."

His arms came around her, gathering her close. "You're perfect for me," he said gruffly.

Nell melted into his embrace. "Oh, Miles," she breathed. "I do love you so."

As they held and kissed each other, a looming shadow spread over the hall. Miles's and Nell's heads turned in unison to discover that it was cast by Shadow herself. The little tabby was padding cautiously down the stairs.

The cats had made themselves invisible during the dinner party, as they always did when strangers were about, but now the last guests had gone, they emerged one by one. Horus descended the steps behind Shadow. Virgil and Absalom crept out of the library, and Smoke materialized from beneath a chair.

"It's all right," Miles told them. "You're safe now." His mouth hitched briefly as his gaze returned to Nell's. "They're relieved to have the place to themselves again."

Nell encircled his neck. "They're not the only ones."

In a short time, the house in St. James's Square had become her home. The place where she truly belonged.

But it wasn't the house.

It was Miles.

He was her home. Her whole world.

"Shall we retire, Mr. Quincey?" she asked.

Miles's smile spread into a swift grin. "An excellent idea, Mrs. Quincey." And sweeping Nell up in his arms, he carried her up the stairs.

AUTHOR'S NOTE

The Marriage Method includes several plot points that were inspired by Victorian history—from the comical to the criminal. For more about these inspirations, see my notes below.

CATS, DOGS, AND WIRE CAGE CRINOLINES

Invented in 1856, wire cage crinolines were constructed of hooped wires and fabric tape that stood out from the body, supporting skirts that were (by the early 1860s) sometimes as much as ten to fifteen feet in circumference. A curious animal venturing beneath these enormous skirts could easily find itself caught in the crinoline's framework. And, according to several newspaper articles from the era, many such animals did.

The animals in these nineteenth-century reports were primarily small dogs. One article in particular sparked my imagination. Printed in an 1859 edition of the *Bedfordshire Times*, it's the story of a man traveling by train with his little dog, Pincher. Seated across from him were "two young ladies, dressed in the prevailing fashion." Shortly after the train left the station, Pincher disappeared. At the same time, the man noticed one of the young ladies "moving and shifting her position." After calling for Pincher repeatedly—an action which provoked even more shifting by the young lady—the man realized his little dog was stuck under her skirts. As the *Bedfordshire Times* relates:

> *"[Pincher] was fairly caught in the crinoline. His fore paws and head had got through one of the small divisions which compose those frameworks of the outer attire of the lady, and, as he could neither proceed nor retire from the net, there he was."*

After some machination, the man was able to free Pincher from the crinoline, but not without great humiliation to the young lady. According to the newspaper, she was so mortified by the scandalous experience that she "covered her face with her handkerchief" while the dog was removed.

There are lots of similar reports in nineteenth-century papers, including many where the young lady was injured by the trapped animal. But I found much more inspiration in Pincher's story, since he was a gentleman's dog and since it was his male owner who had to untangle him from the young lady's crinoline. A scandal indeed!

LONDON BROTHELKEEPERS AND THE EVILS OF PROCUREMENT

The character of Lily Pritchard first appeared in my novel *The Siren of Sussex* (Belles of London, book 1). She was a villain even then, but in *The Marriage Method*, I wanted to reveal the full extent of her evil character. Her story and that of the abduction of Flora Brent were drawn from several nineteenth-century reports of unscrupulous madams who went to incredible lengths to procure comely young girls for their brothels.

Victorian newspapers (of both the legitimate and sensationalist varieties) weren't shy about reporting these stories. Lurid tales abounded of guileless country lasses being lured to London under false pretenses, only to find themselves trapped in a brothel.

An article in the 1847 edition of *The Leeds Times* reports on an "influential" meeting that took place to address the issue. The attendees, who were seeking to suppress "houses of ill fame," as well as improve and support the laws protecting women, had studied the issue and ascertained that:

> *"Unwary young females and mere children are frequently entrapped, and sold into the hands of profligate libertines. Agents are sent into the towns and villages of the United Kingdom, whose ostensible object is to engage young girls for domestic service or other female employments, but whose real design is to degrade and ruin them. Female agents are also employed in London and many of our large towns, to watch the public conveyances, and decoy the simple and inexperienced into houses of moral pollution and crime, by offers of advice, or temporary protections. By such and other means, the entrapping of innocent young women is reduced to a regular trade. . . ."*

The description of the methods Victorian brothelkeepers used to entrap their unwitting victims is echoed in more modern publications. As author Kathleen Barry explains in her 1996 book *The Prostitution of Sexuality*:

> *"Girls were often procured through newspaper advertisements offering positions of employment, usually for domestic work, or they were approached in railway stations, where young girls coming to the city from the country were easily identifiable."*

Given these reports, it wasn't too outlandish for me to imagine that Mrs. Pritchard had similarly identified Flora Brent when she encountered her at the railway station.

WOMEN'S SELF-DEFENSE IN VICTORIAN ENGLAND

The students at Miss Corvus's Academy receive a thorough education in self-defense. This includes instruction in fencing, jiujitsu, and boxing. All of these pursuits are authentic to the nineteenth century—though, at the time, still rather revolutionary for the female sex. Indeed, the very idea of women practicing self-defense was all but unheard of in the mid-Victorian era. Instead, women were meant to rely on gentlemen for their protection, and on the rigid rules of polite society that confined their movements and restricted their company.

Despite this, women *were* beginning to take up the responsibility for physically defending themselves. They were also utilizing (what had previously been considered) masculine athletic pursuits as a means of keeping fit. Women's boxing had been around since the 1700s, but by the dawn of the Edwardian era, there were women's fencing clubs, martial arts classes, and suffragettes performing "suffrajitsu."

I envisioned the students and teachers at Miss Corvus's Academy as being very much ahead of this historical curve. It's part of the incendiary nature of the charity school, teaching its students subjects that were still deemed unsuitable and even unnecessary for women.

ACKNOWLEDGMENTS

I owe endless gratitude to so many who assisted, encouraged, and advocated for me as I wrote this book.

To my dedicated and dauntless mom, Vickie, thank you for reading early drafts of this story, for running interference with difficult people, for handling Stella's and Jet's (many) trips to the animal emergency room, and for staying on top of who gets what medication and when. More than ever this past year, your love and support have enabled me to do my best work. I'm so thankful for you!

Thanks are also due to my amazing agent, Kevan Lyon, who always fights for me and my stories (and who is never too busy to offer reassurance when I have moments of self-doubt). To my brilliant editor, Sarah Blumenstock. And to Liz Sellars, Yazmine Hassan, Anika Bates, Lynsey Griswold, Marianne Grace Aguiar, Rita Frangie Batour, Kelly Wagner, and the rest of the fantastic team at Berkley/Penguin Random House, who do so much to get my books in front of readers.

An enormous thank-you to my wonderful critique partner, Isabel Ibañez, whose feedback helped me in crafting Nell and Miles's love story. To my invaluable assistant, Rel Mollet, who offered such great advice as I was revising. To the mighty Lyonesses, for their insight and encouragement. And to the lovely (and very generous) authors who were kind enough to read and endorse my Crinoline Academy series: Mary Balogh, Kate Quinn, Chanel Cleeton, Madeline Martin, Evie Dunmore, Sarah Adler, Syrie James, Hester Fox, and Harper St. George. I am touched, honored, and so grateful!

Thank you as well to my readers for sticking with me through all the twists and turns in this crazy business. On the darkest days, your emails and social media messages are what keep me going.

Last but never least, all my love to my precious little animal family—Stella, Tavi, Bijou, Asteria, and Jet. None of this would mean anything if I didn't have you.

THE MARRIAGE METHOD

Mimi Matthews

READERS GUIDE

QUESTIONS FOR DISCUSSION

1. As a girl, Penelope "Nell" Trewlove damaged her leg when she fell from the roof of the Academy. How does Nell's injury influence the decisions she makes as an adult? Why might she wish to remain at the school? Why might she desire to leave it?

2. Newspaper editor Miles Quincey sets great store by his reputation. Why is it so important to him that his good name remain unblemished? How does the fact that he's a self-made man play into this?

3. When Nell is compromised, Miss Corvus dismisses Nell from her position as deputy headmistress. Why does Miss Corvus make this decision? Should she have allowed Nell to remain, even if the ensuing scandal damaged the school?

4. After losing her job, Nell accepts Miles's proposal of marriage. What reasons might she have for marrying him rather than remaining single? What does she risk in trusting Miles? What does she hope to gain from their arrangement?

5. Nell has spent her life at the Academy, first as an orphan girl, then as a teacher. How does her history at an all-female institution influence her ability to connect with the women in the London slums? How might her experiences help or hinder her when dealing with men?

6. Miles has five cats, each of them rescued from the streets. What draws him to cats? What does his kindness toward them reveal about his character?

7. Nell and Miles agree to be partners in their investigations. What actions do each of them take to support this partnership? In what ways do they circumvent it?

8. How does Nell's discovery about Lady Belwood influence Nell's decision to return to Whitechapel in search of Flora Brent? What might Nell have been trying to prove to herself?

9. As Nell falls in love with Miles, she begins to share more of the Academy's secrets with him. How do these confidences help to strengthen her bond with Miles? How might they betray her Academy sisters?

10. To repair her reputation with the Academy's benefactors, Nell invites Reverend Pettiman to a dinner party at her and Miles's home. For what reasons is she willing to endure his company? Would you open your home to someone who had done that much damage to your reputation? Why or why not?

May 1864

Gabriel Royce leaned back in the oxblood leather wing chair behind Viscount Compton's carved walnut desk as though the desk, the library, and the stately Grosvenor Square mansion itself belonged to him. The jacket of his immaculate black-and-white evening suit was open, exposing the white tie and black silk waistcoat beneath. "Seems easy enough to me," he said.

His casual posture was belied by the menace of a Birmingham drawl edging his words. Over the past decade, he'd taken great pains to cultivate an upper-class accent—a necessary skill when dealing with the narrow-minded aristocrats with whom he regularly did business—but whenever his temper threatened, the truth of his origins always managed to seep out.

In those moments, there was no hiding where he came from. Though Gabriel had made a kingdom of St. Giles, it was the Black Country where he'd been born and bred, and where he'd spent the first years of his life. He'd only come to London as a scrappy orphan lad of twelve, eking out a place for himself in the Rookery with his wits—and with his fists.

Lord Compton paced the library carpet in front of Gabriel, his brows pulled into a furious scowl. He was a well-favored man in his middle fifties, with graying brown hair, a full graying beard, and a slightly thickened, but still athletic, figure that spoke of good wine, aristocratic sport, and a life of unutterable privilege. Like Gabriel, Compton was clad in elegant evening wear, though his suit of clothes had likely been made in Savile Row rather than by a struggling back-slum tailor.

"Easy, you call it?" Compton echoed in dismay. "To welcome you into my home? To permit you to associate with my friends? My *family*?"

Gabriel was mildly entertained by the viscount's distress. The man was usually unflappable—a model politician, with a thoughtful tone and a somber manner. "Come now, your lordship. It isn't as though I'm asking to marry your daughter."

Compton turned on Gabriel in the circle of light cast from the oil lamp on the desk. His face was transformed by fatherly outrage. "You go too far, Royce."

"Not far enough, it appears, if you think you have the choice of refusing me."

Compton snorted. "And have you unleash your band of ruffians on me?"

The distant strings of an orchestra drifted from the ballroom above. It was mingled with the muted murmur of voices, and the thump of footsteps as late-coming guests continued to arrive. A polonaise had been playing when Gabriel had first entered the library, followed by a country dance. Another dance was starting now. A spirited galop, which (by the sound of the stomping upstairs) had been joined by a crushing number of couples.

Compton's ball was the first truly tonish party of the social season. The grandest people in London were reputed to be in attendance—illustrious lords, wealthy ladies, and powerful politicians. Compton and his wife had already welcomed most of them when Gabriel had turned up, unannounced and uninvited.

For a few coins, an obliging footman had shown him to Compton's library. The viscount had marched in moments later to find Gabriel seated behind his desk, dressed for the evening's entertainment, and possessing all the deceptive patience of a hungry wolf waiting to strike.

Watching the viscount now, Gabriel's mouth curved in a lazy smile. "If you don't do as I ask, my ruffians will be the least of your troubles."

Compton's expression turned stony. He was no coward. It took guts to walk the reputational tightrope he'd been traversing these many years. But, audacious as he was, he knew his limits. He would do as Gabriel wished in the end. The result was inevitable. It was only the speed at getting to that result that appeared at issue.

Unfortunately for Compton, Gabriel's patience was wearing thin.

"Is it not enough that I keep the law away from your dealings in the Rookery?" Compton asked in a last attempt at reason. "That I protect your interests from those who would drive you out of St. Giles?" He set his hands on the edge of the desk. "You and I had an *agreement.*"

Gabriel stood to his full and not inconsiderable height. "Yet still you insult me."

Compton straightened. He took a step backward. It was less out of fear than it was a refusal to submit to Gabriel's physical dominance. The viscount would let no man loom over him, least of all one he considered so far beneath him.

"It's not an insult to insist you and I keep to our proper spheres," he said. "My guests this evening are a different breed from what you're accustomed to. They're gentlemen of influence—"

"Just as I am." Gabriel strolled out from behind the desk. "Which is why you're going to introduce me to them." He smiled again. "I have a sick fancy to become respectable."

Compton's lips flattened. He shot a glance at the closed doors of the library. The music filtered through, an audible reminder of his duties to his guests, and to his position in society. "Your jests are ill-timed, sir."

"It's no jest. I'm formulating a plan for changes in the Rookery. When the time comes, I'll need the freehanded support of wealthy benefactors."

Compton exhaled a contemptuous gust of breath. "Is that what this is about?" Stalking past Gabriel, he jerked open a drawer in his desk and withdrew his checkbook. "If it's money for the poor you're after, your request need go no further than me." He picked up his steel-nibbed pen, poised to dash off an order on his bank. "I'm not opposed to investing in a new workhouse."

Gabriel's jaw tightened on a reflexive surge of anger. Workhouses were the last thing the poor of St. Giles needed. Workhouses that separated mothers from children. That broke up families. Workhouses were where good, decent folk went to sicken and die. As sure a sentence as the hangman's noose, but lacking the dignity of the rope. Unlike a walk to the scaffold, admittance to a workhouse required no judge or jury. It recognized no defense.

After all, what defense was there to the crime of being poor?

No. Gabriel's plans didn't involve workhouses. He had other ideas. A vision for honest, aboveboard reforms to benefit the people of the Rookery and, ultimately, himself.

"I'm not interested in charity," he said.

"Call it a business contract, then," Compton responded.

"A business contract with you?" Gabriel's tone was silky with disdain. "I'd sooner crawl into bed with a scorpion."

Compton's face went rigid. He set down his pen.

"Put away your money," Gabriel told him. "All I require from you this evening are introductions to my betters." He gestured for Compton to precede him to the door. "If you would be so obliging."

Compton thrust his checkbook back into the desk drawer. He slammed the drawer shut. "Haven't the good people of this city already done enough to clean up St. Giles? And succeeded, too. The slum is all but eradicated."

It was a common misconception among the well-to-do. St. Giles was located in the heart of fashionable London, surrounded on all sides by the wealthiest communities. Many years prior, part of the slum had been cleared away to make room for the construction of New Oxford Street. But the wretches who had formerly occupied those long-removed lodging houses, gin shops, and prostitutes' hovels hadn't miraculously vanished into thin air. They had merely been pressed back into an even smaller area, the squalor of their living conditions now hidden from greater public view.

"Just because you can't see us anymore, doesn't mean we ceased existing," Gabriel said. "The people of the Rookery are still there—only now they're crowded one hundred to a cellar."

Disgust crossed Compton's face. "Such filth and depravity. I curse the day Tobias Wingard ever found his way there."

"But he did find his way there," Gabriel said. "And straight into my betting shop. Quite an impressive stack of papers he had with him, too."

Compton flinched at the reminder. "Very well," he said, coming forward. "I shall do what I can for you." He stopped in front of Gabriel. "But I warn you, Royce. If you at any time expose me to even a hint of impropriety—"

"You're warning *me*?" Gabriel took a step toward the viscount, bringing them face-to-face.

This time Compton held his ground. "Let it be mutual destruction, then."

Gabriel met the viscount's threat with a fleeting smile. "Don't flatter yourself. You might destroy my business, but you could never destroy me. Street rats always survive, one way or another. While fine lords like you—" He gave a humorless chuckle. "There won't be much welcome for Lord Solomon in Whitehall, will there, not once proven accusations of fraud are hung round his neck."

The color drained from Compton's face. "How *dare* you mention such despicable slander in my home, where my wife, or one of my servants might—"

"Rest easy, my lord." Gabriel slapped him hard on the back. "I've no intention of speaking a word of it." Again, he gestured for Compton to precede him. "Not so long as you behave."

Compton glared at him with a flicker of unvarnished hatred before, at last, grudgingly opening the library door. Gabriel had him by the throat and Compton knew it.

Gabriel had no intention of letting him go, not now, nor at any point in future. The viscount's support was too valuable. More valuable yet than Gabriel was willing to admit to the man. A politician in one's pocket was a precious thing. It was in Gabriel's interest that Compton's reputation remained unblemished and intact. The survival of the Rookery depended on it, and Gabriel's survival with it. There was no separating the two.

Together, he and Compton passed from the library to the house's opulent marble-tiled entry hall. A sweeping Italianate staircase led to the first-floor ballroom above. Gabriel climbed the steps alongside his reluctant host.

Two young ladies in full-skirted pastel silk dresses passed them on the ascent. Seeing Gabriel, they blushed and giggled behind their fans, quickening their pace down the stairs. A balding manservant in a plain black suit followed not far behind them. The butler, Gabriel surmised. He was a brawny chap, and one who (judging by the crooked lump masquerading as his nose) wasn't opposed to physical violence.

It was a good thing it had been a pliable young footman who had opened the door when Gabriel had come calling this evening and not this sinister-looking fellow. The outcome might have been very different.

"Do you require assistance, my lord?" the butler asked Compton.

"It's no matter, Parker," Compton said without breaking his stride. "A late-coming guest. I shall introduce him to the others myself."

Parker fixed Gabriel with a suspicious frown as he passed.

Gabriel offered the man a sardonic wink in reply.

Like recognized like. It was a tenet Gabriel had never failed to see proven true, and one that had helped him tremendously in his rise from the slums. He'd learned to recognize a fellow wolf in lamb's clothing.

The butler was one of them.

So was Compton.

Yes, despite the pomp and the pageantry, and the milk-faced young misses giggling behind their fans, Gabriel had every reason to feel at home here.

Upstairs, the ballroom's entrance was marked by two towering marble columns. Footmen flanked the opened doors. They bowed to Gabriel and Compton as they entered.

There were too many couples dancing to count. They moved over the polished wood floor to the strains of the music in a twirl of tail-coats and impossibly wide ruffled skirts, the ladies' jewels shining in the blaze of light produced from the gas wall sconces and the twin crystal gasoliers.

Compton guided Gabriel along the edge of the room, where spectators lined the walls, both sitting and standing. "That's Lord Trefusis," he said, jerking his chin in the direction of an elderly man seated by the bank of green velvet–draped windows. "A charitable gentleman by all accounts. His estates are in Northumberland. And that gentleman, there by the fern, is Sir Newton Cobble, a man of property from Cornwall."

Gabriel registered the two men with immediate skepticism. Aged country gentlemen were something less than the rich London progressives he'd envisioned rallying to his cause.

Compton pointed out another fellow, even older than the first two. "That gentleman with the ear trumpet is Lord Upton-Frye, a Yorkshire baron of good family. If it's alms for the poor you're after, he's the one to speak with." He glanced back at Gabriel with barely veiled contempt. "Well, sir? Which of them shall I introduce you to? I presume they are all of them strangers."

Gabriel coolly returned the viscount's gaze. After their confrontation in the library, he had assumed Compton would fall into line. Instead, the viscount believed he could take Gabriel for a fool. Why else would he be attempting to fob him off on doddering men of little influence, rather than introducing him to those gentlemen with actual power?

The offense couldn't be overlooked. To pardon one affront was to invite a host of others.

Gabriel fully intended to address the issue. To forcibly remind Compton of the very real harm he could do to him. But not here. Not tonight. This evening was for finding benefactors for the people of St. Giles. Not just men of property, but men who understood how to get things done in London, and who had the coin, and the political capital, to do so.

Turning away from his insolent host, Gabriel searched the room for himself.

It was unforgivable ignorance to assume the paths of the poor and the well-bred wealthy never crossed. Indeed, Gabriel himself had placed former denizens of the Rookery in many of the great houses in Mayfair. They worked as scullery maids, stable hands, and footmen, washing pots, mucking out loose boxes, and stoking the fires.

And the flow of cross-class commerce didn't only move in one direction.

The sons of the aristocracy regularly made their way to Gabriel's betting shop in St. Giles. They visited the gin merchants, the flesh peddlers, and the public houses, indulging in all of the worst vices and inventing a few new ones along the way. Often, it had been up to Gabriel to deal with them at the end of their revels, administering his particular brand of Rookery justice.

He recognized some of their faces among the fashionable guests this evening. Upright citizens all, by the looks of them. One would never know that handsome, young Baron Mannering had once wagered the clothes he stood up in on a losing bet, only to find himself spending the night in a Rookery alleyway in nothing but his underdrawers. Or that Lord Powell, heir to the Earl of Ingram, was so deeply in debt to a backstreet moneylender that he'd twice come to Gabriel's betting shop, stinking of cheap wine and sobbing like a baby, begging for Gabriel to intervene.

Which Gabriel had, of course.

Better the young lords were indebted to him than to a poxy wine merchant or moneylender. Influence was currency to Gabriel. He knew how to wield it. To weaponize it. It was invaluable to him, especially now, when the square footage of the Rookery was shrinking by the year. If it shrank any further, the slum threatened to disappear completely. Gabriel had no intention of finding himself displaced and powerless. Not so long as there was something he could do about it.

The orchestra closed the galop with a flourish of strings and horns. Another swirl or two, and a few lively chassés across the room, and the dance was over. Several couples departed the floor and several more came to take their places before the next dance began.

It was then, through a break in the crowd, Gabriel observed two late arrivals enter the ballroom. One was a society matron—blond, buxom, and bejeweled. The other was a younger lady of exceptional poise. Clad in a ball gown of deep blue silk, she stood straight and proud beside her older companion, her chin lifted slightly as she surveyed the room with a dispassionate gaze that spoke more of jaded royalty than of a girl in her middle twenties. So might Cleopatra have regarded a crowd of unruly Romans.

The similarity was only enhanced by the young lady's striking good looks. She had gleaming raven hair, bound in an elaborate roll at her nape, and a flawless expanse of warm, golden ivory skin revealed by the short sleeves and low neckline of her bodice.

Gabriel marked her presence with the same ingrained detachment with which he marked anything out of the ordinary in his environment. He noted her beauty. Her uncommon self-assurance. But he wasn't moved by them. He'd seen countless attractive females in his lifetime. They may differ in their allurements, but one was ultimately interchangeable with the next.

A fair-haired lady in amber silk swept over to greet the late arrivals. It was Compton's wife. Gabriel had never met her formally, but he recognized her pallid face by sight. She'd been an heiress when she and Compton had married, one with a sizable fortune and a notoriously dim intellect. Easy prey for a man like the viscount, on the hunt for money and power.

After an exchange of curtsies, and a short dialogue with the older blond lady, Lady Compton turned to the crowd in search of her husband. She easily found him.

"It seems I'm not the only latecomer," Gabriel said as the three ladies made their way toward them.

Compton followed his gaze. "That is my lady wife," he said tightly, having no idea Gabriel already knew exactly who she was. "And that is Lady Belwood, wife of Sir Walter Belwood. As for the younger lady . . ." This time Compton stared. "I've not yet had the pleasure." He stepped forward. "Doubtless her ladyship wishes to provide an introduction."

Gabriel's expression hardened. He had as little interest in being introduced to society ladies as he had in meeting aged Northumberland squires. But it was too late to avoid the tiresome obligation. Lady Compton was already bearing down upon them, her two guests in tow.

"My lord!" she said to her husband. "Thank goodness you've returned. I trust this means your business in the library is completed for the evening? You've already missed the arrival of Lord and Lady Martindale, and the Marquess of Whitby. And here is Lady Belwood, just come. She has brought her protégé, Miss Flite, to grace our party."

"My apologies, madam." Lord Compton bowed to the two late arrivals. "Lady Belwood. Miss Flite." His eyes lingered on the younger lady's face for a moment before he grudgingly acknowledged the necessity of introducing Gabriel. "Allow me to present Mr. Royce, an acquaintance of mine. We've been discussing a charitable endeavor, but all is settled now. I've invited him to join us. Mr. Royce? My wife, Lady Compton. And this is our near neighbor, Lady Belwood, and her companion, Miss Flite."

Masking his growing impatience, Gabriel bowed to the three ladies as civilly as if he were a gentleman himself. "Lady Compton. Lady Belwood. Miss Flite."

As he straightened, he held Miss Flite's gaze a fraction longer than was proper. Her eyes were the deepest blue he'd ever seen. More akin to a deep midnight purple in the gaslight.

"Miss Flite has just returned from finishing school in Paris," Lady Belwood said, with a flutter of her ostrich feather fan. "She's staying with me in Brook Street for the season."

"A relation of yours?" Compton asked. "I seem to remember one of your second cousins married an Italian. Or was it a Spaniard?"

Lady Belwood wafted her fan with increased vigor. "Miss Flite is not a blood relation. I was, ah, acquainted with her guardian when I was a girl. I promised, when the time came, I would introduce Miss Flite into society. It is the least I can do for her."

"I'm amazed I've not encountered you before, Miss Flite," Lady Compton said. "Is this your first visit to London?"

"It is, my lady," Miss Flite replied. A faceted glass hairpin in the shape of a dragonfly was nestled in her hair. It sparkled as she moved.

Lady Compton flicked a dubious glance over Miss Flite's elegant face and figure. "You don't strike me as a country girl. But if you've been finished in Paris—"

"Finishing schools accomplish marvelous things these days," Lady Belwood interjected. "The girls they turn out have remarkable polish. One can take them anywhere."

Gabriel directed a cold glare at Compton. It was bad enough to have his time wasted by old country squires and frivolous, fan-fluttering ladies, but now he must affect an interest in *finishing* schools? Until Gabriel had intervened, the children of the Rookery had had no school at all. Boys and girls of five had already been working. The alternative was starvation.

Compton pretended not to notice Gabriel's ire. He kept his attention fixed on his wife—and on Miss Flite.

"You must bring her with you to the musicale next week," Lady Compton said. "My daughter, Carena, will be back from Hampshire. She's to perform an aria for us from *Lucrezia Borgia*. There will be a dinner to start." She touched Lady Belwood's arm. "You *are* still planning to attend?"

Miss Flite exchanged a wordless glance with Lady Belwood.

Lady Belwood appeared distinctly uncomfortable. "Er, yes. That is, I had thought—"

"Oh, but you must," Lady Compton insisted. "We see too little of you. And Miss Flite will certainly wish to make the acquaintance of other young people."

Lady Belwood smiled thinly. "If you insist, then naturally, I shall bring her."

The two older ladies lapsed into a short discussion about the dinner, and about the many events to come before the season's end. Compton was included by virtue of his wife, who sought his opinion on every subject.

Miss Flite and Gabriel were temporarily left outside the conversation. They stood silent across from each other—Miss Flite attending to what the others were saying, and Gabriel poised to make his exit.

He hadn't come here to engage in polite small talk about dinner parties and musicales. His time would be better spent in conversation with one of those aged country squires. At least then there would be a hope in hell of gaining influence for the people of the Rookery. Here there was nothing.

A civil word or two to Miss Flite and then he would take his leave.

Their eyes met briefly.

"A finishing school in Paris, was it?" Gabriel inquired.

"That's correct." Miss Flite returned her attention to the others.

"And were you?" he asked.

She glanced back at him again, distracted. "Was I what, sir?"

"Finished?"

Her mouth curved into a slow, feline smile. "On the contrary," she said. "I'm just getting started."

Gabriel smiled in return, mildly amused by what he perceived as ladylike flirtation. He was about to reply, when he realized Miss Flite hadn't been looking at him when she'd spoken.

She'd been looking at Compton.

• • • • •

Effie made her way down the gaslit, richly carpeted corridor on the house's ground floor, her steps unhurried but purposeful. Lord Compton had said the library was where he conducted his business. A fortuitous admission, and one Effie's mind had latched on to like a vise the instant he'd made it.

She'd waited most of the evening to extricate herself. Until now, her dance card had been too full to allow for any moments of freedom, except for a short visit to the ladies' retiring room. A marked success, considering the circumstances. It had been Nell, not Effie, who had been destined to ensnare men with her loveliness. A destiny that had been snuffed out that fateful day on the Academy's roof. If not for Effie's weakness, it would be Nell standing here, preparing to bring about Lord Compton's downfall, not Effie herself.

But so long as Effie *was* here, she was determined to do her best.

She may not be sweet or gentle or possessed of perfect porcelain skin, but five years in Paris had taught her to respect her strengths. What she lacked in classical beauty, she more than made up for with confidence, and with the gift of originality.

The moment the supper dance had ended, and the guests had departed for the dining room, Effie had slipped away to pursue her own agenda.

The enormous skirts of her Parisian ball gown rustled silently over her wire crinoline as she approached the library's double doors. She'd bought the gown at a salon in the Rue de la Paix. It was a beautiful garment, made of Prussian blue silk, with a bodice cut low at the neck and shoulders, and an unforgivingly narrow waist that made a bounty of Effie's modest curves. Along with the distinctiveness of her looks, and the resoluteness of her manner, it had helped her achieve her goal this evening. She'd made herself memorable, a young lady whom Lady Compton, and every other society hostess, would feel bound to invite to all their future events during the season.

It had also ensured she'd caught the attention of the gentlemen in attendance. According to Miss Corvus, Lord Compton was an admirer of beautiful women. It had behooved Effie to at least attempt to appeal to his masculine senses.

A failed attempt, as it happened. The gray-haired viscount hadn't betrayed the least interest in Effie. Neither had he revealed himself to be a particular villain. He'd been excessively civil, addressing her with a fatherly air rather than that of a male admirer. He hadn't asked her to dance. Indeed, aside from a single heated look (which

Effie was beginning to wonder if she'd misinterpreted), he'd steered well clear of her.

Unlike the younger gentlemen.

If Effie's aching feet were to judge, she must have danced with every male in attendance between the ages of eighteen and forty.

Well. Perhaps not *all* the males in attendance.

The enigmatic Mr. Royce had stood out among the assembled company as starkly as a feral dog amid a pack of lap spaniels. It wasn't only because he'd failed to beg a dance from her. And it wasn't on account of any deficiencies in his dress. It was something in his posture, and in his pale blue eyes, so cold, hard, and remote.

Effie recalled the way he'd looked at her when they'd been introduced in the ballroom. There had been a certain distance in his gaze. Coupled with the brooding set to his jaw and the skepticism evident across his brow, it had made him appear far removed from the wealth and excess of the glittering lords and ladies surrounding them.

Like Compton, Mr. Royce hadn't shown any marked interest in Effie. He hadn't even bothered to linger in her company. After an introduction, and a fleeting exchange about her time in Paris, he'd disappeared into the crowd. Effie had seen him only once after that, engaged in solemn conversation with a much older gentleman by the ballroom windows.

Pity, he might have made the evening interesting.

As it was, Effie felt tonight's challenge was all too simple. She couldn't believe she'd indulged in any anxiety over it. Those first nights in Lady Belwood's guest room in Brook Street, Effie had fretted for hours in her bed, hugging Franc close and worrying herself to ribbons.

She hadn't been lying when she'd told Nell she hadn't picked a lock in five years. She hadn't crept into any forbidden rooms, either, or stolen anything from anyone. What if . . . ?

But her worries had all been for naught.

Opening one of the wood-paneled doors, Effie passed into the library. Any anxiety she'd had about encountering Lord Compton, or anyone else there, was promptly put to rest. The room stood dark and silent. The gaslights had been turned off, and there was no fire lit in the hearth. The sole source of light came from the tall windows beside Lord Compton's heavy walnut desk. A full moon shimmered through the curtains, shining softly over the inkpots, blotter, and stack of unread correspondence littering the desk's surface.

The rest of the large room was sunk completely into shadow. At one time, that mightn't have been an issue. As a girl, Effie had been accustomed to finding her way without a lamp. It had been one of Miss Corvus's earliest lessons, to master the darkness. An Academy student was never to be dependent on anything, not even a candle. She must find her way, stealthily, fearlessly, with complete self-sufficiency.

But Effie had been too long in the City of Light. Though she didn't fear the darkness, she'd long lost the habit of peering into it like a cat. She exhaled a soft breath of relief to find Compton's desk illuminated.

It was a big piece of furniture, heavily carved, with plenty of drawers, small doors, and other nooks and crannies. She trailed her bare fingertip in a languorous line across the edge of the desk until she reached the stack of letters. Sweeping them up in her hand, she riffled through the envelopes in the moonlight. They were waiting to be posted, addressed to various gentlemen. Not a one of them looked nefarious, but how could Effie tell without breaking their seals?

She quietly returned them to the desk. She was a long way from exposing herself by opening and reading Compton's outgoing post. First, she would search his desk. If Miss Corvus was to be believed, the viscount's crimes were in the past. It seemed more likely Effie would find evidence of them hidden away somewhere rather than willingly written down in a letter to another person.

Perching on the edge of the leather chair behind the desk, skirts billowing out all around her, Effie's attention was entirely focused on the drawers. The first one she tried was locked. So was the second. She rattled it quietly, privately cursing her luck. Drat Nell! She of the lockpicks and coded samplers. It figured she would be proven right.

Effie reached for her glittering dragonfly hairpin. One of a set of three, it was comprised of faceted glass affixed to a sturdy black wire. Like her dress, it had been made for her in Paris.

She was just inserting it into the lock of the first drawer when the silence in the library was broken by the unmistakable strike of a friction match.

A flame blazed forth from the darkness, illuminating a gentleman's face as he lit his cigarette. He was seated in one of the leather armchairs across the library, his jacket and gloves discarded and his cravat loose at his neck.

Effie went still. It was Mr. Royce. She didn't need a lantern to make out his face. His harshly hewn countenance, with its high cheekbones, sunken cheeks, hard jaw, and coldly piercing blue eyes, was readily identifiable even in the fleeting glow of phosphorus and sulfur.

"Are you lost, Miss Flite?" he asked.

She slowly stood from behind the desk, tucking her dragonfly pin back into her hair. Her composure didn't slip an inch. "Not at all, sir. I was looking for someone."

His gaze held hers. Wafting out his match, he cast it into the crystal ashtray on the table beside him. "Perchance you've found him."

Photo by Vickie Hahn

USA Today bestselling author **Mimi Matthews** writes both historical nonfiction and award-winning Victorian romances. Her novels have received starred reviews in *Publishers Weekly*, *Library Journal*, *Booklist*, *Kirkus Reviews*, and Shelf Awareness, and her articles have been featured on the Victorian Web, in the *Journal of Victorian Culture*, and in syndication at *BUST* magazine. In her other life, Mimi is an attorney. She resides in California with her family, which includes an Andalusian dressage horse, a sheltie, a miniature poodle, and two Siamese cats.

VISIT MIMI MATTHEWS ONLINE

MimiMatthews.com

MimiMatthewsAuthor

MimiMatthewsEsq